# KELVOS'S
# TESTIMONIAL

---

*Surviving the aftermath
of human first contact*

## PHIL  BAILEY

ISBN
978-1-7781024-1-7 (Hardcover)
978-1-7781024-2-4 (Paperback)
978-1-7781024-0-0 (eBook)

1. FICTION, SCIENCE FICTION, ALIEN CONTACT

To Cora for challenging and supporting
my crazy notions, including this one.
Also to Sarah for far exceeding her programming.

I would like to acknowledge all of the individuals
who added so much value to this book.


Thank you, Dave, for your valuable feedback.


To Bret for introducing me to the publishing process, to Jordan for
shepherding me along each step of the way, to Kevin for your expert editing
and improvements to the flow of the story, to Jodi for your beautiful design
work, to Oriana for your valuable marketing insight and to Suzanne and Jan
for getting my book across the finish line.


Special thanks to Alain Berset, 3D character artist extraordinaire, for
putting up with all my revisions and producing the amazing rendering of
Kelvoo on the cover.

# NEED TO KNOW—THE PREFACE TO KELVOO'S STORY

**Contributed by Samuel Buchanan (Terran human)**

I was deeply honored when my dearest friend, Kelvoo, asked me to write the preface to this book. As a kloormar, Kelvoo has done a remarkable job of writing in a style that humans like me and other members of the Alliance can understand and appreciate. Kelvoo asked me to write this preface to fill in gaps in the story and provide additional background information, especially for readers who lack thorough knowledge of the kloormari and their planet.

I offer the Planetary Alliance my deepest gratitude for granting Kelvoo the opportunity to provide this story to you. For many years I have tried, with little success, to advocate on behalf of the kloormari. I am confident that your request for Kelvoo's testimonial will have a profoundly positive impact on the kloormari and their planet.

**The Planet Kuw'baal**

When Kelvoo's home planet was originally charted by the twenty-second Terran planetary survey, it was designated as *Ryla 5*. From the vantage point of a passing vessel, the planet appears to be a perfectly smooth bright-white sphere due to its complete cover of water vapor tens of kilometers thick. The planet's mass is 1.08 times that of Terra.

The following illustrations are provided for reference:

# Terra and Kuw'baal
## External Appearances and Relative Sizes

Terra                    Kuw'baal

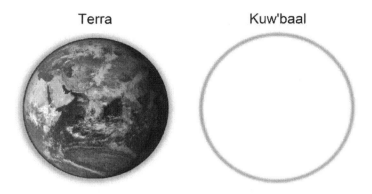

# Solar and Rylar Star Systems
## Relative Orbits of Innermost Planets

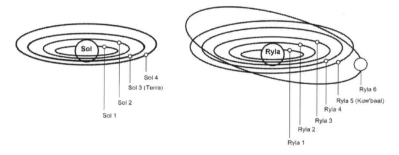

Note: *Star system diagrams are for illustrative purposes only and are **not** to scale*

A day on Kuw'baal lasts about 23 hours and 2 minutes in Terran time, and the planet orbits its star every 380.3 Terran days. In the initial drafts of Kelvoo's story, Kelvoo indicated whether Terran or Kuw'baal time units were used whenever duration was mentioned. I thought that this was cumbersome and unimportant to the story. It took some effort, but I was able to convince Kelvoo to drop these references when dealing with time. I suggest thinking in terms of Terran time units when reading Kelvoo's story.

Kuw'baal has a rocky surface ranging from vast plains to undulating hills. The planet's atmosphere contains oxygen, a variety of inert gasses, and traces of carbon dioxide, making it breathable by humans. The planetary survey noted Ryla 5 as being able to support life-forms, including the potential for future Terran colonies.

Rain occurs on most days, usually in the mid to late afternoon. The rains are heavy, and they generally come about suddenly, lasting from a few minutes to two hours. Lightning sometimes accompanies the rain. There are no oceans on the planet, but there are vast mineral salt flats. The rain flows onto the flats, depositing minerals there and quickly evaporating to replenish the constant clouds. Some of the deeper valleys contain long, serpentine lakes of high salinity water.

There are circumstances in which massive disruptions occur on the planet. After Kuw'baal, the next planet out from the star is Ryla 6, a large, frigid planet (10.4 Terran masses). Ryla 6 can pass close enough to Kuw'baal to subject the planet to massive tidal forces, resulting in violent quakes and landslides. These episodes last for several weeks.

Kuw'baal's orbit is on the same plane as its star's rotational equator. Fortunately for the kloormari, Ryla 6 has an orbital plane that differs by about twenty-three degrees. As such, close encounters with Ryla 6 occur only thousands of years apart. The kloormari word for these encounters cannot be represented in written Terran since the word is a low-frequency rumble that resembles the actual sound of an earthquake or rockslide. We simply use the term "upheaval."

## First Contact

Sixty-three years after the twenty-second survey, first contact was made indirectly via an autonomous, unpiloted lander positioned a short distance from Kelvoo's village. After 175 days of observation, the lander was retrieved. Days later, the lander's mothership, the *Pacifica Spirit*, touched down in the same position with a scientific team. I was a member of that landing party.

Kelvoo's story nearly ended before the *Pacifica Spirit* touched down on the surface of Kuw'baal. Out of an abundance of curiosity and exuberance, Kelvoo rushed toward the *Pacifica* as it touched down and came close to being incinerated by rocket exhaust or killed by blunt trauma from flying debris.

If Kelvoo had not survived, our mission would have been canceled, and the Terran First Contact Authority would have had a long-term responsibility to keep Kuw'baal isolated from outside contact while trying to mitigate the damage already done to kloormari society.

The particulars of our first-contact mission are included in Kelvoo's story, so there is no need for me to go into further detail.

**Physical Appearance of the Kloormari**

Gross External Kloormari Anatomy
Plate 1 - Anterior/Posterior View [1]

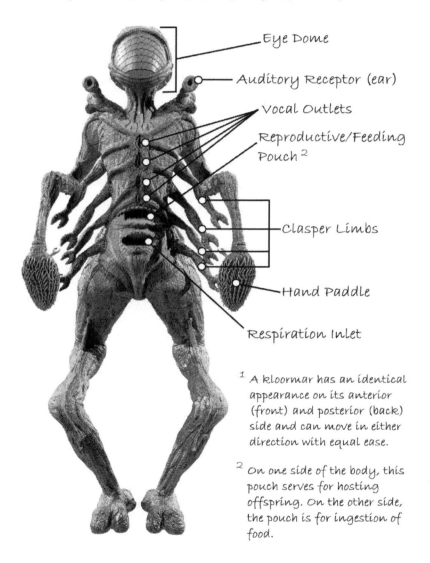

Eye Dome

Auditory Receptor (ear)

Vocal Outlets

Reproductive/Feeding Pouch [2]

Clasper Limbs

Hand Paddle

Respiration Inlet

[1] A kloormar has an identical appearance on its anterior (front) and posterior (back) side and can move in either direction with equal ease.

[2] On one side of the body, this pouch serves for hosting offspring. On the other side, the pouch is for ingestion of food.

# Gross External Kloormari Anatomy
# Plate 2 - Oblique View

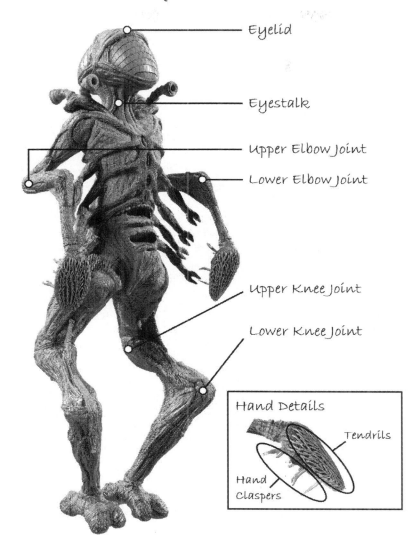

Eyelid

Eyestalk

Upper Elbow Joint

Lower Elbow Joint

Upper Knee Joint

Lower Knee Joint

Hand Details

Tendrils

Hand Claspers

A full-grown kloormar, when standing, is similar in height to a full-grown Terran, perhaps slightly shorter on average. The kloormari are bipedal most of the time, though they can move surprisingly quickly in a prone position using their multiple limbs. A kloormar can run forward or backward at the same speed and with the same ease.

A kloormar is extremely dextrous, able to perform precision work using each limb independently, making the kloormari unparalleled multi-taskers.

**Language and Communication**

The kloormari possess the ability to produce an incredible range of sound due to the number of vocal outlets and the ability to control each outlet independently to produce polyphonic sound. This level of control lets a kloormar have conversations with more than one other being simultaneously. Due to the varying sizes of the vocal outlets, the kloormari have a vocal range of 8 Hz to about 40,000 Hz. Humans perceive a loud 8 Hz tone as buffeting air. Most humans cannot hear tones below 20 Hz or above 20,000 Hz.

Due to the flexibility of their vocalization, a kloormar can effectively imitate any sound that is audible to humans, from standard Terran speech to sounds produced by any natural phenomena or even machinery.

One of the first questions to arise when studying kloormari words in written Terran is "What's with all of these 'K' words—Kuw'baal, kloormari, Kelvoo, etc.?" In most cases, kloormari nouns begin with a click sound. Terran linguists have chosen to use the letter "K" at the beginning of translated words that start with a click. Due to the limitations of the standard Terran alphabet, Terran versions of kloormari words are extremely crude. For example, in kloormari, the name "Kelvoo" is pronounced with a click, followed by a buzz similar to an "E" sound in words like "pet." This is followed by a clipped "L," transitioning into a humming "vvvvvv" sound, transforming again into a much higher pitched pure tone, "ooooo." All of this happens quickly with "Kelvoo," taking about 0.3 seconds to enunciate.

It is impossible for a human to imitate the sounds in the kloormari language. The kloormari, however, can imitate standard Terran or any other known spoken language with ease.

All kloormari speak the same language regardless of their location on Kuw'baal. This is because the species originated in one general area of the planet before dispersing across their world. With their perfect memories, each kloormar has full knowledge of the standard kloormari language.

One of the benefits of a monolingual planet-wide society is a standard written form of the language. The written language shows multiple layers, similar to Terran musical notation but with eight layers (one for each vocal outlet). Symbols in each layer represent the position of each set of vocal cords.

The variety of sound and the ability to produce multiple sounds simultaneously allow a kloormar to convey detailed information in a fraction of the time that standard Terran would require. In written form, Kelvoo's entire story could be represented in just nineteen Z-RES screens of text using the equivalent of a ten-point Terran font.

Note of interest: During our team's extended first-contact visit, we wanted to come up with a name for the planet to replace "Ryla 5," using a kloormari word out of respect for the inhabitants. Their name for the planet is unpronounceable, so we looked for words with meanings such as "home" or "place of the inhabitants." The team settled on the Terranized form "Kuw'baal" ("our place of origin"), because several members of the team were amused by the word's similarity to "cue ball." They thought that, when viewed from orbit, the planet looked like a cue ball from the old Terran tabletop ball-and-stick game known as "pool".

## Sustenance

There are just twenty-five known plant and seventeen animal species on Kuw'baal. The non-kloormari animal species are small and resemble Terran insects. The kloormari have no need to interact with them in their everyday lives. As such, Kelvoo's story makes no mention of other animal species on Kuw'baal.

The biomass of one plant species far exceeds that of all other vegetation combined. "Algel" is the common name that we Terrans use for the dominant plant species. The name is a shorthand combination of "algae" and "gel."

There are no carnivorous species on Kuw'baal. Rich in protein, minerals, and other nutrients, algel is the sole food source for all animal species on the planet.

Algel grows on rock along the banks of streams containing clean water. Like phytoplankton on Terra, algel is composed of single-cell plants that use photosynthesis for energy and minerals from rocks for nourishment. Each cell manufactures and exudes copious amounts of clear protein with a consistency between the "whites" of uncooked Terran chicken eggs and congealed gelatin. Due to its clarity, algel can grow up to two meters thick while still allowing light to penetrate and support the algel on the bottom layer.

To take samples, members of the scientific team usually dug their fingers into the algel and pulled out a handful of the substance. A handful of algel feels heavy. On close inspection, the gel is speckled with greenish-purple colonies of plant cells.

Algel flows slowly downhill, as do glaciers on colder planets. When an algel flow reaches a cliff, it hangs over the precipice and stretches down slightly. Slurping sounds follow as chunks fall off and impact the ground or algel pile below with a distinctive wet plop. Algel falls are rare on Kuw'baal, but one such fall is located a short walk from Kelvoo's village.

The kloormari word for "algel" sounds like the slurping sound of the substance itself. The sound cannot be accurately vocalized by Terrans, and as such, cannot be represented by the Terran alphabet.

Tests of algel indicated that it is not harmful for Terrans to consume and would make an excellent source of nutrition. After the test results were received, eight members of the first-contact team were served bowls of algel at suppertime as a social event and to record one another's reaction when eating the substance. Six team members spat the algel out within two seconds. The remaining two swallowed the algel. Four of the eight participants vomited forcefully within fifteen seconds. The team's objections were based on the texture of algel in the mouth and throat. One team member remarked that algel resembled grass that had passed through the digestive tract of a Terran slug, blended into rancid, semi-solidified fat, and subsequently eaten again and regurgitated by the same slug.

To remedy this, samples of algel were spread onto a fine mesh and dehydrated, reducing it to chewy strips, similar in consistency to a Terran human snack known as fruit leather. Four members of the scientific team tried the algel leather. All agreed that it was a great improvement over the untreated form, though still unpleasant. The leather was determined to be suitable as emergency nourishment for Terrans who would otherwise face starvation.

**Reproduction and Lifecycle**

Gender does not exist among the kloormari or any other organisms on Kuw'baal. This presented a challenge to Kelvoo when writing the story in Terran. Kelvoo did not use the pronouns "he," "she," "him," "her," or "his" when referencing other kloormari. As a result, some of Kelvoo's writing (and some of mine, for that matter) is a bit stilted. Kelvoo did not want to use "they" because it implies more than one individual, nor did Kelvoo use "it" since a kloormar is not an inanimate object.

The idea of requiring genetic material from two genders to produce offspring is a strange concept to a kloormar. Any full-grown kloormar can host and incubate an embryo in a reproductive pouch. Any kloormar can also contribute genetic material; however, a kloormar who hosts an embryo does not provide genetic material and has no genetic influence on the offspring's traits. The single privilege the host is granted is the right to name the child.

To reproduce, a kloormar volunteers or is selected to be a host. The host pulls the reproductive pouch open. Other kloormari deposit genetic material into the pouch via a flexible siphon that can be extended from any of the vocal outlets. Anywhere from seven to twenty-five donors typically provide genetic material. At least two kloormari must provide genetic material to the host; otherwise, conception will not take place. The scenario of only two genetic donors is considered to be offensive and reckless in kloormari society, as a larger number of donors greatly decreases the likelihood of genetic defects.

Kloormari do not experience any compelling lust to reproduce. Acting as a host or a donor is neither pleasurable nor unpleasant. Duty to community is the driving force behind reproduction. As such, pregnancy is always planned and is based on the size and age of the local population and the availability of resources.

After gestation lasting about four weeks, a new kloormar emerges from the pouch. Infants grow and learn quickly. A newborn can consume algel immediately and does not require a great deal of care. Infant kloormari will roam freely in a village and may receive assistance from any member of the community. There is no parent-child bond between any adult and child kloormar.

A kloormari child becomes fully grown after about forty-three years and is capable of taking either reproductive role at approximately forty-eight years. The average lifespan is about 304 years, give or take a decade.

Disease is unknown to the kloormari, so death does not come about through illness. Injury is the only cause of premature death; however, loss of a limb is not usually fatal, and limbs will grow back over time. Natural end of life occurs suddenly due to the shutdown of any one of the four interconnected neural hubs or "brains" in a kloormar's body. The causes of brain shutdown are unknown.

Members of some kloormari communities, such as Kelvoo's village, will carry their dead to a lake or streambed and deposit the corpse where the water will dissolve the nutrients in the body to replenish and return nourishment to the environment.

## Technology

When humans cite examples of their species' earliest landmark innovations, they tend to refer to development and use of the wheel, the ability to make fire, or the use of stone tools. Of these, stone tools were the only innovation used by the kloormari at the time of first contact. On the other hand, written language has been used by the kloormari since early in their evolution.

When discussing kloormari technology, the standard Terran expression "Necessity is the mother of invention" is apropos since, as a species, the kloormari have rarely had need of anything to ensure their survival.

The meticulously preserved historical accounts written by the kloormari tell us that innovation came about in short bursts, correlating directly to the planet-wide upheavals that occur whenever Ryla 6 makes a close pass to Kuw'baal. The accounts recall that a written form of the language was invented after an upheaval in order to pass information along to future generations. These accounts describe the warning signs of an impending upheaval, preparations to increase chances of survival, and strategies for coping with and recovering from upheaval events.

Writings were originally made on parchment-like material made from the k'k'mos plant (roughly pronounced *[click]-[click]-moss*). The plant has long, spiky leaves, similar to a Terran yucca plant. Long, straight, tough fibers are pulled from the leaves, laid out on a flat rock, and soaked in a thin layer of algel. Over several days, the parchment dries and becomes brittle. It is then wiped with the sticky juice from the succulent leaves of the "kobo" plant, which makes the parchment flexible and preserves it against decay.

To write on the parchment, a kloormar uses the tendrils on the back of the hand paddles to form the necessary shapes. The kloormar then dips the shapes into pigment and presses them onto the parchment.

Thousands of years after the advent of writing, a subsequent upheaval event led to another innovation. In that event, the ground began to shake, leading a large crowd of kloormari to gather on a plain that was sheltered by a rock face. The crowd knew not to get too close to the hillside due to possible rock-slides. A large rock-slide did occur at the base of the hill, exposing an almost flat ledge most of the way down the hill. Moments later, thousands of rocks broke free from a vertical face at the top of the hill. The rocks struck the ledge and bounced skyward and away from the hill, raining down onto the crowd, killing scores and injuring hundreds. This event led to the invention of structures to provide shelter from such projectiles.

A kloormar's home is constructed from a mixture of clay from mineral flats and rainwater, reinforced with k'k'mos fibers and coated with kobo juice. This "ksada" substance is formed into bricks that are stacked into a circular structure with a door and a window opening, then coated in a smooth layer of ksada. The conical roof is framed and supported by k'k'mos leaves, laminated together to form beams that are topped with tiles formed out of ksada. Each house provides shelter for a single kloormar.

A side benefit of kloormari structures is that they provide shelter from the rain. This is useful for the production and drying of parchments, which previously took place in caves. In addition to houses, villages have at least one larger structure that hosts group functions and shelters documents from the rain. The larger structures can be thought of as a combination of a community hall and library.

The kloormari originally lived in just one area of Kuw'baal, but the upheaval that led to the development of houses also made the kloormari decide to disperse, in case a future upheaval caused the entire population to be swallowed up by a giant crack in the earth or a volcanic eruption. From that moment on, groups of kloormari ventured from the village, following streams and finding valleys and lakes and places where algel was healthy and plentiful. After several day trips, a group would settle a new area. From there, new groups would repeat the process to establish new settlements farther afield.

A network of villages was established. Sometimes a village would be abandoned for one close by that had more resources, so most villages grew farther apart over time. Over the millennia, every part of Kuw'baal ended up with a village within a few days' travel of any given location. The villages are small, so the overall population remains sustainable.

As part of their education, some adult kloormari spend a few years traveling on foot between villages to learn from other kloormari and to share their knowledge.

## Intelligence

Assessing the intelligence of a species is subjective. If a particular criteria is used, it is simple to apply standard tests to measure overall intelligence. One such criteria could be the sophistication of the species' technology. Another criteria might be the species' ability to interpret, retain, and apply knowledge.

If we measured the intelligence of the kloormari by their technology at the time of first contact, we would conclude that they are probably the least intelligent of the sentient species that we know. In my opinion, using the technology standard to assess the kloormari would be egregiously misleading.

It is my absolute belief that the kloormari are by far the most intelligent species that we are aware of.

A kloormar never forgets. The kloormari remember every sound, every sight, every smell, every touch, every sensation, and every piece of information from the moment they leave their host's reproductive pouch until the moment of death.

The kloormari possess *hyperthymestic* memories. This differs from a photographic or eidetic memory, which relate more to the way that memory is processed. In humans, hyperthymesia is nearly unheard of, occurring in about 1 out of every 100 million individuals.

The capacity of a kloormar's brain appears to be unlimited. My own scientific team initially theorized that brain shutdown and death occurs when a kloormar's capacity for information is exceeded. This was not borne out by evidence, since individuals who had more diverse experiences and stimuli in their lives—and therefore, more information to process—did not have shortened lifespans.

When a kloormar is provided with information, it is learned immediately. New information can be combined with existing data to infer further data and draw conclusions.

When a Terran speaker asks a kloormar to repeat Terran words, the kloormar may do so at first with an accent, but after two or three tries, the kloormar will be able to repeat the words so perfectly that they are indistinguishable from the original speaker's voice.

The kloormari learn manual tasks almost instantly. Due to their multiple limbs, manipulators, and tendrils, the kloormari are extremely dextrous. They can learn and repeat tasks with ease and can improvise while performing tasks to improve efficiency.

Prior to human contact, the kloormari were prolific writers. Each village had a team of scribes that recorded every major and mundane daily event. Any community member could relate any information to a scribe in spoken or written form, and it would be placed into the village record.

Kloormari education begins at birth. Usually, a member of the community acts as an initial educator for an infant. They begin by vocalizing basic sounds, words, and phrases, which the infant learns to repeat. The educator will show objects, mime actions, and take the child to witness community activities or geographical features and vocalize the corresponding words and concepts.

After seven to ten days, an infant is capable of having a basic conversation with any other kloormar. At that point, the child is taught the kloormari alphabet and how words are sounded out. At about forty days of age, a kloormar is able to read and write.

Before human contact, a kloormar would—after becoming literate—study written historical accounts. History is learned mainly in written form because, in the same time span, the kloormari can receive several times more information by reading rather than by hearing spoken words. Occasionally, communities would gather around to hear an oral account of important stories, mainly to form closer community bonds. Stories were always factual and unfailingly precise. The concept of concocting and telling fictional stories did not exist among the kloormari and would have been dismissed as harmful and irrational.

Although the capacity of a kloormar's memory is seemingly unlimited, an individual will never know the entire history of the species, simply because, in their 300-year lifespan, there is only time to read or hear a small fraction of the recorded history. As such, after several years, a kloormari child would choose a specialized area of knowledge and learn under the tutelage of one or more kloormari with similar expertise.

The kloormari live to learn. Having no stimuli to process and nothing to study is highly stressful for a kloormar. Historical texts and specialty material were traditionally used to compensate for any lack of sensory inputs.

A common question by other species is whether the kloormari ever give their brains a rest. Sleep, or a similar transition to an alternative state of consciousness, is common to all known sentient species, and the kloormari are no exception.

A kloormar will enter a meditative state after receiving large amounts of information that needs to be processed. The kloormar will cease all physical activity and will shift the mind to analyzing, cataloging, and sorting recently acquired data. During this process, a kloormar's external senses will remain active but detached. If danger or anything else requires attention, the kloormar will cease meditation and resume the process at a later time. After meditation, the kloormari can recall the recent information faster and make connections with other data to deduce new facts.

***

If you have taken the time to read the preceding section, thank you for bearing with me. I promise that the information will give you the necessary context to appreciate and understand Kelvoo's story.

On a personal note, it felt strange to review the sections of Kelvoo's story that were about me. In part one, I thought that Kelvoo was being far too kind and complimentary toward me. In the final part, Kelvoo has a more accurate assessment of my character. As you will read, I am a deeply flawed human with many faults, but those flaws are important to the story. Despite my failings, Kelvoo has supported and stood by me.

# MY STORY

## BY KELVOO OF KUW'BAAL (KLOORMAR)

### Foreword

Thank you, members of the Planetary Alliance, for requesting my account of my interaction with the human species. Writing this account has been difficult for me, not only from an emotional point of view but also because, as a kloormar, my default writing style is far too detailed and pedantic for human readers. I am grateful that my human friend Samuel Buchanan agreed to assist me in making my story more readable and relatable.

It is of utmost importance to me that humans in particular take an interest in my story and retain important elements of my message. Human-kloormari interaction has caused a major upheaval in the lives and culture of the kloormari, and there are many important lessons to be learned by all.

With this in mind, and with the knowledge derived from my intense interest in human literature, I will adopt the style of an autobiographical novel, written to appeal on a personal and emotional level. Although it is against my nature, I will make use of simile, metaphor, contractions, and other literary devices in the interest of producing something memorable and meaningful to the various species participating in the inquiry.

# PART 1: ENLIGHTENMENT

# ONE: FIRST CONTACT

As the morning horizon of the Kuw'baal sky began its timeless transformation from black to grey, I made my way to the algel falls where I assumed my meditative stance, closed the lid over my eye, and let the slurping and plopping of the falls lull me into a deep state of meditation. I began the process of sorting, cataloging, and cross-referencing the inputs since my previous session as I prepared myself for another day or two of work, reading, and satisfying my primal urge for learning.

As the grey sky brightened to its full whiteness and intensity, my auditory senses picked up the growl of distant thunder. Although thunder that early in the day was unusual, it was not unheard of, so my meditation was not interrupted until the sound continued for far too long without fading away.

My external senses took over, jolting me into full consciousness. I swiveled my auditory receptors toward the sound, which was becoming a roar reminiscent of intense rain pummeling a roof. I scrabbled up the steep gravel path to the top of the falls, having to use my claspers to assist my lower limbs as pebbles slid beneath me and kicked out behind me. The rise of ten meters afforded me a better view.

I scanned the distant land. To my left was the gentle slope where the village homes were perched. The slope ended in the stream of water and algel that meandered and slid past the village. The opposing bank was lined with loose boulders, some of which had been arranged as stepping stones for fording the stream. Beyond the stream and farther to my right was a vast mineral plain with crystalline and powdery deposits brightly reflecting patches of white, yellow, red, and rich browns. Farther right, the distant ridges bordering the plain were closer, revealing bands of black, beige, and yellow where surface rock had fallen away during ancient upheavals. This narrowed the plain to a valley between my position atop the falls and the ridge. A rocky moraine of jumbled, jagged boulders sloped from my location down to the plain.

The roar continued to increase in intensity.

As I concentrated on the farthest land close to the horizon, a dark speck on top of a bright light appeared in the sky on the other side of the ridge. This

3

was astonishing. Apart from a thrown object, I had never seen an object moving above the land unless it was falling directly down like raindrops or a rock. The speck sped toward the village above the ground and yet below the sky as if it had been thrown but would not fall back to the ground. This was confusing.

The speck grew larger and louder. Then, as it approached, it slowed and moved closer to the ground. The speck became a black object, resembling a rounded cube. It rode atop a bright light as though the light from the entire sky had been replicated and concentrated into a single point. The object rotated and then descended vertically toward a flat shelf of ground slightly higher than the mineral plain adjoining it.

From my vantage point, I saw eighty-seven villagers running onto the plain. I joined the rush, slipping, bouncing, and painfully scraping my way down the boulders to the plain and then breaking into a run toward the object's apparent destination. The roar became so painfully loud that we had to stop at 124.3 meters from the object's target point. I was relieved that we stopped short as huge clouds of dust and chunks of mineral deposits radiated out from below the object like a powerful wind blowing straight down. My eyelid closed shut, and my inhalations stopped short as we were engulfed in dust and debris. I folded myself into a ball as a wave of heat, gravel, and sharp mineral crystals scoured my skin. Acrid, unfamiliar odors stung my olfactory receptors.

The roaring did not fade away as thunder would; it simply stopped instantly. The hot wind halted, replaced by a natural breeze. Through my eyelid, I sensed the ambient light getting brighter. I blinked away dust from the surface of my eye as the cloud cleared and the dust settled downwind, revealing the object. It rested solidly on the plain, supported by four straight sticks, each extending at the same angle from each corner of the object. The object's outer surfaces not covered with dust were as black as night and yet as reflective as water or algel. Shapes extended from the overall cube with bulbous or angular profiles. Black marks radiated from the ground below the object's center, fanning out in every direction.

For those of us gathered around the object, our senses were nearly overwhelmed. Our species had no prior experience with such events. Our group circled the object, making observations from each angle. We chattered with other villagers as we peppered one another with raw observational data. The chattering grew as hordes of additional villagers came running toward the object.

Kwazka, an elder, approached the front of the crowd. The tightly packed blue speckles on Kwazka's upper limbs and eyelid indicated great age and implicit wisdom. Instead of participating in the chatter, Kwazka circled the object slowly, taking in the scene. The only sounds that Kwazka made were short, pure tones of varying frequencies directed at the object in order to

4

process the echoes to determine the object's hardness and various structural attributes.

We had no fear of the object, because we had no experience of danger from unmoving objects on flat ground. We kept several meters away to process the object's overall features before moving in for closer, more detailed analysis.

A villager named Ksoomu stepped closer. When Ksoomu was within 5.2 meters from the object, it produced a buzzing sound, growing louder as Ksoomu drew closer. At a distance of 4.3 meters, we heard a short snap. A thin strand of blue lightning extended from the object to the center of Ksoomu's mass. Along with Ksoomu, we all jumped back, trying to make sense of what had just happened.

"Are you intact?" Kwazka asked.

"I experienced only mild irritation," Ksoomu replied. "I jumped back because I was startled."

Ksoomu made a second, slower approach. At the same distance as before, a more intense buzz sounded, and then a louder snap rang out with a brighter strand of lightning. Ksoomu emitted an exclamation of pain while falling to the ground. "I felt a sting, but I am otherwise undamaged," Ksoomu remarked. "I shall make one more attempt."

A child named K'raftan, twenty-three years of age, stepped forward. "I will approach at the same time to see how the object reacts to simultaneous advances."

The same events repeated. This time, at 4.3 meters, a bang as loud as lightning rang out. A blindingly intense bolt extended in two directions as both kloormari were propelled back several meters. At first, we feared they were dead. Black marks were clearly visible on their skin, surrounding a blistered wound. On closer inspection, we realized that both of them were unconscious, in a state resembling meditation but not responsive to external stimuli. Ksoomu and K'raftan began to stir, slowly regaining their senses.

K'raftan's inquisitiveness was clearly stronger than the will to avoid pain. "I shall try again with a faster approach."

"No!" Kwazka shouted. "This object presents a potential danger to those who approach. We cannot allow our curiosity to cost the life of any member of our community. We shall remain 4.6 meters from the object, and we shall move farther away if it buzzes. Is there any dissent among us?" Nobody raised any objections, so Kwazka continued. "I propose that we record and process all that we have experienced so far. Let us form a group that includes the scribes to record our preliminary observations and experiences. A second group can commence meditation to process and refine the preliminary data. When that is completed, let us record and redistribute the refined information. In the meantime, those who are not in a group can return to the village, and a small group can remain here to monitor the object. Is this agreeable to all?"

We all vocalized our agreement and began sorting out our groupings as we started to disperse.

"Look!" K'raftan exclaimed.

We turned around to see a limb unfolding from the top of the object and assuming an upright position. A cylindrical "hand" with a reflective end rotated and then stopped. We gathered around the object. To get a better view, I walked to one side. The hand rotated to stay pointed at me as I moved. When I stopped, the hand stopped. A couple of villagers moved together in the other direction, and the hand rotated to follow them.

"Could that be an eye that has only a limited arc of vision?" a young villager speculated. "Is it, perhaps, observing us?"

"Could the buzzing and lightning from the object have been a warning and a self-defense maneuver?" another villager suggested.

These concepts were an epiphany and a shock to us all.

This was no object; this was a living creature!

# TWO: THE LIGHTNING CREATURE
# AND ITS OFFSPRING

Due to my previous vantage point from the falls, I was in the group whose purpose was to relate our observations to the scribes. After my report, I spent the rest of the day going about my regular routine but keeping the creature within my sight.

On the second day, a flap opened on top of the creature, and another creature emerged. It had four outstretched arms with a flat, semi-clear circle at the end of each one. The "child" creature ascended and held its position above the host creature. This was confusing. It was as though an object had been thrown skyward but failed to return to the ground.

As the child moved over us, we felt a wind blowing down from it. The child creature moved to the end of the village closest to the falls, skirted the village in a straight line, turned at a right angle for a few meters, then moved back in the direction it came from. When it reached the stream at the edge of the village, it turned and moved a few more meters along the village perimeter, then crossed the village again. The creature repeated this zigzag pattern until it had passed over every section of the village. Then the child returned to its host and descended back through the flap into the interior of its parent. The flap closed, and all was silent again.

Each day, the child creature emerged once or twice. It did not make any trips when rain was falling. Sometimes the child moved in a pattern, usually staying over or close to the village, but sometimes it would disappear into the distance and then return later.

Six days after the host creature's arrival, the three eldest villagers—Kwazka, Kahini, and K'losk'oon—called a community meeting. Such meetings, in which the villagers gathered in one location, would occur after eventful happenings when the community members' body language, gestures, and subtle intonations could convey more nuanced information than written information could provide.

"What might we conclude from our observations of these recent eventful days?" Kahini asked.

"The host creature came from the sky," a voice called out. "It makes lightning. Perhaps, whenever the sky lightning comes, it is created by creatures like this."

"The host creature can reproduce, but its offspring looks nothing like it," another voice said. "Perhaps other types of creatures provide it with seed, and it serves as host for many types of creatures that we have never seen before."

Other voices were raised.

"In the last six days, we have seen two creatures that have no mention in any historical accounts. It may be that more new creatures will be coming."

"Perhaps there is a sky world, and something is happening to make the creatures come to the ground."

"We do not know whether the host is sentient, but the child appears to be intelligent since we have observed how it sometimes moves in methodical patterns."

"Could it be that the creatures have come to warn us? Could a new upheaval, unlike any other before, be imminent?"

"Maybe the creatures were sent by other beings to protect us."

"Could it be that there are superior creatures who created us?"

"Have these beings been observing us?"

"Maybe they are sending a message."

"Perhaps we have displeased them!"

"That's enough!" K'losk'oon interjected.

"We called this meeting out of concern about exactly the type of speculation that we have just heard," Kwazka said. "Our own long experience and historical texts have shown that theories and guesses do not lead to positive outcomes. They cause us to convince ourselves of falsehoods and waste time and thought on spurious information. This spawns confusion and can lead to community discord.

"This much we can be sure of . . . The new objects are, in fact, living creatures. The host creature came from the sky. The host creature makes lightning. The host creature gave birth to a different type of creature. These creatures can move above the ground, which we would never have believed possible.

"We have the supporting observations and evidence to confirm these findings. Any other significant conclusions are only speculation. We do not have the inputs or any existing frames of reference to ascertain additional facts.

"We must accept that there are some things that we do not know. Perhaps we shall never have all of the answers. We must continue with calm, patient observation of the creatures, and we must record and share our observations with the goal of learning more over time. I advise that we refrain from assumptions and speculation. Do K'losk'oon and Kahini concur?"

"Yes," the elders replied.

"Do all villagers agree?" Kahini asked.

We all agreed.

I had never doubted that we would come to a sensible conclusion, and I was certain that the ideas thrown around at the meeting were just a fleeting intellectual exercise that nobody would take seriously. I did, nonetheless, feel a mild sense of relief that my community would not go down such a murky, uncertain path.

In the following weeks and months, daily life gradually returned to a more normal state. We gathered algel, built or repaired homes, kept in touch with other villages, and read, wrote, and meditated like before. Each day, a few citizens would take their turn staying close to the lightning creature, observing it, and documenting its child's trips.

After 175 days, the lightning creature started buzzing spontaneously. Small streams of lightning jumped between the creature and the ground in a circular area around the creature. The buzzing grew in volume, and the radius of the lightning circle grew. The observing kloormari backed away to avoid the lightning. Once the creature had cleared the surrounding kloormari to a radius of one hundred meters, a hiss emanated from the creature's base, followed by a roar, a blinding light, and another barrage of dust, debris, and heat.

The lightning creature rose toward the sky on a pillar of flickering light. In a column just below the light, our view of the distant hills shimmered as if reflected in rippled water. The creature shot higher while slowly tilting to move away. The lightning creature and its child within disappeared over the horizon on its journey back to its home in the sky world. A vast and empty silence followed.

The lightning creature was never seen again on Kuw'baal.

# THREE: SECOND CONTACT

Six days after the lightning creature departed, I completed an evening meditation session by the falls. My sessions had been taking longer since the lightning creature's visit, and I found myself having to hurry back to the village before darkness set in.

I was making my way back to the village on a path along the stream bank when I stumbled over some loose stones and fell. As I got back to my feet, a faint, low-pitched roar caught my attention. As the noise grew in intensity, it seemed to come from every direction. I moved to a sitting position, bracing for a quake and dreading the possibility that an upheaval was starting. When the shaking didn't happen, part of me wondered whether the lightning creature had returned, but this noise was different. It was much deeper and interspersed with crackling sounds. I moved my eye so that its base was level and tried to concentrate on the areas just above the horizon, but in the nearly complete blackness, I could only guess the direction.

I sensed the sudden appearance of light almost directly above me. I didn't see the light appear because my eyelid was covering the portion that looks skyward. When I moved my eyelid down, I saw six lights evenly spaced as though positioned on the points of a hexagon. By then the roar was intense. The flickering lights grew larger and brighter as they moved closer. An additional light, this one totally steady in its intensity, cast a cone of illumination through the atmosphere and formed a perfect circle in the exact spot where the much smaller lightning creature had rested.

The light from the new creature was illuminating the mineral plain and the raised area that the lightning creature had occupied. I was compelled to observe the new creature as closely as I could. I wasn't close to any of the stepping-stone paths over the stream, so I simply jumped in. I landed on top of an algel pile as my lower limbs flipped out from under me. I assumed a prone position and scuttled on all of my appendages as I flopped, slid, and writhed across the stream to the edge of the plain.

I heaved my bulk up the bank, weighed down by clinging algel. Then I stood, shook off the algel, and broke into a run. As the creature neared the ground, boulders on the plain cast long, flickering shadows. The contrast of the intense light against the black shadows was disorienting, but somehow, I managed to keep running at full tilt.

As the creature touched down, I realized I had seriously underestimated its size, and I was dangerously close to it. I stopped when the blast of air and dust hit me. I noticed loose rocks of up to several kilograms shooting out like projectiles. I experienced a sharp pain in my lower torso accompanied by the sense of being pushed backward with great force.

I coaxed my mind back toward consciousness and opened my eye. Some of my ocular segments were out of alignment, so I was seeing multiple images. I was lying on my side, which turned the ground into a wall. Sticking out from the wall was a huge black object adorned with several sources of bright light, illuminating the ground. Based on reflections from some of its lights, the object's surface was shiny, indicating it may be the same type of being as the lightning creature.

Were the images real or were they being manufactured by traumatic injury to one or more of my brains? I didn't know.

A flap was open on the creature's side, with the end of the flap on the ground. I saw the silhouettes of several child creatures rapidly emerge from the flap. I couldn't determine the exact number due to my visual impairment. Each child appeared to have only four large limbs, two of which were for walking upright, resembling the way that my species travel. An approximately cylindrical object was located where a kloormar's eye would normally be. Light emanated from the highest point of each child creature. An additional source of light shone from one of the upper limbs on each creature.

The creatures ran toward me. As my vision started to resolve, I saw that there were six of them. One was carrying a flat object about two meters long. I felt no fear, perhaps because of my impaired state, or maybe because my curiosity overwhelmed all other responses.

When the child creatures reached me, they stopped and stood around me. Their skin was wrinkled and bright white and made crinkling sounds as they moved. The creatures were vocalizing. Their sounds were simple and had a narrow range of tone that seemed to me like a near monotone. I concluded that they were likely intelligent beings since they seemed to respond to each other's voices.

One of the beings placed the flat object on the ground beside me. Using their upper limbs, the beings rolled me on top of the object. Three handles were located on each long side of the flat object. Each being grasped a handle and lifted the flat object, and me, from the ground and made their way back to the parent creature's open flap.

On the way back to the parent, the beings walked in silence until one of them vocalized. I didn't know the meaning of the sounds at the time, but the words were, "Bloody hell, guys, we sure botched this goddam mission!"

I was carried up the flap, eye first. The creature's interior was bathed in light. I bent my eyestalk to look down past my lower limbs. The flap closed with a steady whining sound, followed by a solid "click."

I was, as the Terran expression goes, "in the belly of the beast."

11

# FOUR: HELLO

*Note to reader: In this chapter, I use terms such as "corridor," "room," "stretcher," "bench," and "chair." Readers should be advised that I was unaware of, or did not have the full concept of, these things until learning about them later from the visitors. Since readers will be acquainted with these objects, I will use the familiar terminology in the interest of expediency rather than trying to describe each of these objects as I sensed them at the time. I do not use conventional terms for many other items because I want readers to understand my state of mind as I attempted to comprehend and make sense of these things.*

The beings carried me down a short corridor and turned into a small room. They placed the stretcher on a bench, left the room, and closed the door behind them. I was sore in many parts of my anatomy. I slowly and stiffly sat up on the bench. My vision had resolved, and I felt as though any damage to me would not be permanent.

The walls, ceiling, floor, and bench were white and pristine. A window was in the wall opposite the bench. A table and a chair were in place, allowing a seated individual to look through the window.

I stood tentatively, walked the two paces to the desk, and peered through the window. The six beings were observing me. As we regarded each other, I reached out to the opening. I was startled when a force stopped my manipulators. When I looked at the window from an angle, I could see reflected light. Somehow, unlike a kloormari window, the opening framed a substance that allowed light to pass through but was absolutely solid. The substance, I learned later, was called "glass."

I sniffed the atmosphere and realized there was no variation in the smell from the moment that I was brought inside the creature, though the air had an unfamiliar dryness.

I observed the floor, walls, and ceiling, looking for an exit. I felt the seams of the door and the window frame. I pushed and pulled the surfaces in these areas but could tell that they were solid, and I would not overcome my confines by physical force. I went back to the window to view the beings again. They vocalized to one another, then left the corridor, closing a door behind them.

I was alone.

My rational, inquisitive mind fled, and fear flooded in. Why did the child beings take me to their parent? What were they going to do with me? Was the big creature going to leave and take me away to the sky world, so I would never see my species or my village again? My body responded to my panic in ways that I had never felt before. My extremities tingled with hundreds of points of sharp pain. My respiration became shallow and strained, and the contrast of my vision intensified, making the whiteness of the room painful to my eye.

A deep purple light and a high-pitched tone grew in the corridor, snapping me back into a semblance of rational thought. My panic faded, but my overall fear did not. The purple light intensified until it flooded the entire corridor. A moment later, the purple light and the sound were gone, and the child beings filed back into the corridor and did something amazing.

One of the beings grasped a small protrusion at the base of the cylinder on top of the shoulders of another being. The first being pulled the protrusion part of the way around the base, opening a slit in the skin. The being opened another slit down the length of the other being's torso. That being then pulled off its own skin!

Inside the skin of the top cylinder was a roundish object, topped with thousands of thin fibers, which extended down one side. On the other side were two holes with ball-shaped objects recessed in them. A triangular protuberance stuck out below the ball holes with two holes in the end. Below that was a horizontal slit with plump edges. When the beings vocalized, the horizontal slits opened and moved. On either side of the roundish object were two stationary flaps. This entire object was supported on a stalk that resembled a kloormar's optical stalk but smoother and less symmetrical.

When the beings had removed their outer skins, they revealed themselves to be less bulky. Their upper limbs had flat ends with five small, flexible appendages. Except for the round object and stalk above the shoulders and the ends of the upper appendages, the beings were covered in what appeared to be another layer. The coverings were bright orange with a round shape containing symbols on one side of the torso, along with black-striped shapes on a shoulder. The coverings were identical on each being except for the number and shape of the shoulder stripes. The orange covering ended near the bottom of the lower limbs, where the limb narrowed the most. Below that were coverings that seemed to be of a much stiffer, thicker material with a thick, black, solid material on the surface that touched the ground.

One of the beings vocalized to another and held an object toward the second being. The second creature turned its entire body so that the round object on top had its holes facing the first being. The second being took two steps toward the first being. The ball holes rotated down to face the object, which the second being reached out and took.

Could it be that the ball objects were used for vision? They were tiny, and since they were both on the same side, it seemed as though the creatures could only see in the general direction that they were pointing. This idea was supported by the fact that the being turned toward the other being when communicating. This, combined with the way the lower limbs were jointed, led me to conclude that these creatures could move their bodies rapidly and effectively in only one direction!

My fear lessened as a new feeling grew in its place: pity. When I considered these creatures' existence, I wondered how they could possibly cope with such handicaps.

The beings were verbally communicating with one another in soft tones. One of the beings moved a chair, positioning it across from me on the other side of the window, and directed its eyes toward my eye. It pointed one of its upper limbs at the center of its upper torso. "Samuel Buchanan." It pointed the limb toward the same location on my torso, then waited, staring at me. It repeated the action, this time using its other limb to point to its vocal opening as it repeated, "Samuel Buchanan."

When it pointed to me again, I pointed to the center of my torso. "Samuel Buchanan." When I heard myself say the words, I knew I was not duplicating the sound properly. The pace of the chattering between the beings picked up.

The being repeated the action. Again, I said, "Samuel Buchanan." I knew my pronunciation had improved this time. The creature's vocal slit turned up at the sides and opened slightly, revealing an upper and lower row of shiny white objects inside.

I knew that I could do better. I pointed to the same spot. "Samuel Buchanan." This time my audio receptors told me that I had replicated the being's voice perfectly with identical frequencies, speed, intonation, and emphasis. The being's vocal and vision holes opened wide, and all talk between the creatures ceased. After a moment, they started vocalizing loudly and rapidly. Each being's vocal slit turned up and exposed the rows of white objects. The creatures turned to one another, raising their upper limbs and slapping the flat ends together. I sensed that the creatures were pleased with our interaction. I felt rather pleased with my performance too.

I now knew that "Samuel Buchanan" meant "upper torso."

The creature that had spoken to me motioned to the others, and they quieted their chatter. This time the creature pointed to itself again. "Samuel Buchanan." The creature then stood and touched another being on the shoulder, saying, "Lisa Thomas." I surmised that "Lisa Thomas" meant "shoulder." I was confused when the being pointed at the top center of a different being's torso. "Rashid Gulamali." The creature placed its hand on top of another. "Li Huang."

I started to think that perhaps the creature was not reciting body parts but was providing the name that identified each being. The being who spoke must be named "Samuel Buchanan." The creature continued with "Pauline Scott" and "Michael Stone." The creature sat again, looked directly at me, and gestured toward its vocal slit and then to me.

"Kelvoo," I said.

The beings became excited again. I placed a hand against the clear material in the opening. Samuel Buchanan stood and slapped the flat end of its upper limb on the other side of the opening opposite my hand. I surmised this was a congratulatory gesture.

Samuel Buchanan sat again and gestured at the other creatures, once again signaling them to cease their chatter. I decided to reverse the situation by speaking my name and pointing at Samuel Buchanan with the expectation that the being would repeat my name. The being made a click sound by opening its vocal orifice quickly. This was followed by a buzz and then a "voo."

I repeated my name, and Samuel Buchanan tried again. Sam's vocal range was limited and could not reproduce the "el." The "voo" was recognizable but was in far too low a register. We tried two more times, but I realized these primitives lacked the sonic range and the skill to communicate in the kloormari language. If we were going to communicate by voice, I would have to learn the creatures' language. This seemed as though it would be a relatively easy task given the simplicity of their vocalizations.

Samuel Buchanan briefly spoke to the others and then pointed to its torso and looked at me. "Sam." Then it looked at one being at a time. They pointed to themselves, and each vocalized in turn.

"Lisa."

"Rashid."

"Li."

"Pauly."

"Mike."

Sam pointed at me, and I said "Kelvoo." I wasn't sure whether I was supposed to shorten my name, but in kloormari, the word "kel" means path, and "voo" is a form of the verb "to eat," so a shortened name would make no sense.

One of the beings brought a box on a small table into the corridor. The box had a slot and various lights on it. Sam produced a flat stick. It opened its vocal slit and scraped an interior surface, then held the stick close to the window, showing me some liquid and buildup of material on the edge.

Sam took an identical stick and placed it in a tray beside the window, then pushed the tray. On my side of the wall, a hatch opened, and the tray slid toward me. I picked up the stick, and Sam pointed at me. I moved to put the stick into one of my vocal openings. Sam waved and pointed to my food pouch, mimicking the opening of the flap. I opened my food pouch and scraped the stick along its interior surface, collecting a small quantity of liquid and tissue on the edge of the stick. Sam pointed to the tray. I placed the stick in the tray, and Sam pulled the tray back to the humans' side of the wall.

The being called "Li" placed the stick in an opening of the box with lights and touched some square shapes on the box's surface.

Sam took out a flat, rectangular object. It had a frame around a shiny surface. Sam touched the surface, and it lit up with white on the entire surface except for a red circle in a corner. Sam took a black stick with a pointed end and dragged it across the surface. A black line followed the point of the stick. Sam touched the red circle, and the line disappeared.

Sam took out an identical object and stick and passed them to me via the tray.

Sam started to draw pictures on the object, resembling members of Sam's species and actions being taken by them. Sam drew the lightning creature and what I assumed were huge creatures like the one that we were inside of. I couldn't tell for certain because I had only seen the creature in darkness. While drawing, Sam spoke, trying, I assumed, to help me understand the words by relating them to the images.

I learned several words, including "Infotab," which referred to the object in my hands, and "stylus" for the drawing stick. The lightning creature was called a "lander," and the massive creature that we were in was a "vessel."

Sam's Infotab drawings included vessels and landers with many dots and a few circles behind them. I had no idea what this was intended to convey.

Sam seemed to be encouraging me to draw, so I did. I drew pictures, and I also wrote kloormari words and spoke them, but it seemed that Sam would never understand or be able to pronounce my words.

The box out in the corridor started emitting a steady tone. A rectangle on the front of the box lit up, looking like a smaller version of the device that Sam had provided to me. The rectangle was green, and symbols were displayed on it, which I thought might be components of the creatures' written language. "Li" touched the screen and then uttered the words, "All tests are complete. The subject is clear on all levels." I did not understand these words, but moments later, Sam stood and opened the door to the room confining me.

Sam stepped in. Sam's upper limbs were spread down and away from the body. The digits on the ends of Sam's upper limbs were spread apart. I had the impression that Sam was indicating peaceful intent. Sam slowly reached an arm toward me, using the other arm to point to my hand. I reached out my hand. Sam grasped it. "Hello," Sam said, then exposed the white objects in its vocal slit.

Sam motioned me to follow. I stepped out of the room and into the corridor. One by one, each of the beings extended their arms, and grasped my outstretched hand, and said, "Hello." I responded in kind.

We proceeded down the corridor toward the parent creature's external flap. We turned and passed through a door into a much larger room. A long table was in the center of the room, and the table was encircled by twelve chairs. Each of the six beings lowered themselves into a chair and motioned me to do the same. I complied, but I was very uncomfortable. The chair did not do a good job of accommodating all four of my knees. Leaning against the back of the chair blocked half of my vocal outlets and one of my two respiration inlets. As I shifted and leaned to find a more comfortable position, the chair shot out from under me, clattering into a wall and sending me sprawling on the floor!

The creatures moved rapidly to my side, seemingly distressed. Rashid and Lisa took my upper arms and started lifting me. I got my feet under me, and they let go as I steadied myself. Lisa pulled the chair back, and I assumed a high kneeling position, bending only my lower knees. The floor was covered with a soft substance, so I was very comfortable in my position. It also placed me at about the same height as the seated creatures.

On the wall at the far end of the table was a flat rectangle that looked like a much larger version of the Infotab. Sam pointed a thicker stick toward the rectangle, and it lit up. Sam pointed to the rectangle and said, "panel."

Sam proceeded to display a series of images on the panel, accompanied by words. I sensed that Sam had done this before and that a pre-planned series of pictures and words were being shown as part of a method for teaching communication.

After several hours, I had learned a great deal. For example, when referring to Lisa, Li, or Pauly, Sam used the term "she." "He" was used for Rashid and Mike, and for Sam when another being referred to Sam. To indicate possession of something, "her" was used for the former three and "his" for the latter. "Him" also seemed to be used for Sam's group. I surmised that these terms must have indicated status or perhaps an attribute that was not apparent to me.

Sam indicated that creatures of his type were called "humans." He also taught me the names of some human body parts. After viewing the images and the accompanying words, the humans said in unison:

"Head and shoulders, knees and toes, knees and toes, knees and toes. Head and shoulders, knees and toes, eyes, ears, mouth, and nose."

The humans chanted these words while pointing to parts of their bodies. The humans elongated the duration and tone of the words in a curious way. Sam brought out a device that produced similar styles of sound. He used the words "song" and "music" to describe this manner of speech.

I started to realize that my anxiety was gradually melting away, replaced by fascination, and I was becoming less wary of the humans.

Sam murmured to the other beings and then looked at me. "Lander . . . eye," he said slowly and with intensity. He touched the stick that controlled

17

the monitor. A picture emerged, and the picture moved as though we were seeing a partial view through another being's eye! The image started as all white with darker parts starting to fade in. The white faded away, and I could see ground, as though viewed from a hill of great height. The distant ground below grew closer as though the being was falling. As it did, I could make out a plain. I could also see falls of algel and water feeding a stream. The stream flowed between the plain and a rise with houses on it. I saw eighty-seven kloormari running from the village, across the stream, and onto the plain. I saw another kloormar scrambling down a hill of boulders from the top of the falls.

I was stunned to realize I was witnessing the past arrival of the lander! The figure descending the boulders was me! Sam had said, "Lander eye!" It made sense—I was witnessing what the lander creature saw, as if the humans had been able to reach into the lander's visual memory and display it at will!

At that moment, something happened that I had never experienced before, and as far as I knew, neither had any other kloormari. The volume of information, the intensity of the sensory inputs, and the realization of what I saw overwhelmed me to such an extent that I entered an involuntary meditative state. My mind turned inward as I struggled to catalog and cross-reference the data that I had been exposed to since the large parent creature had appeared.

I do not know exactly how long I was mentally absent. I snapped back to a conscious state when Pauly clapped her hands near my auditory organs. I was far from processing all of the queued-up data, but enough was cataloged that I could function again.

The humans were gathered around, examining me closely. I sensed that they were very concerned for my well-being.

After a few moments of rest, Sam made some movements on his Infotab. Six flat panels on one of the walls hummed and slid upward, revealing windows. I could see the mineral plain and distant hills of my world. Since the moment I entered the parent creature, enough time had passed that the scene was illuminated under the bright-white midday sky.

I approached the windows and peered down and to the side toward my village. The plain around the vessel was covered in kloormari! Perhaps the entire village was there, watching the massive beast.

Sam looked at his companions. "Get ready," he said. The humans looked at one another and pulled their orange "clothing" (a new word Sam taught me) down to remove the wrinkles. Some of them checked their "hair" (another word from Sam) and smoothed it down. Some of the group did something on their Infotabs and stowed them in a pouch on their outer layer.

Sam opened the door, and we exited into the corridor next to the vessel's closed flap. Sam positioned me in front of the center of the flap. The humans placed themselves with three on either side of me, so we were positioned like the leading edges of a triangle with me in front.

Sam stepped out of formation for a moment and pressed his hand against a panel on one side of the flap. As Sam took his place again, the flap hummed and slowly opened outward, touching the ground to serve again as a ramp. The moist, fragrant atmosphere of Kuw'baal wafted in, shrouding me in comfort. I strode down the ramp with the humans behind me into the presence of a multitude of astonished, welcoming kloormari.

# FIVE: WELCOME

The villagers kept their distance from the vessel, shouting questions to me as I approached.

"Are you unharmed?"

"What are those orange creatures?"

"Are you being held captive?"

"Are the creatures dangerous?"

Once I was most of the way to the crowd, they surged forward. The humans halted a few meters behind me. I held out my arms and spoke. "These creatures are called humans. I was too close to the large parent creature when it touched the ground. As a result, I was hurt. The humans were concerned for my safety. They took me inside the beast. They may look hideous and frightening, but I believe the humans are of no threat to us. We have been learning to communicate with one another. Where were you when the beast landed?"

The villagers replied that since darkness had fallen shortly before the visitors' arrival, they had been inside their homes. When the villagers heard the roar and saw the lights coming from the sky world, they gathered in the center of the village to devise a plan of action. Urging one another to stay calm, they used the light from the creature to walk to the edge of the village where they could view the plain.

I explained that I had been beside the stream when the creature appeared. I crossed the stream right away and ran toward the beast. "Did you not see me?" I inquired. They explained that the vessel was low by the time they had a good view. The column of light below the vessel was so bright, and the shadows were so dark that they could hardly see anything at all. When the column of light suddenly vanished, they had to get back to their houses by feeling their way along. Some kloormari had spent the night in others' houses, and some just waited in the dark. At first light, the villagers had made their way across the stream and the plain. They had been waiting close to the beast and watching. No one had even realized I was missing until they gathered by the beast.

I held my arms out again. "Although these humans have arrived unexpectedly, I believe it is in our interest to welcome them as we would welcome guests from another village. These are simple creatures. They are very limited in their physical and intellectual capabilities, but they can communicate on a basic level. Despite their limitations, I believe we can learn a tremendous amount from them. I propose that we invite them to visit our village as guests. Do we all concur?"

The crowd responded enthusiastically.

"I will now introduce each of the humans by the full name that each uses."

As I spoke each human's name, the corresponding being stepped forward, placed the flat surface of one hand over their sternum, and bowed their head in what I assumed to be a sign of respect. With the introductions completed, my fellow villagers gathered around. The humans reached out to grasp the hands of the kloormari or to touch them on the shoulder. Some villagers felt the humans' clothing, hair, and faces.

The crowd included many kloormari infants and children who were particularly curious, energetic, and unafraid. A tiny kloormar, K'pai (five years of age), tried to climb the lower limbs of the human, Pauline Scott. "Pauly" reached down and gently lifted and held K'pai in her upper limbs. Her eyes opened wide, and her mouth opened and turned up. Though alarmed at first, the villagers were amused and reassured by Pauly's gentleness.

Several villagers prompted me to bring the humans to the village. I motioned for the humans to follow. Our huge group paraded over the plain, across the stream, and up the hill to the village. As we walked over the cracked ground and crunching mineral crystals in the bright light, I related my experiences in the parent creature to many of my fellow villagers. Another large group walked around the humans, observing every action and detail with rapt attention.

When we reached the stream, the smell of fresh algel made me realize how hungry I was. Just before crossing, I took a small detour to the shore of the stream and scooped up a couple of handfuls of the refreshing, satisfying sustenance, putting one scoop into my eating pouch and offering another to the humans. The humans held up a hand or shook their heads, which I took as a sign that they were declining the offer. Being from the sky world, perhaps these creatures did not require food, or maybe they were just unfamiliar with algel. I didn't see an eating pouch, but the humans' torsos were obscured by their orange coverings.

Our excited procession strode over the stepping stones, and we made our way up the gentle slope to the edge of the village. I turned to Sam, pointed to a dwelling, and spoke the kloormari word for "house." Sam tried but could not form the sounds to repeat the word. Then he provided the translation, "house," as I had expected. As I led the group into the village, I pointed to the path, and Sam said, "Path." This prompted other kloormari to engage with each of the humans by pointing to or touching various objects and listening to the translation.

Several villagers were gesticulating to each human, trying to get their attention, pointing to various objects, and in my assessment, nearly overwhelming the humans. We arrived at the large community structure in the center of the village. When Sam entered, he regarded the surroundings, consulted with his fellow humans, and then pressed the sides of a small black cube attached to his shoulder and spoke into it. "Stand by for deployment of intro presentation."

"Affirmative," a voice said from the box. The words were, of course, meaningless to my species.

Sam motioned the group down the path back toward the plain. When we reached the edge of the village and had a clear view across the plain, Sam touched his "talking cube" again. "Deploy the intro presentation." We watched in fascination as a new flap opened on the side of the distant vessel, this one much larger than the last. A black, rectangular platform with yellow sides emerged from the new ramp, positioned a few meters above the ground, similar to the child that had come out of the original lightning creature.

The platform made its way toward us, remaining above the plain. Sam pointed to the platform. "Hoverlift." As the hoverlift drew closer, we saw a railing around the perimeter. A podium was positioned in the center of the hoverlift's leading edge. My fellow kloormari and I were astounded to see two more orange-clad humans on the hoverlift's platform, one standing behind the podium.

I had assumed that a total of six humans had been inside the parent creature since I hadn't seen any additional beings. I got Sam's attention and motioned that I wanted to use his Infotab. I made a drawing motion, and he put the device into draw mode. I pointed to Sam and each of his five associates. Then I touched the device six times to make six dots. Next, I pointed at the approaching hoverlift and added two more dots. Finally, I motioned toward the vessel and handed the Infotab back to Sam, hoping that he would respond by indicating the number of humans inside the vessel creature. Fortunately, Sam took the hint and started adding dots. He showed the screen to me with twenty-one dots! I didn't know whether he meant that twenty-one humans were the total or whether there were twenty-one more humans in addition to the eight that I was now aware of. Either way, there were a great many more humans than I had anticipated.

The hoverlift passed directly over the stream without so much as a bump. It silently skimmed over the path up the hill, remaining perfectly level despite the incline. The hoverlift slowed and lowered itself to about 1.2 meters above the ground. Sam spoke to the two humans. The human at the podium put a hand over his sternum and said "Rupert McKenzie." The other human made the same motion. "Rani Vysana."

Sam motioned the hoverlift to follow as he led the way to the center of the village. The hoverlift navigated between the walls of the houses that lined the path. Most of the kloormari followed it.

I walked close behind the hoverlift, off to one side. I saw a stick extending vertically from the top of the podium, held by the human, Rupert McKenzie. He could move the stick from side to side. As he did so, the hoverlift would move in the same direction. Rupert McKenzie moved the stick frequently, appearing to adjust the direction of the platform to avoid hitting the walls of the homes along the route. When we reached the structure at the village center, Sam extended an upper limb to his side with the flat of his hand parallel to the ground, then lowered his arm. I looked up at the hoverlift and saw Rupert McKenzie push down on part of the podium. The hoverlift gently touched down on the ground.

Rani Vysana opened a gate in the railing around the hoverlift's platform. Sam then directed some of the humans to move large objects from the platform into one end of the community structure, assembling them into what was clearly a predetermined configuration. Cords connected a white box to two large black panels (humans seemed to have a great affinity for flat rectangular objects). The villagers crowded around, taking it all in. When the humans completed their task, Rupert McKenzie and Rani Vysana stepped onto the hoverlift, which rose and then sped back to the vessel.

The six original humans formed a line beside the objects that they had set up. Sam motioned for the villagers to gather. I was more accustomed to human gestures, so I asked the villagers to gather. When the crowd had assembled, Sam loudly vocalized, "Hello." The villagers ceased their movements, not understanding how to respond.

Sam directed his eyes toward me. "Hello," he said.

"Hello," I replied.

He turned back to the crowd. "Hello!"

The crowd responded with a hearty but not completely accurate "Hello!" Each villager tried twice more to perfect their pronunciation. They didn't do so in unison, however, producing a disjointed din.

"Hello!" Sam bellowed again.

This time, the villagers replied in perfect unison, using Sam's exact pitch, emphasis, and timing as though hundreds of Sams were speaking in unison. Now that I was more familiar with human body language, I was quite sure that the humans experienced great astonishment.

Sam touched one of the panels. It lit up with white light and the customary red circle in a corner. This was familiar to me due to my Infotab drawing experience. It was not familiar to the other villagers though, as evidenced by their own astonished stances and remarks.

Sam touched the second panel just as the afternoon rain started drumming on the roof. The panel showed a detailed drawing of two humans without

23

clothing or other coverings. The drawings started small in the center of the panel, then grew in size to fill the panel. The crowd was alarmed. A young villager close to the front got up and looked behind the panel and was disturbed to see nothing there. I told the villagers about my previous experience watching the memories of the lightning creature when it visited and explained that the humans were able to access previous visual memories from other creatures and display them on panels. The crowd was aghast and turned their attention back to the panel.

Then the panel spoke! When the two figures were displayed, the panel said, "Humans." It drew a circle around one of the figures. "Female." It drew a circle around the other figure. "Male."

The panel proceeded to show a series of images, including an amazing world covered in huge plant-like objects in an incredible green hue. It showed water for as far as the eye could see. It showed hills that were impossibly high and white particles falling from the sky and covering the land. And the sky . . . what a sky it was! Sometimes the brightest blue, sometimes white or black like on Kuw'baal, and sometimes when it was black, it had a round white object in it and was speckled with small white lights.

The panel showed unimaginable things that looked like life-forms, some on land and some in water! Human forms were shown with the life-forms, indicating that some of the life-forms were tiny, and some were many times the size of any human or kloormar.

The presentation ended by showing a sphere of mostly blue but also marked with whites, greens, and browns against a black background with points of light behind it. A bright, shiny ball of light was prominent in the image. The panel drew lines from the blue ball and outward to other spheres. It showed images of creatures that looked like the large one resting on the plain, moving between spheres.

Every time that the panel showed something or depicted an action, it spoke. It was fascinating to watch but far too overwhelming to make any sense of it.

At about the same time that the images stopped, so did the rain. I noticed that the sky outside would be darkening soon. Sam moved in front of the first panel. He took a drawing stick and made images. He drew a representation of the village, the stream, the plain, and the vessel. He pointed to himself and the other five humans present and then drew six circles on top of lines that represented six human bodies and limbs. These "stick figures" were depicted between the village and the stream. Sam made a walking motion with two of his fingers, and he drew a line from the group of stick figures to the vessel. The crowd murmured their interpretation, with the consensus being that the humans wished to return to the vessel creature.

Next, Sam drew an image of a human's head lying on a surface with its eyes closed. He mimicked this by putting the inner surface of his hands together on one side of his head, tilting his head to rest on his pressed hands, and closing his eyes.

"I think that the human is indicating that his group requires meditation soon," I said. The villagers concurred. As I spoke, I realized I was also on the verge of reaching my mental capacity, and I would require a lengthy meditation cycle. Without a doubt, my fellow villagers would be feeling the same way.

Finally, Sam drew five copies of a simple landscape. He filled in the sky with black on the second and fourth copy. The fifth copy included an image of the vessel. Sam drew stick figures leaving the vessel and a myriad of figures with twelve limbs (kloormari) moving from the village toward the vessel. This took a while for the crowd to figure out, but our most popular guess was that the humans wished to meet with us again after two day/night cycles.

As fascinating as our encounters had been, I was relieved by the prospect of a two-cycle break. I was going to need at least that much time to process and catalog what I had experienced.

The group of humans lined up. Sam signalled his companions, and together they spoke the word, "Goodbye." Sam held his hands out toward the crowd, and they repeated, "Goodbye." With that, the humans turned and walked back out of the structure into the early evening air, damp and refreshed by the recent rain.

We followed the humans to the edge of the village. They turned back toward us, raised an upper limb, and moved their hands from side to side. We reciprocated and then watched as our fascinating guests made their way down the hill and over the stream as twilight set in. About halfway across the plain, lights shone from the humans. Then they walked into the parent creature's flap, which closed behind them.

*Many weeks after first contact, Samuel Buchanan provided me with a copy of a report, relating to the humans' first in-person contact with the kloormari. In the interest of context and perspective, a copy is provided here.*

# TERRAN FIRST CONTACT AUTHORITY

**Mission Incident Report**

---

**Mission:**  Ryla 5 First Contact

**Vessel:**  Pacifica Spirit          *Check if vessel not applicable* ☐

**Location:**  Ryla 5 - Coords: 48.5642 x -123.4449

**Incident Date/Time:** XY 528/03:57 TST

**Incident Category:**   Fortunate O    Unfortunate ⊙

**If unfortunate, select severity:**
Potentially insignificant O   Mild O   Moderate O   Severe O   Extreme ⊙

**Reported by:**   Kwami Thomas Staedtler       **Title:** Captain

**Incident Details:**

With deep regret, it is my duty to report a troubling incident during landing of the Pacifica Spirit on Ryla 5 for in-person first contact with the sentient indigenous species (as yet unnamed).

I have prepared this report following interviews with Navigator First Class Lynda Paige, Exo-biologist Li Huang, and First Contact Administrator Samuel Buchanan.

After a successful and uneventful first contact/surveillance mission using Remote Lander I, the Pacifica Spirit entered the atmosphere of Ryla 5 directly above the designated landing zone, shortly after nightfall. Prior surveillance indicated a strong likelihood that the inhabitants would be located in their shelters for the night.

The vessel descended through the ubiquitous cover of water vapor, obscuring visual observation of the planet's surface until the vessel descended to 1,573 meters AGL. Long-range heat-signature scans were ineffective due to the species' lack of body heat. At 1,500 meters, landing spotlights were activated. At 1,240 meters, motion detectors indicated a possible life-form at a considerable distance and on the far side of a waterway. Three seconds later, the life-form was tracked crossing the stream and then approaching the landing site at a high rate of speed. Navigator Paige issued an immediate command to the flight computer to abort the landing, but the system responded that the LSAP (last safe abort point) had passed. I initiated a ship-wide landing zone infiltration alarm and alerted the crew that a single indigenous inhabitant was inside the blast zone.

First Contact Administrator Buchanan implemented the prescribed procedure, commanding five additional crew members located in his proximity to form a recovery team. Under Buchanan's command, the recovery team removed their landing constraints, donned anti-contamination suits, equipped themselves with head- and arm-mounted lights and a scoop stretcher, and prepared for landing by bracing themselves adjacent to port-side forward hatch B.

I ordered the main vid panel in each section of the vessel to display the feed from the topmost anterior port camera. The feed showed the infiltrator, illuminated by the landing lights and vessel landing exhaust. The infiltrator halted when the outer pressure wave of exhaust reached it. The six landing thrusters produced high-speed ejecta, including rocks, some capable of inflicting serious injury or death on collision with a human.

A rock with an estimated diameter of 20 cm struck the infiltrator. The life-form was thrown backward several meters and did not move. Upon touchdown, Navigator Paige initiated emergency shutdown of all thrusters. The recovery team, led by Buchanan, opened the hatch and made their way to the life-form and placed it on the stretcher. As the team made their way back to the vessel, the indigenous being began to stir but was not fully conscious. I ordered the lower level of sector B to be sealed as per emergency isolation protocols.

After the recovery team closed the hatch, the life-form was placed in isolation pod B-01 off the main corridor. The six crew members moved into isolation pod B-02 and then initiated a UV, ozone, and ultrasonic decon of the corridor. The crew moved back into the corridor and decon'd B-02. Samuel Buchanan was able to communicate with the life-form and persuade it to provide a biological swab sample. Buchanan was able to elicit the subject's name. The name is unpronounceable by humans, but the team agreed to use the approximation "Kelvoo."

Li Huang placed the sample into an AXObi-5 analysis unit while Buchanan initiated further rudimentary communication with the assistance of standard issue Infotab devices.

When the AXObi-5 completed its test cycle, its analysis indicated that Kelvoo was free from biological and chemical contaminants. The recovery team then took Kelvoo to conference room BC-1. When our guest attempted to sit in a chair, a mishap occurred, and Kelvoo fell to the floor but appeared to be unharmed. Kelvoo assumed a kneeling position, which appeared to be more natural for its body configuration.

Buchanan continued his communication attempts using the main conference panel. This continued well past dawn on the planet. Buchanan decided to return Kelvoo to the mineral plain outside of the vessel. Buchanan was concerned that a multitude of the indigenous life-forms now gathered outside would be anxious regarding our guest's whereabouts. Buchanan requested that the team accompany him and Kelvoo since our guest was now accustomed to all members of the recovery team.

The crowd of indigenous beings were extremely curious and non-threatening. Using non-verbal signals, Kelvoo invited the team to walk with the crowd to their village, on the far side of the stream. After a tour of the village, Buchanan decided to accelerate the already disrupted introduction process by implementing Community Presentation 101. The presentation equipment was brought to a communal structure in the village by two additional crew using a hoverlift.

After the presentation concluded, Buchanan attempted to suggest a subsequent meeting two Ryla 5 days later. It was assessed as being likely that the crowd understood. The team made its way on foot back to the Pacifica Spirit as night fell.

## Impact:

Due to the landing incident, mission plans and protocols for a gradual introduction to humanity have been scrubbed. Samuel Buchanan was intended to be our sole representative for establishment of inter-species communication, to be followed by a gradual introduction to other crew members as they assumed their roles for exploration and experimentation on the planet's surface. The need to attend to the human-caused injury of an indigenous being overrode first-contact protocols.

We are fortunate that the indigenous population appears to be welcoming, curious, and completely lacking in hostility or resistance to our presence. We are presently in "uncharted territory" pertaining to first-contact procedures. We will be vigilant, and we shall use our best judgement to mitigate cultural or any other damage to the natural inhabitants of Ryla 5.

It is my expectation that I and members of my crew will be subject to investigation upon our return to Terra.

# SIX: ENROLMENT

When the humans were back inside their vessel creature, I was not in a mental state to handle an onslaught of questions from the villagers. I slipped away between houses. To avoid others, I took a rather circuitous route to my dwelling. Once there, I assumed a comfortable pose and immediately slipped into a deep and lengthy meditative state.

The other villagers were similarly inclined. Most of them meditated on their contact with the humans through the night, the next day, and into the following evening. Due to my additional interactions and the fact that my involuntary meditation in the vessel was fleeting at best, I was unconscious through the whole night plus all of the next day and the following night. I wasn't fully cognitive until the dawn of the day that Sam had requested for our next contact.

In the depths of my meditative state, the sights, sounds, smells, and feelings replayed in my mind. Certain scenes had common characteristics that lent themselves to cross-referencing. For example, the humans used devices: the Infotabs, the box that the mouth stick was put into, the floating hoverlift, and the equipment that it transported to the communal structure. The humans *controlled* these things.

Then there were the strange beings: the lightning creature and its sky-traveling offspring, and of course, the massive creature called "vessel." The humans were able to extract and view the memories of the lightning creature. Inside the vessel beast, the humans could open doors, control displays, retract window covers using their Infotabs, and could touch panels on walls to open the flap to the outside. I also cross-referenced things that I didn't see. I could perceive no respiration or intake of food by the non-human creatures.

An astonishing possibility coalesced in my brains: The lightning creature, the creature that came out of it, and the vessel creature might not be creatures at all! These might be objects—devices that the humans controlled and used!

Perhaps the humans were more sophisticated than I had thought!

I pulled out a fresh parchment and a clay tray of pigment and recorded the details of my interactions with the humans and what I had learned about them, along with my theories and speculations. Then I realized I was ravenously hungry. I left the pigment to dry and quickly made my way along a less-traveled path to the stream, emerging upstream from the village, almost at the algel falls. Downstream I saw villagers feeding. These were just a few stragglers since it was later in the morning than usual for nourishment. I scooped a healthy portion of algel into my food pouch. The algel was rich and had a soothing consistency. I closed my eye and took a moment to savor and take energy from the life-giving substance.

Feeling refreshed and energized, I experienced a boost of motivation to share the results of my meditation with the rest of the village. I ran to my home and retrieved the parchment. I made for the community structure at a full gallop, leaping over wayward infants and children along the way.

The structure was packed with kloormari. Six villagers were examining the equipment left by the humans. Another was excitedly making elaborate diagrams on the drawing panel while others lined up to take a turn.

I strode in and announced my theory about the non-human creatures being inanimate. I was crestfallen by Kahini's reply. "Yes, yes, several members of the community have come to the same conclusion! We do, however, have a great many questions for you!"

In response, I picked up a brush from a communal writing table, dipped it into a pot of kobo juice, and coated my parchment to preserve the writing. Then I posted the parchment on a wall. "Here is my complete account, from the moment of sighting the vessel," I said. Within two minutes the assembled crowd had read my treatise. Some villagers still had a few questions. I answered quickly due to my eagerness to visit with the humans again.

Shortly after the question-and-answer session, a villager entered the community structure and reported that a group of humans had erected some type of shelter outside of the vessel and were milling around, looking toward the village.

"Shall we go to the humans and say 'Hello' again?" I ventured.

We filed out of the community structure, down the hill at the edge of the village, over the stream, and across the plain. About 300 meters from the vessel's entrance flap was a structure that looked like a white skin over a frame of thin connected sticks. The white skin resembled the skins that the humans had been covered with when they first retrieved me from the plain. The end of the structure closest to the vessel was open.

As we got closer, more humans emerged from the vessel until twenty-one of them were lined up next to the ramp flap. I raised an upper limb and moved my hand from side to side. "Hello," I said. The humans responded in kind.

A human with the most shoulder stripes and two extra symbols on the chest stepped forward and extended a hand to me. We clasped hands. "Welcome, I am," he touched his chest, "Captain Kwami Staedtler." With the assistance of Sam, Captain Kwami Staedtler counted off twenty kloormari, including me, took us to one side, and motioned for us to enter the vessel. Behind us, I noticed Sam counting twenty more villagers into a group. Each group was led inside the vessel, one after another.

As my group entered the corridor, the doors to all the adjoining rooms were open. The members of my group immediately recognized the corridor, conference room, and isolation room from my written account. Our human guide took us to the end of the corridor, which opened into another hallway, running in a perpendicular direction. The end of the corridor must have been sealed off during my previous visit.

We turned and were directed to stand inside a large box. The human motioned to the box. "Lift." The lower part of the box was walled, and the upper half was surrounded by glass. I pointed the glass out to my fellow visitors, and they recognized the substance from my writings. Our guide touched a panel. "Bridge." A wall appeared out of the side of the entrance to the box. It slid across the entrance, sealing us in. We were troubled by this, but our wariness was replaced by surprise when the box started moving upward!

As the box rose, we could see through the glass as we moved past the level of the entrance ramp and up through six additional levels of rooms and corridors. On the seventh level, the box stopped, and the wall retracted, exposing the opening once again. We hastily exited into a large, curved room. The human motioned across the room. "Bridge."

The oval bridge room had glass windows all the way around it and a large glass covering overhead. Peering through the windows, I saw an expansive shiny black skin covering the lower levels. This indicated that the bridge was smaller than the levels below. The bridge was a bulbous protrusion on top of the vessel.

Around the perimeter of the room below the windows were angled surfaces covered with panels, short sticks, small protrusions, and lights. Some panels displayed shapes and symbols. Chairs were placed facing the surfaces. In the center of the room were two chairs in front of raised surfaces with similar adornments. Three more sets of surfaces and chairs were placed in front of the two center chairs on a floor that was a step down. Our guide pointed to objects and said words such as "workstation," "console," and "panel" (I knew that one).

Once we circled the bridge and were near the lift again, our guide led us through nearby doors where the floor sloped down at a sharp angle. Instead of a steady slope, the floor was a series of horizontal and vertical surfaces. "Stairs," our guide said, also pointing to a railing that ran along one side of the slope. "Handrail," the guide said, then grasped the rail. "Hold the handrail." I grasped the rail and gingerly placed a foot onto the first step. I took two more steps, mimicking the guide. I lost my balance but kept a tight grip on the handrail, preventing a painful fall. I righted myself and finished the descent. I reached out to steady others in the group as they made their way down the treacherous path.

We entered a spacious area with more windows around the perimeter, a glass roof, and chairs, some of which seemed to be folded back to support a human in a nearly prone position. "Observation Deck," Captain Kwami Staedtler said.

From the observation deck, we descended another set of stairs, this time with far more ease. We walked down a long corridor with identical rooms on either side. "Crew quarters," our guide said while passing each open door.

At the end of the corridor was a room full of tables and chairs. A long counter ran along the end of the room with doors, boxes, bins, and devices behind it. "Cafeteria" was the word used to describe this place.

Another level down, we walked into a vast area that was full of air that was much warmer and wetter than the rest of the vessel. The entire ceiling glowed with a white light resembling the daytime sky of Kuw'baal. Tray after tray, from floor to ceiling, bore bright green plants, with species that I had never seen and more variety than I ever would have conceived. Clear tubes, like glass but flexible, dripped water onto the plants. Delightful odors wafted through the room, reminiscent of fresh algel growth after a cleansing rain. "Hydroponics," our guide said.

Farther along the room, tabletops held round glass trays and tubes. Fibrous pink and red substances were immersed in reddish fluids, and tubes in the fluids were emitting bubbles. Each tray or tube was connected by a cord to a panel displaying symbols. An overhead sign bore the symbols "MEAT PRODUCTION."

The next level down held rooms full of panels, boxes, tubes, containers, equipment, and materials that were all new to me. "Lab level," Captain Kwami Staedtler said.

The next level down actually took up two levels. We walked along a shelf, halfway up the side of the space. Massive tube- and sphere-shaped containers lined the space under our walking shelf. Shiny pipes led from the containers into chambers in the middle of the floor. Two gigantic pipes ran to one end of the vessel, and six smaller pipes pointed down into the floor. Thousands of tubes, pipes, and cords snaked in every direction. Consoles, panels, and lights were everywhere. The place had a myriad of strange, acrid odors. "Propulsion," our guide said.

We proceeded forward, on the walking shelf, through a set of doors. This space also took up two levels. Large boxes were stacked from floor to ceiling and secured with straps and cords. Smaller boxes were sitting on shelves. "Cargo hold," our guide said. I estimated that we were close to the flap that the hoverlift had emerged from. At that moment, I saw a closed flap down a path between boxes, with the hoverlift just inside the flap.

From there, we descended a final section of stairs to the lower part of the two-level space. We were led through a door, which opened beside the lift. We turned the corner into the corridor, which led back to the ramp flap and down to the plain. Our guide stood beside the flap. As each of us passed by, Captain Kwami Staedtler bowed his head slightly. "Thank you, goodbye." I returned the gesture and the words, as did the other kloormari as they passed.

As we left the magnificent vessel, a final group of kloormari was ushered in to start their tour.

Our group of twenty milled around, comparing our perceptions of the experience. A few minutes later, the second group emerged, led by Samuel Buchanan. Sam looked at each kloormar in our group and repeated my name. Finally, he looked directly at me. "Kelvoo?"

"Kelvoo," I said, touching my sternum. The expression on Sam's head changed, and he motioned me to accompany him toward the shelter. I was mildly offended that Sam had not recognized me. It was odd that such intelligent beings could be so lacking in perception!

As I entered the shelter, I saw ten soft grey floor mats in two rows of five. I had walked over similar mats during the tour. Each mat extended from under a table. On each table was an Infotab and a vertically mounted panel. At the end of the shelter was a white box connected to two large panels, just like the equipment that the humans had set up in the community structure.

Sam motioned around the shelter. "Classroom," he said.

He touched one of the large panels, showing a line drawing of ten identical kloormari stick figures. Sam pointed to each table and spoke a word for each of them. I thought it likely that he was using a human verbal system for counting. Sam pointed to each stick figure on the panel and spoke the same words. Sam was associating each table with a kloormar.

Sam swept a hand across the panel. It displayed a new image. It was clear that images had been set up in advance. The image showed a representation of the village, stream, vessel, and classroom with a white sky. The image changed—the sky became darker and turned to black. The sky stayed black for several seconds and then turned brighter. Before the sky became totally white, ten kloormari stick figures appeared on the panel between the village and the stream. A line drew itself from the figures, across the stream and the plain, ending at the classroom. I surmised that Sam was suggesting that ten kloormari should come to the classroom tomorrow morning, probably to learn more about humans.

Sam and I turned to each other. "Thank you, Kelvoo," he said, waving his hand. "Goodbye."

"Thank you, Sam. Goodbye," I replied, then turned and walked back into the growing crowd of villagers who were still comparing their observations.

I walked to the three village elders, Kwazka, Kahini, and K'losk'oon, who were attempting to coalesce their information. "Pardon the interruption, elders," I interjected. "The human, Samuel Buchanan, has attempted to communicate with me. If I am not mistaken, he wishes for ten kloormari to visit the new structure tomorrow morning. Samuel Buchanan appears to be preparing to provide new information to the ten kloormari. The human did not specify which kloormari should be in the group. I seek your counsel on the matter."

The four of us stepped away from the crowd. The elders agreed that each of them would select three kloormari and that I, given my added experience with humans, could select the final participant.

"I suggest that the first obvious choice is Kelvoo," Kwazka said. "Kelvoo has had the most exposure to the humans and may have additional insight that can be used to assist the rest of the group."

K'losk'oon turned to me. "Are you willing to take on this role, Kelvoo? When you return to the village, are you also willing to record the information you obtained and teach others what you have learned?"

"It would be my deepest honor and privilege, elder," I replied, meaning every word.

Kahini was next. "I propose you, Kwazka. It is only right that the humans learn our ways. Your depth of kloormari knowledge and your social standing in our village would serve that purpose well."

"You have my sincerest gratitude," Kwazka replied.

"Since Kwazka is an elder, a young member of the community should be included," K'losk'oon suggested. "I recommend K'raftan. This child was innovative when approaching the lander we had called the lightning creature. This showed initiative—"

"Or recklessness," Kahini interjected.

"Be that as it may," K'losk'oon continued, "we should provide a diverse range of kloormari because we cannot tell at this point which traits may or may not fit well with tomorrow's lessons."

The trio added six more villagers: Keeto, K'tatmal, Kleloma, K'aablart, Keesooni, and Kroz.

"Whom do you choose, Kelvoo?" Kwazka asked.

"Kleloma would have been my choice, but since that selection has already been made, I select Ksoomu. I find Ksoomu's writings to be detailed and insightful. Ksoomu was injured by the lander. I don't know whether that has instilled a fear of humans and their devices, but this could provide an opportunity to overcome such obstacles."

We agreed to seek out our nominees to determine whether they would be agreeable and willing to record and share their knowledge. Without exception, they accepted with effusive gratitude and acceptance of their responsibilities.

As night fell and I entered a new meditative state in my dwelling, the privilege and responsibility of representing the kloormari began to sink in. I was going to be one of a select few—one of the first of my kind—to receive instruction from a being from another world!

# SEVEN: GETTING TO KNOW

After the morning feeding, our group of ten met by the stream, bristling with anticipation. As our footsteps crunched across the plain, we were chattering with speculation about the purpose of our meeting and what we might expect. Kwazka advised us not to get ahead of ourselves and not to hope for certain outcomes, which was very much in keeping with Kwazka's judicious demeanor. At the same time, it was not hard to detect that Kwazka's excitement was equal to our own.

Sam was waiting for us. He motioned us to each table. Some of us stood, some knelt, and others locked their legs in a high squatting position. Sam pointed to himself. "I am Sam," he said, then pointed at me. "You are Kelvoo." I was pleased that Sam had learned to pick me out of a group of kloormari. He held up a thin sheet of a substance resembling parchment, only thinner and brighter. "Paper," he said. It bore black symbols. Sam folded the paper so that the symbols were facing him when he placed the paper on my assigned table.

Sam turned to the next student. "I am Sam," he said. "You are . . ." He pointed at Kroz, who said, "Kroz." Sam had to ponder the sounds that he heard for a moment. Then he used a stick with a black tip and wrote symbols onto a new sheet of paper. He placed it on Kroz's table and then tried to reproduce the sound of Kroz's name, with no success. I leaned toward Kroz and suggested that Kroz simply accept the crude pronunciation due to Sam's vocal limitations. The process repeated until each of us had a label. I thought about the fact that Sam had not recognized me yesterday. I wondered whether all kloormari looked similar to humans, making it difficult to tell us apart. This didn't make much sense since the speckling on our skins was unique to each of us.

"Test," Sam said. Then he held up an Infotab and motioned for us to do the same. The contents of his device's screen were repeated on one of the large panels next to Sam's table. Sam motioned for us to pick up our devices. He pulled a finger across the screen, and a stack of seven colored rectangles appeared. One of the rectangles had the symbols "GAMES" on it along with a moving image of two rotating white cubes with various black dots on each surface. He touched the rectangle, and a stack of green rectangles appeared. Sam motioned to us. "Go."

We each pulled one of our manipulators across our Infotabs with mostly the same result. Keesooni got a screen full of symbols. Keesooni held the Infotab up and asked for assistance. Of course, Sam couldn't understand what he was hearing, but he quickly got Keesooni back on track.

Sam tapped a green rectangle that had four squares on it. The screen changed to show the symbols "SIMON'S GAME" across the top. Four large squares filled the rest of the screen. One of the squares became brighter, and the device emitted a short tone. Sam tapped that square. Next, a sequence of two squares lit up and beeped. Sam tapped the same sequence. The same thing happened again, with three squares. When he was done, Sam motioned to us again. "Go."

We followed Sam's lead, and he walked behind each of us, observing our actions. I went through the procedure, repeating the sequence with one, two, and three seemingly random selections of squares. I continued to four, five, six, and seven squares. All of the other students were doing the same.

"Wow!" Sam exclaimed. I looked up and saw that he was not addressing us directly, so I continued. The sequences of squares started to accelerate. I noticed that Kroz was placing a hand just above the screen and tapping it using all six manipulators in rapid sequence. I did the same, and moments later, so were my classmates. When I reached twenty-six squares, I started wondering about the purpose of the exercise. Nevertheless, I kept going. When I reached a sequence of seventy-six squares, Sam held his hands up. "Stop." He slowly shook his head, his mouth hanging open. Our group came to the consensus that Sam was testing the speed of our reflexes. I suggested that he might be impressed.

For the rest of the day, we covered some basic vocabulary, such as "yes" and "no," along with concepts of "I," "you," "we," and "they."

Close to the midpoint of the day, a human walked from the vessel to the classroom, carrying a soft box. Sam pointed the palm of his hand in the human's direction. "Bertha Kolesnikov."

This human was shorter but considerably larger and more powerful looking than the average crew member. The human addressed us in a rougher, less melodious tone than I was accustomed to from humans. We had no idea what the human meant by, "Hiya, fellas, er . . . if y'are fellas, heh heh heh . . . Just call me 'Bertie'—everyone does. I'm the cafeteria lady and bottle washer. I keep this motley bunch of excuses for humans fed an' watered. If ya need anything—a burger, a corn dog, or just some wise advice about life, I'm yer gal!"

Sam motioned toward the garrulous human. "Bertie."

"Anyways, enjoy yer grub, Sammy!" Bertie exclaimed before leaving the box with Sam and lumbering back to the vessel. "See y'all tomorrow!" Bertie shouted.

Sam signaled for us to gather around his table at the front of the classroom. He opened the box and pulled out an object wrapped in paper. He opened the paper, and pointed, "Clubhouse sandwich." The clubhouse sandwich was square and was layered with a spongy substance on the top, bottom, and in the middle. Between the layers were sheets of pink and white along with green and red substances that looked like plant matter. The clubhouse sandwich was sliced in half diagonally. Sam took half of the clubhouse sandwich apart and pointed to the components, saying "Bread, ham, turkey, lettuce, and tomato." Sam reassembled the ingredients. "Food." He lifted the "food" to his mouth. "I eat," he said and then opened his mouth and inserted the clubhouse sandwich!

Sam closed his mouth over part of the clubhouse sandwich, breaking a piece off. He opened and closed his mouth, reducing the food to a mushy consistency. Sam's neck moved, and the food disappeared inside of Sam! We were aghast that a being would use its vocal hole for eating! I correctly suspected that humans would be incapable of speaking clearly while eating. Another human handicap, I supposed.

Sam finished the section of food and pointed to the remaining half. He mimicked putting the food into an eating pouch. K'aablart was braver and perhaps less repulsed than the rest of us. K'aablart picked up the remaining clubhouse sandwich section and tentatively pulled it toward the eating pouch. When the outer bread touched the inner edge of the pouch, K'aablart yanked the "food" away hastily and then gently returned it to Sam as if handling a dangerous object.

Sam pulled some thin yellow objects out of a container. "Potato chips," he said, then inserted them into his mouth. He moved his lower mouth up and down and pointed to it. "I chew," he said in a muffled voice. The potato chips broke with a noisy crunching sound, revealing the purpose of the "teeth" that lined a human's mouth.

Sam took a clear container out of the food box. "Drink," he said. The container held a liquid that looked like water contaminated with rotting algel. "Apple juice," Sam said. He removed a lid from the container and poured some liquid into his mouth. When it disappeared, he pointed to the front of his neck. "I swallow." We all watched how his neck moved as he took another gulp, and the apple juice disappeared.

When Sam finished his food and drink, he used gestures and a few of the words that we had learned to ask whether we would like to walk to the stream or some nearby flat rocks to pick and consume some algel. We used a word that we had learned that day: "No." Unless they were starving, why would any kloormari want to eat outside of early morning or early evening?

We spent the rest of the day learning how to count in Terran. The kloormari use a base-four counting system for numbers up to 256. For higher numbers, we work in base-twelve. It was not hard to adapt to the purely base-ten Terran system. We learned to count from one to nineteen. We then learned about twenty, thirty, forty, and so on, quickly understanding the intermediary numbers. We moved on to hundreds and then thousands, stopping there.

By midafternoon our learning was drawing to a close. None of us wanted the day to end. Sam spoke while drawing on a panel. He seemed to be indicating that we should return tomorrow for another session. We were surprised and delighted, but it got better. Sam illustrated the concept that we should repeat the days of learning in a pattern of five consecutive days, followed by two days with no learning, repeated over and over. We could hardly believe our good fortune!

Sam indicated that there would be a break of 10 days after the 107th Kuw'baal day, when the humans would temporarily depart in their vessel for a task that they had to perform. Finally, Sam gave us a number of great importance: 232. In that many Kuw'baal days, the humans would enter the vessel and would be leaving us. This knowledge brought both comfort and disappointment.

Sam displayed a diagram on the drawing panel. It showed rows with seven squares each. The first five squares on each row were shaded. Sam pointed to the shaded rows. "Classroom, yes." For non-shaded rows he said, "Classroom, no." Sam didn't need to explain; the fact that the diagram indicated classroom days was self-evident to us. Sam called the diagram a "calendar." It included ten consecutive blank squares starting at the 107th position, and there were 232 squares in total.

By the time we left the classroom, it was getting late. We decided to run back to the village since the available time for recording and reporting was shrinking. We were going to make a quick stop by the stream to scoop up some nourishment, but as we approached, a villager told us to report directly to the community structure. "Everything that you need will be provided."

When we arrived, the structure was crowded. Tables were set up at one end of the room with ten bowls of fresh algel, ten parchments, and ten pigment trays. We proceeded immediately to our workstations and started writing while simultaneously being bombarded with questions. When our written accounts were complete, they were posted on the wall where a scribe read them and wrote a summarized account. The scribe's summary would be entered into the village records.

When the questions ended, Kwazka asked Kahini and K'losk'oon to come closer. Kwazka explained that Samuel Buchanan had asked us to meet regularly for the next 232 days. Kwazka was concerned about the impact of the schedule on our ability to perform our regular duties of food gathering, home building, and general maintenance and cleaning in the village as well as our ability to study the historical writings. Kahini and K'losk'oon asserted that other villagers would be pleased to take up the slack, and we would be welcome to make up for our absence and catch up on our studies after 232 days as we saw fit.

I returned to my house as the last glimmers of light faded from the sky. As I transitioned to a meditative state, it occurred to me that I had not read or recorded any historic kloormari texts since the humans had arrived. I felt a certain emptiness and guilt, but I pushed away these thoughts with the rationale that I was learning and passing along knowledge that could transform my species' perceptions of our existence and our place in the grand scheme of things. The privilege of it all filled me with pleasure.

On our second day in the classroom, we learned more about numbers. Sam demonstrated addition and subtraction but soon realized that we had an excellent grasp of the subject. He moved on to multiplication and division, but each of us had mastered that back when we were a few months of age. How else would we know how much algel to harvest to feed a specified number of kloormari? Conversely, if a set amount of algel had to be evenly distributed to a certain number of kloormari, how much would each kloormar receive? Not to know these things would be unthinkable for us.

It surprised us to see Sam trying to explain mathematics in a written form. We kloormari perform all but the most complicated calculations in our minds.

Next, Sam brought up moving images on a panel. He explained that these images were called "vids." Sam connected a device called a "camera," which had a shiny eye called a "lens." As Sam moved around with the camera, we could see on the panel what the camera was viewing. When Sam pointed the camera at each of us, we were fascinated by our own appearance since we had never seen ourselves so clearly. Sam played the vid from the lander as it touched down on Kuw'baal. This was the vid that I had seen before. Sam took out a miniature representation of the lander (a "model") and pointed to four locations where cameras were mounted.

At midday, Bertie brought food for Sam and chattered at us, as before. While Sam ate (discreetly, thank goodness), he played a vid that featured small humans interacting with adult humans and brightly colored furry beings with unblinking eyes. We assumed that the vid was for training human youth. We further assumed that the furry beings were other intelligent creatures that the humans interacted with.

The children's vid covered verbs and the concept of past, present, and future. For example, "Iggles *walked* to the school," "Iggles *is walking* at school," and "Iggles *will walk* home."

When the vid ended, Sam pulled a tube of furry fabric out of a box and then pulled the fabric over his upper arm, revealing imitation eyes and a mouth over his hand. The result was identical to one of the furry creatures in the vid. "Puppet," Sam said.

He stood behind a panel so that his upper body was obscured, then raised his puppet hand over the top of the panel, speaking in a register that was rather high for a human. "Hello, I am Iggles," he said while moving the puppet's imitation mouth. We assumed that Sam demonstrated the puppet so that we would not be misled into believing these things were alive. Nevertheless, we were confused. Why would humans use simulated beings for teaching purposes? Our reaction was the kloormari equivalent of "What the hell was that?"

Our third day was notable. It was marked by a scandal!

Sam was enlightening us regarding the division of humans into male and female. We were not at a stage where Sam could explain the purpose of the two categories, but he could display the now familiar line drawing diagram of an uncovered female and male and he could point out some of the differences.

"Man," Sam said, pointing to the male figure's groin. Then he pointed to the groin and chest of the female figure. "Female." He also reiterated the concept of "he," "his," and "him," along with "she," "hers," and "her." This was followed by Sam naming some of the major external features of the human body in general and each gender in particular.

Our group was gathered around the panel. I shared with my fellow kloormari my observation that some of the humans had the rounded protrusions on the top-forward section of their chests. Kleloma noted that these humans tended to have smaller waists relative to their chests and hips, K'tatmal remarked that the same humans were apt to be smaller overall and spoke in a slightly higher register. We concluded that these were females (she and her). I pointed out that some of these traits were a generalization because Bertie appeared to have breasts but had some traits in common with males in terms of overall body shape and vocal range.

In a remarkable coincidence, Bertie strode onto the scene at that moment. She was carrying Sam's midday nourishment. When she saw us gathered around the panel showing two unclothed figures, she laughed. "Ha-ha! Look at you scamps gettin' yer jollies gawkin' at nekked people! Hee-hee, what a bunch a pervs!"

This time I understood what Bertie was saying with the exception of "scamps," "jollies," "gawkin'," "nekked," and "bunch a pervs."

As Bertie approached Sam's table, K'aablart motioned to Sam to stand beside the panel. Sam complied. When Bertie deposited Sam's meal on the table, K'aablart motioned Bertie to stand next to Sam. When Bertie was in position, K'aablart glanced at the panel for reference and then grasped Sam's groin with one hand and one of Bertie's ample breasts with the other.

"Yow! Gerroff!" Sam spluttered, leaping back.

Bertie's response took a different turn. She reached over and grasped K'aablart's offending limb at the equivalent of K'aablart's wrist, then started twisting K'aablart's arm almost two full rotations. K'aablart let out a deafening screech of pain from all eight vocal outlets, claspers flailing!

"If ya think yer gonna get fresh with me," Bertie exclaimed, "you got another thing comin', ya perv! You pull another stunt like that, and I'll twist off yer lobster arm, boil it in oil, smush it up with a jar o' mayo, spread it on a hoagie, an'—"

Sam interjected with his hands clasping the sides of his head, "Oh God, Bertie, I-I-I'm so sorry! W-w-we were t-talking about males and females and . . . and the differences . . . and I guess K'aablart here j-just wanted to check out the differences directly. W-we hadn't got to the part about privacy and boundaries and such!"

Bertie released K'aablart, who promptly ran behind Sam and crouched to become as small as possible.

"Okay, Sam," Bertie said. "I'll let it go—*this time*. But don' ya let these rascals git the better of ya! If these scallywags give ya any trouble, jus' gimme a holler, and I'll fix 'em good an' proper!" Bertie regarded K'aablart, who was still cowering, and pointed two of her fingers at her eyes, then jabbed them toward K'aablart. She pointed the same fingers at the rest of us as if to suggest that she would be watching us for any further trouble.

Although I was stricken with fear, I wished I had understood Bertie's shouting at the time. This was a remarkable variation on human response and communication that I had not witnessed up to that moment.

We spent the rest of the academic day learning rules of great importance to humans. Sam touched various parts of his body. When he touched his head, arm, shoulder, back, and lower leg, he said, "Yes." When he motioned toward his thigh, groin, and buttocks, he shook his head. "No!" He pointed to the breasts on the female figure and emphatically reiterated, "No!"

In turn, we taught Sam that he shouldn't touch a kloormar's eye or stick his fingers (or other parts) into any bodily orifices without an explicit invitation to do so.

K'aablart didn't have a lot to say. K'aablart knelt at the table on the upper knee joints, making K'aablart appear shorter and trying to be as inconspicuous as possible.

On our way back to the village for our writing and debriefing, we assured K'aablart that we would have been just as likely to make the same error given what we knew (and especially what we didn't know) at the time.

That day we learned four important things:

1.    The anatomical differences between the two major divisions of humans and the pronouns to use (we would learn later about a greater range and fluidity of gender identities).

2.    In Sam's apology to Bertie, he mentioned K'aablart by name, so he was starting to learn to tell us apart by sight.

3.    Based on K'aablart's recollection of the inappropriate palpation, Bertie was female.

4.    Bertie was a formidable human, to be respected and feared. We should only speak when necessary and keep our limbs to ourselves in Bertie's presence.

Our next two days were largely focused on vids about a wide range of subjects. Most of these did not seem to be aimed at Terran children; they appeared to be intended for teaching non-humans the standard Terran language with regard to the life-forms, geography, and technology of Terra and humans. We were enthralled by the diversity of animal and plant life on Terra and the widely varying landscapes. We learned the words for over one hundred life-forms and scores of geographical features. We marveled at Terran structures and were in awe of the devices used to transport the inhabitants of Terra. We also learned that most inhabitants of Terra are human, but nine other intelligent species from other worlds can be found among the population.

Based on attempts by Sam to communicate, dialog that we had seen in vids, and human conversations that we had overheard, we were able to form crude sentences. When I said to Sam, "I like classroom. Thank you, Sam," I recognized that he was smiling and expressing pleasure.

"Thank you, Kelvoo," he replied. "I am happy that you like class." I was pleased that we were starting to engage in conversation.

Toward the end of the fifth day, we watched a vid that introduced the Terran characters used for writing. Each character was shown on the screen along with variations in pronunciation. We learned that letters were grouped into constructs called "words." The vid included sample words and pronunciation of the words. After the vid, Sam displayed some new words on the panel and suggested that we try to pronounce them. If we were correct, Sam would say, "Yes." If not, he would pronounce the word for us. At first, we tended to separate the sound of each letter, pronouncing a word like "pat" as "Puh-ah-tuh." After a few tries, we improved substantially.

Sam pulled up a screen full of text. He read each word aloud while pointing to it. The opening words were, "Once upon a time, there was a planet named Terra . . ." Sam finished the story in two minutes and fourteen seconds. He pointed to us and then the next classroom day on the calendar. We inferred that we would start reading lessons in three days' time. We were beyond pleased with this information but disappointed that we would not attend class over the next two days.

After class we returned to the village community structure and resumed our roles as reporters and teachers. Over the next two days, I helped out around the village, and I tried to study historical kloormari texts. For the first time, I found my studies to be difficult because, in comparison to the intense and fascinating lessons from Sam, the historic documents seemed rather bland. I forced myself to partake in some traditional learning out of a sense of duty to my species, but I struggled with the lack of intellectual stimulation.

# EIGHT: UNLOCKING THE GATES OF KNOWLEDGE

Learning to read opened the proverbial floodgates to rapid learning. In the first classes, we watched language and reading vids for human children and non-human species. The vids showed humans, other beings, puppets, and so-called "animated" figures performing various actions while a disembodied voice narrated an explanation, along with the corresponding text. By the end of the first day of reading, we each had a vocabulary of 217 standard Terran words.

On the subsequent days, our individual vocabularies differed slightly because, for part of the day, Sam had each of us viewing different vids on our Infotabs. After we had each watched individual vids of a similar duration, Sam would show images of objects or scenarios on one of the large panels and ask members of the class to raise their hand if they knew the word or series of words that described the scene.

As the vids introduced increasingly sophisticated words, we were puzzled by the inconsistent spelling and pronunciation of letters in words. Why, for example, was "ough" pronounced "off," as in "cough," but "ow," as in "plough"? Why was "ph" pronounced like an "f" in "phonics" or a "v" in Stephen but neither in "haphazard"? In practice, this was more a curiosity than an obstacle as we would just memorize the spelling and pronunciation of each word when we heard it spoken.

After five days of reading practice, we all had vocabularies well in excess of 2,000 words. We were starting to ask Sam a great many questions. A limiting factor was Sam's inability to engage in simultaneous conversations given his single vocal outlet. When we would ask Sam to define a word or explain a concept, he would reply to the effect of, "I cannot answer your question now because you need to know more words. Please ask me again later."

At the start of the following "week" (one of our new words), we all got some much needed assistance in the form of a "dictionary," which Sam activated on each of our Infotabs. He showed us how, if we didn't understand a word, we could touch and hold the word on the screen, and a written definition would be displayed. We could tap an icon on the definition screen to hear a clearly spoken pronunciation.

Sam had each of us use our Infotab to read a recipe for the preparation of a human delicacy called "macaroni and cheese." He asked us to use the dictionary to obtain the definition of any words that we didn't understand. "Recipe," "delicacy," and "macaroni" were terms that I learned via the dictionary.

After twenty minutes, Sam interrupted us. "I'm curious about the time it's taking for all of you to read the recipe. Typically, a human would take about two minutes to read it. I'm hearing a lot of audio from your dictionaries." Sam walked over to Keeto's table and asked Keeto to show him the steps that Keeto had taken since opening the recipe document.

Keeto explained that the first step was looking up "macaroni." Keeto saw that macaroni is a pasta, so the next step was to view the definition of "pasta." The dictionary defined it as a food prepared from flour and eggs. Keeto knew something about eggs from a previously viewed vid, so Keeto decided to pursue "flour" first. This led to "wheat," which led to "grain," then "agriculture" and so on.

Sam created a diagram on the drawing panel. He wrote "macaroni and cheese" at the top of the screen. A line extended down from "macaroni" to "pasta." Two lines led down from "pasta" to "egg" and "wheat." Sam added new lines and words that Keeto had not mentioned, such as "pasta" leading to "Italy" and then "Europe" and "cheese" followed by "milk," "dairy," and "cow."

Sam drew an "X" through all of the terms that were more than one level below "macaroni" and "cheese." "I know that you, as kloormari, have a strong need to go very deep into the details, so I also know that what I am going to ask will be very difficult for you. I am asking you not to go more than one level down when using the dictionary. You will need to accept that there are words you will not know right away, and you will not have a total understanding of the original words, but things will become clearer when you read related information in the future. If you continue on the path we have just seen, you could spend a lifetime learning about anything associated with macaroni and cheese and come out unable to have a normal conversation with a human."

We didn't understand every word of what Sam was saying, but his intent was clear.

The introduction of the dictionary (and its judicious use) provided a breakthrough.

We spent the rest of the week reading stories and articles selected by Sam to gradually introduce new concepts. At the start of the following week, Sam said he was convinced that we now had all of the knowledge and tools that we would require to take control of our education.

"I was very happy when I learned that I was selected for a voyage that might find intelligent life," he said once we had taken our places in the classroom. "I thought about how pleased I would be if we could communicate with those life-forms. I was so happy when I first saw kloormari on the vids from the lander. I was scared because the kloormari look so different from humans, but your species welcomed us with friendship. My hope was that by the time we left to return to Terra, we would be able to talk with each other in a simple way, but we are already far beyond that!

"The kloormari are the most intelligent beings that I have ever met. All of you have made so much progress that my direct involvement in your education will only slow you down. I would like each of you to take control of your education and help one another. I will be here to assist if you need my help. I will also be happy to talk about anything that you would like to discuss as a group. All I need to do right now is to give you the tools that you need for self-directed learning."

Sam pointed to the white box that the large panels were connected to. "This box is an InfoServer. It contains hundreds of billions of facts, articles, books, audio recordings, vids, and the interplanetary 'standard reference.' This InfoServer contains almost all of the knowledge of humanity up to the moment when our vessel departed from Terra. I have unlocked access to the data on the InfoServer both here and in the community structure. You can access the data on your Infotabs within 1.2 kilometers of an InfoServer and also via the panels in the community structure."

Within ten minutes, Sam had demonstrated how to access and search the InfoServer and its priceless store of information.

From that point forward, our knowledge grew exponentially. I started by selecting random topics and setting a time limit before moving on to a new topic. As students we were often able to assist one another since, among us, one student may have studied a subject where another student lacked knowledge. After a few days, our class discussed the topics that interested us the most. Then we each selected subjects in which to specialize.

We accessed many types of media. Overall, we preferred to read text. As kloormari, we were able to view and retain a full screen of text at a time instead of having to use the usual human technique of scanning lines from left to right. In cases where I did not need to consult the dictionary, I could digest a screen of 500–600 words in about two seconds. As such, we could absorb many times more information by reading than by viewing vids.

Vids, on the other hand, were indispensable for visualization. The kloormari language is descriptive enough that written text can adequately describe objects and vistas in excellent detail. Standard Terran, on the other hand, is limited in that regard, so vids are the perfect medium to fill that void. Only vids can capture human facial expressions and body language, which helped us grasp the arcane nuances of nonverbal human communication. For example, vids and audio were useful to demonstrate how parts of a sentence were emphasized and exaggerated when sarcasm was being expressed.

For the next few months, we filled our brains with subjects ranging from advanced mathematics, human history, linguistics, anthropology, classical literature, commerce, law, economics, chemistry, biology, physics, and astrophysics to comic books, comedy, romance novels, and erotica. I had the most difficulty grasping humor and human relationships as I had no points of reference from kloormari society.

Some other notable events took place during the weeks and months of our education.

Kwami Staedtler, the captain of the vessel (the *Pacifica Spirit*), dropped by a couple of months into our training and asked Kwazka whether he could meet with the village leaders to make an announcement, with Kwazka translating for him. The captain wasn't aware that we don't have leaders per se, although we do involve elder kloormari in important events and decisions.

We left class early that day. The rains had just ended, and parts of the plain were flooded, so Captain Staedtler had to carry his shoes and socks and roll up his trousers to wade while we accompanied him to the village and up the rise to the community structure. Kahini and K'losk'oon were summoned, and once they had arrived, 227 villagers were in the building. Kwazka introduced the captain, explaining that captains were akin to wise elders of their vessels.

"It has been a great privilege and honor to make contact with the wonderful kloormari on your fascinating world of Kuw'baal," Captain Staedtler began. After more platitudes, he explained that the humans were pleased to pass along their "meager" knowledge to the brilliant students. "However," he said, "in reality, we humans have learned even more from you." I had serious doubts about his statement and his perception of "reality," but my studies had made me familiar with political rhetoric, and I considered it possible that Captain Staedtler really believed his assertion.

Finally, he arrived at the true purpose of his speech. "Like the kloormari, we humans constantly seek knowledge. We are honored to be your guests and would be forever indebted to you if you would let us study your planet and your species in greater depth." He proceed to ask permission to set up additional structures around the vessel, to send teams out to take samples from the surrounding area and the village, to interview kloormari and use the students to translate (this was a surprise), and to perform painless and safe physical examinations of the kloormari.

There was no need for Captain Staedtler's political preamble. The gathered kloormari were very pleased that the vastly superior humans would take such an interest in them. Speaking on behalf of all those who were gathered, Kwazka told the captain that he and his crew could do as they pleased with the full support of the entire community.

After that, the crew of the *Pacifica Spirit* sprang into action. The next day, three structures identical to the classroom were erected. Like the classroom, the structures were about 300 meters from the vessel—outside of the vessel's takeoff blast radius in my estimation. Extendible masts, about twenty meters tall and topped by photoelectric panels and lights, were put up in the vicinity. After that evening's writing and reporting session, while making my way back to my dwelling, I saw powerful lights across the plain. They were mounted on top of the masts and flooding the human structures and environs with light. The structures also glowed, their interior lights shining through their thin white fabric shells.

For the next three days and nights, the hoverlift was in constant use, emptying the cargo bay and shuttling equipment and supplies to the new structures.

The humans started venturing away from the vessel during daylight hours, taking samples of rocks, sand, mineral deposits, water, algel, and other plants. Captain Staedtler or another crew member took turns accompanying each of us to the village after class, usually to request that we ask volunteers to come over for physical exams. When it was my turn, Captain Staedtler walked with me. He asked for my impressions, observations, feedback, and challenges. I made an offhand comment that, as our learning accelerated, my fellow students and I were finding it difficult to provide complete briefings after class before darkness set in.

The next day on my way to the classroom, the hoverlift with three crew members passed me, heading toward the village. When I returned to the village, three lighting masts had been placed in the community. Separate photoelectric cells were mounted to the roof of the community structure, powering lights inside the building and preventing the InfoServer's nearly depleted power cells from expiring. After class, the new lighting gave us more time to present our information, and when we were finished, all of the villagers had enough light to walk to their homes after full darkness had fallen. We were very pleased and grateful for this technology. The only downside was that the attending villagers had less time to meditate, and we students had fewer hours to process the day's teachings for ourselves.

Other curious occurrences were visits by kloormari from other villages, many of them having walked for days. One or more kloormari from my village must have traveled to other settlements where some of their villagers must have felt compelled to witness the humans, their devices, and their activities in person. The visitors kept a reasonable distance, so they did not intrude. Most visitors stayed for a day or two before starting the long journey back to their homes. They were welcomed to spend their nights sheltered in the community structure if they wished.

And so, the humans, the students, and the villagers fell into a rhythm and routine, and the presence of the humans became as normal as the afternoon rains and the ebb and flow of day and night.

Apart from struggling to understand the vagaries of human emotions, customs, and society, my fellow students and I had a difficult time with some aspects of astrophysics. While we had extensively studied the theory of gravity, starting with Newtonian physics, it seemed incomprehensible that Kuw'baal was a sphere orbiting an enormous source of heat and light called a star while spinning in a void. It required a great suspension of our lifelong observations to think that we could be standing on any part of a sphere without falling off.

It might have been easier to understand our planet if it was not constantly shrouded in a layer of cloud. If we could observe our star, we might have found a way to simultaneously compare the angle of the star from different parts of Kuw'baal. We knew that day and night occurred at different times and in different places, but we perceived that as a band of light that would travel across our world from one skyline to the opposite horizon. It would also have been different if we could have looked up at night, staring in wonder at nearby planets and distant stars.

It should be made clear that we fully believed the science. Our training and the empirical evidence were irrefutable. Our only struggle was in *visualizing* the nature of our planet, our star system, our galaxy, and the universe that contained it all. Personally, I couldn't even fully grasp the notion of anything existing beyond our sky.

Presumably due to their base-ten numbering system, one hundred has significance to the humans. On the one hundredth day since our training commenced, Sam surprised us with an announcement that would lead to a fundamental change in our perceptions of Kuw'baal and all that the universe holds beyond our world.

"I have an announcement that coincides nicely with our one-hundred-day anniversary," Sam began. "As you know, in seven days, the *Pacifica Spirit* will be leaving on a ten-day mission. Our crew will perform a remote survey of Ryla 6, and then we'll rendezvous with a supply vessel for provisions. Finally, we're going to pay a courtesy call to a planet, Saraya, in a star system just over ten light years from here.

"I've spent many hours lobbying the captain and the chief of security. Due to my efforts, but especially due to the way that all of you have conducted yourselves, I am overjoyed to announce that you're all invited to accompany us on our mission as observers!"

We were so delighted with Sam's announcement that we forgot ourselves and started babbling to one another in kloormari while rapidly pacing back and forth and running in circles.

"Now, I understand if some or all of you wish to stay behind, if you are worried about your safety or if you think that the whole experience would be a bit overwhelming," Sam said.

It took a moment for my excitement to subside enough to communicate in Terran. "Sam," I said, "on behalf of all of us, let me assure you that none of us would pass up such an opportunity! Just when we think that you and the crew couldn't be any more generous, you surprise and honor us even more. We couldn't come close to adequately expressing our gratitude. Thank you."

"Well," Sam said, "it *will* provide a chance for you to visualize a few aspects of astrophysics."

Sam's remark served to solidify my notions of human understatement.

# NINE: ABOVE AND BEYOND

Leading up to the mission, I concentrated all of my classroom time researching interstellar travel, spacecraft, propulsion, and control systems. I studied the operations manuals, maintenance schedules, and schematics for the type of vessel that we would be boarding. Sam also had us watch a short series of standard vids, which were played for all first-time spacecraft passengers.

K'tatmal asked Sam how we'd be fed during the voyage. Sam explained that the vessel's botany and agriculture experts had managed to grow algel in a standard incubation vat and that kloormari volunteers had successfully consumed it. Later that day, we visited the vessel's hydroponics section. Blobs of algel lined the bottom and sides of a clear cylinder about a meter in diameter and two meters high. Bright lights shone from the cylinder's lid, and clear liquid was added as a constant mist that doused the algel. Each student was offered a sample. The farmed algel was palatable but rather bland and lacking in its usual rich aroma.

When the morning of our departure finally arrived, the breeze was light and fresh for this eventful day. Captain Kwami Staedtler met our class in his full dress uniform at the lower hatch. He escorted us to the bridge, then aft and down the half flight of stairs to the observation deck. For safety and stability, we knew that we would have to be prone during takeoffs and landings. We saw that the reclining chairs had been modified with a center strip of the backrests removed so that our breathing inlet and vocal outlets would be unimpeded on the side of us that faced down toward the deck.

A live vid feed provided the sights and sounds from the bridge. Although the hatches closed shortly after our arrival, I knew that the pre-flight checklists would take two to three hours to complete—longer if any issues had to be investigated and rectified. As crew members read their lists, I followed along in my mind, having familiarized myself with all the processes.

Thirty minutes before takeoff, my classmates and I were on tenterhooks.

"Excited?" Sam asked.

"To say the least," I replied.

"Me too," Sam said, "I've done this about a dozen times before, but it never gets old. Leaving a planet for the great beyond is an awesome experience in the truest sense of the word."

Fifteen minutes later, Bertha Kolesnikov entered.

"Bertie! Are *you* giving us the safety briefing today?" Sam asked.

"Yeah, I kinda got volunteered for the job. Fact is, I'm also the appointed guest services coordinator, so I'm supposed ta keep you an' yer gang happy and content. How funny is that? Heh heh heh!"

"Okay, you boys, listen up," she barked (this was not the first time she had assumed that we were male). Bertie started reading the briefing from her Infotab without her usual coarseness and overly familiar style. "Welcome aboard the *Pacifica Spirit*. This vessel is equipped for your comfort and safety."

As Bertie continued, Keesooni (for some reason) decided to speak in unison with Bertie. "In the unlikely event of an emergency . . ."

For some reason, my classmates and I felt compelled to join in. After all, we had seen the briefing vid a few days before. " . . .pressure suits with locator beacons can be found on all decks in lockers marked . . ."

I glanced over at Sam and recognized his somewhat unsuccessful efforts to stifle laughter. I was pleased that he thought we were funny, though I really didn't "get it."

"Alright!" Sam exclaimed when Bertie was finished. "Let's give Bertie a big hand of appreciation." Sam clapped his hands while we snapped our manipulators.

"Aw shucks!" Bertie said. "You lugs sure know where your bread's buttered, don'cha?"

Sam and Bertie asked us to take a seat, recline, and fasten our restraints. They made the rounds to check on each of us, then Sam strapped in, and Bertie left, no doubt to take her station somewhere.

From my reclined position, I could see the village up the hill on the port side of the vessel. To starboard, I could see the rocky ridges that lined the far side of the plain. The windows in the ceiling showed our destination—the pure white sky and all that lay beyond it.

Vid panels rose from the floor on arms, allowing us to pull the monitors closer. Our monitors displayed views from cameras mounted on the bow and the lower starboard and port sides of the vessel. I saw hundreds of kloormari gathered on the plain, outside of the blast radius, waiting to witness the first kloormari ever to leave our world. I took a moment to let that thought sink in.

At one minute before liftoff, a digital countdown appeared in a corner of our monitors and all vid panels.

Thirty seconds . . .

My respiration rate had increased. We students were swiveling our eyestalks, looking at one another, trying to grasp what was about to happen.

Twenty seconds . . .

The manipulators on my upper limbs were clutching the armrests. My clasper limbs were wrapped behind the backrest, tightly fastening my body to the chair.

Ten seconds . . .

Respiration was at maximum. Anxiety level high. Excitement even higher.

Five seconds . . .

I was suddenly calm. Committed to the mission. Every sight and sound profoundly vivid. A low growl started from the bottom deck.

Zero.

The roar of the engines was nothing like I expected, just a soft rumble like distant thunder. Totally different from what the kloormari on the plain must be hearing and feeling.

I watched the monitor for the live feeds from below the vessel. All I could see was intense red and brown dust and a few pebbles jetting past. Next was the sensation of being lifted, faster and faster. On the monitor, I could see beyond the dust clouds. Some of the villagers were crouched nervously. Others were standing and waving up at us.

Within ten seconds, I could see the entire plain, village, stream, and algel falls on a single monitor. Moments later, I could see over the hills that fringed the plain and up into the highlands that fed our stream. As I glanced out of the observation deck's side windows, I saw the horizon getting lower and lower and then disappearing below the window frames.

In my excitement, I lapsed into speaking kloormari. "We're flying!" I shouted. A better Terran translation would be, "We're going upward," since at that time there was no kloormari word for flying. It was a glorious feeling to be doing something that a short time earlier hadn't even been a notion that any kloormari could conceive of! As the *Pacifica Spirit* accelerated, I felt as though I was transcending all that had ever defined me, breaking out of a shell that I never knew I was imprisoned in. Oh, the wonder! Oh, the unlimited possibilities for me and for every single kloormari in existence now and forever into the glorious future!

The g forces shifted as the vessel adjusted to a more horizontal flight path and picked up speed. As I watched the land below us streaming past, I was awed by the vastness of the hills, valleys, lakes, and plains that I had never seen before.

That's when terror struck us.

As we approached the bottom of the sky, we realized it was not a flat, uniform, monochromatic surface. Great bulbous protrusions extended down randomly, white on top and slightly grey on the bottom surface. "Sam, we're getting very close to the sky!" I tried to modulate my voice to imitate a frightened human so that he would know how anxious I was.

"Stay calm and don't worry," Sam replied. "As you all know, what you call the sky is just vapor. We will pass right through it without difficulty."

"Sam, do you not see the parts hanging lower than the rest of the sky? We can't see through these things, Sam. They are solid!" Kwazka said with great alarm.

I looked at the forward-facing image on the monitor. A huge column of descended sky was dead ahead, and we were closing fast. "Stop the vessel! We're going to collide with a piece of the sky!" I screamed. Each of the other students had their eye glued to their monitor and was shouting a panicked warning.

"You need to relax!" Sam shouted. "Just put your trust in the crew and our cap—"

We screamed with terror as our collision with the sky jolted the *Pacifica Spirit*. Silence and blackness followed.

I opened my eyelid. We were still below the sky, streaming along at a blinding velocity.

"You see? We hit the sky!" I barked.

"That," Sam exclaimed, "was called turbulence. It happens whenever we fly through parts of an atmosphere with differing densities. We passed through a column of water vapor, which is denser than the drier air."

As Sam spoke, there was another (much smaller) bump as we rose into a smoother part of the sky, a bright white nothingness. We were engulfed inside the sky world!

As we continued our ascent, the daylight grew stronger and became brighter than any of us had experienced. Gradually, occasional patches of light blue started streaking past the ceiling windows. In a flash, the sky was gone, replaced by a dome of the brightest blue we had ever seen. The monitors showed the sky below us, lumps and puffs and columns of it streaking past!

An incredible ball of light pierced the ceiling windows, casting deep shadows from every chair and fixture on the observation deck. Each of us had to close our eyelid over the part of our eye directly facing the light. Ryla! Our star! Giver of light and sustenance to our planet!

The dome of blue started to darken, and I saw that the edge of the sky below was curved. The dome deepened to indigo and then, as it transformed to blackness, a few points of light pierced through. With each passing second, more lights became visible until thousands upon thousands of lights were draped across the blackness.

Stars! Each one millions of times larger than my entire home planet, each one a massive factory of light and energy, fusing atoms over the eons, and yet each one so distant that it was only visible as a tiny point of light in the vastness of space!

My musings were interrupted when Captain Staedtler announced that we were to accelerate to a high orbital velocity. Our seats adjusted themselves to a more upright position as the g-force of acceleration pushed us against the padded backrests. As the force of our angular momentum counteracted the gravitational pull of Kuw'baal, I felt lighter, as if I could fly without a space vessel! As we approached orbital velocity and zero gravity, Captain Staedtler announced that the graviton field was being activated. The vessel's artificial gravity gradually took effect. When we were at one Terran g, slightly less than one g on Kuw'baal, we were permitted to release our restraints and move about the observation deck.

By this time, the star Ryla was behind and below the vessel. I watched the monitor and saw Ryla disappear behind Kuw'baal below us.

"Performing a one-hundred-and-eighty-degree roll to port," a voice announced over a loudspeaker. "Our guests may want to take a look out the port side of the observation deck." We walked to the port-side windows. As the *Pacifica Spirit* started a slow roll, we saw the stars appearing to rise, pass overhead, and then set on the starboard side.

The curve of Kuw'baal came into view. With Ryla slipping behind it, the planet was a black circle with a magnificent glowing orange fringe. As the vessel completed its roll, my home world appeared overhead, almost filling the length of the observation deck.

There were no words. We planted ourselves in place and allowed the spectacle to unfold as our star seemed to cross behind Kuw'baal and illuminate the other side of my world. In a glorious burst of blinding light, Ryla rose over the horizon. We watched, motionless, until Ryla was below us and the fully lit Kuw'baal was over us, a globe of pure white as smooth as the glass in the windows.

As a kloormar, I had never experienced what humans call "love." Having never been a human, I cannot say that what I felt in that moment was the same thing as love, but in those moments of viewing my home world from the great beyond, I experienced a feeling unlike any other before.

Within the context of my life and limitations, at that moment I fell in love with humans and everything good that humanity represented.

The silence was broken by Captain Staedtler coming down the stairs. "Beautiful, isn't it? I've been spacefaring for over forty years, but a sight like this never loses its magic. I can't begin to imagine what this experience is like for you, but I can see that it is having a profound impact.

"I just wanted to let you know that sustenance will be brought to you in a moment. After that, the internal lighting will be dimmed, and most of the crew members will begin a sleep cycle. I recommend that you do the same, or in your case, enter a meditative state.

"We will remain in orbit until morning while the night crew performs routine systems checks. We have a busy schedule tomorrow, including a couple of surprises. Quarters have been prepared for you on the deck below this one in case you want to make use of them. Your names have been printed, in Terran, on the door to each of your quarters. Please feel free to wander around and explore any open parts of the vessel. Good night to you all, and I'll see you in the morning."

The captain turned and left just as Bertie entered, pushing a hovercart with a small vat of algel, ten bowls, and a large serving spoon. One by one, we each unglued our eye from the spectacle, pulled a handful of algel from the vat, and placed it in our feeding pouches, having no use for the bowls and spoons. Then we moved back to our previous positions to continue staring in wonder at our planet.

"Beautiful, ain't it?" Bertie said as she and the hovercart glided out of the room.

Apart from Sam, we had no use for our quarters that night. We stayed where we were and effortlessly slipped into a deep meditation. As we orbited, our planet transitioned from a complete sphere to a half circle, to a slim crescent, to a black hole in space, and back again in a hypnotic rhythm. As we meditated, our eyes remained fully open for most of the orbital cycle, instinctively closing only when the direct rays of Ryla pierced the observation deck.

At the start of the morning staff rotation, Sam entered the observation deck. Being aware of his presence, we began to stir. The first thing we noticed was that Kuw'baal was gone. K'aablart walked to the rear windows of the deck and recognized our home as a small crescent receding far off the stern, surrounded by thousands of stars.

Sam wished us a good morning. Then he suggested we proceed to the cafeteria, so we could socialize with the crew. "Before we head down, I would ask you to wear these name badges," he said. "I apologize for my species' difficulty telling individual kloormari apart, but these will help your interaction with the crew until they learn to identify you." We donned our "badges" which were actually armbands to wear around our upper limbs.

In the cafeteria, we formed a line behind three humans. They served themselves from a selection of prepackaged foods and drinks. At the end of the counter was a clear urn containing algel. A lever at the bottom of the urn opened an outlet where the algel could slurp out. The outlet hung over the edge of the counter and was at such a height that we could just open our feeding pouch and let the algel flop in. "Down the hatch!" as the Terran idiom goes.

Sam was seated at a table with a plate of sausages in front of him. "Damn fine saussies, Bertie!" he called out.

"I guess a total wiener like you would know a good sausage, eh, Sammy?" Bertie guffawed, as did a few of the other crew members in attendance.

Lynda Paige was the chief navigator and was sitting alone. I had the notion that I should practice small talk, so I knelt beside her at her table. "Hi, Lynda Paige, I'm Kelvoo. How long have you served aboard the *Pacifica Spirit*?"

"Well, hi, Kelvoo." Lynda smiled. "This is my second mission on the *Pacifica*, so I guess I've been here for almost three years now. Before that I was posted to a freighter, the *Bold Venture*."

"I recall reading about the *Bold Venture*," I said. "Length overall: 1.2337 kilometers. Beam: 225 meters, seven crew—"

"I know," she interjected.

"One thousand two hundred and seventy-one days ago the vessel suffered a hull breach caused by metal fatigue," I continued. "Three crew members were lost and have been commemorated for saving the vessel and the remaining crew members at the cost of their own lives."

"Yeah, I know," Lynda said with unexpected forcefulness. Other conversations grew quieter in the cafeteria. In hindsight, I realized the other crew members must have been listening in.

"I'm sure that you would know, Lynda, since you were one of the surviving crew. How fortunate you must have felt. The heroes of the incident were Ensign Mary Westham, Engineer Oleg Paige, and First Mate Ndugu Xao. It's interesting that the engineer had the same last name as you. Was he related, perhaps?"

When Lynda looked up at me, I could see tears welling up on her lower eyelids. "He was my husband, and he died the day before my birthday. Thanks a heap for reminding me!" The cafeteria immediately fell silent as she leaped to her feet and stormed out of the room.

I turned to Sam, who had been consuming a sausage at the adjoining table and was just recovering from a fit of coughing. "Sam," I inquired, "did I just commit a social faux pas?"

"Oh, yes, Kelvoo! I'm sorry to say that you really put your foot in it!" I was thinking of asking Sam about the origin of that Terran saying but thought better of it.

"What just happened?" I asked.

"When a human forms a pair-bond with another person, and that partner loses their life, the psychological impact is extremely painful."

"But, Sam, I've read that talking about that kind of loss is beneficial and can improve the healing process."

"That's only true if the person indicates they want to talk about it. Usually, they'd have that kind of conversation with a family member or a long-time friend or a professional counselor. In a professional setting, these personal matters are usually off limits because humans want to stay focused on their work and not be reminded of their pain."

57

"If I were human, how should I feel after committing such a transgression, and what would be an appropriate course of action?" I asked.

"Typically, remorse and embarrassment are the dominant feelings. The course of action would be to make a sincere apology in private."

"I didn't wish to cause suffering, and I'm concerned that I may have caused crew members to have negative thoughts about me, so I suppose I am having feelings of remorse and embarrassment."

Feeling compelled to make things right with Lynda, I grabbed one of Sam's remaining sausages. "What the hell?" Sam exclaimed as I ran out of the room with the sausage.

I thought I might find Lynda on the bridge, but I didn't have to go that far. She was leaning against a wall in the corridor.

"Lynda Paige," I said. "Please accept my sincerest apology for my insensitive remarks. I feel deep remorse and embarrassment. I did not intend to cause you pain, and I am deeply sorry. I hope that you will find it possible to forgive me at some point in the future."

"It's okay, Kelvoo," Lynda said softly. "I should apologize to you. We all know that human behavior is new to the kloormari and can be confusing. Hell, it's even confusing to humans some of the time! I should have remained calm and professional. You know, I thought I was over the worst of the pain, but sometimes I still get triggered. I hope we can put this behind us, if it's alright with you."

"Thank you, Lynda Paige. As a sign of my sincerity, I have brought what you humans refer to as a 'peace offering.'" I held up the sausage and proffered it to Lynda. Her eyes grew wide for a moment, and then she started to chuckle and then laugh uncontrollably.

When she settled down a bit, she touched my shoulder. "Kelvoo, you're a good guy—I mean person—I mean kloormar. Thank you." Then she bit an end off the sausage and stuck her head through the cafeteria doorway, holding the remaining sausage aloft. "Hey, Bertie! Damn fine sausages," she said as she regressed back into gales of laughter. "See you around, Kelvoo," she chortled as she strode down the corridor.

*Humans seem weird,* I thought.

The captain's voice sounded throughout the vessel. "Kloormari guests, please report to the observation deck."

As we entered the observation deck, we saw that retractable sheets of fabric had been pulled taut over the windows, about fifty centimeters away from the glass. Handrails that had been recessed into the floor and window frames were now extended. The railings from the window frames protruded past the sheets of fabric between the rows of windows.

Captain Staedtler entered. "We would like to conduct a little experiment this morning with any of you who want to participate. We didn't want to announce it beforehand because that could affect the results. We are curious about your ability to adapt and move in a microgravity environment. We would like to disable the graviton field and see how well you can navigate around the room. As you can see, all hard surfaces have been covered for your protection. If you do not want to participate, please say so now. You can then proceed to any other part of the vessel and strap yourself to any fixed surface."

As usual, not one of us considered missing out on such an experience.

Captain Staedtler touched the communication device on his shoulder. "Commence zero g with two-minute standard countdown."

A moment later, a vessel-wide computer-generated voice sounded. "Zero g in two minutes."

"Okay," Captain Staedtler said, "please spread out, and stand with your lower limbs slightly bent. When we lose gravity, I want you to kick off from the floor and move around *very gently*. Once you're in motion, nothing will stop your momentum and trajectory until you contact another object. We're not looking for acrobatics and certainly not speed, so please take it easy. Now if you'll excuse me, I'm going to strap myself into the chair over in the aft starboard corner. Just thinking about floating around makes me queasy!"

As Captain Staedtler strapped in and we took our positions, we heard another announcement. "Zero g in one minute. Secure all objects." The next announcement was a countdown from ten seconds. When the count reached zero, I straightened my lower knees slightly and gently pushed off. I hadn't realized it would take an additional second or two for the graviton field to fade from one Terran g to zero.

When I reached about one meter in height, I began to fall slowly back toward the floor, gradually rotating backward. Halfway down, zero gravity kicked in. I tried to get my feet under me, but I was treading air. One of my feet hit the floor when I was about forty-five degrees off horizontal. I started to spin backward. To avoid scraping against any surfaces, I tucked into a ball, which greatly increased my spin. As I approached the ceiling, I straightened out to reduce my spin. I was just out of reach of any handrails, so I struck the fabric that was stretched in front of the ceiling windows. The fabric stretched and then rebounded, sending me back toward the floor.

Halfway to the floor, K'aablart collided with me, sending us spinning in opposing trajectories. I ended up in Captain Staedtler's lap! He steadied me and then pushed me gently toward a railing that extended from what was normally the floor. As I held the railing, I saw my fellow kloormari spinning, tumbling, and floating in all directions. Sam was among them, trying to steady some of them and demonstrating that he possessed some experience with zero gravity.

I started to pull myself along the length of the railing. As I did, I calculated the force required per unit of speed and rotation. I found that I could use my claspers to grasp objects for stability, and I figured out how to push off with minimal pitch, yaw, and roll. I could see that my fellow students were also getting the hang of things.

After several minutes, Kwazka asked me and three others to form a line at the aft end of the observation deck. We lined up with Kwazka in the middle. Kwazka explained the plan to us. Kwazka kicked off to glide the length of the observation deck. Kroz and I followed on either side of Kwazka. Kleloma and Keesooni followed. We glided in a precise "V" formation across the entire length of the observation deck.

At the same time, the other students were practicing spins and rolls despite Captain Staedtler's admonition to avoid acrobatics. They perfected their spin and roll rates to end up with their original orientation at the end of each glide.

"How much longer, Captain?" Sam asked, his voice unsteady. I saw a sheen of sweat on his face, which seemed to have taken on a pallid complexion.

"I've seen enough," Captain Staedtler said. Then he spoke into his communication device. "Restore gravity to one g." I was concerned when I heard the command since I was slowly drifting just below the ceiling. Fortunately, gravity was restored gradually, and I was able to touch down gently and hold a railing. At about a half g, Sam stumbled to the wall behind the bridge and pulled out a hose from a panel marked "Liquid Recovery." Sam pressed a switch on a funnel at the end of the hose. I heard air being sucked into the funnel as Sam vomited into it.

Personally, I felt fine. In fact, I found the exercise incredibly stimulating and was disappointed that it had ended so soon. Perhaps I had experienced a kloormari equivalent to the human concept of "fun."

Another vessel-wide announcement was made. "All available personnel, report to the cafeteria immediately." Sam and Captain Staedtler left the room.

"I wonder whether that includes us," K'tatmal said.

"Well," Kwazka replied, "the announcement said 'personnel,' not 'crew.'"

We proceeded apace to the cafeteria. The area nearest the counter looked like a scene of mass murder from any number of Terran horror vids. Thick red liquid, flecks of meat, and sinuous white matter covered the walls, floor and ceiling. Bertie was staggering about as if in a daze.

"Bertie," I ventured, "what is that stringy stuff in your hair?"

"It's spaghetti, dumbass!" She wheeled about and turned on Captain Staedtler. "Fer chrissake, cap'n! Two minutes? You gave me two minutes' warning before goin' to zero g? It's a damn good thing I'd just finished pourin' off the boiling water!"

"Bertie!" I interrupted. "It might be advisable to moderate your language to the captain. According to part five of the regulations, section seven point two, the captain may have the option of disciplining you for insubordination."

"Insubordination!" she roared. "I'll give you insubordination! Have some lunch on me!" With that, Bertie scooped up a heaping handful of sauce-laden spaghetti and hurled it at me, splattering my upper torso and looping a few strands around my eyestalk.

The rest of the crew began to smirk, then to shake silently, some of them covering their mouths. Someone in the crowd started tittering. A second later, everyone erupted in paroxysms of laughter.

I looked over at Bertie, covered in sauce, her hair matted with pasta and ground meat. She couldn't help herself. Although her mouth was sealed tight, her lips were turned upward at the corners, and she shook with a combination of constrained mirth mixed with rage that was still simmering—unlike the remains of the marinara sauce.

We all pitched in and had the cafeteria cleaned within twenty minutes.

The spaghetti was a total loss. Lunch for the humans that day consisted of buns, butter, cheese, potato chips, and pudding.

After that we were ushered onto the bridge. "After the zero-g test," Captain Staedtler said, "I was about to address all of you, but then the incident happened where we lost our lunch. Some of us," he added, turning toward Sam, "in more ways than one! What I was going to say is that you all performed in zero-g far beyond any of our expectations. It may have seemed like a cluster of disorganized flailing at the start, but compared with an inexperienced human, each of you adapted far more quickly. By the end of the exercise, you did at least as well as a human with one hundred hours of experience. Amazing performance! Now, we would like to learn about your piloting skills. For that I will turn things over to our chief navigator, Lynda Paige."

Lynda got up from the chair at her station and turned to address us. "In this exercise," she began, "we would like to give each of you the chance to pilot the *Pacifica Spirit*. We will deploy a set of training drones, which will light up to display a path through space. We will switch navigation to total manual control and ask you to guide the vessel along the path. I don't want you to worry about damaging the vessel. Automated safeguards will be enabled, limiting your relative speed and maneuverability. Navigation will be switched back to automatic if you are about to make any dangerous moves. If any of you are uncomfortable with this or you don't want to participate, please stand to one side now."

Of course, nobody moved.

"Okay then," Lynda continued, "to evaluate each of you individually without you picking up on the experience of any kloormari that go ahead of you, I will ask you to wait on the observation deck and then call you in one at a time. I think we'll start with my buddy Kelvoo here. So, Kelvoo, please come over to my station. The rest of you, please proceed through the doors."

As I approached, Lynda met me partway to her station. As we walked, she touched my shoulder and leaned in close. "I wanted to give you a turn first to let the rest of the crew know that we're cool," she whispered. "Cool" was an expression that I had seen on Terran vids, so I got the gist of Lynda's statement. I found reassurance in her remark, and I thanked her.

Lynda released the clamps holding her chair to the deck and moved it aside. I knelt in front of the navigation console, which consisted mostly of a large, sloping panel. "I'm going to speak fairly loudly so that all of the bridge can hear our interactions," Lynda said. "Please do the same." She reached over to a side console. "Releasing nav training drones, pattern alpha one."

A hatch opened on top of the *Pacifica*, just forward of the bridge, and a swarm of over one thousand drones adorned with green lights emerged and moved ahead of the vessel. The drones used their ion-propulsion engines to form squares with five drones on each side. A series of squares appeared ahead, forming a tunnel that receded into the distance. Farther ahead, I saw the tunnel start to turn to port. I looked at the nav console and saw the position of the ship in relation to a representation of the path that was being constructed. The path started straight, then turned left, followed by a series of increasingly tight curves. When the drones were in position, I could see that the path ended back at the starting point, right behind the vessel.

Lynda tapped a control on the nav panel. "Requesting captain's override."

Captain Staedtler touched his panel. "Override granted."

A joystick rose from the nav console beside the panel. Lynda asked me to grasp it. The joystick was shaped to fit human hands, but I was able to make do with the manipulators on my hand with only minor discomfort. Lynda reviewed the motions with me. I could lift or lower the joystick to move the vessel vertically. I could also move the entire stick left or right to slide sideways to port or starboard and tilt the stick in any direction to tilt the vessel in the corresponding orientation. By twisting the stick, I could rotate the vessel around its center of mass. My other hand paddle could slide forward or back over a control on the panel to increase or decrease thrust in the forward or reverse direction.

"So, are you ready to take the joystick and navigate the course?" Lynda asked.

"No," I replied.

"Why's that?"

"Because first we need to set the mode switch from auto to manual."

"How do you think we would do that?"

I reached to the top-right corner of the panel and tapped the "mode" icon.

"Nice! Are we ready now?" Lynda asked.

"No. Now we need to open the flow of propellant to the maneuvering thrusters. After that we must extend the thrusters from the hull."

"Where did you learn all that?"

"I read the operation manuals for this series of interstellar vessels."

"Which ones?"

"All of them."

"All twenty-one volumes?"

"Yes."

Lynda laughed. "Well, I guess you don't need me then! Why don't you show me how it's done and then take us out?"

I started the propellant flowing and extended the thrusters as per the written procedures. I moved my left hand paddle up slightly on the velocity control, and the vessel slowly started to accelerate down the center of the drone tunnel. I didn't move the joystick until a few seconds before entering the first curve. Then I nudged the joystick to the left. After a long delay, the *Pacifica Spirit* began to slide laterally to port. To avoid sideswiping the portside drones with the stern, I twisted the joystick to the left, and the vessel began to rotate to port. The bow barely cleared the edge of the last rectangle before the turn. I narrated my actions as I performed them.

When the vessel was pointing in the right direction. I twisted the stick to straighten out, but I underestimated the momentum that the entire vessel now had to starboard. I pushed the stick hard to the left but not soon enough. The vessel collided with the drones along the right side of three rectangles. That's when the full lateral thrust to starboard took effect, blasting the vessel through the right walls and completely outside of the course.

"I'm sorry. I hope I didn't destroy too many drones," I said, tapping the "Nav Reset" control on the panel to halt the vessel in relation to the course.

"That's what they're made for," Lynda replied. "They'll slide back into position once we're about a kilometer away."

I nudged the vessel back into the course. In my mind, I reviewed my prior movements, the vessel's responses, the forces of momentum, and control delays. My calculations were completed before I was ready to accelerate forward again.

Even though the course became increasingly challenging, I managed to complete it with no further collisions. The bridge crew and Sam applauded as I brought the vessel to a relative halt.

"Not bad," Lynda said. "Let's do that one more time with pattern beta one." She issued some commands using a side console. The drones didn't move, but she said that the course was ready. Some of the drone rectangles moved slightly as I approached. The rectangular tube of the course snaked vertically and horizontally, requiring constant adjustment as I proceeded.

I had a good enough feel for the vessel and its controls that I completed pattern beta one with no collisions. Finally, I came to a stop.

"I think that'll do, Kelvoo," Lynda said. "Thank you for completing the exercise." The crew applauded a second time. I even got a whistle and a couple of "whoo-hoos."

Sam called me over to him near the aft of the bridge. From there, I watched as each of my fellow students took their turn at the nav console and then joined Sam and me. Only Kwazka and K'raftan knew the steps to take before using the joystick because the remaining students had studied other aspects of space travel instead of the specific operation manuals.

Each student's performance was applauded. As the afternoon progressed, Captain Staedtler and the bridge crew became more jovial.

"Any questions?" Captain Staedtler asked when we were done.

"I've got one, Captain," Sam said, raising his hand. "Could I have a go?" The rest of the crew laughed.

"You know, our guests did complete the exercise much faster than I thought they would, and they only used a fraction of the propellant that we had budgeted, so what the hell?" Captain Staedtler said. "Go ahead, Sam, give it a try. We'll use you as a control subject, so we can evaluate how well a kloormar with no experience did against a human with no experience."

"Whoa, I was only kidding!" Sam protested.

"Too bad!" Captain Staedtler said, grinning. "You asked for it, and you got it! I'm sure we'd all like to see this." He issued a command to broadcast the bridge vid feed ship wide.

Sam approached the nav console tentatively. "Don't worry," Lynda said, "I won't bite your head off if you break the ship!" More laughter came from the crew. "Besides," she added, "you've had the benefit of watching ten kloormari do this. It should be a piece of cake."

Lynda manipulated the nav console to get everything ready for Sam to take the stick. Sam gently accelerated down the straightaway. He smiled in relief. When the vessel approached the first gentle turn, Sam twisted the joystick. When the vessel didn't respond immediately, he twisted more. The vessel turned on its axis but continued in the same direction, right through the side of the course on the starboard side of the vessel. Sam panicked, overcompensating at every turn. By the time the vessel was simultaneously pitching, yawing, and rolling a few kilometers outside of the course, Sam raised his hands from the console. "Sorry, sorry. I surrender!"

The crew gave Sam a standing ovation accompanied by raucous cheering. I had to explain to some of the students that the crew was mocking Sam in a collegial way as a form of humor. Sam walked back to us shaking his head, his smiling face partially buried in his hands. Captain Staedtler asked Lynda to stabilize the vessel, recover the drones, and put us back onto our original heading.

When the crew had settled down, Captain Staedtler got up and addressed us. "Another phenomenal performance! Once again, all of my expectations were completely blown away! We are back on course for Ryla 6. As a point of interest, we may have appeared to have stopped during the training exercise, but we still remained on an overall intercept course at high speed. If you would take a look through the upper forward windows, Ryla 6 is the brightest object. While our vessel is not pointing directly to the planet, keep in mind that the planet is also in motion, so both objects will arrive at the same location tomorrow morning."

Nobody on the bridge needed a lesson on such basic concepts, but we listened politely.

After filling up in the cafeteria, all of the kloormari assembled back on the observation deck to meditate as Ryla 6 grew larger over the course of the night.

# TEN: A WHOLE OTHER WORLD

Shortly before breakfast, the *Pacifica Spirit* was in orbit around Ryla 6. The planet looked no bigger from orbit than Kuw'baal had, but we knew that the planet was ten times larger than ours, so we were in a far higher orbit than we had been around our home.

At the poles, Ryla 6 was as smooth and white looking as Kuw'baal due to a frozen layer of carbon dioxide. The rest of the planet was dark grey to black with rock formed from volcanic activity billions of years before. Curved mountain ranges and valleys snaked across the surface. Some of the valleys were filled with frozen water, reflecting a brilliant cyan hue like glacial ice that I'd seen in historical Terran documentary vids.

After breakfast, we kloormari were on the bridge as observers. Large panels displayed telemetry from scanners as the planet's surface, magnetic fields, gravity, atmosphere, and geology were scanned. At the same time, the remote lander that had given us our first contact on Kuw'baal was prepared and launched. Survey specialist Ron Suwannarat explained that the lander would be pushed to its limits due to the planet's massive gravitational force. The lander's drone would not be onboard to save weight and fuel and because the atmosphere was too thin for its turbine fan thrusters to work.

Once the *Pacifica Spirit* moved to a higher synchronous orbit above a potential landing site, the lander was launched. We watched the vid feed from the lander as it plummeted toward its target. The lander performed three deceleration burns as it descended into a valley between walls of black basalt and on toward a frozen lake below. The objective was to land on the ice at the edge of the steep rock face so that samples of ice and rock could be taken and returned to the vessel.

When the lander was just over half a kilometer from the ice, a problem became evident. The lake's surface was strewn with ice boulders and fractured with cracks. These were too small to be detected by the previous sensor scans but large enough to swallow the lander, or at least one of its legs.

"Could we hover the lander over the surface and move laterally to search for a site?" Captain Staedtler asked.

"Under average circumstances, no problem," Ron replied, "but with the increased gravity, having enough thrust to achieve escape velocity is already looking sketchy. I recommend we fly up the side of the gorge and try to find a relatively flat area on top of the ridge."

We watched the lander vid as it labored up the wall of the canyon. The wall was a study in black. Shiny black obsidian reflected Ryla's intense light while rough black basalt absorbed the light, and the black shadows revealed only darkness. Near the top of the ridge, the mountain's slope became rounded as it flattened out. This gave way to spires ranging from five to ten meters high. Between the spires were pockets of gravel that provided a relatively flat surface. Ron deftly put the lander down on a small patch of gravel, directly beside a spire of solid rock.

In the hours that followed, the lander deployed its drills and spades to take samples aboard where it used lasers and chemical reagents to vaporize and analyze the samples. The lander's telemetry lit up the panel with raw statistics, molecular structure diagrams, and detailed analyses. At the same time, humans and software ran scenarios for launching and retrieving the lander.

Captain Staedtler returned from lunch and requested an update.

"I'm sorry, Captain," Ron said, "but our change in plan for the lander required too much fuel. Without being able to achieve escape velocity, the only option would be to set the lander on a semi-ballistic trajectory. The *Pacifica* would have to go sub-orbital and essentially intercept the lander while in a virtual free fall toward Ryla 6. A tremendous amount of immediate thrust would be needed from the *Pacifica* to escape the gravity well. All occupants of the vessel would be subject to a very uncomfortable level of g forces."

Captain Staedtler nodded. "Let's just leave it alone then, Ron. We knew the risks in sending the lander to such a massive body. What do you think about leaving the lander as a data-gathering outpost until sometime in the future when it and its samples can be collected?"

"I think that's the best option," Ron replied. "There's plenty of light for the lander's photoelectric panels, so it should keep operating indefinitely. In the meantime, it's already provided a treasure trove of data that will keep science teams busy long into the future."

"Okay," Captain Staedtler said. "I'll write up an incident report with your input tomorrow." He turned toward the navigation console. "Lynda, break orbit, and set course for the jump point."

Captain Staedtler explained that our journey to the jump point would take slightly over twenty-five hours, at which point we could "jump" through space to a destination where we would make a pre-planned rendezvous with a supply vessel. "You are free to move around the vessel until we jump," he said. "Non-essential crew can take some leisure time for rest and relaxation until two hours pre-jump."

"With your permission, could we ask the crew questions about the vessel and the tasks that they carry out?" Kwazka inquired.

"Much of the crew will be off duty and may not want to get into such discussions," Captain Staedtler replied. "You must also leave the crew alone from 21:00 tonight through 08:00 tomorrow. Outside of that, you may ask any member of the crew whether they would entertain questions. If they're willing to assist, I have no problem with that. I just ask that you respect crew members' wishes if they decline.

"I should also advise you that this vessel's technology is standard for a research ship and is accessible to the public. In the future, if you are on a military vessel or a craft that uses more advanced technology, you will not be granted this level of access."

"Thank you," Kwazka said. "You honor us with your openness."

For the next couple of hours and then after breakfast the next day, we asked our questions. Overall, the crew enjoyed answering them in exchange for asking us about our lives, culture, and planet. We were pleased at how interested the humans were in us.

I spent my time in various parts of the vessel learning about navigation, engineering, and communications. Crew members were very accommodating and proudly showed me their work and equipment. After spending a couple of hours with each crew member, I would access the ship's InfoServer on my Infotab to expand on what I had learned.

The first interaction that Kroz had was with systems engineer Audrey Fraser, who introduced Kroz to software development and systems security. Kroz was so infatuated with these topics that Kroz spent no additional time with other crew members. Audrey Fraser didn't mind. She was pleased to share her knowledge with a being who was so interested in the intricacies of her work, which most crew members took for granted. At the time, none of us realized the pivotal role the skills Kroz was developing would play in the future.

Two hours before arriving at the jump point, all crew members were at their stations. Systems integrity checks were performed and then repeated. When we arrived at the jump point, Captain Staedtler made a vessel-wide address.

"Before we jump, I would like to explain to our guests where we are and what to expect. There is nothing particularly special about a jump point. There is no equipment stationed here, and there is nothing remarkable about space-time in this location. Jump points are simply areas of space that have been thoroughly surveyed and are shown to be particularly empty. This area is almost completely devoid of dust or any other particles. The same is true of any of the jump points that we could travel to. Materializing into a cloud of gas or dust, or worse, solid matter, has proven to be catastrophic too many times in the past, so we always err on the side of safety.

"We are at a jump point that was only recently mapped by a probe that was sent to the Ryla system. We were interested in the system due to a planetary survey conducted sixty-three years ago, which indicated that one of the planets, Ryla 5, could support life. Of course, Ryla 5 is actually the planet Kuw'baal, which we have grown to know and love.

"I will ask all crew members and guests to go and secure themselves now. When we jump, don't expect anything in particular. In fact, as you'll see, jumping is a whole lot of nothing. During the jump, anywhere from a few seconds to a few minutes will seem to pass for you. I hope you find the experience to be interesting. I'll see all of you on the other side."

We buckled ourselves in on the observation deck. I was looking out of the ceiling windows as the ship's computer-generated voice counted down from ten. At zero, all of the stars that I was seeing disappeared, replaced by absolute blackness. The vessel's interior appeared as a still image. Even when I changed the orientation of my eye, the image of the ceiling stayed dead center. All ambient noises, like the humming of the engines or the movement of air through the ventilation system, were gone. In fact, the total lack of sound was disquieting. When I tried to speak, I could feel my vocal reeds vibrate, but no sound came out.

In what I perceived to be thirty-one seconds, my senses returned to normal. First the scene cross-faded to correctly represent the direction that my eye was pointed. Next, a whole new set of stars appeared, first with their light being so bright that it blended into solid white outside the vessel. Then, within a fraction of a second, the blended light shrank back into thousands of pinpoints. At the same time, sound was restored with great intensity as though thirty-one seconds of sound had been compressed into less than a second. I could make out my own voice from the time that I tried to speak during the jump. With a great whoosh, the normal level of sound restored itself.

It was a good thing that we had done our research and had been briefed earlier; otherwise, I might have found the experience to be deeply disturbing rather than absolutely fascinating.

A vessel-wide announcement told us that we could remove our restraints. Captain Staedtler announced that we would now travel for several hours to the rendezvous point to meet the supply vessel. I knew this was necessary because the destination of a jump must never be located close to vessels or any other known objects. Captain Staedtler suggested that we get a good night's sleep or meditation.

# ELEVEN: ADVENTURES AT THE MALL

After breakfast the next morning, we gathered on the bridge. Captain Staedtler had been in touch with the supply ship, the *Orion Provider*, which was ready for our visit. The *Pacifica* had slowed, relative to the *Orion*, for a gradual approach. At first, the *Orion* just looked like a rectangular object, blocking the light from the stars behind it. When we were within ten kilometers, the *Orion's* external floodlights came on, illuminating its silver-grey skin.

The *Orion* was neither sleek nor aerodynamic. There was no need since the massive structure was built in space and would never intentionally be in contact with an atmosphere. The vessel was essentially a metal box. A bridge and adjoining observation deck sprang out of the "top" of the hull, resembling an elongated blister. Four enormous tubes were mounted on each side of the box at the stern. They held massive engines. A smaller box, the landing bay, was attached in front of the bow, connected by two access tubes. It was separated from the main body so that its gravitational field could be switched off separately from the rest of the ship when visiting vessels entered to land.

As the *Pacifica Spirit* approached, the scale of the *Orion Provider* was difficult to judge. When Captain Staedtler previously announced the ship's name, I looked it up on the Infotab. Intellectually, I knew that the vessel's main compartment was 953 by 517 by 207 meters, but the true magnitude didn't sink in until I saw the windows on the *Orion's* bridge and observation deck. When these appeared as pinpoints in relation to the overall vessel, the sheer mass of the *Orion* started to sink in.

Captain Staedtler contacted the *Orion* and requested and received permission to land. Lynda positioned the *Pacifica Spirit* in front of the *Orion Provider's* landing bay. The huge bay doors slowly opened, revealing a vast, empty space illuminated with powerful floodlights. The deck was grey. Six yellow circles were painted on the deck, and two vessels, one smaller and one far larger than the *Pacifica*, were clamped in place on two of the circles. Lynda rotated the *Pacifica* 180 degrees laterally and initiated the process that would automatically guide it backward and land it in the designated circle.

During the landing process, Captain Staedtler addressed us all via a ship-wide announcement. "For the benefit of our kloormari friends, please be advised that the *Orion Provider* is, under interplanetary law, its own sovereign territory. Since none of you have official travel documents, you will be required to provide a small scraping of tissue for identification purposes. That information will be encoded onto a temporary passport card that you will be required to carry in a pouch with a neck strap, or in your case, a strap that you can wear around your eyestalk. Any of you have the right to refuse to provide a tissue sample, in which case you will have to remain aboard the *Pacifica* during our visit.

"For the benefit of our guests and the entire crew, remember that we are *all* guests on the *Orion*. You will be on your best behavior. You will respect everybody on the *Orion*, and you will follow any directions given to you by the *Orion's* crew and authorities. All standard security and confidentiality protocols will be adhered to in accordance with the mission directives.

"As a personal word of advice, don't go blowing all of your pay in the shops, restaurants, lounges, and entertainment facilities. Speaking of pay, in recognition of their graciousness as guests and in light of all of their assistance and all that they have taught us, I am pleased to say that each of our kloormari guests will be provided with 150,000 units of SimCash to use and enjoy on the *Orion*. This is not a great deal of money, but it will let you experience some aspects of commerce and pick up a souvenir or two.

"When we land, please disembark in an orderly fashion and proceed through customs unless you are on the roster for the first shift. At 14:00, all procurement personnel will report to the vessel for loading. All crew members and guests must report back at 18:00 for departure at 19:00. Let's all take this time to relax and enjoy the *Orion's* hospitality."

When the *Pacifica* was just above the deck, the landing bay's graviton field was switched on at a very low level, causing our vessel to touch down on the landing deck with only the slightest bump. Our internal graviton field was gradually reduced as it was counteracted by the *Orion's* landing bay field, resulting in no perceptible change in gravity.

We watched the massive doors close. Air started flooding into the landing bay, silently at first and then with an increasingly loud roar as the atmosphere increased in density.

We made our way down to starboard-side Forward Hatch A, while the air pressure in the landing bay increased. Next, crew from the *Orion* clamped the *Pacifica* to the deck. The hatch opened, and we filed out. At the bottom of the ramp, the vessel's purser, Max Magnusson, handed each kloormar a "neck" pouch with a currency card. Sam led our group as we hiked across the landing bay to the aft wall. A catwalk ran halfway up the side and aft walls of the bay, about one hundred meters up. The two access tubes entered the landing bay at the catwalk, one labeled "Passengers" and the other "Freight."

We boarded a huge elevator on the passenger side and were whisked up the aft wall. Customs officers were stationed just outside the access tube. Members of the crew walked through a scanner, which read information from the passports they were carrying while cameras matched their faces to the corresponding images in a database.

Each kloormar was asked to open their food pouch for a scrape sample and to stand against a background for image capture. Seconds later, a temporary passport card was dispensed from the sampling machine. We each added our passport to our pouch, and the customs officers welcomed us to the *Orion Provider*. We kloormari and Sam stepped onto a conveyor belt as a group and were carried through the access tube.

On the way, Sam asked us whether we were familiar with Terran shopping malls. We were, to varying extents. As we exited the tube, we were met with a remarkable sight. A corridor ran for the entire length of the hull. Humans and other species walked along tiled paths down the center, while hoverlifts carried others above. My fellow kloormari and I had never seen grass, trees, or flowering plants before, so it was striking to see such landscaping on either side of the main path. Fountains and ponds were scattered about. On each side of us, waterfalls cascaded from the top of the hull to the main level where we were located. The air was pleasantly humid from the waterfalls' spray.

On either side and for almost the entire length of the hull was a galleria of commercial establishments, soaring fifteen levels high. Retail stores, restaurants, drinking establishments, entertainment venues, medical offices, pharmacies, brothels, casinos, fitness centers, and professional offices lined the vessel. Having never visited any kind of business establishment, I was eager to visit as many as time would allow with the possible exception of the brothels, as I was short of the requisite body parts and urges. Hotels and luxury resorts were situated in the distance at the aft end of the hull along with amusement rides, such as roller coasters and free-fall air-cushion jumps.

Sam encouraged us to split up and enjoy exploring the *Orion*. He said he would remain in place for a while and then be replaced by a different crew member since he would also like a chance for some professional downtime. If any of us needed anything, we could hop onto a hoverlift, press the "Command" button, and say, "Destination main level sector zero one."

I strolled along the main level, where recreational facilities were the main attraction. Swimming pools, racquet-sport courts, low-g bowling alleys, rock-climbing rooms, and live-performance theaters were just a few of the facilities available.

Humans were dressed in a wide range of attire, from loose-fitting casual wear to colorful, sparkling, skin-tight clothes. Some wore outlandish hats. Others wore clothes and hats with pictures and words on them. Many clothes had images of the *Orion Provider* with text commemorating the wearer's visit. I wondered whether the purpose of such garb might be to inform others of the visit to invite inquiries or whether humans (with their inability to remember every event) simply wished to remind themselves of their visit. I couldn't figure out why a human would wear such garb during their actual visit.

As I walked, I was fascinated to view species that I had only seen on Infotabs. Sarayans, with their majestic long-necked stature and flowing robes. Bandorians, which resembled gigantic Terran woodlouse isopods, scuttled along on seven pairs of legs. Two-armed Mangors glided along, their slug-like bodies glommed onto personal hover discs. Based on what I had learned about protocol, I resisted the temptation to stare at these species despite my fascination with them. I did, however, notice almost every passerby staring at me for a moment, then looking away as if suddenly remembering protocol themselves. I was not bothered by their behavior since I understood that they had never seen the likes of me before.

After a few minutes, I saw a particular variant of humans for the first time: children. They were in a group of fourteen individuals plus a human and a Sarayan adult who were leading them across the concourse to a hoverlift station from a facility named "Kiddies' Fun-Time Daycare." Signs in the window encouraged adults to let their children play in a caring, nurturing environment while the adults played in the casinos and pleasure palaces or consumed intoxicating substances.

The children crossed my path directly in front of me, causing me to stop short. When the group saw me, they stopped immediately, the children and their minders gaping at me. The children whispered to one another and pointed at me. A small boy walked up to me, pointing. "What are you?"

Out of respect, I bent down to his level, so I would not be too intimidating. "I'm a kloormar," I said, careful to use the human-friendly pronunciation for my species.

"Are you a boy or a girl?" the boy asked.

"I am neither one, but I can function as both," I explained. "I can bear children, or I can fertilize an ovum. We kloormar practice sexual reproduction as a group when—"

"Whoa!" the children's human minder exclaimed, seeming to snap out of her distracted state. "What the hell is wrong with you?"

I stood up and faced her. "I'm not aware of anything being wrong. Could you please clarify your question?"

"Look," she said, "I'm sorry these kids were staring at you. They've never seen a kloormar or whatever you called yourself. I've never seen your kind either, so maybe you're new here and don't know any better. Here's the thing: You don't talk to children that you don't know, and you certainly don't talk about sex. People will think you're some kind of pervert."

"I was speaking to this boy because he asked me questions. Perhaps it was inappropriate for him to inquire about my sex."

"Do you want me to call security?"

"I don't see any reason for you to do so, but it's clear that I have offended your group. I offer you my sincerest apologies for breaking protocol. I meant no harm, and I am sorry."

"Okay, just don't let me see you near any kids. Understand?"

"I understand," I replied. That's when I noticed that quite a crowd had gathered. I quickly retreated and boarded a hoverlift at a station quite distant from the daycare facility. Twelve humans, two Sarayans, and a Mangor were already on the lift. I could see a list of already requested destinations on the hoverlift's display panel. I pressed the command button. "Destination, top level, sector zero one," I said.

"Top level not understood," a voice replied. "State the level name." The display panel showed a schematic indicating the name of each deck.

"Promenade Deck level, sector zero one," I said.

"Sectors only apply to main deck. State the name of the establishment that you intend to visit." Another schematic showed an overhead view. There were too many businesses to fit onto one screen, so the display panel scrolled along the promenade deck map with a business name displayed for each space.

I sensed impatience and discomfort from the other passengers, so I chose a business at random. "Best Buns Body Sculpting and Depilation Salon."

The hoverlift rose and began depositing passengers at the various stops. I noticed that the passengers were tightly packed together at the opposite end of the lift as if they wished to keep their distance from me. After a couple of stops, a burly man stepped forward. "Hey, you. I don't like how you're staring at me."

"I'm sorry," I replied, "but I think you misunderstand. It probably appears that I am looking at you because my body is facing you. The fact is that my eye has a full three hundred and sixty degrees of horizontal vision. I was actually concentrating on the businesses on each side of the vessel. If it makes you more comfortable, I can shift my stance to face away from you." I shifted accordingly.

"You see, I am a kloormar from the plant Kuw'baal. I have eight vocal openings, four ears, and one eye. I first met humans a few months ago. Today I am struggling to have normal interactions with humans. Just a few minutes ago, I was scolded for having an inappropriate conversation with a group of children."

At the next stop, all of the other beings left the hoverlift despite the fact that seven more destinations were on the list. "I don't know what you are," the burly man shouted as the hoverlift departed, "but I don't trust your kind. Stay the hell away from me!"

After six additional stops, the hoverlift docked at the station a few doors away from the business that I had identified. The promenade deck was far less crowded with only a few beings wandering around. This was a welcome reprieve as I was feeling stress from my previous encounters and disappointment for unknowingly conducting myself incorrectly.

I walked to the bow of the *Orion*, above the area where my group had entered the main hull. On the top level at each end of the vessel, a walkway spanned from the shops on one side to the other. At the bow the walkway passed behind and just under the top of the waterfalls. I stopped below the closest waterfall at a designated viewpoint and watched the water cascade in front of me into the pool far below.

An information panel with text and vids was located at the viewpoint. Schematics showed that the levels below the main deck held administration offices, accommodations for the crew and staff of the businesses, life support, the power plant, propulsion, and most of all, vast warehouses of goods. In addition to being an interstellar tourism hub, the *Orion Provider* made the rounds of developed planets in various star systems to purchase items and supply goods and services. It was the most interesting part of my visit so far, and I felt considerably calmer.

I crossed the walkway and sauntered past various shops. I wondered how these businesses survived with so little traffic. I had 150,000 units of SimCash, so I looked at the displays of goods and promotional vids in each window. I didn't see any products or services that interested me, so I kept walking.

I came across a man of small stature standing on the concourse just outside of a shop. He smiled eagerly. "Come into my shop, my friend." I felt obliged to step inside, not wanting to be considered rude by rejecting his offer. "Welcome, welcome, my friend," he enthused. I was confused by his use of the word "friend" since he and I had never met before. "I don't think I've ever met someone of your species before," he continued. "Please tell me about yourself."

I told him that I was Kelvoo from Kuw'baal, and I explained how his species had made first contact with my people, and that this was my species' first off-world experience. I apologized in advance for any inappropriate behavior on my part and told him about my interactions with other passengers so far that day.

"I hear you, my friend," the shopkeeper said. "You must try to forgive my species. We humans are too quick to judge others. I myself have been subject to prejudices and have had to struggle my whole life." He spoke for twenty-one minutes about coming from an "outlier" colony and being subject to negative attitudes. He also told me about being cast out by his family and working on freighters and in mines and laboring for eighteen hours a day, scraping by and slowly saving enough to open his meager store with the hope of eking out a living for the rest of his days. I told the shopkeeper that I felt sorry for him and hoped he would enjoy some success.

"So, my friend," he said, "what would you like to purchase to help support my quest for success? Perhaps this nice matching *Orion Provider* cap and shirt as a reminder of your visit?"

I explained that I wouldn't need a reminder since, as a kloormar, I would clearly remember every moment of my visit. In addition, a shirt would impede my vocalization openings and my claspers.

"Of course, my friend," he replied. "Here is a scale model of the *Orion*, with great detail. You could display this proudly on a shelf in your home."

"My home has no shelves, and my species is incapable of pride. Furthermore, if I could feel pride about the *Orion*, it would only happen if I was involved in the construction or operation of the vessel."

The shopkeeper showed me various souvenirs, games, Infotab covers, hair accessories, socks, and other items that I couldn't use or wasn't interested in.

"If you aren't interested in my products or in supporting me, why the heck did you come into my store?" he asked finally in exasperation.

"You invited me."

"Why didn't you purchase anything?"

"You haven't shown me anything that I want or need."

"Then why did you waste my time?"

"You invited me in."

"I just spent half an hour with you. I could have been outside inviting customers in."

"No, you have only spent twenty-one minutes with me. Given the number of visitors in this section, I doubt that any have even passed by."

"Do you want me to call security?"

"Why would you do that?"

"We have regulations on the *Orion*. If a merchant invites you in, you are obligated to make a purchase. If I call security, you will be fined one hundred thousand units."

"I will give you a choice," I replied. "You can call security, or I can give you fifty thousand SimCash units, and we can be done."

"Fine," the shopkeeper said. "I'm a good person, my friend. I believe in forgiveness, so I'm going to overlook how you took advantage of me." The shopkeeper punched 50,000 into his Infotab's sales application. I waved my card over it and walked out.

Feeling overwhelmed and foolish, I went back to the walkway by the waterfalls and took a twenty-minute meditation break. I decided I'd had enough and would go back to the sector where a *Pacifica* crew member would be waiting. As I boarded an empty hoverlift, a woman shouted. "Just a moment!" She came running onto the hoverlift and thanked me for holding it for her.

"Hi," she said. "I'm Kaley Hart." She held out her hand, and I shook it.

"Hello, Kaley Hart. I'm Kelvoo."

"Please, call me Kaley. I hope you don't mind me saying, Kelvoo, but I have a tremendous interest in studying intelligent non-human species. I'm not familiar with your species, but if you have a little time, would it be alright if I asked you a few questions?"

"I'm not sure you would want to do that. Today I seem to have a habit of saying and doing the wrong things."

She nodded sympathetically. "I've heard that so many times from non-humans, Kelvoo. Humans have so many quirks, and some of us can't be bothered to give others a chance. I promise I won't object to anything that you have to say."

"In that case, Kaley, I would be delighted to converse with you."

"Great! Let's go down to the main level, find a bench, and have a nice chat."

Kaley pressed the command button. "Main level, sector zero two," she said. That sounded good to me as it was close to the *Pacifica* rendezvous point but far enough from the dreaded daycare center.

When we landed, Kaley led me to an empty bench beneath a tree bearing orange globes, beside a stream that emptied into a small pond. I found the setting to be relaxing, and Kaley's friendly, non-judgemental nature put me at ease.

I had a very pleasant conversation with Kaley. She asked questions and listened intently as I replied. Sometimes I would ask whether I was rambling for too long, but Kaley reassured me that everything I was saying was fascinating. I knew that while conversing with a human, I should also ask the other person about themselves. Kaley gave some short responses and assured me that her life was not particularly interesting.

For the next two hours, we talked about the kloormari and how the *Pacifica Spirit* had made first contact with us. I told Kaley about my fellow students, and I confess that I may have bragged about the kloormari's ability to remember everything and to learn and adapt very quickly. I especially enjoyed talking about our current voyage, the skills that we were tested on, and our newly learned abilities.

I ended by bringing Kaley up to speed on the events of the present day. She apologized again on behalf of humanity and expressed her hope that our long conversation hadn't tried my patience. I assured her that it had been the best part of my day. Throughout the conversation, I did my best to avoid delving into small details. Kaley assured me that I did very well, which gave my confidence a desperately needed boost.

We parted ways with a handshake, and I walked to sector zero one without further incident. Max Magnusson was sitting at the rendezvous point. "Glad to see you, Kelvoo," he said. "I hope you don't mind, but the captain says he wants all guests to report back to the *Pacifica* as soon as they arrive here. I'll get Sam to escort you down." Max spoke into his communicator and summoned Sam, who arrived less than three minutes later.

We walked through the tunnel, rode down in the elevator, and strode into the landing bay. Hoverlifts were loading large crates into the belly of the *Pacifica Spirit*.

"Well, that was an interesting experience," I said to Sam. Before I could elaborate, Sam asked me to hold off on discussing the visit until I was on board, and we could debrief. I couldn't think of what the reason might be, but we continued to the vessel in silence.

Once on the vessel, Sam ushered me into conference room BC-1, where five of my fellow students were already gathered. "I'm sorry to say that some of you might have had some unpleasant interactions with other passengers of the *Orion*," Sam began. "For example, Kleloma and Keeto were both accused of inappropriate behavior around children. Both of them deny ever being near any children, and I believe them."

"I'm afraid that I'm the likely cause of that accusation," I said. "I had such an incident, and since humans seem to have difficulty telling kloormari apart, they may have seen Kleloma and Keeto later and thought they were me."

Sam asked me to recount a broad overview of my experiences, saying he would ask questions if he wanted more detail. I told Sam about walking on the main level and then recounted my conversation with the boy in the group of children. I also told Sam about my hoverlift ride to the promenade deck and my interactions with humans along the way. I described reading information about the *Orion* on the walkway by the falls and my visit to the gift shop, which cost me 50,000 units of SimCash for, once again, breaching protocol. Finally, I spoke about my nice conversation with a human woman and how I felt much better afterward.

"You know, Captain Staedtler and I discussed whether to let you roam around the *Orion Provider* when we decided to take you on this trip. Captain Staedtler was reluctant, but I assured him that I had confidence in all of you. I want to assure you that I still have absolute confidence in you, and I know that none of you did anything intentionally inappropriate. What I did misjudge was how some of my fellow humans would jump to conclusions and be afraid of beings that they are unfamiliar with. When we visit Saraya on our next stop, I think it would be best if we stay together as a group. I hope you don't mind."

None of us minded at all.

I asked the other students whether they had made any purchases. Only K'raftan and Kroz had used any SimCash. Both had the same idea, picking up an arm-mounted flashlight and matching photoelectric charging unit. I wished I had seen such a product, as it could be useful back home.

While we waited for the remaining students to arrive, Sam addressed me. "By the way, Kelvoo, that shopkeeper cheated you. There is no regulation in the universe that would force you to make a purchase just for being invited into a store and having a conversation. It was the shopkeeper who broke protocol and behaved outrageously. I am going to lodge a formal complaint with the *Orion's* commerce department and try to get your money refunded."

"I'd greatly appreciate that," I replied.

"What was the name of the shopkeeper?"

"I don't know. He didn't tell me his name, and I didn't ask."

"Okay, well, what was the name of the business?"

"Honest Henry's Fair 'n Square Gift Emporium."

# TWELVE: LA PLAYA DEL SARAYA

All kloormari were back onboard by 17:04. The final containers were loaded onto the *Pacifica Spirit*, and the waybills and manifests were checked by 18:17. We were cleared for takeoff and departed twenty-nine minutes ahead of schedule.

The *Pacifica* headed back to the jump point that marked our previous arrival. From there, we would jump to a point in the vicinity of Saraya.

On our way to the jump, Ron addressed us on the observation deck. He told us that the astrophysics computer had used the existing data regarding Kuw'baal and cross-referenced it with new data from our survey of Ryla 6 to come up with a prediction of each future upheaval event on Kuw'baal for the next 2,001,876 years.

Ron told us that Ryla 6 would be making a close pass to Kuw'baal in 70 years and 142 days from the present date. Some students were alarmed, but I was excited. The next event would happen at about the halfway point in my lifespan! By knowing the exact dates, the kloormari could prepare and be safe, especially if humans or other species assisted in the preparations. Instead of anticipating the next upheaval with dread, we could look forward to it as a fascinating planet-wide experience!

We neared the jump point just after midnight, ship's time. A chime sounded thirty minutes before the scheduled jump so that the crew could prepare, and we could rouse ourselves from our meditative state. Apparently, experiencing a jump while sleeping can sometimes be terrifying for humans. In the interest of caution, none of us wanted to be the first kloormar to jump while in meditation.

Five minutes before jump time, Sam joined us. "I think you're really going to enjoy Saraya and its inhabitants," he said. "Of all the home planets of the intelligent species that we know, Saraya is the one that most closely resembles Terra. The Sarayans are rather formal beings with strict laws, but they're very considerate and forgiving to new species who are not familiar with their rules and regulations."

After that we fastened ourselves down. The countdown proceeded, and our jump felt very much like the previous one.

We could see Saraya as a small bluish circle in the distance. We could also make out two of the planet's four moons as bright white dots. The crew went back to their bunks, and we resumed meditation after we were informed that breakfast would be delayed until 09:00, and morning shift would start at 10:00 to compensate for the interruption of our rest.

In the morning when our group joined the humans in the cafeteria, their smiles and chatter told me that they were excited to visit Saraya and enjoy up to three days of shore leave. I overheard enthusiastic conversations about sights and attractions that crew members wanted to visit. Audrey Fraser, the systems engineer that Kroz had worked with, was looking forward to visiting her cousin, who was posted to the Terran high commission where we would all be staying as guests.

After breakfast, Captain Staedtler and the crew donned uniforms in preparation for the visit. The captain was an imposing figure with his peaked cap, epaulettes, gold braid, and sash over a double-breasted coat, pressed trousers, and patent-leather shoes. The crew wore the orange jumpsuits with insignia that I had last seen during our eventful first contact. This time, the jumpsuits had been cleaned and pressed.

We were all on the bridge at 11:58 ship time, which was early morning at the landing point on Saraya. The Sarayan visitor control center provided the *Pacifica* with an orbital path to assume. We could hear the Sarayan controller's voice coming from Lynda's navigation console. It was interesting to hear Sarayans speak standard Terran with lilting accents and elongation of most vowel sounds.

As we orbited, the crew prepared for landing while the welcoming delegation on Saraya prepared for our arrival. At different points in our orbit, we could see each of Saraya's four moons. Two had grey surfaces with mountain ridges, plains, and craters of all sizes. Another was smooth, white, and icy and much smaller than the others. The fourth moon was reddish and irregularly shaped. I was told that it was far smaller than the other moons, but from the planet's surface, it appeared much larger and faster moving than the others due to its much lower orbit.

Lynda rolled the vessel so that Saraya was visible through the upper windows. We kloormari, along with Sam, moved to the observation deck for the clearest view possible.

Our view of Saraya was remarkable. Most of its surface was covered with crystal-clear oceans. For the most part, the oceans were less than fifty meters deep with a white sand floor. This gave the water a brilliant azure hue, which gradually transitioned to darker blue over the deeper portions far from land. White sand ringed the coastline, and sandy cays formed swirling lines in the seas.

From my perspective, Saraya appeared to be lacking a sky, with the exception of large areas with dots or swirls or flat expanses of white. I reminded myself that the substance I thought of as sky was, to most beings, cloud.

The land was lush with forests, with the exception of steep outcroppings of black rock thrusting up past the canopy. The higher mountains were topped with snow, as were Saraya's polar regions. With several billion inhabitants, I had expected to see more evidence of cities or other major structures.

When we and the Sarayans were ready, when we were in position and had received clearance, we strapped ourselves into the chairs. The *Pacifica Spirit* was rolled so that its belly faced the planet. The vessel was then slowed to begin its descent into the atmosphere while we watched the scene below via our monitors.

As we drew closer, we saw webs of thin grey strands extending across Saraya's surface. Each strand was made up of tiny dots, all moving in the same direction. The strands soon revealed themselves to be lanes of levitating vehicles, all moving along precise routes to various destinations on Saraya. We saw tall structures poking up through the forest canopy with wide gaps between them. As we got closer, we saw buildings under the canopy, forming a vast city that was mostly obscured below the foliage.

We approached a circular landing pad above the trees, mounted atop a pylon that jutted up from the forest floor. From the landing pad, a walkway stretched to an impressive structure with multiple glassy towers surrounding a raised courtyard. Our flight was absolutely smooth from entry into the atmosphere to a gentle touchdown on the pad.

After systems were shut down, and the vessel was secured, we made our way down to Starboard Hatch A. Captain Staedtler positioned himself in front of the hatch, followed by the crew. Bertie was at the rear, holding a loaded hovercart. Sam stayed behind the rest of the crew as part of our group.

The hatch opened, and a rush of Sarayan air breezed in, heavy with the fragrance of foliage and floral nectar. Orange-tinged light from Saraya's rising sun bathed the landing pad and adjacent structure in a warm glow. To the left was the coastline with surf gently caressing a white-sand beach that stretched toward a rugged black headland. Low in the sky, we saw the white crescent of one of Saraya's moons, which would be setting shortly.

The Sarayan regional governor, escorted by the Terran high commissioner, stood twenty meters from the hatch, waiting to greet Captain Staedtler. Various staff members and dignitaries stood in a line behind the governor.

Captain Staedtler strode down the ramp, followed by the rest of the crew, who fanned out to form a line behind him. Bertie followed but then turned to the right, skirting the crowd and pushing her hovercart over the walkway, no doubt taking supplies into the building. We hung back just inside the hatch.

To the right of the walkway, a large, illuminated sign bore the Terran word "Welcome." The word faded away, and to my astonishment, the sign displayed kloormari writing spelling out our word for welcome, "Awustin."

"How do the Sarayans know our language?" I whispered to Sam.

"No doubt you remember me asking you to write the word for 'welcome' on the second day of this trip. I simply transmitted an image of your writing to our Sarayan friends. Surprise!"

Captain Staedtler approached the governor, then stopped and dipped his head in a manner that fell somewhere between a nod and a bow.

"Welcome to Saraya, Captain Staedtler," the governor said, speaking clearly and deliberately. "You and your delegation grace us with your presence."

"We are honored and humbled by your gracious welcome, Governor Linsuma," Captain Staedtler replied, speaking loudly for all to hear.

The two beings looked directly at one another, neither betraying any emotion on their faces. Five seconds later, they both broke into a grin, then each reached out with their right hand and gripped the left shoulder of the other in the Sarayan equivalent of a handshake.

"How the hell have you been, Kwam?" the governor asked.

"Oh, a little worse for wear but glad to see you again, Gov!"

Captain Staedtler turned to the Terran high commissioner and extended his hand. "Nice to meet you, Commissioner Rathtrevor."

"Good to meet you too, Captain Staedtler. Please, call me George."

"Thanks, George. Kwami's good for me, or 'Kwam' if you want to follow the lead of this rascal," Captain Staedtler said, gesturing toward the governor.

"So, Kwami, where are these guests we've been hearing so much about?" Governor Linsuma inquired.

Captain Staedtler straightened up. "Governor Linsuma, it is my pleasure to introduce our first-contact administrator, Samuel Buchanan, who in turn, will present each of our guests." He gestured toward the hatch with his palm extended.

Sam stepped out and walked smartly down the ramp with us following in single file. He introduced each of us to the governor and the high commissioner. Then Governor Linsuma and other dignitaries led us over the walkway to the adjoining building.

As we walked, I observed the Sarayans. They were slender, graceful beings. Their torsos were shorter than a human's by a third, but their long limbs made up the difference. Their legs moved slowly when walking, but the Sarayans walked as quickly as any human due to the length of their stride. Their skin was smooth and grey with undertones ranging from pink to dark brown.

The Sarayans had necks with a texture and flexibility resembling the trunks of Terran elephants, which I had seen in nature vids. Their necks were usually no longer than a human's but could be extended to reach about twenty centimeters. They also had larger heads than humans with small facial features set in the center front. Like humans, the Sarayans had two eyes, two ear openings, two nostrils, and one mouth. Their eyes were large and round with yellow irises and eyelids that blinked from the bottom up. Their ears and nostrils didn't protrude; they simply consisted of elongated openings. The Sarayans' mouths were simple lipless slits, which exposed short, pointed teeth. Later, when we visited a Sarayan beach, I learned that Sarayans are hairless, and females have two rows of mammaries with three per row. In all, I found them to be a rather handsome species.

The Sarayans were dressed in white robes resembling kaftans with side panels in a vibrant color. I recalled reading that the color denoted their rank or standing in society. Ornate necklaces dangled down to the mid-torso. Each Sarayan wore a white hat that swept back and up to two points. While observing this, I became self-conscious about being unclothed. I had a similar feeling on the *Orion Provider*. Nobody seemed to mind, leading me to believe there was no expectation of clothing if a species had no external reproductive organs or parts for child feeding.

We made our way into a towering reception hall where the humans and the Sarayans were served by staff bearing trays of food and beverages. Announcements and toasts were made while a quartet of performers played unfamiliar but pleasant background music. Bertie stood behind a table serving us algel in fluted glasses. I wasn't especially hungry, having had a full breakfast a few hours before, but I felt obliged to hold a glass and attempt to mingle.

At first, I was anxious about making small talk with a species that I had never interacted with, so I planned to stand on the sidelines. Instead, I was approached and invited to chat by many Sarayans. I was sure to complement their planet, the building, the entertainment, and the Sarayan hospitality. The Sarayans had many questions for me, and when they talked, I listened intently.

Governor Linsuma made sure that he spoke with each kloormar. He told me that when a member of the Planetary Alliance made first contact with a new intelligent species, it typically took several years before that species was deemed ready to leave their home world. The governor indicated how impressed he was by our ability to learn so quickly.

As the reception wrapped up, Sam gathered the kloormari together to inform us that George Rathtrevor, the high commissioner, had kindly offered to take us on a guided tour, ending at his official residence.

Sam led us outside where we saw a streamlined vessel with large windows. Winglets protruded from the sides of the body, and fins were mounted on the stern. I couldn't discern the purpose of these features except perhaps for decoration. Sam jumped aboard. "Everyone on the bus," he said. When we entered, we saw that High Commissioner Rathtrevor was already onboard and had changed into casual Terran clothing.

We lifted off and glided just over the treetops. We slowed or stopped outside of notable buildings and feats of engineering and dipped below the canopy along a preprogrammed narrow path between majestic trees to see preserved ancient buildings and ruins. We traveled inland into the mountains, rising high above flocks of huge reptiles flying in V formations. We descended into a steep gorge and over a river, hovering barely above the water as we followed its winding course back to the ocean. Furry animals leapt and glided between the treetops overhanging the river while emitting a cacophony of vocalizations. All along the way, George narrated, delving deep into the minutiae of facts and figures. It was my understanding that humans didn't typically want such details, so I wondered whether our guide had been briefed on the fact that we would be fascinated by this engrossing tour.

We exited the forest as the river transformed into a swampy estuary. White-sand beaches formed huge crescents on either side of the estuary with surf piling in, giving way to azure waters beyond. We turned right and followed the beach to a headland of black cliffs. As we passed close to the cliffs, we saw walkways and rooms carved into the rock face. George explained that these structures were the basis of Sarayan communities hundreds of thousands of years in the past.

After we rounded the point, we dropped down to a sheltered bay. We were surprised when George commanded the bus to perform a water landing, and it gently settled onto the surface. The vessel was obviously built to float and was clearly stable as it bobbed gently in the small waves.

"I have a little surprise for you," George said.

"Trust us and don't be alarmed," Sam added, smiling. "We don't want another panic like when we flew through the clouds over Kùw'baal!"

"Descend," George commanded.

The ocean started to rise, lapping at the lower frame of the windows. We were tense, but after a successful interstellar voyage we were more than ready to trust humans. Within a minute, the water had risen over the windows and closed over the skylights. Bubbles streamed past the windows, and then, as the bubbles cleared, we could see the white sandy bottom. The seafloor had ripples that looked like tiny dunes running parallel to the shoreline. Shafts of light beamed through the blue, forming ever-changing patterns of light playing on the sand.

Hovering a meter or two off the seafloor, the bus started moving out of the shelter of the bay and under the open ocean's waves. Now I understood the purpose of the winglets and other control surfaces on the bus. As we moved forward, the surge of each wave pushed us sideways in one direction and then the suction of the next approaching wave pulled us the other way, producing a zigzagging path.

As we neared the undersea portion of the bluff, the sand gave way to a field of boulders. Red aquatic plants were anchored to the rocks, their thin stalks swaying in the surge and reaching for the surface where broad fronds spread out to absorb light and cast long shadows below. As we rode beneath the canopy through a fascinating undersea forest, I felt as though we were visiting an entirely new world within a single planet.

All around us, creatures swam, some in organized schools, some in vast swarms of random movement, while others swam solo. Creatures darted in and out of the spaces between the boulders below us. Some crawled or slithered over the boulders, and others hovered above, near the canopy.

We descended along the bottom, past the point at which the plants grew and beyond the surge of the waves above. We moved out over flat sand interspersed with semi-transparent pinnacles resembling quartz. Sam told us that these structures were called "pandrygals" by the Sarayans and "silicate reefs" by human zoologists. He also told us of how he loved diving and snorkeling in some regions of the Terran oceans where minute creatures called "polyps" build shells of calcium carbonate around their bodies, resulting in structures called "coral reefs." He explained that the formations we were seeing were made by billions of similar creatures, which used silica fibers to build their tiny homes, creating huge overall structures.

The silica reefs were home to a myriad of creatures that we hadn't seen before. One of the more striking examples were "pilipikis," which (according to Sam) resembled Terran ribbon eels, though the pilipikis were much larger. They appeared to be dark red with dark blue and faded yellow mottling. George switched on an external spotlight and turned it toward the reef, which sparkled and reflected iridescent hues. The light also revealed the true colors of the pilipikis and other creatures, which consisted of dazzlingly bright reds, blues, yellows, and every other color in the spectrum.

After about twenty minutes of touring the reefs, the bus slowly rose to the ocean's surface and into waves about two to three meters high. As we bobbed there, I saw the cliffs and headlands about a kilometer away. The sea sparkled, and a fine spray of water blew from the tops of the waves, producing rainbows of refracted light.

George turned the floating bus so that it faced downwind, then nudged it forward so that it rode along in the trough between waves. He eased off the velocity control, and the bus started to "surf" down the face of a wave. He engaged the vertical power axis, and the bus gently lifted into the air with water streaming off the windshield, winglets, and fins. "Automation is great," George said, "but I do love taking manual control whenever I get a chance."

George switched back into automated navigation and spoke a command. "Destination, Terran high commissioner's residence, scenic approach alpha." The bus turned and rounded the headland, skimming close to the ocean's surface. We passed the beach that we had crossed on our way from the river, followed by the estuary and the beach beyond it. Once past the estuary, the bus started rising and moving toward the top of the next towering headland.

At the top of the headland, a series of buildings and landing pads jutted from the sides of the razorback ridge, with terraced, manicured grounds between the structures. A circular building with glass sides was perched on the side of the headland facing the ocean with the roof also serving as a landing pad. In the distance, poking through the forest canopy, we could see the taller structures of the city below, including the governor's residence, where we had first set foot on Saraya.

"Welcome to the Terran high commission," George said as we touched down. We disembarked and were immediately buffeted by gusts of wind. "This is one of the drawbacks of living at such an elevation!" he shouted above the gale. "The late-afternoon winds can be kind of brutal."

"What's our elevation?" I shouted back.

"Two thousand four hundred and thirteen meters above ocean level!" George replied, his jacket puffing up and his slacks flapping in the wind. Behind the group, I saw the bus lift off to fly back to its base or perhaps to serve another group of passengers.

George opened a door into a small stairwell-access structure. We descended a gently curved set of stairs into an expansive room below with a high ceiling and tall curved windows all around. The room was bright. Classical Terran music played, providing a sense of calm in stark contrast to the blustery conditions outside.

Everything about the room was curved. Curved conversation pits were carved into the floor and lined with curved sofas and tables. The ceiling had rounded bulkheads and recessed areas with curved light fixtures. Circular tables with chairs were positioned close to the windows. On easels and pillars around the room, art was displayed, and Terran artifacts were exhibited.

We were located in the side of the structure that faced the ocean with the city on our left and the twin beaches to the right. A wall separated us from the other half of the building, which housed a large kitchen, bathrooms, and the accommodations where the crew would spend the night. Outside our half of the building, a spacious deck curved out over the bluffs.

Groups of people were conversing with one another. Some of them were crew from the *Pacifica*, and others were strangers to me, including a smattering of Sarayans. I made my way around the room's perimeter, looking at the displayed art and other objects. Each piece had a plaque with information about the artist and details regarding the origin and background of the piece. I was impressed by the skill of some of the painters who, using only liquid paint on a canvas surface, were able to capture the color, subtleties of light and shadow, scale, and perspective that made them look like images from a camera.

When I moved to look at an abstract painting, I came upon Lynda. She had been looking at the work for several minutes. "Good afternoon, Navigator Lynda Paige," I said.

"My goodness, aren't we being formal, Kelvoo of Kuw'baal," she replied.

"I thought I'd give it a try."

"I love this piece," Lynda said. "When I look at it one way, I see churning rapids cascading down mountains into a red desert below. From a different perspective, I see a crowd of beings, some crying out in despair and others full of joy as they peer down into a lava-filled volcanic crater. What do you see, Kelvoo?"

"I see a background layer of blue paint, darker at the top and lighter at the bottom due to blending in of white pigment. The artist seems to have used a stiff brush with strokes that add downward, slightly curved textures. White paint was added in a diagonal stripe with a stippling action. Red and yellow was added in an approximately circular area in the bottom third bordered with black blobs. Random strokes were used for added texture around the bottom circle."

Lynda laughed. "Wow, Kelvoo, you really need to get yourself an imagination!"

"I don't think I have one of those."

I mingled with more crew members and beings that I hadn't met before, each of them with interesting stories.

Saraya's star, Sah, hung low in the sky. Scattered clouds started to take on pink edges. I saw six of my fellow kloormari along with a dozen others out on the deck, waiting for Sah to set. I stepped outside and noticed that the air was completely still.

As Sah sank lower, the clouds became brilliant shades of orange and red. Beams of light streamed outward from the horizon as I heard several humans telling one another how wonderfully beautiful the scene was. I didn't understand what "beauty" was, but as I reflected on the day's events and the sights I had seen, I too was in a state of wonder over how interesting a day it had been. I was sure that my wonder must have matched the appreciation of beauty that the humans were expressing.

When dusk was taking hold, we were called in for dinner. Humans and Sarayans sat in chairs while we knelt at the round tables. During the day, the algel incubation vat had been moved from the *Pacifica*. The kloormari were served algel that had been compressed into dome-shaped molds with patterned sides and then unmolded onto plates glazed with fanciful and colorful patterns. Ornately presented foods and beverages were served to the humans and the Sarayans.

While the non-kloormari were enjoying a selection of desserts, I could see some of the brighter stars through the windows. I excused myself and made my way through the glass doors onto the deck. My fellow kloormari had the same notion, and we all assembled outside.

In the ocean below, we saw the surf as slowly moving blue-green light caused by the bioluminescence of microscopic organisms. Farther out, random concentrations of the organisms created softly glowing, drifting islands of light. Above, thousands of stars sparkled. On the horizon toward the planet's polar regions, curtains of red and green aurora shimmered as Sah's radiation pierced the planet's protective magnetic field. I saw Saraya's smallest moon rise and make its way across the sky over the course of an hour, gently tumbling end over end.

It occurred to me that never before had I been able to stand on the surface of a planet and peer up at the night sky to view the heavens and look toward infinity.

After such a day, and with such a fascinating scene before us, my fellow kloormari and I assumed comfortable positions and entered a deep meditative state.

I don't know how much time had passed, but at some point that night, I vaguely recall Sam shaking me by my upper limb and shoulder. This was unusual, because every previous recollection that I ever had was crystal clear. I also recalled great pain throughout my body, especially in my joints.

A few hours later, I became aware of a problem. I had to fight my way back to consciousness. My body and my limbs were stiff and sore and difficult to move. When I was getting reacquainted with reality, I realized I was no longer on the deck but lying on my side inside the high commissioner's residence.

Sam explained to me that we kloormari were still in a state of meditation when the gathering had died down, and all guests had settled into their rooms. Sam had assured any concerned guests that it was normal for the kloormari to be in such a state and that we would likely not move until the next morning.

"We had such a great day yesterday that I couldn't sleep because I was recounting the events," he said. "I got up to relieve myself and to find something to drink when I saw all of you out on the deck, but something about your eyes didn't look right. When I stepped outside, the air was very cold, and in the light from the moons, I saw condensation from my breath. In the past, any time that I had spoken to you during your meditation, you were always able to respond, so I asked if you were alright. When you didn't reply, I shook your arm and shouted, 'Kelvoo, are you okay?' You responded in kloormari, but it didn't sound right. Your speech was slow and slurred, and you didn't regain consciousness.

"Some of the guests heard me shouting and came to investigate. I asked them to wake the crew and bring them to me. I explained that you were catatonic and that the low temperature might be the cause. We carried each of you inside, two crew members per kloormar. We placed you on your sides, propping you up with cushions and blankets so that your breathing inlets were unimpeded. We covered you to gradually warm you up. We summoned the resident human doctor and brought in a Sarayan physician. Neither of them were familiar with your physiology, so they agreed that we should just watch you and wait."

Sam then introduced me to Dr. Harris and Dr. Totorix. Dr. Harris asked me to try to move. "Slowly," Dr. Totorix added. I struggled but managed to move my limbs, and the doctors were pleased that I had mobility in all of my extremities.

The other kloormari had started to wake up, so Sam and the doctors moved on to attend to them along with other crew members who had not yet returned to their beds. At the same time, an autotaxi landed on the roof, and Captain Staedtler hurried down the stairs. He asked the group to forgive his absence as he had been in high-level meetings that ended very late and had only just been informed of the situation.

When we kloormari were fully conscious and the stiffness and pain had passed, Governor Rathtrevor came to see us. "You folks sure gave us a scare!" he said. "I want to apologize for not warning anyone that, at this high an altitude, the temperature outside often plummets at night. Right now, it's a chilly five degrees Celsius outside. Sah will rise in about four hours, so I suggest that we all try to get some rest and sleep in or meditate until late this morning. I hope you will all just relax for the rest of today and enjoy some down time."

Sam came back to me and asked why I had never mentioned the effect of cold on kloormari physiology. I replied that, due to the stability of the climate on Kuw'baal, none of us had ever experienced cold before, so none of us even thought to consider the effects. At that moment, I realized that, for the first time in my life and possibly kloormari history, I had a memory gap spanning several hours!

We kloormari stood or knelt in a circle and re-entered a much more comfortable and restorative meditative state while the other beings left to try to get some sleep.

Long after Sah rose over the city, we rose from our rest. That day and the next were to be days off for the *Pacifica's* crew and for us. During breakfast, crew members were discussing the places they wanted to go and the people they wanted to visit. Captain Staedtler was scheduled to play the ancient Terran game of golf with other captains and officers. One by one, the crew members and the captain dispersed to go about their activities.

We kloormari stayed behind with Sam. Some of us read books or articles on our Infotabs, especially where information about Saraya was involved, and some watched current news broadcasts on the building's large display panels. I did a bit of each.

In the early afternoon, shortly after Sam made himself a snack in the kitchen, he went to his room and came back carrying a towel and wearing shorts, a T-shirt, and footwear called "flip-flops." His communication cube hung from a cord around his neck. "I'd like to go to the beach to unwind a little. If any of you would like to come along, you're welcome to do so. Otherwise, feel free to wait here."

We all indicated that we would like to accompany him.

"Please understand," Sam said, "I just plan to sit on a beach chair or lie on a towel and soak up some light and warmth, so you may find the whole experience to be a bit unstimulating. You can bring your Infotabs if you want to do some reading, but there won't be a whole lot else going on."

We were interested enough in seeing a new place that we still wanted to accompany Sam, so he fetched a large towel for each of us and hailed transportation for eleven. We walked up to the landing pad, and within five minutes, a bus (much like the one we'd boarded the day before) touched down.

When we boarded, Sam gave the command: "Destination: Beach three, local sector 57."

"Is 'beach three' the actual place name used by the Sarayans?" Kwazka asked.

"Oh yes," Sam said. "In many ways, the Sarayans are very creative, but when it comes to geographical locations, they prefer numbers or map coordinates. Personally, I have my own name for our destination: 'La Playa del Saraya'!" he said in an artificially grand manner while making a flourish with his right hand.

A moment later, the bus touched down on a small platform at the boundary of the treeline and the bright white sand.

I remarked about the rhythmic sound of the waves, the moisture of the air, and the unique smell. Sam explained that the smell of the ocean was due to small concentrations of magnesium sulphate, known as Epsom salt on Terra, as opposed to sodium chloride or "table salt" in the Terran oceans.

Several hundred Sarayans were in the water, but almost none were on the beach. A few beach chairs and umbrellas were set up, but they were all empty. I asked Sam why this was the case, since images and vids of Terran beaches that I had seen showed packed beaches with just a few beings in the water.

"The Sarayans only see the beach as a feature that provides easy access to the ocean," Sam replied. "They don't understand why a being would want to spend any time on the sand. For example, let's say we were on a path that led to a magnificent and interesting sight, but it was only the path that we found to be interesting. In fact, the beach chairs and umbrellas that you see are only set up for the benefit of non-Sarayan visitors."

To me, the logic of the Sarayans was inescapable. Still, we wanted to experience the beach as Sam did, so we found a beach chair that Sam liked while the rest of us placed our towels on the sand next to him. Then we sat, knelt, or stood on our towels.

A few Sarayans passed by. They regarded us briefly but kept their distance. Sam told us that every Sarayan had been informed of our visit via their media and were ordered to respect our privacy and engage with us only if we approached them first. I felt great appreciation and admired how organized the Sarayans were, given the problems that we'd had on the *Orion Provider*.

Sam removed his T-shirt. He told us that on a Terran beach he would have to apply a protective unguent to his exposed skin to protect it from Sol's damaging ultraviolet rays. This wasn't necessary on Saraya due to a thicker layer of ozone in the upper atmosphere, which blocked almost all UV rays.

Keesooni peered at the Sarayans in the ocean. "Are those Sarayans unclothed?"

"Yes, they are," Sam replied. "Sarayans have strict rules and standards, but some of those standards do not apply to large areas of recreation, including the ocean. Wearing clothes at the ocean would be considered aberrant by the Sarayans, though they don't care what other species want to do. Personally, as a self-conscious human, I think I'll keep my shorts on. And if you don't mind," Sam added, "I didn't get a lot of sleep last night, so I'd like to get some rest now."

"Sam, could I ask you just one more thing?"

"What?" Sam replied.

"Your T-shirt has an image and writing on it saying, 'Thirty-first Symposium on Extraterrestrial Anthropology, Artemis Conference Center, Luna.' Did you attend that symposium? If so, did you obtain the T-shirt to help you remember that function?"

"Remember?" Sam said. "I don't recall anything about that symposium. Hell, I don't even recall buying the damn shirt!"

"Why's that?"

"Because the entire event was nothing more than a colossal piss-up!"

With that, Sam pulled a pair of sunglasses out of his shorts pocket, put them on, then reclined his chair and ignored any further attempts to communicate with him.

Kwazka suggested that the rest of us try to emulate Sam. We took up comfortable positions on our towels, closed our eyelids, and relaxed our bodies. We all found the sound of the waves and even the bright light to be soothing. I wondered whether this type of activity (or lack thereof) served as a human equivalent to our meditation.

About three hours later, Sam stirred. I had started looking at my Infotab, as had others in the group. Sam said he wanted to take a quick dip in the ocean and then head back to our accommodations. I accompanied him as he waded up to his waist and started swimming. The waves had become rather light. I waded in until the waves ranged between my upper and lower knees. The shifting sand covered my feet, and the sensation of the waves moving the sand around my feet was pleasant.

As I stood in the waves and looked out across the expansive ocean, I once again reflected on the incredible events of the past week. I felt so fortunate to have had more amazing experiences in a few days than other kloormari probably had in an entire lifetime.

After Sam's swim, we walked back to the group, where we gathered our towels and Infotabs as well as Sam's shirt, sunglasses, and communicator necklace. Sam used his communicator cube to summon transportation, which landed at the pad where we were waiting.

On the ride back, I noticed that clouds were gathering, and Sah was beginning to set behind them. I figured that the magnificent hues from the setting star would put on a repeat performance that night.

When we touched down at the high commission, a staffer whom we hadn't seen before came running toward us. "Your captain and the high commissioner need to see you immediately," he said with great urgency. "This way please."

As we descended the stairs, we saw a few of the crew members who had already returned. None of them spoke a word as they watched us enter. The staffer led us to High Commissioner Rathtrevor and Captain Staedtler, who were sitting on a sofa in front of a large display panel. The captain's head was bowed slightly, and he was holding it in his hands. I interpreted the look on his face as "grim." He motioned to Sam, who sat beside him. We kloormari gathered beside and behind the sofa.

"One of the governor's aides was monitoring the live vid broadcasts and thought we needed to see something," High Commissioner Rathtrevor said. "She sent us a recording. You *do* need to watch it." With that, he started the replay.

On the vid, a human male behind a news desk began speaking: "We have breaking news from the supply vessel, *Orion Provider*. We have just received the following exclusive recording, transmitted two days ago from our correspondent, Kaley Hart."

"That's the human that I had such a nice conversation with!" I exclaimed.

"Just watch the vid," Captain Staedtler groaned.

"As a travel and leisure reporter stationed on the *Orion Provider*, I get a chance to meet all kinds of interesting beings from all kinds of planets," Kaley began, "but I never would have expected to be the first to report on contact with a whole new species! I am pleased to bring you my exclusive interview with a charming member of this newly discovered species!"

"Oh God!" Sam muttered.

"I had the pleasure of meeting Kelvoo from a planet that star charts call 'Ryla 5' and Kelvoo's species calls 'Kuw'baal.' I'm sure I didn't pronounce that correctly, but I'll let Kelvoo set the record straight."

A shot showing my eye and upper torso appeared on the screen.

"It's so great to meet you, Kelvoo. Please tell me all about yourself and how you came to be here on the *Orion*."

"Well, Kaley, I'm here because a Terran research vessel called the *Pacifica Spirit* came to my planet several weeks ago to make first contact."

"Oh God! Oh God!" Sam said.

We watched as recorded images of me proceeded to tell Kaley the timeline of our first contact, starting with the remote lander and how we thought it was a creature, followed by the landing of the *Pacifica*. I mentioned Sam and Captain Staedtler by name.

Sam jumped up off the sofa and started pacing in circles. "Oh God! Oh God! Oh Jesus, Mary, and Joseph! Oh God! I think I'm going to puke!"

"Sit down," Captain Staedtler ordered.

Sam sat and then turned to me. "Kelvoo, why did you agree to an interview with a member of the media?"

"I didn't!" I exclaimed. "Kaley just seemed like a nice person who was interested in learning about me!"

"Look at the constant angle of the camera," Sam said, turning to Captain Staedtler. "The vid was taken from the reporter's chest level. She was probably wearing a hidden brooch cam!"

"Yes," I said, "she did have a very ornate brooch that looked like it was made of black glass."

The first ten minutes of my meeting with Kaley was played. After that, the vid cut back to the male news announcer. "What you have just witnessed is only the first few minutes of Kaley's in-depth interview. We are pleased to present her extraordinary, ground-breaking interview in its entirety in a two-hour primetime special tomorrow night at 19:00 in each local time zone. You won't want to miss this historic broadcast!"

High Commissioner Rathtrevor stopped the vid. Sam sat in stunned silence, along with everybody else in the room.

"I don't understand why this is distressing," I said. "The conversation was interesting, I was totally honest, and I only said complimentary things about your mission, the crew, the *Pacifica*, and how wonderful all of our interactions have been."

"We will talk about this later, Kelvoo," Captain Staedtler said.

"What do we do now?" Sam asked.

"Whatever the hell the Terran First Contact Authority tells us to do," Captain Staedtler replied. "I sent a top-priority encoded message almost an hour ago. Given the current configuration of the communication relays, we should have our instructions sometime in the next hour or two."

He called over to the *Pacifica's* purser, Max Magnusson, who was at a table nearby. "Max," he said, "We don't know what TFCA will require us to do. It's possible that we'll be ordered to leave immediately. Broadcast a message to all crew members who are still out. Tell them to return to the high commissioner's residence immediately—captain's orders!"

Captain Staedtler stood to address everyone within earshot. "Go to your rooms, pack your belongings, and pile your bags over by the stairs. We need to be ready to move on a moment's notice."

I already had all of my personal possessions on my "person": one neck pouch, one temporary passport, and 100,000 units of unredeemed SimCash.

Just over an hour later and shortly after dark, a taxi landed on the pad, and Bertie got out and stumbled down the stairs, both hands gripping the railing in a rather intoxicated state. "There better be a damned good reason for this," she slurred. "I had two hot Sarayan studs competing for me and tellin' me all the nasty things they were goin' to do to me. Did someone die or somethin'?"

"No," Captain Staedtler replied. "The complete details of our mission are all over the primetime newscasts!"

"Oh God! That's even worse!" Bertie replied.

"Better get a liter or two of coffee into you and then pack up," Max advised. "We might be ordered off this planet at a moment's notice."

A response from Terra was late in coming, leading to much speculation about what Terran Command must be thinking and what their strategy might be. The only benefit of the delay was that all crew members had arrived, and their bags and equipment were packed. By then, the clouds had accumulated outside, blocking out any view of the moons and stars.

An alert chime sounded on Captain Staedtler's Infotab. He stood up and read it. "Orders have been issued by Terran First Contact Authority and are as follows: 'You are to board the *Pacifica Spirit* immediately and leave Saraya as quickly as possible. You will proceed directly to Ryla 5 where you will stay for the remaining duration of your original mission. When your mission is complete, you will return directly to command headquarters on Terra.'"

George pressed an assortment of high commission vehicles into service to shuttle us to the governor's residence where the *Pacifica* remained parked. Captain Staedtler ordered the engineering crew to depart first so that the *Pacifica's* engines could be primed and readied. Larger pieces of equipment, such as the algel vat, were loaded onto a flat-deck transport.

When my turn came, I piled into a vehicle with four other kloormari. A light rain was falling, streaking through the beams from the vehicle's headlights during the two-minute trip.

Once we were inside the *Pacifica*, the crew was subdued. I understood why they were morose, given the loss of their final day of shore leave on Saraya. The crew went about their duties in a purely professional manner, reading off checklists, performing and re-performing systems diagnostics, and securing equipment and themselves in preparation for departure.

It took two hours and twelve minutes from the time Captain Staedtler read the orders until we were ready for liftoff.

Without fanfare or farewells, we stole away from Saraya under the cloak of night in a driving rainstorm.

# THIRTEEN: IT'S COMPLICATED

The *Pacifica Spirit* tore back toward the Sarayan jump point. When the required velocity was reached and all systems were nominal, Captain Staedtler made a ship-wide announcement, giving the all-clear and announcing that the next rest period would commence in thirty minutes.

Sam unbuckled himself and asked me to speak with him in private. We walked to the stern windows of the observation deck away from the other kloormari. We stood at the railing, watching as the crescent of Saraya shrank into the distance.

"You may have noticed that the crew aren't their usual cheerful selves tonight," Sam said.

"Yes. Is the reason that they won't be enjoying the final day of their planned shore leave?" I asked, rather pleased that I was so perceptive about human nature.

"That's just a small part of the distress they're feeling. The captain and every member of this crew care deeply about our mission. Every successful first-contact mission marks a turning point for our home planet and every other planet in the Alliance. Missions like this can mark the height of a crew member's career. That reporter's interview has put the success of our mission in jeopardy."

"Because I gave information to Kaley Hart?"

Sam was about to respond when Captain Staedtler appeared in the doorway to the bridge. "Ready?" he asked.

"Come with me," Sam said, beckoning me to follow.

Captain Staedtler held the door for us as we walked onto the bridge and then through a door into a small office in the bulkhead between the bridge and the observation deck. He looked grave as he asked us to sit. Sam took a chair, and I knelt at an appropriate height.

"Kelvoo," Captain Staedtler began, "back on Saraya, I told you that we would talk later about the incident that caused us to leave early. While I would prefer to address this after a good night's sleep, I think we need to get it said now. The first thing I want to say is that I do not blame you for our situation. I'm sure that Sam feels the same way."

Sam nodded, and Captain Staedtler continued. "As for the crew, I recommend that you give them some space. We're all professionals here, but

I can't guarantee that there will be no hard feelings from the crew. Please tell the rest of the Kloormari to keep to themselves for the next couple of days. Best to wait until crew members approach you before engaging them in conversation. As captain, I'll be taking responsibility. I should have provided clear guidance before the *Orion*."

Sam reached across the desk and put his hand on Captain Staedtler's forearm. "You mustn't blame yourself, Kwami. As first-contact administrator, not only should I have briefed our guests better but I also should have accompanied them in person. If I had been with them, I would've shut down any questions about the details of the mission."

"Well, Sam, since we're talking about 'could've, would've, and should've,' I'm the one who approved the excursion."

"After I pushed for it," Sam replied.

"Well, we can point fingers at ourselves all night long and get nowhere. In the end, there will be inquiries and testimony, and the Terran First Contact Authority will apportion the blame."

"Why *did* you approve our visit to the *Orion Provider*?" I asked.

"Because we were so impressed by you and your species," Sam replied. "In most cases, at the time of first contact with intelligent species, they have already developed and are using sophisticated technologies. In some cases, they possessed innovations that we had never even conceived. Even though the kloormari don't have advanced technology, your species blows all of the others out of the water when it comes to the ability to learn and retain information and put that knowledge into action and instantly adapt it to changing situations. We were so taken with your species' abilities and goodwill toward us that we allowed our enthusiasm to get in the way of protocol. We really like you . . . and we wanted to do something special for all of you."

"We need to keep in mind that the TFCA did give us the go-ahead for the *Orion Provider* field trip," Captain Staedtler said.

I looked at him in surprise. "Really?"

"Sure. Since Kuw'baal is fourteen light days from the nearest quantum entanglement relay, we sent our proposal for the visit and the reasoning for it over a month before the trip. We told you about it only after we received approval. You see, sometimes the TFCA will intentionally let first-contact information leak out. They do it to promote their work and help ensure funding. They'd have anticipated that rumors would spread and create a buzz. They just didn't realize that specific details of our mission would be broadcast across the galaxy!

"Anyway, that's where we stand. If there's nothing else, I think we should get some rest. Are we good?"

"No," I replied. "There's one thing that hasn't been explained to me at all."

"What's that, Kelvoo?" Sam asked.

"Even if every detail of the *Pacifica Spirit's* mission was made public to every citizen of the Planetary Alliance, why should it matter? Why should any of the details be secret? Is there something about the mission that is unlawful or unethical?"

"Kelvoo, I'm . . . I'm so sorry. I didn't realize that you wouldn't understand the problem. Of course, now that I think about it, I don't see how you *could* have known." Sam paused to choose his words. "Kelvoo, please believe me, the secrecy has nothing to do with wrongdoing—at least not on our part.

"The point of the secrecy is for the protection of the kloormari. The problem is that sentient beings are complicated. The Sarayans, the Mangors, the Bandorians, the Silupas, the Grovnexuns, the Xiltors, and all of the other species in the Alliance . . . all of them are complex, and each individual has their own unique personality and motivation, but when it comes to humans, we take complexity to a whole new level!

"I now realize that, prior to the *Orion Provider*, we gave you a very incomplete picture of human nature. You see, when it comes to first contact, every crew member on this vessel has plenty of experience or training. We are highly disciplined in this area, and we're all focused on the mission. Sure, there are different personalities and traits among the crew, but even someone as eccentric as Bertie knows how to conduct herself within the constraints of a mission.

"Humans are competitive, and some are self-serving and greedy. The shopkeeper on the *Orion* was like that. Kaley Hart was too. She had an ethical responsibility to identify herself as a reporter, not that it would have changed the outcome, but I'm sure she was only interested in getting the news scoop of the decade! Based on your recounting of the events, I'm guessing that she might have been tipped off by the shopkeeper, since you told him some of your story first.

"Our established protocol is to introduce new species to humans and other Alliance species gradually. A first trip beyond a non-spacefaring species' home world usually doesn't happen for at least two years, so we can prepare the species for contact with outsiders. At the same time, we release information to the Alliance gradually. The location of the new species' planet is the final piece of information to be released.

"The reason we do this is to avoid exploitation. In the past, when there was no official body to handle first contact, opportunistic humans or other beings would flock to the planet of the newly discovered species and look for resources that could be mined or harvested, beings who could be put to work, or land to settle on or sell or show to tourists. Sooner or later, the new species would realize they were being exploited. Conflict, suffering, and death, sometimes on a massive scale, would follow. The same things happened countless times in Terran history when lands were discovered by humans of one culture whose interests conflicted with the existing inhabitants."

"So, the problem for the First Contact Authority is what to do now that the location of Kuw'baal is known," Captain Staedtler added. "The good news is that the Ryla system is far enough away from Alliance planets that it would take years for a vessel to make its way to the area."

"But a few hours from now, we're going to instantly jump there!" I retorted.

"That's true," Captain Staedtler replied, "but only we know the coordinates of the safe, pre-surveyed jump point near Ryla. The probe that mapped the jump point took fifteen years to get there from a previously known jump point. Nobody would be stupid enough to set their coordinates to the general area of the Ryla system and risk jumping into a dust cloud or other debris."

"Thank you for explaining these things to me," I said. "I just need to know one thing: Are you expecting me to keep any information secret with regard to my fellow kloormari, both onboard and back on Kuw'baal?"

"Absolutely not," Captain Staedtler said, shaking his head. "Unconditional transparency is the only way for us to maintain trust with the kloormari. For that reason, I encourage you to disclose this conversation and all of your recent experiences with all of the kloormari."

I thanked Captain Staedtler and Sam, and then we parted ways, so we could all get some rest.

Back on the observation deck, I delayed my meditation so that I could update the other kloormari when they were roused before the jump. I stood at the stern windows and watched Saraya and its moons dwindle to dots of light. When the thirty-minute warning sounded, I updated the other kloormari and passed along the advice to give the crew space.

After the jump, the other kloormari resumed their meditation, and I started mine. I had a great deal of information to process. I found it especially difficult to reconcile the unpredictability of the human species. My meditation was focused on calming my anxiety. Even though my experiences after first contact had been astounding and fascinating, I couldn't help feeling a vague doubt about whether our relationship with humans would lead my species to ruin.

After they completed their meditation session, the other kloormari could see that I was deep into my contemplations, so they didn't stir me until close to midday, ship time. Shortly after that, Bertie came up from the cafeteria. "How ya doin', sweetie? We missed you at breakfast," she said, speaking in an uncharacteristically soft voice while handing me a bowl of algel.

Bertie's concern had a greater impact on me than I would have thought. I felt relieved that I wasn't alienated from the entire crew. If I were human, I might say I was touched by her concern.

99

"I'm alright, Bertie, thank you so much for your interest. This is an aspect of your personality that I haven't experienced before."

"Well, don't get too used to it, hon," she replied. "It's prob'ly just my throbbing hangover talkin'!" She gave me a backward glance with a wink and a smile as she shuffled out of the room and back to her station.

The rest of the day was uneventful. We were due to arrive at Kuw'baal in the pre-dawn hours of the next day. My group busied itself reading our Infotabs. At dinner time, the crew was quieter than I had ever seen them. I asked Sam whether they were angry. "No," he replied. "It's been a long and eventful trip for everyone, and we're all very tired."

The crew started their main sleep cycle early, as we did with our meditation session. The *Pacifica* switched ship time to match the local time and duration of the day at my village on Kuw'baal.

We were roused at 03:30 and found ourselves in orbit around my home planet. Unlike the planets and moons that we had seen on our voyage, Kuw'baal was just a plain white orb. And yet, I was relieved to be returning to the familiar, and I looked forward to sharing my experiences with my community.

We re-entered the atmosphere in full darkness. I couldn't see the clouds, but I could feel the slight turbulence as we fell through them. *How odd*, I mused. *Before first contact I thought that these puffy collections of water vapor made up a single, solid sky. Not only did I think there was nothing beyond the sky but I didn't even think about considering the concept of "beyond the sky"!*

On its landing approach, the *Pacifica Spirit* took a different trajectory. We approached the village and the mineral plain from an angle with a slower rate of descent so that, if there were any obstacles in the landing area, such as an errant Kloormar running headlong into the blast zone, the *Pacifica* could travel farther and pick an alternative landing site. I watched my monitor intently. The crew did the same while also monitoring the short-range sensors. As we approached, I saw the three sets of lights in the village and the masts that they were attached to along with the illuminated structures below them, all gifts from the wonderful human visitors.

No obstructions were detected, so the *Pacifica* settled onto Kuw'baal without as much as a bump. I learned later that the *Pacifica* landed twenty centimeters from its previous position on Kuw'baal. Apparently, this was considered to be very impressive.

At first light, a few kloormari started across the plain toward the vessel. Others followed after pausing by the stream to have their breakfast. I asked Captain Staedtler's permission to greet the villagers. When he concurred, Sam suggested that the students take the next three days to get used to being home and to get the other kloormari caught up on our story.

On my way to the lower decks, I made sure to thank each crew member that I saw, in accordance with human custom. Then I diverted to the cafeteria to express my gratitude to Bertie as well. "Not gonna have a little breakfast first?" she inquired.

"Thanks, Bertie. Your algel has been excellent, but if you don't mind, I would very much like to taste some algel fresh from the stream."

"Knock yourself out, kid!" Bertie said.

I opened the hatch and inhaled the fresh, humid air of Kuw'baal and all of the scents that I had never noticed before. The first group of kloormari were just arriving at the vessel. Everyone wondered why we had returned a day earlier than planned. Most of all, they wanted an account of our voyage. I said that there was a great deal to tell, and I'd be pleased to do so back at the community structure. We milled around until my fellow students joined us, and we ambled across the plain back to my hometown.

\*\*\*

The next 116 days came and went. Sam had changed, as had Captain Staedtler and crew. Those changes were not negative; they were just changes. All of the humans were morose for the first few days, but as each one came to terms with the uncertainty that awaited them back on Terra, they became more relaxed and open.

During our absence, life continued in the village as before. The only change was that the decline in the villagers' studies of kloormari historical texts had accelerated. Most kloormari were more interested in studying the information available via the InfoServers and the large panels in the community structure. Each day, groups would gather around the panels to learn about subjects that the group had mutually agreed upon.

Captain Staedtler had a surprise for the village. Unknown by the kloormari and most of the crew, he had procured a few extra supplies from the *Orion Provider*. This included enough photoelectric panels, lights, and cables to equip every home in the village with interior lighting. He also provided lights on stakes that could be pushed into the ground and used to delineate the edge of the paths through the village. Sam said that such lights had been used in Terran gardens for centuries. I don't understand the appeal of gardening to humans, but the provision of artificial light was very appealing to the kloormari.

Finally, Captain Staedtler provided an Infotab to every kloormar in the village, including the youngest offspring. This was welcomed by the villagers with great enthusiasm—something that humans might call "joy."

In keeping with the mission, my group's education continued. We would assemble in the classroom each morning for group learning, but the rest of each day tended to be more free-form and self-guided. Sam felt that, since our world and species were no longer a secret, we would likely encounter more humans sooner than planned. This made him more interested in teaching us lessons about human nature.

Now that the crew had grown accustomed to us, the students interacted with them to a far greater extent, learning from all of them. Kroz continued to work with and learn about systems and software development from Audrey Fraser. Some of us worked with the science teams and would occasionally assist with fieldwork far from the *Pacifica*.

I spent a lot more time with Sam, one on one. He began to open up and share details about his personal life. From that, I learned a tremendous amount about human nature and customs, more than I had during the previous times of intense study.

One hundred and seventy-three days after the *Pacifica Spirit* and its amazing crew left our planet, a terrible series of events befell me, my species, and my world. The lessons that I learned from Sam played a key role in how those events unfolded, how I responded to them, and the effect that they had on me.

Before I describe the events, I will provide context by recounting the key lessons that I learned.

# FOURTEEN: LESSONS IN IMAGINATION

"How many Terran species speak Terran?" I asked Sam during my early school days.

"What do you mean?"

"Humans speak Terran, but according to some of my reading, so do dogs and cats and mice and bears, horses, donkeys, cows, and goats—"

"No, Kelvoo, on Terra, only humans speak Terran, along with other intelligent species that have moved to Terra from other worlds."

"But stories I've been reading show many non-human Terran species talking. Some of the illustrations show these species wearing human clothes and living in Terran houses with furnishings. On the other hand, vids depict these species as animals that appear to be incapable of mental sophistication. I do not understand."

"Well, Kelvoo, I think you've been reading and seeing these things in stories that were written for children. These stories are fiction."

"Please explain 'fiction' to me, Sam."

"Fiction is something that is not fact. On Terra, the only beings who speak Terran or wear clothes or live in residences are humans and intelligent species that originated from other planets. Stories about talking animals are fiction because those creatures don't speak Terran or wear clothes or live in houses."

"But why would anybody write a story that isn't about real things? Would this not be deceptive, especially to children who are in the early stages of learning? Would this not cause damage to the readers?"

"Not at all. Children are already familiar with animals, especially dogs and cats. Even if they were not, they would ask an adult who would explain that these things are what we call 'make believe.' Children enjoy seeing real animals, so fiction about animals behaving like humans is amusing to them. To encourage children to read and learn, we provide them with stories that interest them.

"In addition to this, humans actively encourage children to engage in activity that we call 'play.' When children play, they often pretend to be adults and pretend they are having adventures. They might mimic activities such as being a teacher or a doctor or a spy or searching for buried treasure or traveling to outer space. They may also speak to their toys, such as artificial humans called 'dolls' or artificial animals made of fabric, and they will pretend that their toys are talking to them as well. These are examples of humans using something that we call *imagination*. Does that make sense?"

"No," I replied. "This seems like a misleading activity with no benefit."

"Imagination is a very beneficial activity, Kelvoo. It has allowed intelligent species to make great advances. For example, there was a time when humans had no way of traveling through the air, but people *imagined* flying machines that could transport humans. This inspired humans to figure out how such a machine could work. This led humans to try building flying machines. They failed many times, but they tried and tried again until finally, they built such machines. They continued to build flying machines, and as they did, they *imagined* improvements to the machines and then made those improvements. Eventually, they built machines that could take humans beyond Terra, ultimately leading to us making contact with other worlds and intelligent species. *If we lacked imagination, we would never have accomplished these things.*"

"That makes sense," I replied.

After a moment of thought, Kwazka spoke up. "Sam, I previously asked you why humans had such advanced technology while the kloormari did not. You said the reason was that Kuw'baal was so well suited to us that all of our needs were provided for. You said we had not developed technologies because we had no pressing need for them. As proof, you said the technologies that we did develop, like writing and creating structures, were in response to upheaval events that produced a need to innovate."

"That's right, Kwazka."

"Would you think that another reason for innovation by humans, and perhaps by all of the other technologically advanced species, is the fact that they can imagine? I do not think that we kloormari are capable of imagination. When you suggest thinking about things that are not real, you describe something that is . . ." Kwazka paused, searching for the right word.

"Unimaginable?" Sam asked.

"Yes, I suppose that is right. So, is imagination another thing that makes humans so superior to us?"

Sam was taken aback by Kwazka's question. "Kwazka . . . all of you . . . please do not think for one moment that humans or any other intelligent species are superior to the kloormari! Technology is just one method of comparison. You far exceed humans in your ability to learn and remember. As we get to know you better, I am sure that there will be other measures where you surpass us. Anyway, Kwazka, your question is thought provoking. I would say that the answer is yes. *Need* and *imagination* are both things that have enabled my species to innovate and develop technologies."

Sam chuckled. "Well, that was quite the discussion to have come from a question about how many Terran species speak Terran. I do think it's important for you to study imagination. Doing so will help you understand other species better, and it might benefit all kloormari if you can think about possibilities and how to make those possibilities real."

I didn't pay a great deal of attention to Sam's suggestions. How could I think about things that were only possible? It just wasn't *possible* for a kloormar like me.

***

Ten days after the return from our voyage beyond the sky, Sam decided to revisit the topic of imagination. He said it would be very beneficial toward our goal of understanding humans better, and he had devised some exercises to help us.

"If any of you have studied human literature, and I know you have, you'll be familiar with William Shakespeare," he said, "a pioneering playwright and poet whose work is still held up as an inspiration to aspiring producers of literature and entertainment.

"One of Shakespeare's works was *A Midsummer Night's Dream*. Within that play a group of people depicting actors perform a different play named *Pyramus and Thisbe*. The actors within the play are portrayed as being rather untalented. *Pyramus and Thisbe* was intended to be a tale of tragedy, but due to their ham-handed, exaggerated performances, the audience within *A Midsummer Night's Dream* is more amused than saddened by the performance. Anyway, I think that many of you already know that.

"One of my favorite passages from *Pyramus and Thisbe* is Thisbe's soliloquy, when she comes upon the dead body of her lover, Pyramus. Pyramus mistakenly thought that Thisbe had been killed by a lion, so in his grief, he stabbed himself through the heart, killing himself. Thisbe, who was alive all along, finds Pyramus and expresses her grievous sorrow.

"I would like each of you to recite Thisbe's lines. Try to express the emotion that she must have been feeling. Keep in mind, the emotional attachment that pair-bonded humans have and how painful it would be for a human to lose the one person they love. When you perform these lines, please don't be embarrassed to let loose and go 'over the top' with your emotions. After all, the actors depicted in *A Midsummer Night's Dream* were supposed to be ridiculously over the top. If you can picture yourself in Thisbe's position and convey her feelings in the way that you speak, you will be using your *imagination*! Let's give it a try."

Sam asked for a volunteer. As always, all of us offered. Sam chose K'aablart. "Lie down on one side, and close your eye," Sam instructed. "You see, K'aablart, you are *pretending* to be Pyramus and *pretending* to have died."

"If you say so," K'aablart replied.

Sam walked up to K'aablart and looked down. "Asleep, my love?" He looked up at the rest of us. "That was Thisbe expressing puzzlement. Notice how my voice lilted up at the end, inquisitively."

"'What, dead, my dove?' Now her emotions are changing to fear and dread. I spoke those words softly as if not wanting to hear my own voice speaking them.

"'Oh Pyramus, arise!' His death would be too awful. Thisbe won't allow herself to believe it. She commanded him to get up. She spoke loudly to make sure that Pyramus could hear her."

"'Speak, speak. Quite dumb? Dead, dead? A tomb must cover thy sweet eyes.' Thisbe has come to the terrible realization that her lover is indeed dead. Note how I spoke the last line with a tremor of sadness in my voice."

He read the next stanza.

> These My lips,
> This cherry nose,
> These yellow cowslip cheeks,
> Are gone, are gone:
> Lovers, make moan:
> His eyes were green as leeks.

"Thisbe is remembering Pyramus's physical attributes—all the things about him that she found beautiful. All gone forever. I looked up as Thisbe recounted Pyramus's appearance, so that she would not gaze upon his bloody corpse. I put a moan in my voice when I said, 'Lovers, make moan.'"

He moved on to the next stanza:

> O Sisters Three,
> Come, come to me,
> With hands as pale as milk;
> Lay them in gore,
> Since you have shore
> With shears his thread of silk.

"The sisters three refers to the three fates who were part of Greek and Roman mythology. They were said to weave a tapestry depicting each person's life. Thisbe is saying that the fates have cut the thread of Pyramus's tapestry by allowing his death. Thisbe is now inviting the sisters three to do the same to her so that she may join Pyramus in death. I will speak the next passage calmly and resolutely to reflect Thisbe's unwavering determination."

Tongue, not a word:
Come, trusty sword;
Come, blade, my breast imbrue:
And, farewell, friends;
Thus Thisbe ends:
Adieu, adieu, adieu.

"Thisbe steels herself and stabs herself in the heart. As her life fades away, she bids the world goodbye. I continued to speak calmly and with purpose. After 'Come, blade, my breast imbrue,' I motioned to *pretend* to stab myself and took a sharp inhalation of breath to portray great physical pain. As I fell, I paused between each remaining word as though struggling to breathe and speak through the pain.

"So, what you just saw was me *pretending* to be a fictitious character and using my *imagination* to convey what she would be feeling. Okay, who's next?" Sam asked.

For the first time, none of us volunteered.

"Okay, K'aablart," Sam said, "you've had a front-row seat. Let's switch positions. I'll be Pyramus, and you can be Thisbe. By the way, you can open your eye now!"

Sam laid on his back. "Now go over there and walk toward me. You're Thisbe, and you're about to discover that I'm dead." Sam closed his eyes. "Okay, go."

K'aablart walked over to Sam and looked down at him. "Asleep, my love? What, dead my dove? Oh Pyramus, arise. Speak, speak. Quite dumb? Dead, dead? A tomb must cover thy sweet eyes."

"K'aablart, you're reciting the words, but where's the feeling in your voice? Remember, you're Thisbe and—"

"But I am K'aablart," K'aablart protested.

"You can do this, K'aablart. Say the words like I did."

K'aablart spoke the words and gestured in an exact imitation of Sam's performance, omitting the explanations between verses. In fact, K'aablart performed a perfect impersonation of Sam's voice.

Sam opened his eyes and turned to the class. "What do you think of K'aablart's performance?"

We all snapped our manipulators in applause. "Wonderful," Ksoomu said.

"A great performance," K'raftan agreed.

"Perfect," I added.

"No, no, no!" Sam said. "If K'aablart had used imagination, the performance wouldn't have been an exact duplication of mine. The performance would be different, because it would have been based on K'aablart's impression of the scene."

107

Sam repeated the exercise with Kleloma and Keeto with exactly the same results.

"Okay," he said afterwards, "maybe the works of Shakespeare are just too far removed from your personal experiences. Let's go to Plan B. I'm sure that Kelvoo has told all of you the story of the shopkeeper on the *Orion Provider* and his deceptive business practices. Since this is an event that really happened to one of you, why don't we re-enact that scene? Kroz, you'll play Kelvoo, and K'tatmal, you'll portray the shopkeeper. K'tatmal, stand here outside the door to your shop, and Kroz, walk toward K'tatmal."

"But there is no door and no shop," K'tatmal complained.

"Just try, okay?" Sam said, sounding frustrated. "And don't repeat the dialog that Kelvoo repeated to you. You must use different words that convey the story. Go!"

The following is the resulting dialog:

"Welcome to my shop, potential customer. I request that you come in."

"Thank you, shopkeeper. I shall enter your establishment now."

"Look at my merchandise. Would you like to buy this?"

"No thank you."

"Would you like to buy this?"

"No thank you."

"Would you like to buy this?"

"No thank you."

"You have wasted my time by refusing to purchase my merchandise."

"But you invited me in."

"I shall call security, and they will fine you one hundred thousand SimCash units."

"I offer to pay you fifty thousand SimCash units, and then I will leave."

"That would be acceptable, because I am a very kind human."

"Goodbye."

"Goodbye."

"That is the end of the performance," K'tatmal said.

The other students and I stood and applauded. We were very impressed that Kroz and K'tatmal were able to take the story and creatively adapt the dialog.

"Oh God!" Sam moaned. "Okay, Plan C," he said, sounding utterly exasperated. "Music. One of the great products of human imagination is music. Not only that but music can evoke moods and emotions, which can lead to imagination. Since I know that, as kloormari, you like details and complexity, let's take a look at classical music performed by large orchestras.

"I have some things to do on the *Pacifica*, and I'll be gone for about an hour. Your assignment is to select a piece of classical orchestral music that you think would evoke an emotional response in humans. We can discuss the piece when I'm back." With that, Sam walked off toward the vessel. I figured he needed a break.

Considering the length of some classical pieces, Sam hadn't given us much time to select one. Fortunately, every one of us had spent at least a few hours listening to human music, including classical selections. I had been interested when I saw how music could be used in vids to stir emotion in human viewers.

In the interest of time, each student suggested a piece of music that they had previously listened to. I suggested "Ride of the Valkyries" by Richard Wagner. Kwazka thought that "Symphony No. 5" by Ludwig van Beethoven would be acceptable. Kahini put forward "Eine kleine Nachtmusik" by Wolfgang Amadeus Mozart. In the end, we chose K'raftan's suggestion, the "1812 Overture" by Pyotr Ilyich Tchaikovsky. We thought that the multiple changes in pitch and tempo would have been intended to evoke a wide range of emotional responses.

As we listened to the music via the classroom panel and discussed the various passages in the piece, we vocalized those parts of the music. Due to the complexity of some parts, we would ask other students for help. For example, one of us might replicate the flutes and piccolo while another voiced the horns, trumpets, and trombones. Another student would reproduce violins and other stringed instruments, and another student would take on the percussion section. We would play a passage and then discuss and decide the mood and emotion that we thought were intended. Much of this was guesswork on our part, which was quite an accomplishment given our natural aversion to speculation.

Out of curiosity, we decided to attempt to vocalize the entire "1812 Overture" with all ten of us participating. Sometimes we couldn't tell which instruments and how many of them were producing certain sounds, but we managed to break the piece into its composite tones and intensities and produce a facsimile of the music.

Sam took longer to return than he had estimated. It was nearly two hours before he emerged from the vessel. *Sam really needed that break from us,* I thought.

"So, what have we come up with?" he asked. I thought that Sam's use of "we" was slightly presumptuous, but I wasn't about to antagonize him.

Since we had chosen K'raftan's selection, K'raftan spoke for the class. "We selected the '1812 Overture' by Pyotr Ilyich Tchaikovsky."

"Good," Sam said as he sat down. "What emotion do you think the '1812 Overture' stirs in the listener?"

"Many emotions," K'raftan said. "For example, here is the first minute and thirty-five seconds of the piece."

With that we began our recitation of the music. Sam's eyes opened wide, and his mouth opened even wider. Then he furrowed his brow and slowly got up, circling us to listen from various angles. He stood by the display panel and put an ear close to it as if checking to see whether it was the source of some of the sound. Then Sam took his seat again and resumed his shocked expression.

At the one minute and thirty-five second mark, we stopped. "The piece begins slowly with limited tonal range," K'raftan explained. "We suppose this might reflect a calm and somber mood—"

"Sorry, sorry," Sam interrupted. "Were all of you just performing the '1812 Overture' using only your mouths? I mean, your voices?"

"Yes," K'raftan replied. "We have a far greater vocal range than humans as well as polyphonic capabilities."

"I know that," Sam said, "but what I just heard was beyond amazing! If it's okay with you, could you continue with the rest of the piece, and then we can discuss it after you're finished."

"Certainly," K'raftan said, and we continued.

At four minutes and fifty-seven seconds into the piece, Bertie walked in, carrying Sam's lunch. At that point, the music had a much faster tempo, more instruments, and a more sophisticated, multi-layered sound.

Bertie handed Sam's lunch to him. He reached out and took the lunch bag without breaking his astonished stare at us.

"Heh-heh, nice stuff yer listenin' to," Bertie said. "Good to see ya gettin' a little culture!"

Sam swiftly held a hand up, indicating that Bertie should stifle herself. She made a peculiar face and then stuck her tongue out at Sam from behind, where he couldn't see her. She turned to leave and then stopped in her tracks. Bertie turned around and did what Sam had done. She slowly circled us, then walked to the display panel and cocked an ear. "Well, slap me silly an' call me Sally!" she muttered to herself.

Stepping lightly, Bertie took a chair next to Sam and listened to the rest of our performance with rapt attention. When we finished, Sam and Bertie stood and applauded with great fervor. Bertie shook her head in amazement. "Well, butter my butt an' call me a biscuit!"

Bertie asked Sam whether she could "borrow" me for a moment. She took me aside and told me that she was tasked with setting up a birthday celebration for Sam, scheduled for the coming Friday evening, two days in the future. She asked whether I could arrange for the class to come to the observation deck at 19:00 to join the event and perform the same music as entertainment.

I asked Bertie whether the celebration would be similar to the reception that we'd attended at the governor's residence on Saraya. "Kinda," Bertie said, "but not as formal. Just a get-together with a few eats an' drinks."

Having never attended a casual get-together before, I assured Bertie that I would make the arrangements with the other students and let the village know that we would be absent that evening.

"Okay, but make sure nobody tells Sam," Bertie said. "He knows there'll be a party for him, but I wanna keep your attendance secret, so we can surprise him."

"But Bertie, don't secrets end up causing problems?"

"Not always. This'll be a good secret, and he'll know everything in a couple of days. Besides, people *love* surprises."

Bertie left, and I rejoined the class and their very interesting discussion of the "1812 Overture" and the human emotions that it invoked. Sam didn't seem to be fully engaged in the discussion. He said he was still "blown away" by our performance.

After the discussion wrapped up and we were dispersing, I asked Sam what his favorite piece of music was. He said that so many songs and instrumentals "spoke" to him that the question was hard to answer. He also said that his favorite might depend upon the kind of mood that he was in at the time.

"One piece of music has stuck with me my entire life: 'Canon in D' by Johann Pachelbel. Most people call it 'Pachelbel's Canon.' I don't think the piece would be of great interest to the kloormari, since it's not especially complex. It's typically performed by just one cello and three violins. Despite it being simple, 'Pachelbel's Canon' has a great deal of meaning to me on a very personal level."

As I wandered off, I didn't think we had made any progress toward learning how to imagine, and I thought that Sam must have reached the same conclusion.

\*\*\*

In the evening two days later, the other students and I assembled by the stream just outside the village. We followed the new path across the stream and to the vessel, delineated by the new lighting.

The exobiologist, Li Huang, saw us coming. She scurried out of the vessel and led us to the cargo hatch. It opened, and Li led us on a circuitous route to the observation deck, so we wouldn't accidentally "bump into" Sam.

The observation deck had been emptied of the reclining couches that we had strapped ourselves to during the voyage. Instead, chairs lined the sides of the room, and small tables had been set up at random. A slightly raised platform had been placed toward the stern end of the deck. The main lights were shut off. Illumination came from a small lamp on each table. The platform, however, was brightly lit, mainly from spotlights that had been mounted on the ceiling.

Several crew members were milling around, and others were arriving. Bertie brought in a large decorated cake on a hovercart. She asked my fellow kloormari and me to stand in one corner and then said she would fetch Sam.

A few minutes later, Bertie walked in from the bridge with Sam, the remaining crew members, and Captain Staedtler in tow. They all burst into a short, simplistic song called "Happy Birthday."

"Aww, come on, guys, you shouldn't have!" Sam said when they were finished. "I said I didn't want anything special!"

Bertie led Sam to the cake. "Sorry there weren't any candles in the pantry."

"You baked me a cake? Aw, Bertie, you didn't need to do that!"

Bertie cut a piece for Sam, and he took a big bite.

"Hope ya don't mind that I invited these scallywags," Bertie said, motioning toward my group.

Sam saw us and smiled broadly, then swallowed the cake in his mouth. "Of course, I don't mind! Welcome, guys! How nice of you to come! I just wish I could offer you some of this incredible cake!"

"Well, this'll have to do 'em," Bertie said. She lifted a cloth on the hovercart, revealing ten sets of algel on plates, molded into miniature representations of Sam's birthday cake. We felt privileged that Bertie would make such an effort to accommodate us. We were especially pleased when she told us that she had personally collected the algel from a nearby stream that afternoon. "Way better 'n that fake stuff from the vat, eh?"

Sam came over and welcomed us. Then we mingled with the crowd. The fact that Li welcomed us made me realize that, with the exception of Sam, I had hardly interacted with the crew members that first brought me inside the vessel. During the voyage, I had rarely ventured to the lower decks where they worked. I made sure I chatted with Li, Rashid, Mike, Lisa, and Pauly.

Later in the evening, Bertie got up onto the raised platform. She made a ringing sound by tapping a spoon against the side of a glass and then invited all of the attendees to gather around as she invited the students onto the "stage."

"Now, I'm sure Sammy's been tellin' all of you about the musical talents of his students, so I wanted you all to see fer yerselves what all the fuss is about. Here fer yer listenin' pleasure: Sam's students. Hit it, fellas!"

We performed our rendition of the "1812 Overture." The audience was transfixed. Sam stood at the front of the gathered crew with a beaming smile and mouthed the words "Thank you." When we finished, the audience applauded, cheered, and whistled to express their appreciation.

As my fellow students left the stage, I stepped forward and asked the crowd for their attention. "I have a surprise for Sam. He told me about a piece of music that is very special to him."

Sam's eyes grew wide, and for some reason he appeared to be concerned.

"It is my pleasure to perform 'Pachelbel's Canon.'"

As I began, I saw Sam close his mouth tight, his lips becoming very thin. He balled his right hand into a fist, bowed his head, and rested his chin on his fist as he stared at the floor. A few seconds into the piece, he shut his eyes tight.

The spotlights above the stage spilled some of their light into the front of the crowd. When the music reached its peak, I saw some of the light refracting in a drop of liquid below Sam's left eye. I wondered whether I should stop. I decided to continue, because I'd learned that sometimes humans don't want to show emotion in a gathering of people, and I didn't want to draw attention to Sam's unexpected reaction.

As the music settled toward its conclusion, tears streamed down Sam's face, sometimes hanging from his nose and chin. When I finished, and the audience was applauding, Sam wiped his eyes and approached me, keeping his back to the gathering. He touched my shoulder. "Please walk with me." The crowd seemed to know to give us space.

We walked away from the crowd as Sam guided me to the stern windows where we looked out into the night. "Sam, I hope my performance wasn't bad. You didn't appear to enjoy it."

"Oh no," Sam said. "Your performance was wonderful. It just brought up a lot of bittersweet memories for me."

"What memories are those?"

"Now is not the best time to talk about it, Kelvoo, but we will discuss it soon—in private. Thank you, Kelvoo."

Sam regained his composure, straightened himself up, and re-immersed himself in the crowd.

When the party was wrapping up and most of the crew had left, Sam approached me. "Kelvoo, before we made first contact, what kind of hobbies did you have?"

"Reading and studying the ancient kloormari texts, just like all of the other kloormari," I replied.

"On Terra, I liked to go on long hikes—usually out in nature to places I had never seen before. I was thinking about taking a hike up the streambed where the water sometimes flows onto the mineral plain. It looks as though it takes a turn to the left between two high hills. I'd like to take a look and see what's up there. Have you ever been there?"

"No."

"Have you ever been curious about what's there?"

"No. I've never had a reason to go. It likely looks much like the rest of Kuw'baal. If you wish, I could ask some of the villagers about the area, or I could look through some of the historical texts. I would guess that somebody might have had a reason to go there at some point."

"Actually, Kelvoo, I'd rather just go there and discover the place without knowing anything about it beforehand. What I'd like to know is whether you would like to accompany me. It'll give us a chance to talk."

I thought it was strange for an individual to visit a place just because they hadn't been there before. At the same time, I always found conversations with Sam to be very interesting, so I agreed to go hiking with him. We decided to meet back at the vessel at 08:00 the next morning.

On the way back to the village, I told my fellow kloormari about my appointment with Sam and asked them to explain my absence to the villagers the next day. I was looking forward to my upcoming day with Sam. Perhaps I would even learn the reason why my musical performance had affected him so profoundly.

# FIFTEEN: LESSONS IN FAMILY, FRIENDSHIP, AND LOSS

The next morning, I consumed more algel than usual in anticipation of a day requiring considerable exertion. As I crossed the mineral plain to the vessel, the crystals didn't crunch beneath my feet as much as they had before. The path marked by the light posts was now well trodden, so the crystals were compressed into a hard walkway.

Sam was leaning against one of the vessel's landing struts. He wore a pair of solid-looking boots, a rucksack, and a bandana. "Ready?" he asked as I approached. I confirmed that I was, and we began walking briskly toward the upstream end of the plain.

The dry streambed became more defined as the plain narrowed. Finally, the streambed disappeared at the base of a great rockfall. Up the rockfall to the right was the top of the algel falls. The falls were in the stream that ran past the village. I had never seen the village stream run dry. The streambed that we followed ran parallel to the larger stream, but as we could see from the plain, it veered off to the left farther up the slope.

We began to climb the rockfall, scrabbling over jagged rocks that were up to thirty centimeters across. Some rocks were loose, so we had to test their stability as we climbed. Farther up, the rocks gave way to large boulders up to two meters across. A couple of times, Sam and I had to give each other a boost or a helping hand to scale the boulders. The streambed disappeared intermittently below the boulders and reappeared elsewhere.

Eventually, the grade became less steep. We turned left and followed a ridge along the top of a steep gully. We looked into the gully where we saw and heard rushing water. Sam said the stream appeared to be even larger than the village stream, but once it entered the rockfall, it probably ran underground below the rocks and the mineral plain. Only during and after a substantial rainfall would the lower portions be visible and flood the plain.

Along the ridge, we walked on a surface that alternated between gravel and smooth bedrock. Sam untied his bandana and mopped his perspiring face with it. "I have to slow down a bit," he said, "or I'll get overheated." I welcomed the break since my limbs and joints were quite sore.

After a brief rest, Sam looked up and ahead. "I think we're nearly there."

From the time we left the vessel, I had wanted to know what Sam was planning to talk about, but based on some of my previous interactions, I thought he may want to discuss personal matters. I'd learned that it would be best to let him initiate the conversation.

The ridge gave way to the side of a hill about thirty meters above the gully. The stream flowed over much more accessible ground before it entered the gully.

As we rounded a corner of the hill, we got a complete view into the valley and over the lake that fed the stream. Sam stopped in his tracks. "My God!" he exclaimed. "This is incredible!"

"How so?" I asked.

"The land, the water, the colors! It's amazing! Look at how the lake is nestled in a magnificent bowl. Look at the jagged peaks surrounding it, giving way to the moraine below. Look at how the rock is layered. That vivid yellow, that's probably sulfur. The streaks of turquoise may be oxidized copper. The ochre sedimentary layers, they're probably, well, ochre. The bright white . . . there are many possibilities. And then below the moraine, the bright pink, purple, and red plants, all randomly mixed. Here are some at our feet. I don't know whether these are flowers, but they're absolutely gorgeous! And then the lake with its milky blue water. It reminds me of glacial lakes that I've seen in the alpine levels of the Rocky Mountains on Terra."

"Yes, I see those things," I said, puzzled about what was causing such wonder.

"Kelvoo, on Terra, places like this are revered as planetary treasures. On Terra, access would be greatly restricted, laws would be written, and any development would be banned in the interest of preserving something like this. You know, if I ever ended up residing on Kuw'baal, I would want to live out my days up here!"

Sam led the way down the loose gravel slope to a sandy spot where the stream flowed from the lake. A nice stretch of algel lined the banks. Sam opened his pack, took out a blanket, then unwrapped some food. "Remember Bertie's clubhouse sandwiches?" he asked.

"I remember everything."

Sam ate his lunch and drank a beverage while I consumed some tasty algel. When we were finished, Sam decided it would be the appropriate time to talk.

"Kelvoo, I'd like to explain why your performance last night affected me so much. 'Pachelbel's Canon' is something that I closely associate with my mother. She was an undergraduate student when she met my biological father, Hans Buchanan. Hans was a young, accomplished professor. They chose to have a baby, but when I was born, Hans decided he had better things to do than hang around with a kid. Hans busied himself. He took off to as many conventions and seminars as he could. Mom cut back on her classes to take care of me.

"Hans told Mom that she should get a nanny or put me in daycare and go back to school full time instead of wasting time with me. He called her stupid for wanting to be 'just a mom' rather than 'bettering' herself. When I was two years old, Hans found a new student to chase after, and he was gone.

"We got no support from my father, so Mom had to quit school to take care of me. As a small child, I remember her listening to 'Pachelbel's Canon' whenever she was feeling down. She told me that it had been her favorite piece of music for as long as she could remember.

"When I was old enough to attend school for most of the day, Mom took a job at a private interplanetary school as a teaching assistant for newcomers from other worlds. She helped them learn how to speak, read, and write in Terran. Her mom lived close by, so sometimes I'd spend a couple of hours on a weeknight or half a day on the weekend with 'Gran' while Mom took odd jobs tutoring new arrivals.

"When I was twelve, Mom met a man named Norman. He was a consultant who facilitated the process of getting newcomers settled on Terra. Applying for visas, finding a home, buying furnishings, and learning Terran customs . . . these were all things that Norm and his staff facilitated. Mom met Norm at a banquet that was hosted by a Sarayan diplomat. Norm had assisted the diplomat and her family. Mom had tutored the diplomat's youngest daughter.

"In most cases, kids are very wary and protective when their mom gets into a new relationship. It was different with Norm. I liked him from the moment Mom introduced us. He could relate to anyone. He was considerate and interesting, and he had a great sense of humor. He and my mom seemed like a perfect match. They loved each other very much, but they never neglected me.

"These days, most Terran couples dispense with the old practice of marriage. Not so with Mom and Norm. They had a traditional ceremony. Gran made most of the arrangements. She let me help out. I picked out the music. I'll give you one guess as to the musical piece played at the wedding."

"Well," I replied, "Mendelssohn's 'Wedding March' would be the most commonly played music at a wedding."

Sam shook his head and chuckled. "Oh, Kelvoo! You're right that the 'Wedding March' was played while Mom walked down the aisle, but I'm talking about 'Pachelbel's Canon.' It was played softly in the background by a string quartet while my mom and Norm exchanged their vows. As I watched the ceremony, the music just seemed to capture the very essence of Mom."

"So, this was another way that 'Pachelbel's Canon' reminds you of your mother."

"Yes," Sam replied, nodding, "but that's not all. Mom and Norm settled into life as a loving married couple. Norm never belittled my mom. He encouraged and complimented her and helped her self-confidence blossom. When I was in high school, Mom went back to university and finished her degree in less than a year. After that, she and Norm worked together as equals in the newcomer consultancy that Norm had started. Sometimes I helped out part time. That allowed me to meet newcomers from other planets. Sometimes my mom and Norm would take a working vacation to other Alliance planets. I got to accompany them on two trips to Saraya and another to Bandor.

"Most teenagers think of their moms as 'uncool.' I guess I did too, but she always had my admiration. In many ways she was a hero to me.

"After high school, I took inspiration from my mom and entered university. I majored in teaching and minored in linguistics and anthropology at the University of New Liberia. I graduated with honors and then enrolled in a master's program in education. A few days before I was to submit my thesis, I got word of a terrible accident. Mom and Norm were on a trip to Mang in the Toriod System. A vehicle had been loaned to them and had a malfunction, plunging one hundred and fifty meters into a rock face. Only some of the vehicle's safety measures deployed.

"Norm was killed on impact. My mom regained consciousness before help arrived. She opened her eyes to see Norm's head broken open right in front of her. She was soaked in his blood. My mom was stabilized, physically at least, and sent home along with Norm's remains on the next express flight. Mom was placed in an excellent hospital to recover from her wounds.

"I attended a memorial for Norm, organized by his friends and colleagues, but Mom was too injured to go. We planned to have another memorial for Norm once Mom recovered.

"Two weeks after her return to Terra, Mom started to get a fever. An infection tore through her body. At first, the doctors weren't concerned. A little medi-ray treatment, and if necessary, medications and nanobots would remove an infection in less than forty-eight hours. My mom didn't respond to the treatments though. Experts were called in. Using the latest molecular scanning equipment, they found a new type of infection from a microbe that is endemic to Mang. They figured that the microbes had infiltrated Mom's bloodstream through her wounds. The medical experts requested assistance from the Mangors, but the microbe didn't cause infection in their species, and they couldn't figure out how it interacted with human physiology.

"My mom deteriorated rapidly. She was medicated for pain, but she kept slipping in and out of consciousness. In a moment of clarity, Mom told me that she knew our lives had been complicated and difficult at times, but she was proud of the man that I'd become. She told me to take care of myself and pursue my dreams. I told her that she was my inspiration and my hero, and I wouldn't know what to do without her. 'You'll find a way,' she said sadly. At the end, I held my mom close as her life slipped away.

"I did my best to arrange a fitting memorial for my mom and Norm. I had no idea how many people's lives had been touched by Mom. Hundreds of people came to say goodbye. They were all so kind. People took turns speaking to the crowd, sharing their experiences with Norm or my mom. In the background, a string quartet softly played 'Pachelbel's Canon.' So, Kelvoo, that's why hearing the music affected me so strongly."

"How long ago did your mother die?" I asked.

"Only eight months ago, so the memories are still vivid."

"How did you deal with your grief?"

"For several weeks, I didn't. I put my education on hold, I isolated myself, and I didn't know whether I could go on living. Finally, one of my professors reached out to me. She told me about a first-contact mission to Ryla 5 that was being put together. She said that if I'd get my butt out of bed, submit my thesis, and complete my degree, she could get me on the mission team as first-contact administrator."

"How did you manage to become part of such an important mission? Did the professor have special connections?"

"I'm sure she did to some extent, but being the first-contact administrator on that kind of mission isn't as desirable as you might think. Just because a planet has the right conditions for life doesn't mean there will be any life. Most of the time, there isn't any. When there is life, it's usually restricted to microscopic organisms and sometimes plants. First-contact administrator is said to be the most boring job in the universe when there is nothing to make contact with. It's just through pure luck that this mission has been so remarkable.

"When I was offered the job, what appealed to me was the thought of running fast and far away from my grief. I submitted and successfully defended my thesis, got my diploma, and joined the mission. That's why you and I are here by this lovely stream in this spectacular valley."

"I've been trying to understand human grief," I said. "When a kloormar dies, their community regrets the loss of that kloormar's work and other contributions to the village, but we don't grieve. From stories about death among Terrans that I've read or viewed, it seems that the level of grief is different depending upon the relationship that the grieving individual has to the dead person."

"That's usually the case, Kelvoo. If a casual acquaintance dies, it's sad but not usually as upsetting as the loss of a life partner or a sibling or parent."

"Is the loss of a parent the most painful of all?"

"No. The absolute *worst* loss is when a parent loses a child. Parents are supposed to outlive their children. When a parent is elderly, their death is anticipated. The death of a child is the most unimaginably painful loss that a human can endure. Fortunately, that kind of loss is rare."

"So, your gran must have been devastated."

"I don't really know, Kelvoo. Each human has their own way of processing grief. I wanted to support Gran however I could, so I visited her almost every day. After a couple of weeks, she started avoiding me by making excuses about having things to do or people to see. One day I decided to go to her place unannounced and ask her what the problem was.

"Gran told me that it was painful to see me because I reminded her too much of my mom. She said that she was getting lots of support from her nephews and nieces, and she thought it would be best to put a little distance between us for a while. I've been distant from Gran ever since then. Now that I think about it, Gran's rejection of my companionship was probably the lowest point of the entire grieving process."

Sam stood and looked out over the lake, appearing to be deep in thought. After several minutes, he broke the silence. "Kelvoo, I want to thank you for coming with me today. I'm especially grateful to you for listening. I haven't told that much of the story to anyone else. I feel better now, as though I've turned a corner and can start to get past my loss."

Sam reached into his rucksack and took out a metal cylinder. He told me there was something he had wanted to do when the time was right. "This feels like the right time, Kelvoo."

Sam asked me to stand in place, facing the lake and to sing "Pachelbel's Canon" "nice and strong."

As I started, Sam walked to the shore of the lake, where the stream began. He slowly turned his head to take in a view of the entire valley. Next, he removed the lid of the cylinder and slowly poured out some grey sand and dust. The sandy parts fell into the water and meandered down the stream. Most of the dust was caught in the breeze and drifted toward the gorge.

As the music built to its most powerful stanzas, it echoed from the surrounding hills, resonated through the valley, and filled it with sound.

When Sam's container was empty, he bowed his head, and I saw his shoulders shaking.

When my recitation ended, Sam turned back toward me. His eyes were red, but to my surprise, he was smiling. "Thank you, Kelvoo."

Sam packed up and put on his rucksack. As we started the trek back down to our starting point, the skies opened, and the afternoon rains drenched us.

"Sam, when we studied the story of Pyramus and Thisbe, it made me think about the human practice of suicide. When you told me about your mother's death, you said that you didn't know whether you could go on living. Were you thinking about taking your own life?"

"I have to admit, it did cross my mind a few times."

"I don't think that I could ever understand that," I said. "The thought would never occur to a kloormar. There would be no more opportunities to learn, and worse, such an unnecessary death would be a loss to the community."

"Kelvoo, when you understand humans, you will have a great deal to teach my species!"

Sam's words of wisdom made him chuckle. In fact, he seemed to have taken on a new persona. He chatted amiably with me, told me amusing stories, and laughed often.

By the time we got to the plain, the ground was flooded up to Sam's ankles. As we waded back to the ground where the vessel stood, I asked Sam a question.

"I've learned much about the concept of friendship, Sam, but humans seem to differ on the definition. One common thread is that a friend is someone that you can comfortably talk to about personal matters—someone you can open up to about your feelings. Do you consider me to be your friend?"

Sam stopped and turned to me. "To me, friendship exists between two individuals if each trusts the other and considers them to be a friend. I would be pleased to call you my friend if you were to consider me to be yours."

"I do indeed, my friend."

With that, we sloshed our way back to the *Pacifica Spirit*.

# SIXTEEN: LESSONS IN HATE

One morning in class, Keesooni asked, "Sam, while studying human history, I've found the same thing over and over again: war. War seemed to be happening somewhere on Terra all the time until a few centuries ago. Why would groups of humans want to destroy other groups of humans?"

"You bring up a tough subject, Keesooni," Sam said. He turned to the group. "Are we all willing to take the time to dig into this subject?" We indicated that we were, so Sam began.

"The topics that we're about to discuss have been very contentious and divisive among humans. There are many perspectives and subtle differences within those perspectives. I want you to keep in mind that I'll be giving you *my* perspectives, which are pretty much in line with the consensus among Terran humans today. Prevailing theory is that war is a by-product of early humans' need to compete for survival. Maybe the simplest way to explain it is to ask why the kloormari *don't* engage in warfare.

"Here on Kuw'baal, your planet provides all that you need to eat and to live comfortably. Also, since your offspring are self-sufficient from birth, there are no special attachments to children who contain your genetic material or whom you gave birth to, so an overwhelming urge to reproduce never existed. This means your planet has not become overpopulated.

"The kloormari originated in one part of Kuw'baal. On the scale of evolutionary time, it was only recently that the kloormari expanded their geographical range, so different kloormari races haven't evolved.

"It's also important to note that, since dispersing, the kloormari still have a common language, so communication is not a problem, and ongoing communication means that customs remain much the same between villages.

"Finally, your species is logical—the things that you believe to be true are backed up by facts. Sure, you may be incorrect sometimes, but you do not have superstitions that divide one group of kloormari from another. So, let's take a look at each of those factors and see how they were different for humans."

Sam wrote "Resources" on one of the panels at the front of the classroom. "For early humans on Terra, survival was very difficult. There were only limited areas where humans could thrive due to climate and availability of food, water, and other resources. As hunters and gatherers, my people had to live in cooperative groups or 'tribes.' Since the members of the tribe depended on one another to survive, the tribe would consist of people who trusted one another and knew one another well, so tribes might consist of a small number of extended families.

"Depending on the availability of resources, tribes would have an optimal size. They needed to have enough people with various survival skills, but they also had to be small enough that it was easy to move to a new area when resources were running low. When a tribe was successful and grew beyond a sustainable size, it would often split into two tribes. These tribes were usually friendly with one another, cooperating when it was advantageous and exchanging people for marriage or some kind of equivalent, to maintain genetic diversity and health.

"Tribes were adapted to the climate and ecosystem of their part of Terra. They did not possess the skills to do very well in other ecosystems, so they tended to stay within a region. Every so often, disaster would strike. It could have happened because of a drought or a flood. Perhaps a disease would wipe out many of the plants or animals that they used for food. Maybe a volcano erupted. There were many reasons why a tribe might no longer have the resources that they needed to survive.

"The urge to survive is paramount in humans. A starving tribe would have been forced to move into a new area, which another tribe used. The other tribe might also be starving. This is where a war might start, purely for survival.

"Now, let's say that each of the tribes had different origins. Let's also say that their customs were different, their appearance was different, and so was their language, preventing them from communicating some kind of agreement. Humans had an unfortunate tendency to view people that they didn't understand as inferior—less human than they were, perhaps not much more than animals. Humans have a natural tendency not to kill their own kind, but killing is easier when you see another being as inferior to your kind."

Next, Sam wrote "Race" on the classroom panel. "Ignoring the differences in gender for a moment, when you, as a kloormar, look at a human visitor's skin color, hair, and eyes, you probably think we look much alike."

We told Sam that we disagreed.

"Okay, let me rephrase that," Sam said. "We have more physical differences than a group of kloormari may have, but in comparison to humans just a few centuries ago, we now appear much more similar to one another. In days long past, some of us would have had very pale or very dark skin. Some humans' hair might have been bright yellow or totally black. Our eyes may have had blue or green or dark yellow or brown irises, and our eyes may have been narrower or rounder in shape.

"The race with the lightest skin and hair were 'Caucasians' or 'Whites.' Races with darker-skinned people included 'Blacks,' 'Melanesians,' and 'Aborigines.' Other races with various skin tones included 'Asians,' 'Native Americans,' 'Indians,' 'Middle Easterners,' 'Polynesians,' and so on.

"A long time ago, for reasons I can't comprehend, it was considered to be socially unacceptable and even illegal in some cases to pair bond and reproduce with a person who was not of your race.

"War often broke out along racial lines. This was especially true when humans on one continent developed the technology to travel back and forth across oceans. They considered themselves to have 'discovered' new lands, even though other humans had lived there for tens of thousands of years. For the most part, the existing inhabitants welcomed the newcomers, but the newcomers viewed them as inferior and took over their lands and resources. This led to wars and outright massacres.

"Humans have learned from those terrible times. That's why we follow strict procedures on first-contact missions. It's also why we are very concerned about word of your existence leaking out before you are fully prepared to deal with newcomers.

"The racial differences between humans started to change when it became easier for us to travel around Terra. Humans had the opportunity to meet a wider range of people and to relocate to other parts of the planet. Marriage or similar arrangements between races, or for that matter, between partners of the same gender, became accepted and were no longer considered to be abnormal. Many children of mixed race were born.

"The process sped up after a series of devastating wars and massive population reduction. As a result, countries were abolished, and restrictions on the movement of people were lifted. Life became too precious to destroy it on the basis of another human's race. Today, virtually all humans on Terra have tan skin, brown eyes, and slightly curly black or dark brown hair.

Next, Sam wrote "Language and Customs."

"Language," Sam said, "was a terrible barrier to humans trying to understand one another and make agreements. Centuries ago, hundreds of distinct languages were spoken on Terra—thousands if you include dialects of those languages, not to mention different accents from one region to another.

"Research indicates that, when a child learns a language, the structure of the language has an effect on how the human brain develops and how the person perceives the world and its people. Different languages often relate to different cultures. This presents two barriers to cooperation: an inability to communicate clearly and different values. For example, one culture may have been revolted by another that ate the flesh of animals. One culture might have thought that marriages arranged between families were appalling while others may have found the practice to be highly logical.

"These are examples of how a group of humans may think of another group as being barbaric or inferior, making it easier to rationalize waging war against them when conflict arose.

"Once again, the movement of people on Terra and the intermingling of cultures in recent times has led to a single culture. Terran culture is a mix of customs from previous ethnic groups. The standard Terran that we are speaking now is a blend of many older languages, such as English, Hindi, Swahili, Mandarin, French, Japanese, German, Russian, Arabic, and so many more.

"In olden times, you could guess a person's race and ethnicity based on their name. Someone with the surname 'Buchanan' would have been Caucasian with ancestry likely going back to the country of Scotland. Our captain's first name, Kwami, would likely be a Black person's name, but his last name, 'Staedtler,' would indicate a Caucasian. At one time, our crew members Yuki Sakamoto and Li Huang would certainly have been Asian. Yuki would have been of Japanese ethnicity and Li's ancestors likely Chinese. Today, names are meaningless for identifying a person's race since racial differences have been reduced to nothing more than slight variations in each person's DNA."

Sam wrote "Superstition," then pointed to the word. "This one was perhaps the most destructive and certainly the most puzzling aspect of humanity. Superstition has led to untold bloodshed, war, and even outright genocide.

"Some superstitions were benign. For example, the idea that bad luck would follow if you walked under a ladder, if a black cat crossed your path, or if you broke a mirror. Other superstitions were far more complex and insidious.

"Some superstitions were based on a belief in one or more all-powerful, all-knowing invisible beings who created the universe and either controlled our lives or judged each of us according to how we lived our lives. Billions of people once believed that they must bow down before these beings, who must be worshipped, appeased, and obeyed. These superstitions were called 'religions,' and the supernatural beings were called 'gods.'"

"Why would any human have believed this sort of thing?" I asked.

"Two reasons," Sam said. "Gaps in knowledge and fear of death. One of the things that has led to human advancement is the need to know—the need to understand the world, the universe, and themselves. It is the quest for knowledge that compels humans to learn and build their intellect."

"Is that one of the factors that has made humans more technologically advanced than the kloormari?" Kleloma asked.

"I don't think so," Sam replied. "The kloormari are clearly just as curious as humans and are certainly far superior in their ability to learn.

"The problem with many humans is that the need to understand was so strong and the gaps in their knowledge were so wide that they filled those gaps with something that was made up. For example, early humans had no idea how the universe came into being, and frankly, we still don't fully comprehend it. With the question being so big and so far beyond the understanding of human beings, they filled that gap by reasoning that supernatural beings must have created the universe.

"The human trait of wanting knowledge and filling the gaps was so strong and so universal that every ancient culture had the idea of 'god' and a religion built around that idea. They were, however, inconsistent with one another when it came to the specifics.

"Some religions were *polytheistic*—they believed in several and sometimes even hundreds of gods. Each god might be responsible for certain aspects of life or nature: gods of the sun, the moon, the sky, rains, thunder, and the harvest. Gods of love, hate, celebration, suffering, fertility, and death.

"In polytheism, the gods were in conflict or competition just as each human had internal competing desires and challenges. It was the conflict between the gods that was believed to keep the universe in balance, and so, people tried to live a balanced life.

"Some religions were *monotheistic*. These religions were the most damaging. Under monotheism there was just one god, one doctrine, and one absolute truth. People who followed the doctrine were believed to be righteous. Those who did not were considered evil.

"Fear of death was the other factor that made religion so powerful. Religions put forward the belief in an afterlife. This was based around the idea that each human—and in some religions every animal, plant, and even geographical feature—has a 'spirit,' an invisible entity containing their consciousness, their 'essence' . . . their life force.

"Many religions dictated that when a righteous person dies, their spirit continues to live eternally in a paradise, a perfect place of eternal joy and contentment, with no suffering. For people who were not compliant with the religion, some religions stated that they would cease to exist, while others proclaimed that their spirit would be cast for all eternity into a place of fire and pain and excruciating, unbearable suffering. This helped to ensure compliance from members of society."

"Why would anyone want to believe in this sort of thing?" K'raftan asked.

"I don't really know," Sam replied. "Perhaps it was to feel like part of a larger, powerful community. Perhaps it was just out of fear. Maybe children were raised by parents who were believers, and those children never took the time or never dared to question their beliefs.

"As religions became more powerful, anything that was contrary to the religion's teachings was declared to be evil. For example, there are periods of history in which the Christian religion declared that Terra was the center of the universe and 'Sol,' the Terran star, revolved around Terra, as did all of the planets and stars in the universe. Science was able to prove otherwise, but scientists who put forward this information were forced to retract their statements or be subjected to torture or put to death.

"Religions sometimes operated under the guise of promoting peace and social justice, but to do so they had to moderate their position. They had to disregard the parts of their doctrine that justified violence. This met with resistance from adherents who insisted that the entire religious text must be taken literally despite the fact that many parts of the text contradicted one another.

"Religious wars were waged, and countless humans endured unspeakable suffering and death because of religious absolutism. Religions dictated that they were following the will of their gods and that their gods required them to destroy their 'evil' enemies. All of this suffering at the hands of religion was so needless, and all of it was based on a belief in imaginary beings.

"I would like to encourage all of you to read the religious texts of the humans. The main Christian text is called the Bible, and the main text of Islam is the Quran. You might also want to read the Hebrew scriptures, which relate to the religion of Judaism. Christianity and later Islam formed after Judaism and worship the same original god. If you have the chance, broaden your knowledge by reading religious texts from the Terran continent of Asia. Examples include Buddhist, Confucian, and Hindu texts. Familiarize yourself with these and any other religious documents. It is important to be acquainted with other species' mythology in order to understand their thought processes and how those processes may have been affected in the past.

"Fortunately for humanity, religion slowly faded away. Again, with greater travel and more interethnic relationships, each person's conflicting religious beliefs sort of canceled each other out. Gods that once filled the gaps in our knowledge began to fade as our knowledge grew, and the gaps became smaller. At one point, in desperation, the three Abrahamic religions—Christianity, Islam, and Judaism—actually merged into the 'Universal Church,' hoping that unity would bolster their numbers.

"Finally, early evidence of other intelligent life forms captured people's interest and gave them something else to marvel about."

I decided to speak up. "Sam, you've said that religions start based on gaps in knowledge and fear of death, but what specific event could start a religion?"

"I can tell you about one that happened right here on Kuw'baal a short time ago! Kwazka, several weeks ago, you recounted the speculation that was put forward by some of the villagers after our lander arrived."

"Yes," Kwazka replied. "One kloormar speculated that the creature was here to warn us of a pending upheaval event. Another suggested that it was evidence of superior creatures. It was also hypothesized that other beings

127

were observing us, which actually was true. Another suggestion was that the superior beings were sending us a message and that perhaps we had displeased them. I put an immediate end to this speculation, but I did incorrectly surmise that the lander was a creature that lived in the sky, that it causes the lightning, and that it gave birth to a smaller flying creature."

"Okay," Sam said, "so what if you hadn't suggested stopping the speculation? What if the speculation continued and grew? What if the *Pacifica* had never arrived to show you that there are worlds beyond the sky? What if a majority of kloormari started to believe this was evidence of a superior being—a god who required you to take certain actions?"

"I am pleased that I don't have an imagination," Kwazka said, "because I don't want to think about what could have happened to our species."

Sam smiled. "I'm not too worried about it, Kwazka. The kloormari are highly rational and always in pursuit of the facts and truth. The fact that your species has never developed superstitions gives me a great deal of confidence that you won't go down that path."

"Speaking of imagination," Kwazka said, "isn't religion a product of imagination? If so, don't you think that imagination could be harmful to the kloormari?"

Sam thought for a moment before he replied. "You make a valid point, Kwazka, though I think that ignorance is more of a cause of human suffering than imagination. Nonetheless, imagination has been used to invent gods and also to devise weapons of war and ways to inflict pain and suffering on others. Many things can be used for purposes that are right or wrong. For example, spacecraft can be used to make contact with new species for the greater good of all. They can also be used to wage war against other beings. I don't know whether the kloormari will ever be able to utilize imagination, but I know that you're good beings with or without it.

"Anyway, I've gone on far too long about superstitions, and I would like to summarize. So, we've looked at resources, race, language and customs, and superstitions. These are just a few things that ancient humans have used to rationalize hate. Of course, there have been others like economic standing and ridiculous excuses such as how a person defines their own gender or which gender a person has intimate relations with. Some people thought that these deeply personal traits were other people's business, and they would sow hatred toward people who didn't conform to their own traits. Anyway, Keesooni, I hope that answers your questions about humans and war!"

"It does *that* at the very least!" Keesooni said.

Sam asked us whether we had any questions. I asked whether any humans had resisted the societal changes that ended widespread hate and wars.

Sam said, "Oh yes! To this day, there are millions of humans who resist, but you won't find many of them on Terra." Sam went on to explain that human explorers had discovered two inhabitable planets, one of them had been found 147 years ago and the other 153 years ago. The planets had forests, oceans, and a few species of animals but no intelligent life forms.

"There were enclaves of humans on Terra who wanted the races to live separately to preserve their racial identity, way of life, and heritage. There were others who were religious and claimed to be persecuted because the majority of humans didn't accept their beliefs. Then there were people who thought that humanity had become too 'soft' and accommodating toward others who were different from the majority. There were also criminals who often operated in gangs that would supply addictive substances to people and terrorize members of the community through extortion and violence. These groups of humans were known as the 'Outlier people.'

"Leaders of the Terran government knew that something had to be done to remove the threat that the Outliers posed to a just and egalitarian society. At the same time, as reformed humans, we couldn't just kill these people or imprison them indefinitely.

"Our people found the answer in the newly discovered planets. The antisocial elements of humanity would be offered the chance for freedom on these planets. These planets became known as the 'Outlier Colonies.' At first, only a minority of Outliers chose to make the journey. The Terran government sent experts and great amounts of aid to assist the Outliers to establish sustainable and prosperous settlements. When word came back from the early settlers, the rest of the Outliers gradually decided to make the move. To this day, the Outliers live as they see fit while the rest of humanity enjoys a peaceful existence on Terra, in harmony with other beings through the Planetary Alliance."

"Forgive me for casting doubts," I said, "but while it's commendable that your species has made great progress and has created an admirable society on your home planet, you have described some appalling acts committed by your species. Clearly, humans are capable of terrible things. As much as I trust you and the crew of the *Pacifica Spirit* personally, can the kloormari trust your people? How can we be sure that they won't revert back to their old patterns?"

"Honestly, Kelvoo, there are no guarantees. As we gradually introduce your species to humans and other members of the Planetary Alliance, it will be entirely up to the kloormari whether to proceed with each step in the process.

"After this mission, you can expect further visits from humans and other Alliance species, both to this village and others across Kuw'baal. We will suggest that the kloormari form local committees and a planetary committee, if you are willing. Under the processes of the Planetary Alliance, your species will decide the extent of your interaction with humans or any other Alliance species. You may choose to terminate contact at any time if we demonstrate any reason why you cannot trust us. Do keep in mind that we also have oversight from the other species in the Alliance. It would not be in our interest to revert to our prior hateful ways and risk expulsion from the Planetary Alliance.

"Please understand that every species in the Planetary Alliance has shameful parts of their history that parallel the history of humanity. The fact that the kloormari have no such past makes your species truly unique and extremely precious."

Sam's lessons about humanity's past were both horrifying and fascinating.

# SEVENTEEN: SCHOOL'S OUT

S am was pensive on the final day of class.

The area around the *Pacifica Spirit* was bustling with crew members and hoverlifts. The contents of the cargo bay were being unloaded and repacked as the crew made room for the equipment being retrieved from the three structures near the classroom. Groups of two or three crew members fanned out into areas farther afield to retrieve scientific equipment and samples for detailed analysis back on Terra.

Sam addressed the class. "Tomorrow, the other humans and I will be leaving Kuw'baal and returning to our homes." I didn't understand why Sam was telling us that. We had known the departure date for months, and the nearby activity was a dead giveaway.

"Getting to know each of you has been the most rewarding experience of my life. Before I go, I want to leave you with some advice. I have to say, it feels strange giving *you* advice when you are the smartest, wisest beings I know, but as someone who knows humans, I feel compelled to share these thoughts. Please pass them along to all kloormari.

"First, always question whatever you are told by outsiders. I'm not saying you should be cynical, but always look at the contrary perspectives. When an outsider wants you to do something, try to determine the motivations behind their request. Understand exactly what's in it for them.

"Second, take care of your precious world. Compared with other inhabited planets of a similar size, Kuw'baal is sparsely populated. You still have vast areas where no intelligent beings have ever visited. That is incredibly rare and precious. In the future, if you decide to welcome other species to your world, understand that they may want to exploit its resources. Doing so can be economically rewarding to them, and if you handle things wisely, the kloormari will benefit at least as much, but you must understand the costs. Planetary ecosystems are fragile, and the damage can have a cascading effect that takes hold so suddenly that nobody knows what's happening until it's too late. Don't let greed be the cause of the kloormari losing everything.

"Finally, and most important of all, love one another and love yourselves. I know that 'love' is a strange and ambiguous concept, but what I'm trying to say is this: Be true to yourselves and your species. Don't ever think that you are in any way inferior to others. In the future, outsiders may come along trying to convince you that you would be better off being more like them. Never believe that. If you do, you will be truly lost, and our visit will have marked the beginning of your end. Don't become so enamoured with another culture that you lose your own. Keep studying the ancient kloormari texts and keep writing new ones. Take what you have learned from our visit and make it part of *your* history. Be the authors of your future. I truly *love* each and every one of you. Thank you."

I thought it would be appropriate to stand up and clap. The other students joined me as we snapped our manipulators in applause. Then we filed to the front of the classroom and took turns shaking Sam's hand and thanking him.

For the rest of the morning, we hung around the classroom chatting with Sam and one another. In the afternoon, we pitched in to assist the crew as they prepared for departure. I hadn't been to any of the field research sites before, so I accompanied Lisa Thomas and Rashid Gulamali a few kilometers downstream from the village to retrieve a seismic, meteorological, and water-sampling station. It was pleasant to have a distraction from the impending departure.

By nightfall, all equipment had been stowed, and the *Pacifica Spirit* was ready for launch procedures to begin the next day. The captain and crew hosted the students on the observation deck. For the most part, we just talked and reminisced.

Bertie made sure that the humans were supplied with food and drink, and she served us fresh algel that she had personally harvested a short time before. "I'd do somethin' a little more special for all of ya, but yer dietary needs are kinda limited," she said. I could see Bertie's eyes getting a bit red and wet. I realized that if someone as hardboiled as Bertha Kolesnikov would feel emotional about leaving us, the entire crew must feel a great deal of love for us.

We talked until late in the night, and then we kloormari followed the lights back home.

***

At daybreak, the entire village made its way to the *Pacifica Spirit*. Even the infant, K'pai, was running around. K'pai ran to Pauly and reached up toward her. Just as she had done on the day that the crew first met the villagers, Pauly bent down and gently picked up and cradled K'pai.

Captain Staedtler addressed the crowd while the crew milled around in their uniforms. He expressed his gratitude toward the kloormari, how privileged he and his crew were to be welcomed, and so on. In other words, exactly the kind of thing that one would expect a captain to say.

While he was giving his address, I went over to Sam. "How are you feeling?" I asked in a hushed voice.

"I'm feeling a massive burden, Kelvoo. It's only just sinking in that our visit has changed your world forever. Even if the kloormari had no further contact with other species, you now know that there are worlds beyond your sky and unlimited opportunities to learn. That's going to change every kloormar, and I don't know whether we had the *right* to do that to you."

I assured Sam that giving us such a wonderful gift didn't require any *right* at all, though in the back of my mind, I did harbor some degree of worry.

"You know," Sam said, "even though there are going to be investigations and hearings on Terra about this mission, most of the crew are happy to be heading home to their families and friends. Don't get me wrong; they're all going to miss the kloormari very much, but homecomings after long missions are wonderful things for most people.

"As you know, it's a little different for me. I don't have anybody special waiting for me. I no longer feel like I have a place in Terran society, but I'll tell you this: I feel like I have a purpose and a home here. Here is also where I have the best friend I have ever known.

"Kelvoo, I am going to do everything in my power to return to Kuw'baal as soon as possible—assuming the kloormari will have me, of course!"

"Of course, we will," I replied.

"Promise me this, Kelvoo: if humans or other outsiders come and want favors from you or want to make you an amazing offer, please wait until I come back or at least until I can get word to you. I would love nothing better than to spend the rest of my life advocating for your people."

"That I promise you, my friend," I replied solemnly.

Captain Staedtler finished his speech to much applause. Then he turned and strode up the ramp into the vessel, looking very crisp and proper in his uniform. The rest of the crew started filing back into the vessel.

"It's time for me to go now," Sam said. We shook hands, and he tried to embrace me, rather awkwardly due to the differences in our anatomy, but I appreciated his sentiments.

When the hatch to the *Pacifica Spirit* closed, every kloormar backed away and waited outside the blast zone. We knew it would take about two to three hours for the crew to run through all of the necessary checks. I closed my eye and replayed the memories of being on the bridge or the observation deck while the crew brought their magnificent vessel to life, if only figuratively.

While we waited on the mineral plain, not a word was spoken, not even from little K'pai. Two hours and thirty-eight minutes from the time the hatch closed, the *Pacifica Spirit's* engines roared back to life. As the vessel rose, every villager waved to the crew.

The vessel rose perhaps five hundred meters into the air. It hovered, then turned on its axis toward the hills opposite the village. The vessel started moving horizontally toward the hills, then slowly banked and turned to follow the perimeter of the plain. Then the *Pacifica* disappeared behind the village where we could only hear the roar of its engines.

Suddenly, the vessel reappeared over the village rooftops, flying low and straight back toward us. The air crackled with sound, and we felt the powerful vibrations as the *Pacifica* shot over us. *A final farewell from the captain and crew,* I thought as the vessel arced up toward the sky world. With a final fiery blast, the *Pacifica Spirit* and my best friend, Sam, pierced the sky. Although I could no longer see the vessel, its roar continued from the sky and echoed off the surrounding hills for the next two minutes. As the sound faded away, an emptiness that I had never known before grew within me.

I surprised myself by speaking out loud.

"I miss you, Sam."

# PART 2: AWAKENING

# EIGHTEEN: BACK TO THE RHYTHM

After the humans departed, life in the village returned to a regular rhythm—just not quite the same rhythm as before first contact.

As always, the villagers would wake from meditation, consume some algel by the stream, tidy their homes or the village, possibly assist with building or repairing structures, have some algel in the evening, and meditate again. The difference was during the times in between.

The villagers neglected their studies of the ancient kloormari texts and the writing of new texts—a trend that had started after first contact but had become much more pronounced now that every villager had an Infotab. Some days it seemed as if each eye was metaphorically glued to a screen. Of course, this wasn't true for Kwazka, Ksoomu, K'raftan, Keeto, K'tatmal, Kleloma, K'aablart, Keesooni, Kroz, or me. As Sam's former students, we referred to ourselves collectively as "Sam's Team."

On our last full day with Sam, he had implored us to embrace the things that define us as kloormari and to avoid the urge to become more like humans or any other species. He warned that imitating others would result in us losing our identities, and subsequently, control over our own destiny. Sam's specific words that resonated with me and all the other members of Sam's Team were: "Don't become so enamoured with another culture that you lose your own. Keep studying the ancient kloormari texts and keep writing new ones. Take what you have learned from our visit and make it part of your history. Be the authors of your future."

We spread Sam's message throughout the village, and Kwazka made sure to pass word along to visitors from other communities. The message had little effect in our village. Trying to figure out the reason was puzzling to me. Perhaps Sam's final lesson had such an impact on our team because we had spent so much time with Sam, had grown to know him so well, and trusted him implicitly.

So, the rhythm of the village came to include kloormari standing, kneeling, and wandering about the village staring at their Infotabs. None of the villagers wandered far away since they wanted to stay within range of the InfoServers in the community structure and classroom.

Captain Staedtler had been kind enough to leave a few things behind in case we could use them. That included the classroom and the three other structures, along with the classroom InfoServer and display panels, the algel incubation vat, a hoverlift, miscellaneous gear, and the charging equipment to keep it all running.

Between the InfoServer in the community structure and the one in the classroom, an Infotab could be within range for relatively long distances out on the plain, so on a typical day, a few kloormari could be seen wandering aimlessly around the plain, gawking at their Infotabs where they were less likely to bump into another kloormari or trip over a rock or a child. It astonished me that a kloormar with a 360-degree horizontal field of vision could be so engrossed with a small portable display that walking into an object or another kloormar was even possible.

In addition to an Infotab, each kloormar possessed a belt and pouch, allowing them to carry their Infotab easily. Some kloormari had learned basic weaving from a human how-to vid and had fashioned "Infotab belts" from the leaves of k'k'mos plants. I supposed this was another example of kloormari innovation born of "necessity."

I didn't view the excessive use of Infotabs as being entirely detrimental. After all, for the most part, at least the kloormari were learning *something*. I was, however, distressed when I would see a kloormar viewing something of little intellectual value such as unsophisticated human "sitcoms" or "game shows" or inane entertainment using animated characters or puppets with insipid personas. *What possible value can this dross provide to our people?* I wondered.

It's not as though I didn't understand the appeal of human knowledge and culture. It was far more interesting to learn about human exploits than to read old accounts of when the rain started and stopped on a certain day or how many kobo plants were found in year X and area Y. Nevertheless, those of us on Sam's Team forced ourselves to read the ancient texts and then write out our interpretations and summaries.

So, the rhythm of the village included frequent admonitions from Sam's Team to our fellow villagers, pleading with them to take more interest in the history and heritage of our species. The kloormari, however, were free beings with no leaders to enforce any kind of behavior, so they continued to immerse themselves in human knowledge and entertainment.

Since the Infotabs had given the villagers the ability to learn the Terran language, some of them would practice Terran dialog with one another. For example:

"Good morning, Kaplaq."

"Good morning, K'matani. How are you this fair morning?"

"I am well. Do you like my new Infotab belt?"

"Yes, it is very interesting. I got a new cat today."

"What is a cat?"

To my ears, the villagers' attempts at speaking Terran were stilted and based on Terran things that most villagers had no knowledge of, such as cats.

After several weeks of fruitlessly pestering the villagers, Sam's Team changed tactics. We decided to focus on a subset of Sam's advice: "Take what you have learned from our visit and make it part of your history."

So, we started writing out the details of what we had learned in class and during our nine-day voyage on the *Pacifica Spirit*. We drew lessons from our knowledge and experiences and tried to create autobiographical stories that would be interesting and could provide future guidance for the kloormari. We even made a few vids.

During the humans' first-contact mission, Kroz had come to know the *Pacifica's* systems engineer, Audrey Fraser, due to their shared interest in software development. Kroz had an intense interest in computer technology, along with an abundant natural talent. When the humans left Kuw'baal, Audrey gave Kroz one of her personal computers as a gift.

Sam's Team created video versions of the stories that we wrote. It was simple enough to record vids using Infotabs, but it took Kroz's skills and the computer to transfer the vids to the InfoServer and make them available to the village. We were pleased that our vids were (to use a term from the Terran entertainment industry) "a hit!"

The altered rhythm of the village continued for 173 days after the *Pacifica Spirit's* departure until a small black vessel came from the sky and touched down next to the village.

# NINETEEN: THE INVITATION

The vessel landed on a small flat area next to the homes closest to the algel falls. An imposing human male stepped out of the spacecraft. He was tall but very thin for a human. His black hair gave way to grey sideburns and closely trimmed white facial hair. He was dressed in an ornate uniform. The man smiled. "Greetings from Terra and the Goodwill Initiative," he proclaimed. "Do any of you speak Terran?"

"Good morning. I am kloormar," a villager said.

"Hello, Terran, me is Karunia," another replied.

"Greeting you happy," a third piped up.

By this time, a member of Sam's Team had emerged. "Hello, sir. Welcome to Kuw'baal and our humble village. It is my pleasure to welcome you. May we be of assistance to you?"

"Kelvoo?" the visitor asked.

"No, my name is K'aablart."

"Your Terran is excellent, K'aablart, and I'm very pleased to meet you. I'm Captain Roger Smith. Please forgive me if I didn't pronounce your name correctly. I have come to deliver a message to Kelvoo. Do you know where I could find Kelvoo?"

By this time, I had joined the crowd, along with most of the village. "I am Kelvoo!" I shouted from the back of the gathering. The crowd parted and let me through.

"Captain Roger Smith," the visitor said, extending his hand in greeting. When I shook it, I felt a slight shudder pass through the captain's body. My hand paddles must have felt strange to him.

"Is there a place we can chat?" he asked.

"Do you want to talk in private?"

"No, Kelvoo, that won't be necessary. Honesty and transparency are the hallmarks of my visit to you. Bring as many of your friends as you wish."

I was excited as I led Captain Smith down the path to the community structure with the entire population of the village trailing behind. Along the way, several villagers tried to practice their Terran on Captain Smith. With their kloormari memory, they knew several Terran words but had not yet viewed vids showing how to string the words together into proper sentences. I admonished several villagers not to distract Captain Smith.

Once inside the community structure, Captain Smith told me that he had a proposal for the kloormari who had been Sam's students. I asked all the members of Sam's Team to join the captain and me at the front of the structure. I also asked elders Kahini and K'losk'oon to come up to the front in case their wisdom was needed.

"Thank you so much for your warm hospitality," Captain Smith said, addressing the gathering. He turned toward me and the other members of Sam's Team before continuing. "I bring warmest personal regards from Samuel Buchanan. Sam and I met when we attended the New Liberia University."

Our level of excitement jumped at that piece of news.

"Kelvoo, I hope that the other members of your group will forgive me for asking to speak with you specifically. I just feel as though I know you best because Sam talked so much about you, and I saw your excellent interview from the *Orion Provider*."

Many questions sprang to my mind. "How are Sam and Captain Kwami doing?" I asked. "How much trouble were they in with my interview leaking out? Has there been a formal inquiry?"

"Let me put your minds at ease," Captain Smith said. "Yes, the Terran First Contact Authority was gearing up for a full inquiry and were ready to press charges to the full extent. The Terran public, on the other hand, wouldn't hear of it. Kelvoo, your interview won the public over! You represented your planet and your species admirably. The people of Terra— and other planets, for that matter—were hungry for details. The captain and crew of the *Pacifica Spirit* have been pleased to share stories of their mission, and they're all celebrities—especially Sam."

"Captain Smith," I said, "I am very pleased with the outcome that you are reporting. Is the sole purpose of your visit today to bring us this news, or is there more?"

"I already like you, Kelvoo. Direct and to the point!" Captain Smith declared. "Yes, there certainly is more to my visit. I'd like to tell you about the Goodwill Initiative—GI for short, a Terran charitable organization. Our purpose is to elevate the reputation of humanity by providing aid and assistance to beings on planets that aren't members of the Planetary Alliance. I am representing the 'GI' on a new mission."

"Is the Goodwill Initiative providing assistance purely in the interest of helping others, or are there other motivations?"

"Ah, I see that you must be acquainted with human politics! With any charitable endeavors there are always secondary motives! The honest truth is that we want to be on good terms with the citizens of these planets. At some point in the future, if we decide it would be mutually advantageous for them to join the Alliance, good relations could certainly smooth that arduous process."

"Is that why the Terran First Contact Authority sent the *Pacifica Spirit* to us?" I asked. "Was it to build a relationship with the kloormari in the interest of our possible membership in the Alliance?"

"Not at all. The *Pacifica* came here on a science mission of exploration. My friend Sam was on the crew in case intelligent life was found. Could the kloormari end up eventually being in the Planetary Alliance? Sure, but honestly, membership is a long way off. The Goodwill Initiative is an entirely separate project that only deals with species that we've already had plenty of contact with."

Kroz, who had been busy using an Infotab, spoke up. "I've searched the InfoServer and can find no mention of a 'Goodwill Initiative' that matches what you have described, Captain."

"I'm so glad to know that you folks are interested in performing due diligence," Captain Smith said. "After all, here I am, a complete stranger to you, landing on your planet and asking for a favor, though I haven't actually told you yet what that favor is!

"The reason you can find no mention of our organization is that the data on your InfoServer is at least a year old. Your InfoServer only contains a snapshot of human knowledge, most likely taken just prior to the *Pacifica's* departure from Terra. The GI is a brand-new initiative that wasn't made public until ten months ago."

"Forgive us if we seem to be skeptical, Captain Smith," I said, "but Sam warned us very strongly about trusting anyone who comes to us offering or requesting favors."

"Look," Smith replied, "Sam and I didn't know each other really well in university, but we reconnected months ago when he returned to Terra. I can tell you that he cares deeply for each and every one of you. His kindness is why I admire him so much.

"Of course, you're wondering about the mission that I'm on and exactly what I'm asking for, but rather than hearing that from me, I'd like you to hear directly from someone that you're a bit more familiar with. With your permission, I'd like to link my Infotab's output to your display panel."

"Permission granted," Kroz replied.

Captain Smith made the connection, and a familiar, smiling face appeared on the screen: Sam Buchanan.

"To my wonderful kloormari friends, I am pleased to send you this recorded message at the request of my good friend, Roger Smith. First, I miss each and every one of you, and I look forward to returning and seeing all of you again. I have a great deal of business to deal with here on Terra, so it could be another year before I can get back to Kuw'baal. In the meantime, Captain Smith has a very interesting mission that I think could provide a wonderful opportunity to learn and give you invaluable experience dealing with other cultures.

"By the time you see this, Captain Smith—Roger—will be about to start a six-month mission delivering supplies and services to people in need on a variety of disadvantaged planets. Roger is looking for honest, reliable crew to assist on the mission. I immediately thought about my ten students on Kuw'baal. I see this mission as a way to enhance your knowledge and experience to better equip you for further dealings with humans and other species.

"Whether or not you decide to join Roger on the Goodwill Initiative is entirely up to you. All I can say is that Roger Smith is my friend, and I trust him.

"I'm looking forward to reuniting with all of you as soon as possible, and I hope that everything is going well for you. Goodbye . . . for now!"

Seeing Sam's image and hearing his voice reminded me of the void that his departure had left in me, but I also felt something else.

"Captain," I said, "Sam seemed a little bit different in the recording . . . perhaps a little bit awkward in his presentation."

"Yes," Captain Smith said. "Sam wasn't quite his usual self. He was smiling when he made the recording, but he misses all of you. He wanted to present a cheerful façade for your benefit."

"You know, it isn't difficult to take a vid of a human and manipulate it to make it appear that the person is speaking words that were never said," Kroz pointed out.

"Again, I admire your skepticism," Captain Smith said, "so perhaps I should ask *you* a question: How do you suppose I got here less than six months after the *Pacifica's* departure? Without knowing the coordinates of the nearest jump point, it would have been a years-long voyage! To answer my own question, Sam got the coordinates for me, with the full permission of the TFCA."

*Well, that confirms that he's legitimate*, I thought.

During Captain Smith's proposal and our questions, the villagers in the community structure had been chattering amongst themselves. Having a limited understanding of Terran, they were able to pick out some of the words, and a great deal of speculation was passing back and forth. Kwazka had also been conversing with the other elders, Kahini and K'losk'oon, translating for them.

"Is it just Sam's students that you want?" Kwazka asked. "They are of great value to our community. Perhaps other members of the community can assist you."

"I'm afraid not. We need crew members who can communicate with our existing crew and with the beings that we will visit, many of whom speak Terran. Experience with space travel is another crucial skill. In terms of the value of Sam's students to your community, we fully recognize their value. That's why I'm delighted to say that we're willing to pay your community ten billion units of SimCash for their services!

"Paying crew members for missions of mercy is not a typical practice, but in this case, the TFCA is willing to fund the payment. They think it will provide you with experience in commerce, but most of all, you can think about it as financial aid to give the kloormari resources for future contact with humans and other species. No doubt, merchant vessels will be stopping by with all manner of goods—after Sam's return, of course.

"Ten billion can purchase several transport vehicles, letting you travel to dozens of other villages in under an hour. When your citizens become more familiar with Terran speech and knowledge, think about the opportunities to send them out to educate kloormari in other villages. Perhaps you can use the funds to buy machinery to convert minerals into useful materials, such as construction supplies for better homes or a larger community structure. You might even be able to buy a spacecraft and take trips to other worlds. The opportunities are endless!"

"Your proposal has much merit," Kwazka said, "but we must confer before we can give you a decision."

"Of course," Captain Smith replied. "The only problem is this: I have a ship and crew in orbit right now. My vessel is loaded with medication that is urgently required to cure a disease that has run rampant on the first planet on our itinerary. I must have your decision within twenty-four hours, or I'll need to make do without you. I will return tomorrow at the same time for your decision. If you would like to be part of this exciting mission, we will need to leave immediately.

"When I return, I will do so in a cargo shuttle with room for ten passengers plus one large cargo container. You must bring all of the supplies that you'll need for the trip." He provided us with the dimensions of the space available for cargo.

"I hope you'll be able to assist our important mission, and I know it would make Sam so happy. I look forward to your response."

The captain rose and turned toward the exit. We followed him back to his vessel, thanked him, and many of us shook his hand. He smiled and waved from the cockpit of his small spacecraft. We stepped back as he started his engines. At about twenty meters above the village, he fired his main engines and roared away through the sky.

# TWENTY: DELIBERATION

The three elders and Sam's Team discussed Captain Smith's proposal well into the night—another reason we were grateful for the outdoor lighting left by the *Pacifica*.

Out of our group, Kleloma was the most enthusiastic and took the lead in pushing for our participation. My unintended interview on the *Orion Provider* made me the most hesitant. Each time I raised a concern, Kleloma jumped in and provided convincing counterpoints. We ended up being satisfied that the mission was legitimate, but we had conditions that would have to be met.

First, we would need food to sustain us physically. We would have to take the incubation vat, loaded up with algel.

Second, to sustain ourselves intellectually, we would require one of our InfoServers, assuming that Smith's vessel didn't have an InfoServer that we could use. Based on the dimensions supplied by Captain Smith, we calculated that we would have just enough room for the vat, the InfoServer, and one basket of belongings per kloormar.

Third, we would need access to several standard DL-32 power outlets on the vessel since we wouldn't be able to use any of our photoelectric panels to keep our equipment charged.

Finally, we would require Captain Smith to sign a legal contract. Just as Kroz had decided to specialize in systems development during our previous education, K'tatmal had taken a great deal of interest in governance and law. K'tatmal volunteered to draw up a contract based on Terran common law and Planetary Alliance regulations.

We also decided that nine of us would serve on the mission. "I'm nearing the end of my lifespan, and I wouldn't want to disrupt the mission by expiring before it's over," Kwazka said. "Furthermore, one member of Sam's Team must remain here to try to maintain and promote the practice of studying the ancient texts and creating new ones. As much as I would like to join you, I can best serve this community by staying here."

Kwazka's point about keeping up our practices certainly had merit. Kwazka was insistent about staying behind, so we agreed that Captain Smith could have nine of us. If that wasn't good enough, we would refuse his offer.

Late in the night, after our deliberations were completed, Sam's Team, with the exception of K'tatmal, who stayed behind to draft a legal contract, made its way across the plain via the lit path to the structure that housed the hoverlift and incubation vat.

We knew that time would be short when Captain Smith returned, so we moved the vat and the classroom's InfoServer to an area adjacent to his previous landing spot. We took a basket to store personal equipment, but the only item placed there was Kroz's computer. Everything else, our Infotabs, passports and SimCash cards, all fit into our Infotab belts.

Captain Smith arrived thirty-two minutes ahead of schedule. He seemed to have some minor difficulty getting the cargo shuttle positioned properly over the landing site. When the rear starboard landing strut gently touched the ground, he cut power immediately, causing the rest of the vessel to plop down rather roughly.

Captain Smith apologized for his early arrival, explaining that he was under great pressure to get underway. He smiled when Kleloma said we were willing to assist, but his smile diminished a bit when I added that we had conditions.

We walked briskly to the community structure and got straight to business, describing the equipment that we needed. The captain agreed and assured us that the necessary power outlets were available throughout his vessel.

Next, K'tatmal asked Captain Smith to accept a document transfer to his Infotab. Smith glanced at the contract and chuckled. "Well, well, we have a great legal mind in our midst! We could go to the farthest reaches of the galaxy, and there'd be a lawyer hiding behind an asteroid somewhere!"

"I have kept the contract simple," K'tatmal said, "only fifty-three pages."

Despite the time constraint that he was under, Captain Smith took the time to review every paragraph. The contract codified our equipment requirements and other needs. It also included a clause stating that we could refuse to continue on the mission at any time, and in that event, would be returned promptly to Kuw'baal. Most of the content was what K'tatmal called "boilerplate" text—standard clauses concerning working conditions, sentient being rights, labor standards, and so on. Page forty-one listed the kloormari personnel. "There are only nine of you listed here, but Sam had ten students," Captain Smith said.

Kwazka explained the reasons for not joining the mission. The captain didn't look pleased, but he continued reading to the end.

"Are you sure you want to join our mission?" he asked.

"Yes, sir, absolutely!" Kleloma said.

"Alright then. Between the legalese and you shorting me a crew member, I would normally thank you for listening and be on my way, but you have me at a disadvantage. A beggar can't be a chooser, and I need your help. Sam told me that I can trust you, and that's good enough for me."

He touched the biometrics icon at the bottom of the contract and transferred the signed document to K'tatmal's Infotab. K'tatmal pressed a hand to the screen, adding a biometric signature on behalf of the kloormari. Then K'tatmal transferred a chain-verified copy back to the captain and then to the community structure's InfoServer as a legally binding record.

During our discussion with the captain, fifty-one villagers had been using baskets to shuttle fresh algel from the streambank and the algel falls into the incubation vat, ensuring that our supply was fresh and ready to grow.

We stowed our equipment in the cargo shuttle within twenty minutes. While loading, I noticed that the outside of the hull was covered with a thin, uneven layer of paint, letting the underlying silver-grey color show through in patches. The pilot's chair also looked well worn and out of place. So did the navigation console, appearing as though it had been taken out of a different vessel and shoehorned into place. There were no passenger seats, just a bench along each side in front of the cargo section and behind the cockpit.

"Are you certain this vessel is in good repair?" I asked.

"She may look a little rough around the edges, but her bones are good. Besides, we're going to trade her in after a couple of stops on this trip," Captain Smith said. "Trust me, this is going to be fun!"

There was no time for farewells, which was just as well since ceremony is not exactly ingrained in kloormari society. We took our places along the benches and buckled in, using the frayed restraints.

There was no safety checklist; the captain just performed a perfunctory engine-start sequence. It seemed to take a couple of tries before the six engines came to life, one of them sputtering as it spun up. The vessel's nose lifted off first due to the weight of our food supply in the rear. The captain adjusted the vessel's trim accordingly. Once he achieved a stable hover, he slammed the manual thrust levers forward. We slid on the benches as the shuttle accelerated forward and up. Within fifteen seconds, we had disappeared into Kuw'baal's ever-present clouds.

Shortly after the sky outside was black, we felt a shift to zero gravity, but we were held in place by the shuttle's continued acceleration until we approached the main vessel. There were no windows or exterior view monitors in our section of the shuttle, but we could see straight ahead through the cockpit windows over Captain Smith's shoulder.

The mission's main vessel came into view. The ship had a configuration that was different from any I had seen in my previous studies. The most striking features were four gigantic engines mounted to a huge cluster of fuel tanks. The part of the vessel that the crew would use only accounted for about 20 percent of the vessel's overall length and perhaps 5 percent of the total volume. Like the shuttle, the ship seemed to be cobbled together. The engines and fuel tanks looked as though they could have come from a behemoth like the *Orion Provider*, while the rest of the vessel was unidentifiable.

As the shuttle slowed to approach speed, Captain Smith turned around to face us. "Welcome to *Jezebel's Fury*—fastest ship in the scrapyard!" he said, laughing.

The *Jezebel's Fury* didn't have typical landing bay doors, nor did it have a separate bay where the graviton field could be switched off. Instead, a hatch opened on the upper surface of the vessel, behind the bridge. The shuttle hovered above the open hatch and slowly lowered itself. "Here's where it gets interesting!" Captain Smith shouted. "When the graviton field grabs us, I'm going to have a fraction of a second to fire the landing thrusters. Too late or not enough, and we'll slam into the deck. Too much thrust, and we'll bounce back up and hopefully don't hit the hangar ceiling. Here goes . . ."

The graviton field did indeed "grab" the shuttle with jarring suddenness as the landing thrusters roared. The shuttle delicately touched down on the deck, to everyone's relief. "Nailed it!" Captain Smith proclaimed. "Okay, everybody out! I need to introduce you to the crew."

"Excuse me, sir," K'aablart said. "It's important that we unload the incubation vat and power it up to ensure that we have our food supply for the mission. Could we please meet the crew after that?"

"Sure, why not," Captain Smith replied. "Just get it done quickly. Chop! Chop! Grab that hoverlift over there," he said, motioning to a corner of the bay.

As we slid the vat out of the shuttle's rear door, I saw a variety of vessels in the hangar in varying states of repair. One was just a collection of parts—being scavenged, no doubt, to maintain the other vessels. When the vat was on the lift, Captain Smith led us to a cargo elevator, and we descended two levels to a large open room with a high ceiling. "Welcome to your quarters," he announced.

We moved the incubation vat to a corner that had a DL-32 power outlet. We plugged it in, confirmed that the settings were correct, and powered it up. When the internal lights glowed to life, we were relieved that our food supply appeared to be taken care of.

Our quarters were equipped with ten metal-frame beds with a thin mattress, one sheet, and one pillow each. Clearly, Captain Smith didn't know that we do not lie down to rest. There was also a washroom with a sink and a waste-disposal unit. Since our bodies do not produce waste, the disposal unit was of no use, but we were glad for the water supply, which would be needed to top up the incubation vat from time to time.

From the hangar to our quarters, the vessel was dirty. Dust and grime had collected in the corners, and previous spills had obviously been left to evaporate. We saw three waste receptacles, one of which was full and two of which were overflowing.

"Alright, that'll do!" Captain Smith said after the incubation vat was operating. "Follow me to meet your crewmates," he added, leading us down a long passage.

From the moment we started loading the shuttle to the time when we were shown our quarters, a nagging doubt had been growing in my mind regarding whether we had made the right decision. When I saw the crew, all doubts were gone. In that moment, I knew for certain that we had made a profoundly bad choice.

# TWENTY-ONE: MEET AND GREET

As Sam's Team, led by Captain Smith, reached the end of a long corridor in the belly of the *Jezebel's Fury*, we could hear the din of the crew talking, laughing, and shouting behind a heavy set of metal doors.

The captain flung the doors open. His crew was packed into a darkened room, perhaps ten meters square. At the far side of the room was a bar with a substantial variety of bottled liquids behind it. A couple of couches were on the left and right side, but for the most part, the crew was standing next to tall, round tables where they rested their mugs and glasses when they weren't consuming the contents. Layers of misty vapor hung oppressively throughout the room and spilled out into the passage. The source of the fog was a glass cylinder with bubbling liquid in the bottom and tubes coming from its top. Crew members were inhaling the vapor through the tubes. The entire tableau was reminiscent of a typical "dive bar," as depicted in old Terran vids.

In contrast to the well-groomed captain, the crew looked disheveled. They wore their hair in a variety of lengths but with a consistent level of oiliness. The exceptions were two bald men. The stubble on their scalps indicated they were intentionally shaved. The crew's clothing was grubby, frayed, and torn. Some of the crew members had piercings with ornamental metal inserted through their earlobes, nostrils, chins, and eyebrows. Many had subcutaneous ink depicting skulls, daggers, blasters, snakes, Mangorian death cats, and other objects that humans fear. Their dermal art also included scantily clad or unclad human females, which I assumed were not considered frightening.

A wide variety of odors oozed from the heavy atmosphere, none of which were pleasant to our kloormari senses.

I was puzzled by the fact that I did not see any females in the room.

When the doors had opened, four crew members noticed our group. They stopped talking and gawked at us. I supposed they had never seen beings who looked anything like a kloormar. After a moment, the four snapped out of their astonished state, nodded, and raised their mugs, saying "Cap'n Skully." Captain Smith nodded back. The rest of the crew members were shouting or laughing raucously, not noticing us.

Just inside the door, a giant gong hung from an ornate stand with a mallet dangling from a hook. The captain grabbed the mallet and beat the gong three times. The crew fell silent immediately and faced the doors. They fell back as

Captain Smith led us in. "Lads, I return to you bearing gifts! Nine gifts to be precise. Fellas, meet your new crewmates!" I noticed that his voice had a completely different and gruffer tone in the presence of his crew. I also noticed that the remaining crew members had the same astonished expression as the first four.

"Before we commence with the introductions, I call upon Reverend Hol to deliver the blessing."

A short, stocky man with a red yarmulke and a long, even redder beard stepped forward. "Oh, great creator," he pronounced, "bless us, your children, as we welcome newcomers into our presence. Grant us prosperity, preserve us, and endow us with the strength to smite our foes. In the name of the holy duality of Yahweh-Allah, his son Yeshua, and his prophet Mohammad. Aye!"

"Aye!" the crew replied.

"I expect all of you to welcome your new crewmates," Captain Smith said. "Remember, they're here to share the workload and make your lives easier. Now, I'm going to have to work on telling these fellas apart, so I'm going to let each of them step forward and give their names."

Each of us in turn stepped forward and spoke our name. Then Captain Smith invited his crew members to step forward and introduce themselves. When they did, they didn't extend a hand toward us, but they gave a quick nod, which seemed to be the custom on the ship. The crew had names that didn't seem to fit with a typical human pattern, including names like "Bazz," "Spaggy," "Tank," "Torm," "Wanky," "Mec," "Snowy," and "Ebo." I knew that the crew included a religious leader named "Hol," and crew members had called the captain "Captain Skully."

Some of the crew didn't come forward to meet us. Captain Smith pointed to them and told us their names. "You may have noticed that some of the crew aren't exactly inclined to greet you with open arms. Don't pay them any heed. They'll come around once they see how hard you're going to work here."

The crew member known as "Snowy" caught my eye. He looked like a Terran male, but his skin had a pinkish-white hue, his hair was yellowish-white, and his irises were pale blue. I approached him and asked what species he was.

"Species?" he shouted, grasping my eyestalk in his fist. "I'm a bloody human, obviously!"

"Forgive me," I pleaded. "I have never seen a human with your skin, hair, or eye coloration."

"I'm a white man, you moron! Why don't you ask Ebo here what species he is?" Snowy motioned toward an approaching crewmate. Ebo's skin was dark brown, bordering on black. His eyes were also brown, and his hair was remarkable. It was jet black and had such tight curls that it looked like thick fuzz.

I was about to take Snowy's advice when I realized he was probably being sarcastic and daring me to make a serious social gaffe.

"You must be a black man," I said to Ebo.

"Well, look what we've got here," Ebo said. "A freaking genius!"

"I hope you'll excuse my lack of experience interacting socially with humans. I had thought that black and white humans had become very rare on Terra."

Ebo pinned me against the side of a table while Snowy put his face within five centimeters of my eye. "Don't you ever let me hear you use that word again!" Snowy hissed. "Ever!"

"What word are you referring to?"

"The effing 'T' word, obviously! That planet is called *Earth*. We don't speak its fake, politically correct name. It's Earth, and it always has been!"

"You'd better be effing careful when you talk about Earth," Ebo warned. "Our ancestors were exiled from that pit of elitist vipers three generations ago! We're from the Outlier colonies and goddamn proud of it!"

A wave of terror washed over me. The Outlier colonies! The place of banishment for the worst and most incorrigible humans!

"With the exception of old Skully," Ebo continued, "this entire human crew is from the colonies. Snowy and me, we come from an Outlier planet called Perdition. Whities like Snowy live on one continent, and blackies like me live on another. We work together here because there's a mutual benefit, but on Perdition, we keep apart to keep our races pure. That's our sacred heritage, and that's why the effing Earthers hate us!"

"So," Snowy said, leaning in close again, "what are you going to call the human home world?"

"Earth, of course," I stated emphatically, "given the delicacy of the matter!"

Ebo and Snowy scowled at me, their faces close enough for me to experience their foul breath. Finally, they turned and faced one another and then burst into raucous gales of laughter.

"We're just giving you a hard time!" Ebo said. "Welcome to *Jezebel's Fury*, you freaking weirdo!"

"Yeah, welcome you crazy-eyed goofball!" Snowy said. "But seriously, don't go using the 'T' word on this ship. Just keep your head down, don't say too much, and you might just survive this mission!"

By the time our interaction was over, Captain Smith ("Skully") was finished with the introductions, and the din of conversation had resumed. Captain Smith slammed a large metal mug on a table three times to regain the crew's attention.

"Let's give our new friends a proper *Jezebel's Fury* welcome! What do you say, lads?"

With that, the captain slapped out a drumming rhythm on the tabletop. The crew joined in and then accompanied the beat with a rousing song.

We're the boys of *Jezebel's Fury*.
We're rotten, lowlife scum!
We're dirty sons of dirty whores.
Riled up and full of rum!

Full of rum, we're full of rum!
Hide your women, here we come!
Join with us, we'll have some fun,
if you won't, you'd better run!

We're the boys of *Jezebel's Fury*.
We'll kill you while we smile.
We'll wear your guts like garters,
full of sass and style!

Full of style, we're full of style!
Add a dead man to our pile.
Oh yes, we're sick, oh yes, we're vile!
That's what makes our lives worthwhile!

We're the boys of *Jezebel's Fury*.
We're misfits one and all.
Join our great adventure.
Come on and heed our call.

Heed our call, come heed our call!
If you want to fight and brawl,
full of grog and full of gall,
join with us, we'll have a ball!

We're the boys of *Jezebel's Fury*!
Aye!

Upon concluding their song, the crew stared at my kloormari companions and me. We were at a complete loss for words. After a moment of tension, I shouted "Aye!" out of desperation and then stood as tall as possible and snapped my manipulators in applause. The other kloormari followed suit, and the crew howled with laughter.

When the noise became too much for clear communication, Captain Smith motioned for us to follow him to an opening in the wall beside the bar. He picked up a mug of "grog" that had been poured for him as he passed the bar. The opening led to an alcove with a long table down the center. The floor was raised a couple of steps above the barroom floor. A half-height wall separated the alcove from the rest of the barroom. There we could communicate, though we still had to raise our voices considerably.

"Welcome to the captain's table," Smith said. He sat in an ornate old-style brass-studded wingback chair at the head of the table and invited us to join him. "Have a seat or a kneel or stand or whatever it is that you lads do. So, what do you think so far? Any questions?"

"Captain," I said, "I've noticed that you've called us 'fellas' or 'lads.' Did you know that we are not males?"

"I know that you're not technically males or females, but I suggest you just go with fellas, lads, boys, men, whatever, because you'll want the crew to accept you."

"Does that have something to do with the fact that there are no females here?" I inquired.

"Oh, there are females on board, lad. Reverend Hol has his wife onboard. Murph has two young daughters. In addition, we have three concs."

"Concs?" I asked.

"You know, concubines. Lovely ladies trained in how to keep a crew content."

"Are they onboard willingly?"

"Of course, they are! My lads may be a bit rough, but we're not savages! These fine females are trained in the erotic arts and look forward to serving a grateful crew."

"And what about Hol's wife and Murph's daughters? What are their positions in the crew?"

"Positions?" the captain asked. "Preferably on their hands and knees scrubbing a deck! Maybe bent over a sink of dishes! Perhaps stirring a pot of grub in the galley!" He let out a laugh. "You lads need to understand; these Outliers have clung to a centuries-old mindset. Females don't work as regular crew. They cook and clean and raise babies. They don't get paid, and they don't get an education. Personally, I don't understand their views, but who am I to interfere in Outlier culture?"

Like the captain, I couldn't understand the crew's perspective given the level of talent that I had seen from Lynda, Audrey, Li, Lisa, Pauly, Yuki, Rani, and of course, Bertie and all of the other female crew members on the *Pacifica*.

"My point," Captain Smith said, "is that, right or wrong, you're going to need some respect from these rogues, so you don't want them thinking you're a bunch of ladies! Any other questions?"

"I have some concerns," said K'tatmal, our legal specialist.

"Fire away!"

"Well, Captain, based on some of the things that I've seen on this ship and in the shuttle, I'm concerned that your mission might fall short of some safety standards and protocols. Furthermore, the song that the crew sang and some of the conversation makes me concerned that you and the crew might engage in illegal activities."

"What is your name, son?" Captain Smith asked.

"K'tatmal."

The captain stood. "Come with me, 'Katmul.'"

Captain Smith and K'tatmal stood behind the half-height wall facing the intoxicated crowd. The captain banged his empty mug on the top of the wall. The crew fell silent and faced him and K'tatmal.

"I think it's very important for all you lads to know that my dear friend 'Katmul' here has a few concerns," the captain said in a grave and serious voice. "*Katmul* is concerned that we might not be following all of the safety protocols, and we might be doing things that are . . . illegal!"

The crew was silent and serious. Slowly, Captain Smith turned his head to look directly at K'tatmal. The captain's grim expression gradually changed as the corners of his mouth turned up. Then he slapped K'tatmal on the shoulder and laughed explosively. The rest of the crew instantly burst into roars of laughter.

The captain escorted K'tatmal back to the table. "I have a few questions of my own," he said. "Tell me about yourselves. Let's start with you," he said, pointing to Ksoomu. Ksoomu proceeded to tell the captain about being hatched in the village where the rest of us came from, studying the old kloormari texts, getting a house, helping build structures, working around the village, and so on. Then Ksoomu described the arrival of the lander, the arrival of the *Pacifica*, and all of the other notable parts of our experience up to the moment of Captain Roger Smith's arrival.

"Alright, let's hear from you," the captain said to K'raftan. K'raftan started into a story that was almost identical to Ksoomu's. After the first thirty seconds, I could see Captain Smith's eyes glazing over, and I suspected he was no longer listening.

When K'raftan finished, the captain addressed the group. "Are all your stories going to be pretty much the same?"

"Yes," I replied. "We all come from the same village, we followed the same daily routine, and we were all students of Samuel Buchanan."

"I have something different!" Kleloma announced enthusiastically. "Fifty-seven days prior to your arrival, I slipped on some algel next to the falls near our village. When I rolled downhill, my second clasper limb on one side fell between two boulders and was torn off!" Kleloma extended and waved a tiny partly regrown limb.

"So, you lads can regrow missing parts?"

"Oh, yes, Captain! Missing or damaged parts can regrow."

155

"Yes, but losing a limb is extremely painful," I added. "If we lose multiple limbs or have extensive injuries, the pain and shock can be fatal."

"Well, isn't that something," Captain Smith said. I wasn't sure whether he was making a statement or asking a question.

After a few moments of silence, he looked up at us. "Well, don't you want to know anything about me?"

"Yes, I'm sure we would," Kleloma said.

Captain Smith launched into his life story. We learned of his upbringing and how he'd excelled as a student, all of the places his family traveled to, all of the interesting people he'd met, and his entry into the Commercial Spacefarer's Academy, graduating top of his class. As he spoke, I realized the captain had an extremely high opinion of himself.

He continued to speak of rising through the ranks of the merchant fleet of "Earth." His story became far less detailed when he talked of his brief stint as captain of a bulk freighter. "I wanted to do things my own way," he said, "but the 'powers that be' felt threatened by my superior methods. That's when I decided to go where my talents would be appreciated. So, here I am leading a motley assortment of ne'er-do-wells and scrimshankers on many an exciting adventure!"

I realized that flattery might be useful in my dealings with Captain Smith.

"It's late," he said finally, "and I'm going to call an end to the celebration. We always end our festivities with a hymn. The hymn is a sacred song about being exiled to the Outlier colonies and yearning to return to Mother Earth. Ensure you stay quiet during the hymn and *do not* applaud afterward. The crew will take offense to that. Okay, let's all stand by the wall."

We moved from the table and lined up along the half-wall on each side of the captain. He turned to me. "Kelvoo, right?"

"Yes, Captain," I replied, somewhat glad that he had learned how to recognize me.

"You ever seen a grown man cry, Kelvoo?"

"Yes, I have."

"Oh, well, you'll probably see a few more wet eyes when the hymn is sung."

He got the crew's attention again. "It's late, lads, and we've a long way to travel tomorrow. Let's call it a night and get some rest. Would you do the honors, Spaggy?"

The crew member, Spaggy, reached behind the bar and pulled out a well-used violin. He played a few slow, sad, mournful bars, and the crew sang a heartfelt lament:

Home on the Yangtze, great river I treasure,
long may your course twist and turn.
Peace and contentment and wealth beyond measure.
To your broad shores I'll return.

Boating and fishing and swimming and staying
carefree in warm summer sun.
Pandas and lions and antelope playing.
Blue whales on their downstream run.

Yangtze oh Yangtze, they sent us away
far from your ice floes so grand.
Ripped from your warm embrace,
flung away into space,
off to a sad, distant land.

Home on the Yangtze, the girls are so pretty,
willing to please every day.
Doing as they're told, whether young or old,
I'll be back with them someday.

Basking in sunshine, drinking your waters,
I'll be the picture of health.
Panning your gold or picking your diamonds,
endlessly living in wealth.

Yangtze oh Yangtze, they sent us away,
far from your ice floes so grand.
Ripped from your warm embrace,
flung away into space,
off to a sad, distant land.

Home on the Yangtze, I'm coming back to thee
brimming with vengeance and wrath.
I'm going to smite those that took you away from me,
striking them down in my path.

Some fine day, we'll attack; I'll get my Yangtze back,
with God's grace vanquish the foe.
Rivers of blood, shall form a great flood,
blending with your glorious flow.

Yes, rivers of blood, shall form a great flood,
blending with your glorious flow.

As Captain Smith had predicted, there were many moist eyes in the crowd. Some of the lyrics made no sense to me. Others I found to be disturbing.

As the crew dispersed into the passageway, I turned to Captain Smith. "Captain, my colleagues and I must converse about many things, and then we *must* meet with you."

"Kelvoo, you must understand that I am a very busy man with many responsibilities. Our mission is starting, and I don't have the time for discourse with all of you. I like you, Kelvoo, and I think we share a similar intellect. I would like you to speak for your kloormari companions and be their representative. With that in mind, let's you and me meet in my cabin, shall we say at 09:00 tomorrow?"

"Thank you, sir. I will be there."

He escorted us back to our "quarters" where we would engage in much-needed discussions, and hopefully, a modicum of rest.

# TWENTY-TWO: IT IS WHAT IT IS

In the large space that was to serve as our quarters, Sam's Team had important matters to discuss.

"Would it be fair to say that this 'Goodwill Initiative' mission seems to be differing from our expectations?" I asked.

We all concurred that it was. We also agreed that the mission was unsafe in terms of the vessel, the equipment, and the human crew members.

"Fortunately, I included an important clause in the contract that the captain signed," said our legal expert, K'tatmal. He proceeded to read us Section 3.1 of the agreement:

> At any time during the Mission, as defined in Section 2 of the Agreement, the kloormari members of the Mission (the "Kloormari Members") may decide, by a majority vote of the active Kloormari Members, to cancel their further participation in the Mission. Upon verbal or written delivery of said cancellation to the Captain or the most senior officer of the Vessel, any further obligations on the part of the Kloormari Members to serve the Mission shall be rendered null and void and the Kloormari Members shall be safely returned immediately to their original place of departure on their home planet of Kuw'baal.

"I put forward a motion to invoke section 3.1 of the agreement to cancel our participation in the mission and to inform the captain of our cancellation," K'tatmal said. "All those in favour say, 'Aye.'"

We clearly said, "Aye," with the exception of Kleloma, whose posture indicated dejection.

"Do you disagree, Kleloma?" I asked.

"No," Kleloma replied quietly. "I also vote 'aye,' but I do so with the belief that I'm responsible for getting us into this situation. I was the most enthusiastic about this mission, and I trusted Captain Smith or Captain Skully or whatever his name is. I'm feeling a burden that I believe humans refer to as 'guilt.'"

I assured Kleloma that we were all willing participants. I pointed out that I had the same feelings when I realized the consequences of the interview that I had unknowingly given to Kaley Hart on the *Orion Provider*. I also reminded Kleloma that Sam and Captain Staedtler had absolved me of blame due to my lack of relevant knowledge. I told Kleloma that, likewise, feelings of guilt were neither appropriate nor necessary.

I told the group that I would notify the captain of our decision when I had my scheduled meeting with him at 09:00.

"I'm concerned about the first stop on our mission," Keesooni said. "If we assume that the captain was truthful, we're currently on our way to deliver life-saving medication to a planet to save its inhabitants. I would be reluctant to delay such an important mission if lives of sentient beings would be lost. Of course, we have no way of knowing the truth."

We discussed Keesooni's concerns and agreed that I would ask the captain for proof of the purpose of the first stop. If he could provide it, we would assist with the delivery, and then we would require our immediate return to Kuw'baal.

With business done for the day, we assumed our positions for meditation. As I slipped into my altered mental state, I wondered why Sam had made the recorded message and given the jump coordinates to Captain Smith. Perhaps Smith had tricked Sam, as he had deceived us. Or maybe the unthinkable had occurred, and Sam had been corrupted! Maybe Sam had been working to exploit us all along! I dismissed such thoughts as paranoia and drifted into an unsettled but somewhat restful meditative state.

At regular intervals, my subconscious would open my eyelid slightly to view a display panel mounted high on the wall, so that I could check the time. At 08:35, I returned myself to wakefulness, then scooped my breakfast from the algel vat and consumed it. At 08:55, I walked down the long passageway, wondering where I would find Captain Smith.

I saw a female human sweeping the floor with an old-style manually operated broom. She was dressed in a floor-length frock with long sleeves and a collar that looked tight around her neck. Her hair was covered by a kerchief. When I said, "Hello," the woman looked up and let out a screech of alarm. Then she slapped a hand over her mouth. "Forgive me, sir, you startled me. You must be one of the new crew members that I've heard about." She cast her eyes downward.

"Please forgive *me*," I said. "I didn't mean to startle you. My name is Kelvoo."

"My name is Mary. I belong to Reverend Hol," the woman replied, shaking slightly and continuing to look at the floor.

"I am sorry if my appearance disturbs you. If you wouldn't mind looking at me, it may help you to become accustomed to the way I look."

"Forgive me, sir, but in these parts, it is considered unseemly for a lady to look directly at a male."

I wondered why Mary would assume that I was male but decided not to inquire. I thought that I should reply in a formal manner to try to avoid any further breaches of protocol. "It is I who must request forgiveness, madam, for I am not yet familiar with your customs." As I spoke the words, I couldn't help feeling revulsion at having to acknowledge such objectionable customs. "Could you please direct me to the captain? I have an appointment with him at 09:00."

"Certainly, sir, follow me, if you please."

Mary led me up a companionway, down another passageway, and up another level to a short corridor that led to the bridge. "This is the farthest that I'm permitted to go, sir," she said, motioning to the end of the corridor.

I thanked Mary and then made my way to the opening onto the bridge. I stood in the entrance and observed the scene. A man I hadn't seen at the previous gathering was sitting at a console that appeared to have been bolted in place. A second crew member, named Bazz, was reclined in a metal-framed chair with patched fabric seating. His feet were resting on top of a short storage locker, and he was inhaling vapor from a short cylinder. "Mec" was seated on top of a long metal box labelled "Evac. Suits" and eating a bowl of scrambled eggs. He let out the longest, loudest belch that I had ever heard emanating from a human, after which he smiled as if relishing a notable accomplishment.

"Excuse me, gentlemen," I said. "I have an appointment with the captain."

The man at the console continued staring at the display. Mec continued to consume his food. Bazz took a cursory glance my way, then flicked the back of his hand toward me. "Can't you see we're busy here? Captain ain't got time for the likes of you."

A scolding voice came from the starboard side of the bridge, "Oh, Bazz, that's not very hospitable of you!" Captain Smith emerged from a door. "Good morning, Kelvoo. Please come in. I've been looking forward to our meeting. Please forgive these fine young lummoxes," he said in a jovial yet serious tone as I entered his office. "They can get a bit cranky after a late night."

Captain Smith closed the door, took his seat behind a large desk, and motioned to me. I took a kneeling position across from him.

"I hope you got some sleep and had a good breakfast," he said.

"Yes, it was quite adequate, sir. I hope you don't mind if I get straight to business."

"Of course, my friend," he replied, smiling. I had grown wary of being called "my friend" by people whom I hardly knew.

"After serious deliberation last night, my fellow kloormari and I unanimously voted to enact section 3.1 of our agreement with you. We require you to return us to Kuw'baal immediately."

His smile remained mostly intact, but a couple of new furrows found their way onto his brow. He tented his fingers under his chin and nodded slightly. "I understand, Kelvoo. I did, after all, rush you and your people into making your decision. I also confess that I may have overstepped in the assurances that I gave you. I also acknowledge that the conditions on this ship must be a cause of discomfort for your group.

"I'm prepared to order the ship to turn about and return you to your homes. Doing so will delay our mission by about thirty-six hours. On the other hand, if you complete just this one mission for me, I can have you back home in about a week, and I will consider our contract to be terminated. I have just one question for you. How many lives are you willing to save by delaying your return to Kuw'baal by a few days? Ten thousand? Twenty thousand? Fifty thousand?"

"Captain, my group discussed the first part of your mission and whether we had a moral obligation to participate. The problem is, we feel that you have deceived us, and we don't know whether to believe that we are on a humanitarian mission. Forgive our doubts, Captain, but we require proof of the nature of the first stop of your mission."

"That's only fair, Kelvoo. I do have something I can show you, and I hope it will suffice."

He retrieved a vid to his Infotab. "The place we're heading is a human colony named Friendship. Their population is about two million, or at least it was at its height. Here is a vid communique that we received four weeks ago. I would call the colony right now if I could, but we are nowhere near a quantum entanglement relay for real-time communication, and we are still two days from the nearest official jump point."

The captain slid his Infotab across his desk to me and played the vid. A female human, probably in her mid-twenties, started speaking. "*Jezebel's Fury*, this is Friendship Colony replying to your previous message. We are grateful for your gracious offer of assistance. Please proceed as agreed. We have made all necessary preparations here, and we anxiously await your arrival and delivery of 17.5 million doses of Vinamibefentyn.

"The urgency of our situation cannot be overstated. We are currently losing about five thousand citizens per day, though we expect that to be considerably higher by the time you arrive. God bless you, Captain Smith, and Godspeed."

I pulled out my Infotab and was relieved that it had a solid connection to our InfoServer two decks below. I looked up "Friendship Colony" and was able to verify the colony's existence. As of the reporting date over a year ago, the colony had 2,105,044 residents. It was self-sustaining and mostly

162

agrarian. Contact with other beings was limited due to the founders' ideology of self-sufficiency. The colony had a gold extraction and refining industry, used to trade for essential supplies when necessary.

I asked the captain to spell "Vinamibefentyn" for me, and I entered it into my Infotab, with no results. He explained that the disease broke out in the colony about a year ago and that the treatment was formulated three months after that. He said I would hear the drug referred to as "vina" by the crew, and if we agreed to participate, by the needy colonists. I inquired as to the nature of the disease.

"It's truly horrible, Kelvoo," he said. "It's a terrible torment both physically and mentally. Physically, the body is racked with pain, muscle cramps, and seizures. At the same time, psychotic episodes cause extreme paranoia and hallucinations. Sometimes the pain and stress are too much, and the person dies from shock, but the saddest part of all is that the great majority of deaths are by suicide. The suffering is so intense that the victims reach their breaking point and end their lives to escape their suffering." He looked at me, appearing to be very sincere. "Kelvoo, will you and your team turn your backs on these colonists, or will you assist us?"

"We will assist you on your delivery of Vinamibefentyn to the Friendship Colony as planned," I assured him.

"And I will release you from your contract and return you to your homes upon completion of the delivery," he replied. "As an act of goodwill, I will also transfer one billion SimCash units to your species as payment upon completion of the delivery."

"Thank you, Captain. I have many more questions, but I think it would be best if I provide my team with an update now."

I stood, as did Captain Smith. I nodded my eye slightly, and the captain nodded in return. Then I turned toward the door.

"Wait, Kelvoo," he said, just as I was about to open it. I stopped.

"I haven't been completely honest with you," he said. "I respect you too much to leave things like that. Please come back and chat with me a while longer." I reversed direction and resumed my position at the captain's desk.

"Let me tell you a bit more about myself," he said, confirming my theory that he was engaging in his favorite pastime. "When I was running a freighter for the Terran merchant fleet—and yes, you and I can use the word 'Terra' if there's no crew members around—I did things my own way. I was a tough captain. I enjoyed taking on inexperienced crew members and throwing them into the proverbial deep end. Sure, I'd berate and humiliate them when they screwed up, but they sure learned fast, and they did things my way.

"Anyhow, as you'd expect in a large organization, I got reported to human resources and was called on the carpet for employee abuse. I expected to be able to plead my case and explain that my methods had made my ship by far the most efficient and productive in the entire fleet. That didn't matter to those bloody bureaucrats! They sent me for a psych exam! A goddam psych exam! And do you know what they found? They said I suffer from narcissistic personality disorder!

"Now, I know that a narcissist thinks they're better and smarter than everyone else and that the usual rules shouldn't apply to them, but they didn't take into account the possibility that I actually *am* better and smarter! As for the rules of the merchant fleet, why the hell should I obey a bunch of pointless rules that stop me from making *them* money? Idiots!

"Anyway, I told the merchant fleet what they could do to themselves. When I unloaded my personal effects from the freighter, I just happened to abscond with a suitcase full of palladium ingots. Compensation for my mistreatment is how I saw it. I hopped onto the freighter of a friendly captain, transferred to an old Outlier transport, and set myself up on Perdition with enough palladium to have *Jezebel's Fury* cobbled together from an assortment of derelict and scrapped vessels. I'm no narcissist, Kelvoo, but I do confess that I delight in outsmarting others and manipulating them to do my bidding!"

"Is that where we came into your plan?" I asked.

"It sure is, genius!" He laughed. "A while back, I saw your interview from the *Orion*, and later I saw news coverage of the inquiry and some of the testimony of Captain Staedtler and your buddy, Sam. Both spoke very highly of your species' abilities. The crew and I were on shore leave at the time. You see, I've described this trip to you as a six-month mission. Truth is, it's the second half of a one-year mission. My charming crew thought they had been overworked for the first six months. Since there's no HR department out here, their only option is mutiny. Mutiny is a messy business, my friend, so to avoid it, I promised them that we'd pick up some additional crew.

"I was looking for ten more crew members. Truth is, I could've found them anywhere, but I thought, wouldn't it be fun to go to Ryla 5—or Kuw'baal, as you call it—and see whether I could rope those trained kloormari into serving? You see, Kelvoo, getting your team onboard was a personal challenge. I just wanted to see whether I could pull it off!

"A bunch of the crew thought I was just wasting time and playing games when I ordered *Jezebel's Fury* to the Ryla system. They didn't dare tell me directly, but I heard the grumblings. I told them that I was just catering to their wishes for a little help, so they'd better stop complaining about my little detour."

"Fascinating!" I said, using flattery as best as I could. "So, how did you convince Sam to record the vid?"

He laughed loudly. "Sam? I've never met your old pal Sam in my life! I took some vid of his testimony and had it altered to change his face and words, just as one of your friends suspected in our first meeting. A little Infotab search told me the basics, like where he went to school, just in case you wanted proof that I knew him. By the way, when I said that Sam and the captain were exonerated and treated as heroes . . . I lied! The last I saw, the inquiry was still underway."

"So, you realized that our trust and friendship with Sam could be used against us! That was very clever of you! So, did you trick Sam or somebody else into giving you the jump coordinates to get to the Ryla system?" I asked, feigning great interest.

"No, I figured that out all by myself! I'm not going to tell you how, but later today, you'll find out!" He grinned from ear to ear, clearly enjoying himself.

The conversation reminded me of a Terran "superhero" drama vid that I had viewed months before. In one scene, the hero was captured by the evil "supervillain" who explained to the hero, in great detail, his plans for conquering the galaxy.

At the time, I found the premise ridiculous. Why would the villain reveal the information when there was a chance the hero could escape and use the information to defeat the villain? And yet, here I was, listening to the captain playing a similar role. I came to think that this was a real phenomenon when dealing with a person who lived to impress others. I decided I would keep listening to Captain Smith for as long as he wanted to keep talking.

"You know, Kelvoo, it's been really refreshing having this exchange with you. This is the first intelligent conversation I've had for a long, long time. The fact is, my crew are a bunch of subhuman morons. Half of them can't even read! Can you imagine that? And here you are, having learned a new language and becoming literate in a matter of weeks! Your people may not be very bright when it comes to trusting humans, but that doesn't mean you're dumb!"

It sounded as though Smith was trying to use flattery himself to influence me. He continued to denigrate his crew and to tell me how easy it was to outsmart and control them. I asked him how he kept the crew loyal.

"Oh, that's easy," he replied. "I don't need to manipulate people to make them loyal. I just make them rich beyond their dreams! Any crew member who survives a mission returns home incredibly wealthy. That's how I was able to offer your little village ten billion units of SimCash for your help. After a mission, most crew members simply retire into a life of luxury, though some come back for more. About half the crew on this mission are seasoned veterans. That's why I could have found more crew, but it wouldn't have been nearly as much fun as hornswoggling a whole new species!"

He laughed again and shook his head as if disbelieving his own brilliance. I wanted to keep him talking.

"I noticed that the crew members have unusual names—much shorter than typical Terran names. Why is that?"

"Nobody uses their legal names on these missions. Everyone has a nickname. It seems to help with camaraderie. Most of the time, the name denotes a feature or a skill. For example, 'Hol' is short for 'Holy,' as in 'Reverend Hol,' our onboard holy man. For the crew member 'Tank,' that refers to his body shape. 'Mec' is our ship's mechanic and engineer. We have 'Snowy' because he's so white, and 'Ebo' is for 'ebony' because he's so black. 'Torm' is short for 'tormentor'—he's the ship's disciplinarian. The fellow at the console on the bridge is 'Pilo,' our pilot. As for 'Bazz' and 'Spaggy,' I don't know where those came from. As far as 'Wanky' is concerned, I don't know the origin of that one either, though I have my suspicions. When it comes to me, I'm 'Skully' because of my lovely thin face and deep-set eyes."

"So, should I call you Captain Skully or Captain Smith?"

"Makes no never mind to me, but best to call me Skully on this ship, since the crew wouldn't have a clue who Captain Smith is. Besides, neither one is my real name. I just made up Roger Smith for the benefit of you and your friends! Is there anything else you'd like to know?"

Wishing to keep the conversation rolling, I told the captain that I was confused about the hymn that had been sung the previous night. From my previous studies, I knew that the Yangtze is a major river on the Terran continent called "Asia," and I wondered why a song about the Yangtze would be used to lament the Outliers' departure in general. I also pointed out that wild lions had never ranged into the Yangtze's watershed and had never overlapped with the pandas' habitat. Also, lions and antelope would be unlikely to play together, and ice floes would have been a highly unlikely occurrence on the Yangtze.

"That's how dumb these people are," Smith said. "First, the Yangtze is just a symbol of Terra or 'Earth,' as they like to say. Yes, the song is totally unrealistic, but it doesn't matter. The two Outlier planets, Perdition and Exile, are absolutely beautiful. One is covered in forests and mountains, and the other has incredible oceans, islands, and beaches. The person who wrote the song had never been to Terra. He was a third-generation Outlier. These people embody the old Terran adage, 'the grass is always greener on the other side.' The song represents an idea, not reality, but it gives them a long-term goal and a dream—something else that I can play upon if needed."

"Well, Captain, thanks so much for such an interesting conversation. I must return to my team to update them. I'm sure they'll understand why we need to assist with the delivery to Friendship Colony."

"Not so fast," he said. "We've been having such a great conversation, but I haven't even got to the reason why I called you back to my desk."

"I'm sorry, sir. What did you want to tell me?"

"Kelvoo, in the interest of being completely honest, I want you to know that I have no intention of returning you home after Friendship Colony."

"What?" I asked, incredulous.

He smiled. "Sure, I could string you along, wait until after we're done at Friendship, and then drop that bombshell on you, but why bother? As far as I'm concerned, your contract isn't worth the electrons it's made from. Technically, I'm not above the law, but I sure do enjoy flouting it!

"The bottom line, Kelvoo, is that for the next six months, I *own* you and your entire team, and there's nothing you can do about it! It is what it is, my friend. So, you have a choice: You can go with the flow, and we can carry on having these lovely conversations and be the best of pals for the next six months, or you can resist and suffer the consequences."

"Need I ask you what happens if we just refuse to do your bidding?"

"You don't need to ask, but I'm glad you did," he said, grinning as he drew a blaster pistol from his belt and pulled a cloth from his desk. He started polishing his blaster, pointing it my way from time to time. "You never know what might happen. Perhaps you or your crew end up on the pointy end of a blaster. Maybe someone ends up on the wrong side of an airlock door! The possibilities are endless, my friend.

"By the way, the same holds true regarding this conversation. It's not in my best interest for my crew to know what I think of them. Again, if someone were to tell them, I'd deny it, and that 'someone' might just end up on the wrong side of a blaster or an airlock.

"So, now that you know your situation, why don't you go back down to your friends and give them the lay of the land. I'm sure you'll all have a fascinating conversation! I look forward to you telling me how they responded. Let's meet again at 09:00 tomorrow, but not here. Meet me at my table in the barroom. Effective immediately, the bridge will be sealed and off limits to you and your team."

His grin remained in place as I got up and left without saying another word. I was deeply shaken, and I hoped that it hadn't shown too much during the meeting.

# TWENTY-THREE: EXPLORING, GRIME, AND PUNISHMENT

When I returned to the kloormari quarters, K'tatmal asked me whether we were going to turn back or deliver the medication first.

"We're delivering the medication first," I said. "I wish I could tell you that we will be heading home after that, but we won't be. The captain refuses."

"But that can't be!" K'tatmal exclaimed. "Refusing to honor the contract with us contravenes interplanetary law!"

"That doesn't seem to matter to him," I replied. "Right now, we have no choice but to follow his orders."

I wondered whether hidden listening devices had been placed around the vessel, especially in our quarters. "We need to keep speaking with one another in kloormari despite any desire to practice Terran. We don't know whether we are under audio or vid surveillance."

I recounted my entire exchange with Captain Smith. The others were dismayed, to say the least.

"We need to come up with a strategy to survive this mission and to deal with the possibility that Captain Smith will keep us prisoner beyond six months or simply dispose of us when we are of no further use to him," I said. While saying that, I looked up "narcissist" on my Infotab. "Captain Smith fits the classic definition of a 'narcissist.' He is also highly delusional. Our greatest tool for survival will be information. The captain likes to talk, especially about himself. He thrives on flattery, so by flattering him, we may obtain important data. I suggest that we compliment him when it makes sense to do so despite any revulsion that we may feel.

"We may have to do things that go against our very nature. The captain uses deceit as a weapon, and we may need to do the same. We may need to gather information using clandestine means. I also suggest that we keep information about us to ourselves. Let's not tell any of the humans about any of our mental or physical advantages. We need to formulate our strategy."

At that moment, a ship-wide audio announcement was made. "All personnel prepare for jump in thirty seconds."

We were all astonished, and no one more than me. "This makes no sense," I exclaimed. "The captain said we were two days from an official jump point."

A ten-second countdown commenced.

"Is there such a thing as an unofficial jump point?" K'raftan asked.

Seconds later, the room, the vessel, my fellow kloormari, and my entire body vanished. I was alone in the void of space, surrounded by stars. Without a body, I could feel nothing. I couldn't breathe, but without my body, there was no urge or need to breathe. I was alone in the most complete, profound, and terrifying of ways.

I don't know how much time passed. At some point, bright streaks of light surrounded me, accompanied by a huge "whooshing" sound. I was swept along with the streaks at an unfathomable speed. As I reached the terminus of the streaks, they resolved into our quarters on the *Jezebel's Fury*. When the visual and auditory effects returned to normal, I was in my original standing position on the ship, where I promptly collapsed. I remember seeing the other kloormari fall or slump around me at the same time.

If that was a jump, it was nothing like the ones I had experienced on the *Pacifica Spirit*.

Captain Smith made a ship-wide announcement. "Jump successful. All systems nominal. Bet our kloormari friends enjoyed that!"

We didn't enjoy it at all. Most of us were lying on the deck, disoriented, shaking, and moaning in terror. We stayed there, immobile, too confused and frightened to do anything. After about an hour, while we were still lying on the deck, another announcement from a different crew member was broadcast. "Prepare for hyper-acceleration in thirty seconds."

We didn't know what to expect. A new wave of terror gripped us. After another ten-second countdown, a great roar came from the vessel's aft section. The deck started to vibrate, making our bodies bounce. A powerful acceleration commenced, making us bounce along the floor toward the stern end of the room. Next, a counteracting force sent us bouncing back toward the forward section. The two opposing forces seemed to take a while to balance each other out. They finally synchronized, and at about the same time, the vibration stopped, the roaring faded to background noise, and once again, we could no longer feel the vessel's movement.

Slowly, we got to our feet. "We can't live like this," K'aablart moaned in a tremulous voice. We resolved to find a way back home as soon as possible.

While I was meeting with Captain Smith, some of my teammates had made a brief foray to explore parts of the ship. They retraced our original steps back up two levels to the hangar. From there, they expanded their exploration to the adjoining spaces. We seemed to have the ability to roam freely through the ship, with the recently imposed exception of the bridge. I realized there was nowhere for us to run, so I supposed there was no need for a high degree of restricted access.

I suggested that we continue our exploration of the cargo areas and other places where the crew didn't spend most of their time. I also suggested that we return to our quarters at 18:00 to describe what we had seen to one another to build a mental image of the vessel's layout. We split up accordingly and began our investigation.

I decided to go back to the hangar to see for myself what some of my teammates had described. We had exited the hangar at its aft end. I opened a door on the forward side of the hangar and stepped onto a catwalk at the top of a cavernous cargo hold. Another catwalk circled the hold on each of the three levels below me, followed by the decking on the bottom of the hold, five levels down.

Each catwalk had sets of stairs to the level above and below. I descended the five levels to the floor of the cargo hold. Containers and crates were stacked high, and hoverlifts of various sizes were parked between the stacks. A container labeled "Friendship" soared three levels high. It was constructed of metal several centimeters thick. Each hinge must have weighed 200 kg at standard gravity. The container's door had several biometric and digital combination locks. I was encouraged to know that the captain and crew put such a high value on the life-saving medication.

I made my way to two gargantuan doors on the forward end of the cargo hold, each extending to half the height of the hold. I peered through a small, thick pane of glass in the bottom of each door. On the other side of the doors was a landing bay with a cargo transport that must have been over one hundred meters in length and fifty meters across. I couldn't see a mechanism for opening the doors.

I scanned the walls of the hold for controls, pipes, conduits, panels, doors, or anything else that wasn't just a wall. I walked the catwalk at each level, trying each door and hatch. Most opened right away and were empty or housed derelict parts and equipment. I made a mental catalog of each object.

At 18:00, the team reassembled in our quarters, and we exchanged information about each space that we had explored. Others had already seen the main cargo hold but didn't have enough time to look at every fixture and side area, so I contributed my additional observations.

We had exchanged a substantial amount of detailed information, so after dinner we decided to start meditation early. It would give us more time to process the information and allow us to recall it faster. Our meditation would also help us recover from the trauma of the earlier jump and the rough ride that followed.

We regained full alertness by 06:00 the next morning. We had our algel and then spent time accessing information on the InfoServer relating to the equipment and infrastructure we had observed. Just before 09:00, I made my way to the barroom, which was empty. While I waited for Captain Smith, I made some detailed observations.

When he arrived a few minutes later, he politely apologized for his tardiness, explaining that he'd had to deal with an incident, which we would all find out about shortly. "So, how did you enjoy our little jump?" he asked with a smile.

"It was the most terrifying experience of my life," I replied with complete honesty.

His smile widened as though he was gratified by my response. "Well, it does take a bit of getting used to, I suppose."

I asked him why the experience differed so much from the jumps on the *Pacifica*. "Well, Terran vessels have to include a bunch of extraneous systems for safety and comfort, including force fields that form a bubble around the vessel at jump time, to mitigate the most disturbing effects for the passengers. They're just a bunch of wusses if you ask me. Besides, systems like that just use energy and reduce speed and power."

"I admire your courage and efficiency, sir," I replied. "What I don't understand is how you were able to jump so soon. Yesterday, you said that we were two days from any official jump points. Are there some 'unofficial' jump points? Is that how you managed to arrive at Kuw'baal so soon?"

He laughed and slapped the table. "Tell me, Kelvoo, what's so special about a jump point?"

"Well, Captain, it's an area of space that has been surveyed in great detail and is found to have little or no dust or particles that could destroy a ship that materializes there."

He shrugged. "Who cares?"

"I would think that any captain or pilot or navigator would care. Materializing into debris would likely cause instant destruction of the vessel and all life forms aboard."

"Kelvoo, if I were to jump this ship right now to a random location in this part of the galaxy, what do you think are the chances of disaster?"

"I don't know, Captain. I haven't accessed that information."

"One in two thousand, Kelvoo. A ship is lost only once in every two thousand jumps to un-surveyed space."

The gravity of his words sunk in. I was incredulous.

"Captain, are you saying that our jump yesterday was to un-surveyed space?"

"It sure was, Kelvoo! So was my previous jump to your planet!" He laughed and shook his head. "Sorry, my friend, but it's been very amusing that you've been trying to figure out how I got the coordinates to the Ryla System jump point. Who the hell needs jump point coordinates? Ryla is marked on every star chart. Pilo and I just picked coordinates in the general vicinity and . . . boom! Just a short journey to the fifth planet in the system.

171

Getting to Kuw'baal was the easy part. What we didn't know was where on your planet we would find you. We had no visual clues, thanks to your constant bloody cloud cover.

"Being rather clever though, I did figure that the *Pacifica* might have left behind equipment that radiated some weak RF signals. You know, things like lights or InfoServers. We could only scan narrow swaths of your planet at a time. It took two days to find your village. By then, the crew was getting agitated. That great buffoon Bazz was just about climbing the walls. It was worth the wait just to see him practically wetting himself!

"That, my friend, is the main reason why I was in such a rush to get you signed up and on board! Sure, each hour of delay means some lives are lost at Friendship, but I don't know what would have happened if my little diversion to Ryla had been all for naught. Could've been a full-on mutiny!" He sat back on his chair. "Just remember, Kelvoo, I'm counting on you and your pals to work hard and make me look good."

I was still reeling from the knowledge that the ship was jumping to uncharted parts of space. "Captain Skully, do you intend to keep jumping to un-surveyed space? Isn't that reckless?" His smile vanished. Realizing I had dropped my façade of flattery, I switched to sycophantic mode. "Of course, there's a certain genius to being able to travel immediately to any part of the sector. Now that I think about it, the rewards of instant travel must certainly outweigh such minor risks."

His grin returned. "Kelvoo, you're becoming quite the accomplished BS artist!"

He was quite correct—my praise had been false. I knew that if we performed twenty jumps on our trip, we had a 1 percent chance of dying. To some, odds like that were acceptable. As a kloormar, they seemed abysmally bad to me!

"So, how are you and your lads settling in?" he asked, changing the subject. "Anything you need from me?"

"Well, yes, sir. I have concerns about the general cleanliness of our quarters. I don't want to be a bother, but the dust and odors could affect our respiratory efficiency and hamper our productivity."

"Not a bother at all," he replied. "Let me take care of that right now! Come with me."

We stepped outside the barroom. "Mary?" he called.

"I'm here, Captain. How may I help you, sir?"

"Oh good, she's just down the passageway," he said. "Come with me."

We found Mary sweeping the same patch of floor where I had met her the first time. "Captain, sir," she said while performing a deep curtsy and casting her eyes down.

"My friend Kelvoo here thinks that the kloormari's quarters aren't up to our usual high standards of cleanliness," Smith said. I guessed he was being sarcastic.

"Forgive me, good captain, sir," Mary said timidly. "That area of the ship hadn't been used for a while, and I've been reluctant to clean the area with our guests present. My husband would not approve of me being in the presence of males."

"Fear not, my good woman! Just show me where your cleaning supplies are kept." Mary walked a few steps and opened a door to a closet full of supplies.

"Mary, in recognition of your excellent service, I am giving you some time off! You may rest until we reach Friendship Colony. In the meantime, please give your cleaning cart to my friend here. Kelvoo and the other kloormari will scrub their quarters and every corner of this deck and the decks above until they are gleaming!" He turned to me. "There you go, Kelvoo, problem solved. Plus, you and your friends can now make yourselves truly useful!"

"Thank you, Captain. I appreciate your solution," I said with sincere gratitude. I hadn't realized at the time that Smith was probably intending to demean us. I was looking forward to my team having an excuse to explore the busier sections of the vessel.

He accompanied me back to our quarters. We stopped in the passageway just outside of our room. "Before you get to the scrubbing, Kelvoo, I've arranged for a little entertainment." He showed me an open door marked C-12 across the passageway from our quarters. It was a space much like our quarters, two levels high, but C-12 had a catwalk one level up and around the full perimeter. "You and your team are to report here at 10:00," he said before walking away.

I pushed the cart into our quarters and updated the team. At 09:50 the captain made a ship-wide announcement, asking all crew members to assemble in room C-12. We arrived there at precisely 10:00. A few short rows of folding chairs had been set up facing some type of scaffolding. A black case rested on a small table beside the scaffold. A few crew members were already seated, and others began filing in. We stood behind the rows of chairs. Three additional chairs were positioned against a wall to one side of the scaffold.

Captain Skully strode in wearing his full dress uniform. I suspected that some type of auspicious occasion was about to take place. As soon as he had taken his position to one side of the scaffold, three human females entered from a side door.

The women wore scanty white outfits with gold piping. The top of the clothing consisted of two straps of fabric that crossed over the women's breasts in an "X" configuration, connected to each other behind the neck. The bottom of the straps attached to a skirt that fell well short of mid-thigh. Two of the women wore shoes with thin straps that crisscrossed up to a point above the knee. The heels on the shoes were so high that it must have taken considerable training to walk in them. The other female was barefoot.

All three of the women looked unhealthily thin. They also looked very young. I was not yet capable of estimating the age of humans based on their appearance, but I was quite sure that the women were substantially younger than any females on the *Pacifica*.

The barefoot female was in bad condition. The side of her face was red and swollen with a large black bruise surrounding her left eye. A dried crust of blood was visible under her nostrils. Her arms and the sides of her torso were bruised and lacerated in places. One of her arms hung limply by her side, and one of her legs was crudely splinted to a metal pipe. I wondered what had happened to her.

The young woman's companions were physically supporting her on each side as they slowly made their way to the three side chairs and took their seats.

The captain addressed the assembled crew. "This'll be old hat to the veterans here but a very important lesson to all new crew members, both human and kloormari. On these missions, we depend on each other, not just for profit but often for our very lives. We have to function as a unit for the sake of the mission and for morale. When a crew member disobeys an order or does something that has a negative impact on other crew members and their morale, consequences must result, if for no other reason than to set an example to those who would follow a similar path."

He gestured toward the injured female. "Last night, one of our crew members thought it would be a good idea to smack one of our concs around. That in itself isn't unusual, but restraint, gentlemen, is usually called for."

While I was saddened that hitting a fellow human wasn't unusual, I was appalled that one of the crew members had intentionally caused such severe injury.

"Bring him in, Torm," Smith said.

Torm led a crew member into the room. Torm was wearing a pair of coveralls that had been white but which were now heavily stained with the dried remnants of some sort of spattered liquid. The crew member's hands were restrained behind his back, and he was bare from the waist up.

"Your name's 'Brawn,' isn't it?" Smith said. "More brawn than brains, I'd suggest. Looks like you got a little carried away last night." He pointed his chin toward the injured female.

"I'm sorry, Captain, but I don't see why it's a big deal. She's just a whore."

Smith's reply was unsettling due to its casual tone. "Personally, I prefer the term 'concubine,' though 'conc' would suffice, and you are quite right,

Mr. Brawn; these three are just concs—hardly worthy of respect or privilege. What you fail to understand is that you broke this conc. We don't know how long it will take for her to heal, but in the meantime, I can't use her, and none of your crewmates can either. What if she heals, but you've damaged her looks, and nobody wants her anymore?

"The point is, it doesn't matter if she's a conc or a hoverlift or a shuttle. You willfully damaged property of this ship, and you've put me in the position of having to deter you and your crewmates from repeating such selfish negligence."

I was revolted by the captain referring to a sentient being as property to be used. The fact that she was injured and in pain increased my revulsion. I wondered what form his deterrence would take. Based on my limited knowledge of human crimes and punishments, I suspected that Brawn would be confined to quarters or placed in a brig if one existed onboard.

"Torm, put him in his place," Smith said.

Torm removed the restraint from one of Brawn's wrists and fastened it to the scaffolding. He did the same with Brawn's other wrist. Brawn's back was facing the crew, and his wrists were spread wide apart and fastened at a level slightly above his head. I wondered why the man was being immobilized. Brawn turned his head toward the three women. "Whores!" he shouted and spat in their direction.

"Tut, tut, Mr. Brawn. Such unseemly behavior," Smith remarked. "I can see this is a first for you, given your lovely, pristine skin. Torm, would you please give the fine fellow a taste of what he's in for?"

Torm opened the black case on the table and pulled out a flexible metal cord with a rubber handle. He pressed a switch on the handle and shook the cord. Blue sparks danced on its surface.

Torm moved the end of the cord to within a centimeter or two of Brawn's upper back. A loud crack emanated from the cord, and a blue spark jumped to Brawn's skin.

Brawn screamed. "Oh God! Oh my God, no!" He started sobbing. "I'm sorry, Captain, I'm so sorry! I promise never to do that again! Please, sir, please let me go! I'll do anything you say!"

"Okay," the captain said. "Keep your mouth shut."

Brawn's sobbing diminished to soft whimpers. I was deeply disturbed; this human had just been subjected to severe pain.

"Reverend Hol," Smith said, "would you please deliver the absolution?"

Hol stepped up to Brawn. "Would you like to ask the Almighty for forgiveness?"

"I dunno."

"You need to understand, my son, that there is a chance you won't survive the next two minutes. You have sinned in the eyes of the captain and in the eyes of the Almighty. If you are granted forgiveness and then you die, you will ascend into paradise. If not, you will be cast into hell where, for eternity, you will feel pain far more terrible than you will experience today."

Brawn started breathing rapidly. "Oh no! No, no, no, no!" he said between breaths, and then he vomited.

"Repeat after me," Hol said calmly. During his recitation, he paused frequently, and Brawn repeated his words between gasps. "Oh God of mercy, I declare that I have sinned. I accept you into my heart, and I beg you to wash my sins away. I shall follow a righteous path and spread your word. In the name of Yahweh, Allah, the son, and the holy prophet."

Every fiber in my body trembled with horror. I couldn't get my mind around the purpose of this spectacle. Here was a human who had brutally attacked and harmed another human being who was about to be tortured in some terrifying way. I couldn't understand how adding more pain and suffering would, in any way, compensate for the previously inflicted pain and suffering.

Hol turned to the crew. "Our brother has confessed his sins to the Almighty so that he may gain his heavenly reward someday. Let us give him the strength to endure his worldly punishment through a song of praise. For Brother Brawn's day of reckoning, I have selected an ancient Christian song, based on the prayer of Saint Francis. Those who have been attending my services will know this one well. Let us join together and sing 'Make Me a Channel of Your Peace.'"

About half of the crew knew the song. Torm proceeded to lash Brawn in time with the song, landing a blow at the end of each line.

> Make me a channel of Your peace
> Where there is hatred, let me bring Your love
> Where there is injury, Your pardon Lord
> And where there's doubt, true faith in You

With each lash, a blue flash and a loud snap rent the air, matched only by Brawn's screams of agony. With each blow, a fine spray of blood shot out of the creases that the cord left in Brawn's back, adding to the stains on Torm's coveralls. Sizzling blood and burned skin stuck to the metal cord. Wisps of smoke wafted through the room, smelling of burned flesh.

> Make me a channel of Your peace
> Where there's despair in life, let me bring hope
> Where there is darkness, only light
> And where there's sadness, ever joy

I looked at the captain. His mouth was clenched sternly, but judging from his eyes, I suspected he was smiling inside.

Oh Master, grant that I may never seek
So much to be consoled as to console
To be understood as to understand
To be loved as to love with all my soul

I looked over at the three women. They sat expressionless. Their eyes were glazed with a bland weariness. Was this just one of many horrors they had experienced?

Make me a channel of Your peace
It is pardoning that we are pardoned
In giving to all men that we receive
And in dying that we're born to eternal life

Brawn's screams died down, and he was silent while the beating continued. Most of the crew seemed to be deeply troubled. Some turned their heads away, their eyes closed and their teeth clenched. Those who were singing picked up speed, presumably so the ghastly spectacle would end sooner.

Oh Master, grant that I may never seek
So much to be consoled as to console
To be understood as to understand
To be loved as to love with all my soul"

The speed of the crew's singing reached a fever pitch. I could take no more. I sat on the floor, gripped my knees close to my chest, noticing that the other kloormari had done the same. I closed my eyelid and I tried to block the sounds and smell from my mind.

Make me a channel of Your peace
Where there's despair in life, let me bring hope
Where there is darkness, only light
And where there's sadness, ever joy

The beating finally ended. I stood uneasily and saw Torm removing a damp cloth from a bag in the case. As he wiped the cord free of blood and skin, the liquid in the cloth fried and steamed. Next, Torm took some adhesive strips out of the case. Where Brawn's skin had been split, Torm pinched each side together and placed several strips across the length of each wound. He rolled up lengths of gauze, rubbed ointment into each roll, placed each roll on top of a wound, and then covered them with a dressing. It was clear that he had done this before.

Brawn began to stir as Torm attended to the last of the wounds—I could tell by Brawn's sharp intake of breath and tremulous exhalation whenever Torm touched his back.

"Thanks everyone for attending," the captain said casually. "Dismissed."

As Torm started to unfasten Brawn, the crew got up and left in silence. The two uninjured women assisted their companion to her feet. They passed behind Torm and Brawn on their way out, walking through a pool of blood. The injured woman had only one of her feet touching the ground, leaving half a set of bloody footprints across the deck.

On his way out of the room, the captain touched my shoulder and motioned toward the blood and footprints, smiling. "Do have your team clean that up. There's a good chap!"

# TWENTY-FOUR: TRYING TO MAKE SENSE OF IT

We were badly shaken when we regrouped in our quarters. Kleloma thought we should commence our cleaning duties, starting with room C-12. I thought that, for the sake of our mental well-being, we needed to meditate to try to make sense of our terrible experience.

Kroz and K'raftan agreed with Kleloma, so we compromised. The three of them would work in C-12 while the rest of us meditated. Ksoomu, Keesooni, and I would be awakened in one hour to take over cleaning while Kroz, K'raftan, and Kleloma could start a longer meditation to help them deal with the extra stress of returning to the place of trauma.

One hour wasn't going to be enough to process the horrors I had witnessed, but I hoped it would tide me over until the evening.

I assumed a comfortable position, closed my eyelid, and began my session. It was anything but restorative. I involuntarily replayed the captain's reckless jump practices and his cavalier attitude toward the "entertainment" of watching one of his crew members being beaten. I relived seeing the three young women enter the room, one of them with horrible injuries. Once again, I witnessed the defiance, followed by the sobbing and the pleas for mercy from an insolent and then terrified crew member. I recalled in great detail the flash and snap of each lash and the flying spray of blood, with the captain standing there all the while, smugly entertained by the spectacle.

Oddly, the worst part of my recollection was the singing. Crew members watching the agony of a comrade while singing the praises of their deity. Singing about serving their god through peace and love and pardon. Singing of hope and light and joy and consolation. The song kept repeating in my mind, then another "copy" of the song joined the first one part of the way through. Then a third copy started, offset from the other two like a rondo and similar, in a strange way, to "Pachelbel's Canon." After that, more copies started playing at random, each in a different key and none of them synchronized in any way, just a baffling cacophony of auditory madness echoing through my mind.

Meditation was supposed to be about reconciling information—cross-referencing and matching otherwise disparate data, but I couldn't do it! I

179

couldn't reconcile the values espoused in the crew members' praise with their acceptance of the abuse of females and the merciless violence that the captain employed as retribution. I had so many questions:

How could humans believe in one set of values, enforced by an all-powerful, benevolent god, while their actions were in complete opposition to those values?

Did humans rationalize their actions through a self-delusional mental defect? If so, how could so many humans have the same defect at the same time?

Instead of a mental defect, could it be that, on some level, humans understood their beliefs to be superstition, or were their beliefs not strong enough to counter their nature? Is violence and greed endemic to human nature? Does the worship of a deity mitigate human nature or make it worse?

I had insufficient data to answer my own questions, but I wanted the answers, since they might be crucial for our survival. The situation left me in a stressful state.

After what seemed like just a few minutes, K'raftan gently stirred me into consciousness. "I thought I should rouse you, Kelvoo," K'raftan said. "You've been out for an hour and fifteen minutes." For a change, I was actually grateful to be extricated from meditation.

K'raftan led us to C-12 and explained the contents of the cleaning cart. Mary had been kind enough to explain to K'raftan's trio the basics of cleaning and the purpose of each cleaning product and tool. K'raftan passed the knowledge along to us and then left to join the others in meditation.

Ksoomu, Keesooni, and I were relieved that the blood and the memories that it would trigger had been scrubbed from the deck in C-12. We swept and washed along the outside edges of the deck and up the walls as far as we could reach. When Ebo passed by, we asked him where the chairs and scaffolding were stored. We folded and stowed the chairs and figured out how to disassemble and stow the scaffold. All the while, we made a mental note of each fixture, outlet, door, hatch, and panel. We opened each unlocked door, hatch, and panel in the interest of "cleaning," of course. When we were done, C-12 looked almost as good as it would have in new condition.

At 18:00, we kloormari were all back in our quarters and fully alert. We decided that, in the absence of any contrary orders, we would work from 10:00 to 18:00 daily for five out of every seven days. We would meditate in two eight-hour shifts so that at least half of us would be alert at any given time. We briefed one another on the observations we had made during cleanup. Just before we could finish, we heard the door open.

"Excuse me, gentlemen, I hope I'm not intruding," Hol said, peering from the edge of the door.

"How may we help you, Reverend Hol?" Kleloma asked.

Hol took Kleloma's question as an opportunity to let himself in. He stood in front of our group. "This morning, I could see that all of you were very upset by what you saw." Hol paused as if anticipating a response. Since he had made a statement instead of asking a question, no response was forthcoming.

"When someone is upset," he continued, "it can be of great help to talk about it. Would any of you like to share your feelings? I may be able to offer some comfort."

Hol's words took me back to my first conversation with Lynda on the *Pacifica Spirit*. She had undergone the tragic loss of her husband, but she definitely didn't want to talk to me about it at that moment, especially since I was almost a stranger to her.

"It can help to talk about traumatic events when the individual is ready to talk," I said. "You are a stranger to us. Why would we wish to talk with you, especially when you were an active participant in the events?"

"Well, for starters, I'm a trained counselor. I've provided most members of the crew with guidance and help, including those who are not in my flock. More important than that, as the holy man on this ship, I serve as a conduit to a higher power."

"Are you referring to Captain Skully?" K'raftan asked.

"No, my son," Hol said with a slight smile. "I am referring to the Almighty Lord."

"We do not want to discuss these beliefs with you," I stated firmly.

"I'm merely offering to talk and to give you options, my son. What's the harm in talking?"

"The harm is that if we disagree with you—or even if we agree, but with some minor differences—human religious history suggests that you might brand us as heretics. We have learned how the Jewish, Muslim, Christian, and other religions have dealt with heretics at different times in their histories. We have also seen how Captain Skully deals with beings who break the rules. We suspect that he might react similarly to those who displease him."

"Let me be the first to agree that religions have had a terrible history," Hol replied, "including the three that my beliefs are based upon. You must understand that those religions had to progress over thousands of years until they were ready to merge into the New Religion. My beliefs are founded on the perfect union of three sets of imperfect ancient beliefs. New Religion is based only on love and compassion.

"As far as the captain goes, he is a non-believer, so he doesn't care whether you believe or not. I have tried to reach him, but he is resistant. I believe in my heart that someday he will see the way. You must also understand that anything you say to me stays between you, me, and the Lord. Members of this crew have confessed many a sin to me, but my profession forbids me from reporting their confession to any other living being. I swear to God that you can trust me."

"Is there anything else that you would like to say, Hol?" I asked.

"No, I will leave you gentlemen alone. Just know that you have a friend in me, and I'm always willing to lend a sympathetic ear and provide advice. Before I go, I wonder whether I could transfer some very interesting reading material to your Infotabs. It's clear that all of you are very intelligent, and I've heard that you can all read."

"What reading material are you referring to?" I asked.

"Oh, just some translated Hebrew scriptures, along with the Bible, and the Quran . . . just a few things to help you to understand where I'm coming from."

"We have all read those documents at the suggestion of our human teacher."

"What? All of them?"

"Yes."

"How much of them do you remember?"

"The entire text of each."

"So, if I were to ask you to complete the following verse, what would you say? 'For God so loved the world that he gave . . .'"

"It depends on the version of the Bible. The King James version says, 'His only begotten Son, that whosoever believeth in him should not perish, but have everlasting life.'"

"Alright, that one was easy. How about you quote me from King Solomon, Proverbs 24:16."

"The Talmud says, 'A righteous man falls down seven times and gets up.' The biblical version is, 'for a righteous man falls seven times, and rises up again; but the wicked are overthrown by calamity.'"

"Remarkable! What does Sanhedrin 89b say about liars?"

"The liar's punishment is that even when he speaks the truth, no one believes him."

"Incredible! What about Surah Al-Anfal 8:33?"

"And Allah would not punish them while they seek forgiveness."

At that moment, K'tatmal spoke to me in kloormari at an ultrasonic pitch so that Hol would not hear. "Aren't you giving away the fact that we have perfect memories? You had suggested that we don't want to reveal too much about ourselves."

I replied to K'tatmal in the same clandestine manner. "I acknowledge that I am taking a risk, but I think we may have something to gain by befriending Hol and encouraging further communication."

"I am astounded by your knowledge, my friend!" Hol said, responding to my previous answer. "Perhaps you should consider ministering to others!"

"May I test your knowledge?" I asked.

"Certainly."

"What did Rabban Gamliel say in Pirkei Avot 2:3?"

Hol closed his eyes, lowered his head, and grasped his chin. After a few seconds, he opened his eyes. "I'm sorry Mr.—"

"Kelvoo."

"I'm sorry, Kelvoo, but I must admit, you have me at a loss."

"Rabban Gamliel said something that might explain my reluctance in communicating with you: 'Be wary of authorities who befriend a person for their own purposes. They appear loving when it is beneficial to them but do not stand by the other person in his time of distress.'"

"Kelvoo, all of you," Hol said, "I'm humbled and in awe of your intelligence. I'll leave you in peace now, but I hope that we can talk more. From a purely selfish point of view, I enjoy debating my beliefs and having them challenged. Further conversations with you would help to test and sharpen my skills as a holy man. At the same time, I hope it will help you learn that I am someone you can put your trust in."

The holy man bid us goodnight and then left.

The team discussed how we might go about engaging with Hol to learn more about the crew, the mission, and the ship.

By then, the start of the first meditation shift had been delayed, so those of us in the first shift took our positions and began a longer and hopefully more productive meditation.

At midnight Ksoomu awakened me and the other slumbering Kloormari. "Take a look at this," Ksoomu said.

We walked to a corner where the other kloormari were gathered around Kroz. "While you were in meditation," Kroz said, "I connected my Infotab to our InfoServer at a lower level of its operating system. The InfoServer is much better at detecting local connections. I found a ship-wide network."

"How long do you think it would take for you to connect to it?" I asked.

"I already did, two hours ago! You see, the network has a very commonplace MXV-88 access point. When it's installed, the administrator is supposed to implement quantum encryption. It looks as though they never bothered! I looked up the documentation on the InfoServer, which told me the temporary admin passcode that is set on all units in the factory."

"What passcode is that?"

"Password."

I was astonished. How could the captain and crew be so careless? When I thought about it, I surmised that Smith would have thought too highly of himself to install a piece of equipment. He would have assigned a crew member who might know how to connect an access point but may have been too illiterate to secure it. On the other hand, why bother? The network's range would be limited to the ship. Who would need to hack into its network?

"We have read-only access to the network," Kroz cautioned, "so we can see what's going on, but we can't control anything."

"What happens if someone changes the passcode or implements quantum encryption?" I asked.

"As part of read-only access, we can intercept each input from a user. I am logging the inputs to a data repository on the InfoServer. If a quantum key hash is generated, it will also be intercepted and logged."

"So, what can we see with our new read-only access?"

"How about this?" Kroz swiped the Infotab screen and tapped an icon. A live view from various parts of the vessel were displayed in tiles on the screen. Kroz tapped a tile, and it expanded to fill the screen. "Bridge one," Kroz said. Sure enough, a live view of the bridge was displayed. Only Pilo appeared to be on duty. He was fully reclined, motionless in his chair at the console, probably sleeping.

Kroz showed us views from other cameras. "Bridge two" showed the bridge from a different angle. Another view showed us four crew members drinking in the barroom. We saw an armory room with rows of blasters charging in racks. The name of a human crew member was displayed on a label beside each blaster. We saw the concubines' quarters. One of the concubines was unclothed and appeared to be giving a massage to Spaggy. Another was sleeping, and the injured woman was propped up with cushions in a chair. There were no views into the quarters of the captain or the crew. It troubled me that the crew were afforded privacy but not the concubines, whose activities were considered by humans to be extremely private. Other views showed the galley, C-12, the hangar, the main hold, and the landing bay where the large cargo transport was stationed.

"Are there any views of us?" I asked.

Kroz tapped a tile, and our quarters were displayed. Only some of us were visible. The camera was positioned in the corner of the room directly above us, looking out across the room. We could now identify the blind spots on the vessel where we could avoid surveillance—which included the corner of our room below the camera and a small alcove with closable doors in one wall near the corner.

K'aablart asked Kroz whether we could listen in on the areas covered by the cameras.

"No," Kroz replied. "The cameras don't appear to include microphones, but I'm working on a solution."

Finally, Kroz showed us how to view the vessel's telemetry. This included energy consumption, radiation levels, and velocity. The velocity value was fluctuating between 997.9902 and 998.5441. I wasn't familiar with a scale of velocity in which those numbers would make sense.

The time had come for Kroz and four others to take the second shift of meditation. I pulled up various views from the cameras on my Infotab and stared at them for hours.

We delayed breakfast until 08:00 when all the team members were awake. During meditation, Kroz figured out how to access archived information. Kroz was able to access a basic schematic of the vessel and send it to our Infotabs.

The schematic confirmed my suspicion that there were no windows 'for viewing the stars or planets outside the vessel, with the exception of those on the bridge. One of the cameras on the bridge showed windows, but they appeared to have been covered by metal plates on the outside of the vessel. I understood that windows were unnecessary for the crew, but I wondered why the view from the bridge would be blocked.

"Kelvoo!" a voice barked at 09:20, startling all of us. The captain walked into our quarters and saw all of us gathered in the corner. "What are you lads up to?" he asked as he strode toward us.

Having anticipated such a possibility, Kroz tapped an icon on the Infotab screen, replacing its contents with a documentary vid and clearing all of our screens. "We were discussing the merits of dachshunds," Kroz said as Terran canines frolicked on the screen.

Looking nonplussed, Smith turned to me. "What happened to our daily meeting at 09:00?"

"Please forgive me, Captain. I don't believe that we ever discussed further meetings after the last one."

"Well, I remember making that arrangement. You must have forgotten."

"I suppose that must be the case, sir," I lied.

"Well, come with me, and don't screw up again," he snapped. We made our way to the barroom.

"I understand you've met the ship's holy man," he said. "That must have been a treat!"

"Why yes, Captain, he did stop by. How did you know?"

"He mentioned it to me."

"I'm curious; what impressions did he have of us?"

"Oh, he didn't go into any specifics; he just mentioned it in passing."

The conversation told me that, in all likelihood, the captain or a crew member saw Hol entering our quarters on the camera feed. I doubted that Hol would only mention us in passing when he had been so astonished by my knowledge of scripture. Smith obviously didn't want us to know about the surveillance; he probably knew that we had explored the hangar and cargo hold, but if he mentioned it, we could be tipped off. I concluded that we had to be vigilant in avoiding activity that could be seen as suspicious when we were in view of a camera.

"So, did Hol get you lot to 'see the light'? Have you become his apostles?"

"I'm not sure how to answer that, Captain. Historically, belief is very important to some humans. I'm reluctant to incur your wrath by taking a position on the subject."

"Sounds as though somebody's put the fear of God into you, Kelvoo!" He laughed. "Let me assure you that I don't give a damn what you believe so long as it doesn't affect my mission or your ability to follow orders. Personally, I don't mind saying that I think Hol's a twit. He's tried a few times to turn a subject of discussion toward his superstitious claptrap by throwing a 'God willing' or 'Bless you' or 'Amen to that' into the conversation. The thought that I should turn my life over to God or Allah or Yahweh or Christ or Mohammad—the gall! The idea that I have sinned and need to *beg* some 'higher power' to forgive me? To forgive *me*? Me, the captain of this ship? Come on! You know what, Kelvoo? I take back what I just said about not giving a damn whether you believe. You can believe whatever you want, but if you convert to religion, you'll lose a whole lot of my respect!"

Having the respect of a man like Captain Smith was irrelevant to me— perhaps even offensive on some level, but it was going to be necessary.

"Do you wish you didn't have Hol aboard your ship?"

"Yes, much of the time I do, but he's what I call a 'necessary evil.' Remember, my human crew are a load of mouth-breathing morons. These are people who don't know how to make a decision or have a single independent thought. They want a user manual for their own brain. Hol tells them how to live and what to think. I give my crew the promise of wealth for motivation and the threat of pain or death for deterrence. Hol, on the other hand, gives them the promise of eternal life in heaven for motivation and the threat of eternal suffering in hell for deterrence! Hol's religion is useful to me. It helps me to control an unruly bunch of men. Speaking of deterrence, did you enjoy the entertainment yesterday regarding your crewmate, Brawn?"

"Again, Captain, I'm not sure how to answer that, though I think you could tell by our reaction that we were deeply disturbed. I suspect that this was the reaction you wanted since it would provide deterrence against displeasing you."

He grinned. "So, you didn't enjoy it at all? Not even a little bit on some level? That's too bad. I rather liked it. In fact, I must admit that it even gave me a bit of a boner."

I hadn't encountered the term "boner" before, but I thought it best not to raise the subject.

# TWENTY-FIVE: EYES AND EARS

My meeting with the captain was over before 10:00, so I helped with housekeeping. We decided that Kroz's time could be better spent probing the ship's systems, so Kroz stayed behind and worked in the corner of our quarters that the room's camera couldn't see.

When I cleaned the passageway outside of Spaggy's quarters, he asked whether I would mind tidying his room. When I was finished, he thanked me.

Spaggy asked me whether I would mind cleaning his dirty laundry. I required his assistance in locating the laundry facilities. He explained how to feed each article of clothing into a hopper on the machine and add cleanser. I learned that clothes were made of a variety of fabrics, and the machine would sense each item's composition and apply the appropriate concentration of cleaner and temperature. Then Spaggy showed me how to fold or hang each type of item.

While the cleaning machine worked, Spaggy asked me about my planet. I provided some cursory information and then asked him about himself. Spaggy said he was on his third tour with the captain. He had grown up poor but saw a great opportunity with Captain Skully. After the first tour, he was wealthy beyond any measure that he could have imagined, but he didn't understand why money was so important, and he felt he would be bored living in a mansion with no real adventure.

I appreciated my conversation with Spaggy. It reminded me of all my wonderful interactions with Sam, Captain Staedtler, and the crew of the *Pacifica Spirit*.

By the next day, word had spread regarding my work for Spaggy. My meeting with the captain was brief and unremarkable. After that our team set out to clean some new areas when crew members started asking us to clean their quarters. I cleaned Snowy's cabin, and he was appreciative.

Later, Bazz saw me in the passageway. "Hey, kloomer, get over here," he said. As I approached, Bazz pointed into his cabin. "Clean up that mess, kloomer. I'm gonna be back in an hour, and it better be perfect!"

When I entered the cabin, its contents were in utter disarray, as though Bazz had deliberately strewn things about to make the job more difficult for me.

I had Bazz's cabin cleaned and organized within forty-eight minutes. I spent the rest of the time cleaning the passageway. Bazz returned five minutes early. "Better be perfect," he warned. I watched from the doorway as he looked around. He dragged a fingertip across a shelf and examined it for dirt but saw none. The next thing he did was stand in the far corner, drop his pants, and urinate on the floor. "Missed a spot, kloomer," he said.

I took a cleaning bucket, a brush, and a dry towel, knelt on the floor, and started scrubbing. The odor of human urine was disgusting to me. I made quick work of the cleanup. "That'll do, kloomer," he said, just before delivering a kick to my midsection.

"Have I done something to cause you offense?" I asked.

He scowled. "I don't like you, and I don't like your type stinking up this ship!"

"Then I'll be sure to avoid you. Meanwhile, I suggest you don't call on any of us the next time you wet yourself."

Bazz's response was a kick to the back of my thigh as I walked away.

By the time our day was done, we had, between us, seen all of the occupied areas of the ship apart from the bridge. We exchanged information so that we were all fully up to date.

I updated the group regarding my encounter with Bazz. We concurred that we were under no obligation to clean a crew member's personal quarters, and we would no longer provide any such services to Bazz.

Ksoomu reported looking into Brawn's cabin. Brawn was lying on his front in the darkened room. He winced and inhaled sharply as Torm replaced the dressings on his injuries. Torm invited Ksoomu in and asked whether Ksoomu would be kind enough to tidy the cabin and dispose of the old dressings.

"I suppose you think I'm some sort of monster for what I did to Brawn here," Torm said.

"I think that we may all be in circumstances where we do what we have to do to survive," Ksoomu replied. "As disciplinarian, you have a very unpleasant duty, and it must be difficult sometimes."

Torm nodded. "Thank you for understanding."

Ksoomu reported that Torm had been extremely polite and grateful. Ksoomu's story made me realize that human beings exhibit so many paradoxes. Here was an example of a human who was capable of empathy and kindness but at the same time could inflict incredible suffering on others with great expertise and efficiency.

When we returned to our quarters, Kroz provided some welcome news. We could now access audio surveillance despite the fact that the ship's cameras had no microphones. What the ship did have was wall-mounted communication devices in most rooms. Through a process that no one else could understand, Kroz had managed to switch the devices on so that they were continuously sending the audio from each unit to an unused channel that we could receive.

Kroz modified the audio by increasing its frequency into the ultrasonic range, well beyond the range of human hearing. Within the ultrasonic range, Kroz set the sound from each device to its own sub-range. Kroz switched the audio on. At first, the sound was a jumble of voices and ship noises from all over the vessel, but thanks to our "multi-channel" kloormari hearing, it was fairly easy to focus on one range or another. I brought up the vid tiles on my Infotab. As I viewed the feed from each camera and came across a feed with humans talking, I could easily understand what they were saying.

For the first time since we had learned of the captain's betrayal, I felt hopeful. Now we had virtual eyes and ears throughout the ship. I thanked Kroz for the wonderful work and praised Kroz's talent, but Kroz cautioned me that seeing, hearing, and knowing did not translate to an ability to actually *do* anything about our situation.

"What would it take for us to be able to take action?" I asked.

"Control of this vessel," Kroz replied.

"What would be required to do that?"

"The problem is that all *control* systems are built around quantum encryption. The consoles on the bridge have been linked to the vessel's control systems via an encrypted interface. The systems can only be controlled from those physical consoles, and access to the bridge has been blocked."

"What would it take to link an interface other than the bridge consoles to the control systems?" I asked.

"According to most security documentation that I've read, only the captain can link a new device. He carries a 'command card' with him. When he isn't wearing a jacket, you may have noticed that he wears a lanyard around his neck, which leads into his shirt pocket. The captain would need to place the card in close proximity to an Infotab and then enter a command access code. The Infotab would use software on the card to direct control to another interface."

"Could the Infotab itself have that interface?"

"Yes, provided that some type of compatible vessel-control interface software was installed on the Infotab."

"So, our first step is to obtain the captain's command card."

"In theory, yes, but I can't think of how you would accomplish that. The card is on the captain's person at all times. If he's following standard protocol, he would only remove the card when going to bed for the night, in which case he would place it in a locked vault within his reach. The captain's cabin has a single door that opens onto the bridge. The only way to the captain's quarters is via the bridge."

"Is there no other route to the bridge or the captain's room?"

"Not in any practical sense. There are ventilation ducts throughout the vessel. You would have seen duct cover grates in each room, but they're far too small for any of us to fit through. You'd need a little robot or a small, trained creature to get through that maze."

I resolved to figure out how to get access to the command card. Kroz was pessimistic, but I thought it best to focus on finding a way, if for no other reason than to cling to hope to help maintain my sanity.

The next morning when I met with the captain, I reported Bazz's assault on me.

"That thundering idiot!" he shouted. "I bring you boys in to help lazy lumps like him, and this is how he shows gratitude? Don't worry, Kelvoo, I'll take care of Bazz but not just yet. Tomorrow morning, we arrive at Friendship Colony, and I need everyone alert, ready, and in high spirits. We're already down a man with Brawn in recovery, so I'll deal with Bazz *after* we make our deliveries."

"Is there anything we should do to prepare or practice for the mission tomorrow?"

"Can your team lift stuff and move it from one location to another?"

"Yes, Captain."

"Good. Then you're all eminently qualified for the mission. Don't worry; this one's easy. By the way, our meeting tomorrow is cancelled. The entire crew will assemble in C-12 at 08:00 for the pre-mission briefing. Make sure your team is there."

# TWENTY-SIX: FRIENDSHIP

The crew gathered in room C-12. We sensed a certain energy from the human crew members. I suspected they had been bored waiting for their mission, especially after the detour to Kuw'baal, so now they were eager for a change of scenery and to perform the work that they had signed up for.

My team had a different type of energy. We wanted to return home, but we wanted to make the best of our unfortunate situation. As such, we were eager to perform work that would benefit so many beings.

"I want to start by thanking all of you for your patience in waiting for this part of our mission," the captain began. "You've had to wait a little longer than usual, but we do have some extra helping hands." He motioned to the kloormari team. "The rest of you know this, but for the benefit of our new crew members, the medicine we'll be delivering has the pharmaceutical name Vinamibefentyn, but regular humans just call it 'vina,' so when you hear the crew or the people at Friendship Colony say 'vina,' they're referring to our precious cargo.

"I'm going to describe the plan for today, but if any of you have a question, raise a hand. It's a simple delivery mission, but we need to be clear on everything, so don't hesitate to ask if you're unsure about something.

"We're going to deliver the vina in ten stages using the cargo shuttle and the transport. One vessel will offload the vina while we load payment onto the other. Both vessels will return to *Jezebel's Fury* where the empty vessel will be loaded with more vina while the gold is offloaded from the full one. Spaggy will perform an assay on a few samples to verify the purity, and if everything looks good, we'll make the next sortie.

I raised my hand. "Captain, you said we would load payment. Isn't this a humanitarian mission?"

"Kelvoo! How quaint!" He laughed. "Did you think we'd be delivering the vina for free?"

"No, sir. I assumed the mission was being funded by a government or a charity."

The captain addressed the human crew. "What do you think, fellas?" He chuckled "Shall we become the 'Charitable Order of the Sons of Jezebel'?"

The crew roared with laughter.

"Don't you just love this guy?" he asked. "Kelvoo, you never fail to amaze and entertain me. I might just keep you around for a while!"

He regained control over the crowd and then provided some details about the situation on the ground. The colonists were so desperate that many of them would kill to get vina if they thought their neighbor had some. The health agency on the planet's surface had ten different landing and offloading sites but wouldn't provide the location until our vessels were on the way to avoid having landing sites overrun by frantic citizens.

Captain Skully selected a team of twelve human crew members to ferry the medication to the colony. He named them "Team Vina."

"I'll be personally leading the second team, consisting of our kloormari friends. They'll be handling the gold. They're 'Team Loot.'"

Bazz had a question, though he didn't bother to raise his hand. He just shouted. "Why should those kloomers get to handle the gold? Why should we trust those bastards?"

"Well, Bazz," the captain replied, "since you're so interested, I'll explain it to you. The only reason you're here is for the payout. These kloormari just want the experience and to do something productive. The payment they're getting goes straight to their village. So, who am I going to trust more, a bunch of cutthroats who'd sell their mamas down the river or a team of kloormari who wouldn't know or care how to spend a crate full of gold?

"As for you, Bazz, I know all about your contempt for our guests and your abuse of them, and I don't think much of you questioning my choices, so here's another choice I'm making. I'm taking you off this run. Snowy, you're taking Bazz's place."

Bazz clenched his jaw and his fists. He looked like a volcano, ready to erupt. He stared at the kloormari with an unsettling intensity.

The captain instructed both groups to proceed to the main cargo hold in thirty minutes to begin loading the transport.

Shortly after we returned to our quarters, we watched the live vid feed from the bridge. We saw the captain announcing a thirty-second warning for rapid deceleration and Pilo using controls on the bridge console to initiate the deceleration. The slowing was much like the previous hyper-acceleration with violent shaking and the alternating back-and-forth forces pulling and pushing us.

At the appointed time, we assembled in the main hold. The first thing I noticed was that each human on Team Vina was wearing a blaster in a holster. I assumed this was standard practice for most missions.

The captain had opened the huge safe, which was stacked with cube-shaped boxes, about ten centimeters long on each side. The boxes were stacked 66 high by 50 wide by 100 deep for a total of 330,000 boxes. Each box was marked "50 Doses."

He asked for two large and two smaller hoverlifts. We used the small lifts to offload the top layers of boxes before the lower layers could be accessed. Team Vina was assigned to one side of the container, and we were told to unload the other side. The captain requested each team to stack 17,500 boxes onto each of the two larger lifts so that 35,000 boxes could be loaded onto the transport for the first trip. While we were making the first delivery, the crew members who were to remain on board, including Bazz, would stack another 35,000 boxes for the next trip. For the tenth and final trip, the remaining 15,000 boxes would be delivered.

Team Vina rode the hoverlift to the top of the container and formed a chain. The man at the front grabbed a stack of ten boxes, turned to the next man in the line, and handed the boxes over until the last crew member in the chain placed them on the hoverlift's deck. The team stayed at the top of the container until they had to reach a long way in to get more boxes. They filled their hoverlift to the point at which there was barely room for the team to stand. Then they lowered the lift to the deck of the hold and slid their load off.

Team Loot took a different approach. We had all done the math in advance, with Kroz being the fastest calculator, so we let Kroz direct the operation from below. Unlike the humans, only five members of our team ascended on the hoverlift while the others waited below. We grabbed ten boxes at a time, like the humans did, but we only took a few boxes from the top layers and then took more from each lower level while the hoverlift slowly descended. With only five kloormari on board there was more room for boxes. Crew members could also jump or step off the hoverlift at the bottom levels, allowing for all of the deck space on the hoverlift to be covered when we reached the deck of the cargo hold.

We also had an anatomical advantage over the humans. Instead of twisting our bodies, we could lift a stack of boxes over our eyes and down behind us to hand off to the next kloormar in the chain.

"Hey, not fair!" Wanky said with a smile when he saw us performing the maneuver.

The captain watched the performance while slowly shaking his head with admiration and disbelief. "Not fair indeed!" he remarked with a grin.

I estimated that we outperformed the humans by 72 percent. When we completed our stack of fifty by fifty by seven boxes, we assisted Team Vina, making short work of the first batch. As Team Vina moved the large hoverlifts into the cargo transport, the captain and Team Loot made their way up to the hangar on the top deck.

We boarded the cargo shuttle that had originally taken us to the *Jezebel's Fury*. As the hatch at the top of the hangar opened, I saw the planet that was home to Friendship Colony. The planet appeared to be about 95 percent ocean with a few scattered islands. The polar regions were covered in ice while the equatorial zone was as blue as a sapphire.

The shuttle cleared the hatch and moved to a point beside the vessel's bow where we saw the huge landing bay doors open and the transport emerge. Instead of moving toward the planet, both vessels actually rose to a geosynchronous orbit just south of Friendship Island, where the colony was located. This would let us move directly to the landing coordinates rather than having to wait to complete an orbit. The captain made contact with the planet's health agency. "Ready for first coordinates."

The landing coordinates were provided, followed by a desperate "Please hurry!" We made an unnervingly rapid descent through the atmosphere and into a heavily fortified and fenced area several hectares in size and far from the towns and villages that we could see on the island. The much larger transport landed in the middle of a field, giving the captain a chance to land the smaller, more maneuverable shuttle close by. Its rear hatch opened before we had even touched down.

Through the hatch, we saw twenty-three humans sprinting across the field to the transport as its rear hatch opened. The captain ran to the transport's hatch. "Stand back and let them at the cargo! Don't block them! Just get the hell out of their way!"

The first colonist ran headlong into a stack of boxes and ripped one open, grabbing a dose. The other forty-nine doses were scattered across the deck as the colonist flung the box away and ripped the packaging open on her dose. Each dose of vina was in a plastic tube with a short needle inside a clear, spring-loaded plunger. The colonist slammed the tube onto her upper leg, and the plunger pushed the needle into her thigh muscle.

By this time, the remaining members of the colonist ground crew had reached the transport, falling over one another, scrabbling over the deck on their hands and knees to pick up one of the spilled doses or grabbing a new box and ripping it open. As the colonists injected a dose, they made their way onto the field's grassy vegetation, laid down, and took a moment to weep with relief or close their eyes and lie motionless.

By then, both of our teams were gathered to the side of the hatch, close to the captain. "Poor bastards," he said. "It's going to take ten minutes or so before they actually feel physical relief, but they've got a dose in them, and they know it's going to be alright."

After no more than two or three minutes, most of the colonists stirred. They looked at our group and thanked us profusely for saving their lives. Some cried and some knelt before us, groveling with praise. I had expected at least a few of the colonists to stare at me and my teammates since they would never have seen beings like us before, but there was no such response. Clearly, receiving their vina was so important that anything else was of no significance.

"Don't you have the rest of a planet to save?" the captain asked the colonists with a smirk.

They got up and walked briskly or jogged to a big metal structure, bringing out a large hoverlift loaded with stacked totes. Two empty hoverlifts also moved toward our vessels.

"Team Loot, get those totes loaded onto the shuttle!" the captain shouted.

We moved to the cargo shuttle and transferred hundreds of open-topped totes, each loaded to the brim with shiny gold bars. We finished loading just as the transport finished unloading. Now that the colonist ground crew had taken their first doses, they were extremely calm, very efficient, and no doubt wanting to distribute the vina planet-wide as quickly and as equitably as possible.

With our first delivery complete, each team boarded their respective vessels. The captain was in a buoyant (and I daresay, generous) frame of mind. He invited me to sit with him in the cockpit. As we lifted off, I looked down and could see the colony's ground crew moving the vina-laden hoverlifts into two of the colony's shuttles for distribution.

On our way back to *Jezebel's Fury*, I asked the captain how much time would pass until the colonists required more vina. He explained that the medicine lingered in a human's tissues for a long time. Each dose was usually effective for about six weeks, so when we completed the final delivery that day, the Friendship colonists would have about a year's supply.

When we arrived back at the *Jezebel's Fury*, the onboard crew had become more efficient, and a new load of vina was ready. The captain and I rode the gold-laden hoverlift down to the main cargo deck. We stowed the gold in a large, secure container, much like the one that had contained the vina.

Within fifteen minutes we departed on another sortie. This time we were directed to a different landing zone. We happened to pass over the previous offload site, and I saw that several hundred colonists had breached the perimeter of the site and were roaming through the field. The colony's shuttles were no longer there, and I assumed they had departed safely with their life-saving cargo.

Our second offload was similar to the first, except that we heard a massive, growing crowd outside the perimeter screaming, "Vina! Vina! Vina!"

For the return trip, I asked the captain to give another team member the opportunity to "ride shotgun" with him. With each subsequent sortie, a different kloormar rode with the captain, and the chaos at each landing site was diminished, indicating that the medication was being distributed successfully.

On the way back from the sixth trip, we were starting to feel fatigued. I realized we were burning a great deal of energy. K'tatmal was in the co-pilot seat and asked the captain whether we could go to our quarters quickly to consume some algel. He said we were on too tight a schedule, so he called ahead and asked a crew member to fetch a large bucket of algel, which was ready for us when we landed. We realized that, on future missions, we should each take a small container of algel with us.

Our final sortie landed well after night fell over the colony. By that time, there was no more desperation for vina, and it was safe for us to touch down on a large pad on top of the colony's main health center. The colony's leader and the minister of health met us and expressed their unlimited gratitude. They also invited us to a celebration. Captain Skully thanked them but said we were all exhausted and had to be underway since we were behind schedule for other important missions.

When we disembarked from the cargo shuttle in the hangar, Skully thanked us for the good work. He also told me that we could dispense with the daily meetings. "Just let me know whenever you want to have a chat, Kelvoo."

We returned to our quarters in our most upbeat mood since our first arrival on the ship. Even if Skully had charged the colonists an exorbitant amount for the vina, I felt we had done a good thing, judging by the colonists' immense gratitude. Skully had complimented our work, and we were well aware of how much time and effort we had saved the crew. I thought that perhaps even Bazz was going to see us in a different light and that we might just finish our six months of duty intact.

My thoughts were interrupted by Kroz. "We should all listen to this."

Kroz brought up the vid feed from the barroom along with the ambient sounds from the ship. An animated discussion was happening among several crew members. "I don't trust those effing kloomers, and you shouldn't either!" Bazz said. "Did you see those smug bastards loading that vina, trying to make us look bad?"

"So what?" Ebo replied. "Did you see how much work they saved us? I wish we had twice as many of them!"

"Oh, course you do! That's their plan! They work for almost no pay. They use their freakish mutant skills to outperform us, and next thing you know, we're gone."

"What do you mean, gone?" Spaggy asked.

"Think about it, Spag. Did you see Skully praising those parasites? Practically tripping over himself to kiss their alien backsides! First, they make us look weak and lazy, and then they worm their way into the minds of the people in power. Think about it, all of you. If you're the captain, why would you bother with humans anymore? Just hire a bunch of low-wage kloomer freaks instead, and keep all the profits for yourself!"

"Look, we don't want to make any trouble with the captain," Snowy said. "When this mission's over, I'm going to retire a rich, rich man. So what if more kloormari end up on dangerous missions? No skin off my lily-white nose! Come to think of it, maybe I'll want to hire a bunch of them to take care of my manicured property and pool. Maybe they could clean my mansion, cook my meals, and serve fancy little appetizers at my lavish parties. Yeah, I can see it now!"

"That's exactly what I'm talking about!" Bazz said. "This is just the beginning. First, they worm their way onto this ship. Then the captain tells all the other captains how much better they are. Then they get jobs on Perdition and Exile. And then before you know it, humans are the minority on our planets! These bastards are evil, and they're out to replace us. These aliens are going to sneak up on us, and the next thing you know, we'll be replaced!"

"You know, he might have a point," Wanky said. Tank nodded in agreement.

"What do you think we should do?" Tank asked.

"I haven't figured that out yet," Bazz replied. "We still have a while before the end of this mission. One thing's for sure, we need to get rid of them before we head back home."

Tank and Wanky seemed convinced by Bazz's assertions, but Ebo and Snowy looked skeptical. We couldn't tell which way the other crew in the barroom were leaning.

As the gathering split up for the night, Bazz left the group with the following words: "Think about it, fellas. Let it sink in. We can talk more about it later."

We were all shocked. None of us could have foreseen that our exemplary service could backfire and turn our human crewmates against us. Any optimism we had after Friendship Colony evaporated. We had studied enough human history to know what xenophobia looked like and where it inevitably led. We had to find a way out and gaining control of the vessel seemed like our best option.

As I settled in for the first shift of meditation, the germ of an idea started to form in my mind. In my meditative state, I analyzed my idea and ran various scenarios. When I woke up and the second shift of meditation started, I studied the vessel schematic and developed multiple plans, each of which took many variables into account. My idea would be risky, but the risks presented by the hatred from some of the crew would become much greater over time.

At 08:00, we consumed our morning meal, and then I asked the others to gather around. "I have plans that could help us gain control of this ship. Kroz, when we talked about ways to access the captain's quarters, we talked about the ventilation ducts. You said we'd need a little robot or a small, trained creature to get through that maze. What I'm asking from all of you is this: Please, put a baby in me."

# TWENTY-SEVEN: MR. KELVOO'S CLASS

Disagreement is rare in kloormari communities. When faced with choices, an immediate consensus is usually reached, and the choice proves to be the best option in a great majority of cases. At least that was true on Kuw'baal.

Of course, on Kuw'baal, life had followed the same routine, the environment was stable, and we were a single species whose individuals looked, sounded, and behaved in a similar manner, so there were few variables to consider when making a decision.

This certainly was not the case on the *Jezebel's Fury*. We had widely varying opinions on whether we should produce an infant kloormar to access parts of the vessel that were off-limits to us.

We discussed the length of time it would take to prepare a baby for such tasks. We assumed twenty-eight days for gestation plus up to forty days for learning. Since the offspring would not be running around a village much of the time, I estimated that, with each of us taking shifts, we could educate a baby to follow the necessary instructions by thirty days postpartum. Either way, the baby would require over two months of preparation, so it certainly didn't present a short-term solution. I thought we could keep searching for a quick fix while the baby kloormar was being trained.

The team discussed and debated the risks of my idea. We knew that if the baby was caught before completing its mission, the repercussions for the baby could be terrible and possibly deadly. The same would be true for us, though any other attempt to escape could mean a similar fate.

In the context of the norms of kloormari society, my reasoning for having a child was unorthodox at best. There was no change in the availability of resources, and our population of nine was not advanced in age and in need of a replacement any time soon.

In the end, we all decided against adding a new kloormar, but the option was available if circumstances changed in the near term.

At 09:04, a ship-wide announcement warned the crew of a jump in thirty minutes' time. We were grateful that the captain had chosen to give us a more reasonable amount of time to prepare mentally. I suspected he had only given us thirty seconds the first time just to "mess with our heads," something he had seemed to take delight in.

We were as well prepared as we could be when the thirty-second jump countdown started. Once again, my surroundings disappeared, my body fled the scene, and what seemed to be my consciousness was adrift in space. I kept my panic in check and tried to think about what I was seeing and feeling. This time, the experience was much more interesting than terrifying.

When the jump was over, it didn't take long for the countdown to hyper-acceleration to begin. Kroz watched the vid feed from the bridge and heard the captain request a target velocity of 998. I pulled out my Infotab to monitor the vessel's speed. No speed was displayed.

When acceleration started, it was as bouncy and had as much push-pull force as before. I kept watching the speed readout, which started displaying at a value of ten. It rose rapidly until 995, then the rate of increase slowed until velocity stabilized, ranging between 997.9973 and 998.62.

We were preparing for our cleaning shift to start at the usual time of 10:00 when Reverend Hol decided to let himself in again. We had no interest in further conversion attempts from Hol.

"Lads," he said, "don't worry. I'm not here to talk to you about God or religion, at least not this time. I'm actually here to ask a favor. We have a crew member named Murph. He's a very good man and a devoted member of my flock. I'm sure you've seen him around and cleaned his quarters, but Murph keeps to himself, so you probably aren't acquainted. Anyway, Murph has two young daughters, and he's here with them because his wife went to heaven a couple of years ago."

*Oh no,* I thought. *Here comes another round of preaching.* Fortunately, the reverend didn't go there.

"Murph has heard about how smart all of you are. He asked me whether you could help to make his daughters smart. I reminded him that the education of females isn't exactly encouraged and might not be looked upon favorably by the crew. What I *did* suggest is that you might be able to teach the girls to read. Nothing wrong with a woman reading a recipe book or scripture, that's what I say! So, are any of you lads interested in teaching?"

I considered the possibility. I wondered whether educating not only the children but also crew members might alleviate the crew's paranoia. If we could help empower the crew and set them up for more rewarding and meaningful careers, perhaps they would see us as allies.

My teammates had similar thoughts.

"We might be interested," K'raftan said. "If my teammates agree, perhaps we can all be involved and take turns teaching Murph's daughters."

"That sounds good," Hol replied, "but how would you coordinate with each other so that you aren't repeating the same lessons or skipping ahead too fast?"

"We are kloormari. We can brief the group after each day's lesson, and within forty-five seconds we can be fully coordinated for the next day," K'raftan said.

"That sounds wonderful. Now please forgive me for having to ask this, but which one of you is Kelvoo?"

I stepped forward.

"I hope you don't mind," Hol said, "but the captain knows and trusts you best, so if it's alright, I'd like you to provide the first lesson."

"When would you like me to start?"

"Er, well, actually, Kelvoo, is there any chance you could come with me now?"

"I suppose it would be alright if my teammates don't mind covering for me. Perhaps I could just introduce myself and see whether reading lessons might work out."

"Thank you so much, Kelvoo. Murph and the girls will be so delighted! Please come with me."

Hol led me along the "back route" to a corridor where some of the crew's quarters were accessible. He knocked on a cabin door, and Murph opened it. Murph had a large fleshy face and a large fleshy body. His hair was short and bristly, and he had a stylized heart inked onto one of his cheeks with "Sally" written across it. "Murph, I'd like you to meet Kelvoo. He and his kloormari friends have agreed to teach your little girls to read."

Murph asked us to come in, speaking in a soft voice. His bunk was located on the left. An image of a smiling woman was placed on a small table beside his bed. A length of string was draped across the right side of the room with sheets serving as makeshift curtains. The sheets had been pulled to one side, so I could see two cots placed there.

Two small pairs of eyes peered at me from behind the curtain. "Now, don't be shy girls," Hol said. "This is Mr. Kelvoo. Come on out now and introduce yourselves."

The older girl jumped out from behind the curtain and giggled. The younger one moved to a spot where she was partly hidden behind her sister, then leaned to one side to look at me.

"Hi, Mr. Kelvoo, I'm Brenna," the older girl said. "And this is May," she added, pointing to May's face beside her.

"Hi, Mistoo Keloo," May said. "I'm May an' dat's Bwenna."

"Well," Hol said, "looks like you lot are going to get on like a house on fire! I'm going to get out of your way now."

With that, Hol disappeared. I had no idea how to interact with small children, so I started by asking them their ages.

"I'm ten years old," said Brenna.

"I'm almos' dis many," May added, holding up her thumb and all of her fingers on one hand.

"How old are you, Mr. Kelvoo?" Brenna asked.

"I'm seventy-one years old, Brenna."

She frowned. "How many is seventy-one?" It was clear that advanced mathematics wasn't Brenna's strong suit.

"This many," I said, making seventy-one of the tendrils on the back of my hands stand upright.

"Wowee!" she exclaimed.

I decided to jump straight into the first lesson. "So, before you can learn how to read, you have to know the alphabet."

"I know my alphabet!" Brenna declared.

"Excellent! Can you recite it for me?"

"What's recite?"

"Sorry, can you *say* it for me?"

Brenna got as far as "P" before losing track.

"I know my ABC!" May proclaimed.

"That's great, May. Can you say it for me?"

"Sure. A, B, C!"

Thus began the education of Brenna and May and the illustrious teaching careers of the kloormari faculty. I knew that teaching these girls to read would be a long process requiring exquisite patience. I didn't know much about the development of intelligence in human children, but I thought that perhaps the restrictive environment on the *Jezebel's Fury* might have delayed their progress.

After an hour of reviewing the remaining letters of the alphabet, I announced that the lesson was over for the day. I told the girls that another teacher would continue their lesson at the same time the following day. The girls looked concerned.

"Is the other teacher nice?" May asked.

I assured the girls that the other teachers were exactly like me.

"I'm glad," Brenna said.

Murph, who had been watching the lesson intently, thanked me profusely as I left the cabin.

# TWENTY-EIGHT: WAR

Several days passed uneventfully. We monitored conversations throughout the vessel, but apart from occasional grumbling by Bazz about "effing kloomers," no anti-kloormari conspiracies seemed to be afoot.

May and Brenna's education continued. They couldn't tell their teachers apart or remember our names, but since we were all kloormari, we were collectively known as "Mr. Kloormar" by Brenna and "Mistoo Koomah" by May. They were still learning the basic sounds made by each letter in the standard Terran alphabet.

Occasionally, we saw Brawn up and about. I didn't know whether to feel empathy for the beating he had taken or disdain for the beating he had inflicted on the young woman. We tended to avoid him.

As we approached our next stop in the Benzolar system, the vessel completed the usual rapid deceleration, and the entire crew was summoned to C-12 for a mission briefing. Remembering that we had run low on food during the last mission, we filled resealable bags with algel and put them into a pouch on our belts.

In C-12, rows of chairs had been set up, facing a large display panel.

"Good morning, gentlemen," Captain Skully said. "For those who aren't familiar with the situation on Benzolar 3, we're delivering defensive weaponry to the planetary government."

Thanks to our ability to see and hear throughout the vessel, we already knew the overall situation and much of what he would be saying. We were quite up to date, in part from listening in on the captain's communications with the planet.

"Two years ago," he continued, "a violent terrorist organization was formed with the intention of overthrowing the government. The terrorist insurgency has been making serious gains, so we have the task of getting a couple of thousand blaster rifles and chargers, fifty pulse mortar launchers, and fifty surveillance drones to the government forces."

He displayed an aerial image of our area of operations. A major city was located on a plateau. Patches of forest and scrublands surrounded the city. To the west, on the city's outskirts, the plateau ended where a steep slope and cliffs led down to a wide river valley and forests below. Sentry towers were spaced along the edge of the plateau overlooking the slope, ready to defend against attacks from below. An armory was stationed about 300 meters from the edge of the slope, and a landing pad was located beside the building.

The captain switched to a map showing the features close to the armory and landing pad. The map illustrated berms of rock and dirt scattered between the building and the precipice, providing firing positions against enemies that might approach from the slope.

"We're going to load the cargo transport with the weapons crates. They're stacked in section 1A of the main hold. There have been reports of terrorist activity in the area, so this is a straight in and out mission. We dump the weapons and get the hell out as quickly as possible. Don't worry about collecting payment. Most of the SimCash has already been transferred to our account. The remainder will be transferred when our friends have done a quick inventory of the goods.

"Each human on this mission will carry a sidearm and will form a perimeter around the landing zone. We're not expecting any need for your blasters since government troops will be defending you—your blasters are just a precaution but stay alert. If you run into any trouble, you will defend the mission and your fellow crew members. There are to be no heroics or grandstanding. As for the kloormari, they will only handle offloading of the crates. Let's get this done with as little excitement as possible. Pilo will operate the transport, and Tank will lead this mission. I will remain onboard *Jezebel's Fury* and coordinate as needed."

His last sentence produced a few grumbles from the humans. He provided an opportunity for questions, but there were none.

"Alright, the kloormari will proceed to the main hold and get ready to move the crates from section 1A. The rest of you will collect your sidearms and join our kloormari friends. Spaggy will oversee loading. When the transport is loaded, Tank will take over operations. All of you will work together. Take care of yourselves and each other. Crew is dismissed."

In the main hold, each section was delineated on the deck as a yellow painted rectangle. Section 1A was on the starboard side right beside the large doors to the landing bay. The doors had already been opened along with the transport's rear hatch, so we had a clear path to start loading.

We weren't sure of the packing order or the load balancing that Spaggy might want, so we laid out the cargo in the configuration that we thought would be optimal just outside of the transport's hatch. There were 200 long white boxes. Each had a hinged top with two latches. Along the sides of each box were two strap handles. Based on the size and quantity of the boxes, we inferred that each box housed ten blaster rifles.

Larger crates held the remaining weaponry. We stacked the white boxes in a long line with the larger crates along each side. The stacks were complete and ready for loading in ten minutes, which was when the human crew arrived. We asked Spaggy whether our proposed layout met the requirements for configuration and load balancing.

"Yeah, I guess," he replied. "Okay, let's get the transport loaded." In ten more minutes, the task was completed.

There was an empty space in the transport forward of the hold and aft of the cockpit. A few small windows provided a view out of the sides of the fuselage. We squeezed into the space with the rest of the crew. Bazz had positioned himself as far from our group as possible. We noticed that Brawn had recovered enough to join the group. There were no seats—the space allowed for standing room only. Looped straps hung from overhead railings, which could be held to stay upright during flight. Loops were also positioned on the floor.

The landing bay's exterior doors opened as the transport ascended and hovered. The transport accelerated quickly to clear the landing bay. I could see why. Once the vessel was clear of the deck, it was no longer in the ship's gravitational field, and it shot "up" immediately. By leaving the ship quickly, we avoided having the nose rise suddenly and the vertical thrusters pushing us up into the top of the landing bay opening.

We were suddenly weightless. The humans remained stationary, as they had known to put their feet through the floor loops. We lost our footing and had to reposition our feet back on the floor to use the loops.

As the transport got underway, the humans began to shout out their song. "We're the boys of *Jezebel's Fury*. We're rotten low-life scum . . ." This time, we kloormari joined in out of our wish to fit in with the crew. The humans didn't seem to mind our participation, though it felt odd to me to call myself a dirty son of a dirty whore and to sing that I killed with a smile and was sick and vile.

We plunged directly toward the planet. It was mostly brown land and green forest with a few small bodies of water. Any cloud cover seemed to be over mountaintops. We were too high to see enough detail, but I thought that the rain in the mountains must feed rivers that flowed into lakes.

As we entered the atmosphere, we were accompanied by four small fighter craft from the planet. Two of the craft led the way, and the remaining two flew along each side of us. We started to descend directly to the landing zone. Looking through the cockpit windows, I recognized the armory and landing pad from the aerial images.

A few flashes of blue light appeared ahead of us from the edge of the precipice. A fraction of a second later, balls of blue plasma streaked past us. The two lead fighters accelerated ahead, the left one peeling off while the two remaining fighters laid down suppressing fire aimed at the spot where the flashes had originated. The transport dropped sharply to avoid the plasma blasts. The lead fighter that had moved to the left flew over the edge of the plateau from left to right, dropping incendiary devices. The edge of the precipice lit up with balls of flame, soaring fifty meters into the air.

We landed abruptly. The human crew members moved ahead, taking up positions behind the dirt and rock berms, facing the drop-off. Government troops lined the roof of the armory. The ruins of two sentry towers were visible. I could only guess that they had been destroyed in a previous attack. Our surroundings were strangely quiet.

We began offloading onto hoverlifts that the government troops rode to and from the armory. About halfway through our offload, a plasma ball ripped through the top of a tree beside the transport, splintering branches with an enormous crack and sending charred leaves floating to the ground. That's when, as the humans say, all hell broke loose! Blaster fire erupted from the drop-off to our right. Volleys of pulse mortars landed nearby. On impact, the mortars sent out blue-tinted plasma shockwaves that raised dust from the ground and sent pebbles and rocks flying.

The human crew members who, minutes earlier, had sung about their sass, gall, and love of killing were suddenly transformed into a shouting, screaming agglomeration of terrified men. Some fired indiscriminately toward the precipice or toward an unseen enemy in the trees and bushes to the right.

We kloormari just offloaded crates as fast as possible. Suddenly, we heard the boom of a pulse mortar and felt the concussive wave hit us like a punch to the abdomen. From behind a berm, we heard Mec screaming. "Man down!"

One of the government soldiers grabbed Keeto's shoulder. "What's the matter with you? Go help your buddy and keep yourself low to the ground." Keeto laid down and used all twelve limbs to rush toward Mec, "centipede style."

About two minutes later, we saw Mec and Keeto running toward us with Ebo between them. They each had one of Ebo's arms draped around their shoulders and were supporting him as they ran. Unexpectedly, Keeto was holding a blaster. Ebo had a cut across his forehead and lacerations on his face and upper torso. Mec and Keeto had Ebo's blood on their upper bodies. They threw Ebo into the transport. Keeto put the blaster into Ebo's holster and then joined the rest of the kloormari as we worked frantically to complete the offload.

Next, Pilo came running toward us, crouched low, a look of terror on his face. He jumped into the cockpit and switched on an external loudspeaker. "Bug out! Bug out! Bug out!" he screamed.

The rest of the human crew ran back to the transport. "We've nearly finished offloading!" I shouted.

"Screw the offload, you kloomer idiot!" Mec shouted as he threw a switch that started the rear hatch closing. "All of you, get onboard now!"

Chaos ensued as humans and kloormari tripped over one another to get onboard. I was about to board on the port side of the vessel with Mec behind me. On the starboard side, K'tatmal was about to come around to our side when three figures dressed in black emerged from the underbrush and grabbed K'tatmal from behind. With one swift motion, one of the terrorists placed a black bag over K'tatmal's eye dome.

"They've got K'tatmal!" I shouted as they dragged K'tatmal away. I turned to give chase, but Mec grabbed me and threw me into the transport, then jumped in and pulled the hatch shut. I scrambled to the starboard side and pressed my eye to a window. I caught a glimpse of a small personal vessel skimming over the treetops. It had a two-passenger cab up front and an open box in the rear. Two of the terrorists were in the rear, holding on to K'tatmal. The vessel was being strafed with blaster fire from the roof of the armory. The last I saw of K'tatmal was when the vessel descended over the precipice and fled down into the valley.

As we were about to lift off, we saw two fighter craft return to strafe and burn a line along the drop-off and into the trees. The transport was hovering barely above ground when Pilo put it into reverse and knocked over a lighting pylon on the way out. He spun the vessel 180 degrees and rapidly accelerated away from the drop-off, skimming treetops and buildings as he went. In a minute, we had covered several kilometers. That's when Pilo decided we were far enough from the action that he could pull up and blast the transport almost vertically out of the atmosphere of Benzolar 3.

During our escape, we were bounced around and squashed against bulkheads. Mec and Spaggy did their best to attend to Ebo's injuries. Since the transport didn't carry first-aid equipment, Mec and Spaggy used dirty rags to staunch Ebo's bleeding. As we became weightless, Mec and Spaggy had their feet in the floor loops and held onto Ebo as he floated between them, drops of Ebo's blood floating through the compartment as shiny red spheres.

Nobody said a word. Everything had happened so fast that all of us, human and kloormari alike, were struggling to process what we had just experienced. When the transport touched down in the landing bay, it seemed to take an unbearable amount of time for the outer doors to close, for the landing bay to repressurize, and for the inner doors to swing open.

Captain Skully was waiting in the cargo hold. I assumed that Pilo had briefed him on the situation during the return flight. Murph and Torm had remained on the *Jezebel's Fury* during our mission. They were waiting with a stretcher to take care of Ebo.

The crew filed out of the transport with blank, defeated looks on their faces. I wondered how the captain was going to berate the crew for the botched operation. Instead, he exhibited empathy and concern. As the crew filed by, Skully would touch a crew member's shoulder and say things like, "Are you alright, lad?"

When Ebo passed by on the stretcher, Skully took a moment to offer words of comfort.

"Sorry it all got so screwed up, Captain," Spaggy said as he passed.

"Don't be sorry, Spaggy. You boys didn't screw up—our customers did. They should have provided a safer landing zone or done a better job clearing the site. Look at the big picture. Despite being under fire, you delivered everything but a couple of boxes of rifles. Good enough! Best of all, you did it with none of you getting killed." He looked up and saw me standing behind Spaggy. "Well," he added, "maybe."

I hung back until the rest of the crew had departed. "I guess you know that K'tatmal was taken prisoner," I said. "Is there anything we can do to rescue K'tatmal? Could we maybe negotiate a ransom payment?"

"I'm sorry, Kelvoo. You need to understand that your friend was taken by ruthless, bloodthirsty terrorists. Those people don't value the lives of other human beings, so they certainly won't care about a kloormar. I hate to say this, but if K'tatmal is lucky, they will have killed him by now. If not, they will use the most awful interrogation techniques first. The sooner that you and your friends accept that K'tatmal is gone, the sooner you can heal and move on."

I knew that even if K'tatmal could have escaped from the terrorists, there was only a small quantity of algel in K'tatmal's belt pouch, so it wouldn't be more than three days before death from dehydration or starvation.

As I came to the awful realization that I would never see K'tatmal again, I experienced an emptiness that I hadn't felt since Sam's departure. *This shouldn't happen,* I thought. *On Kuw'baal, when a villager dies, their contribution to the community may be missed, but life goes on. We might place the body in a stream to replenish the planet's nutrients, but we never feel a hollow misery like I'm feeling now.*

I recalled what I had learned about emotional bonding between humans and how humans who have shared joyful or traumatic experiences have stronger emotional connections. Since we had been through much more than any previous group of kloormari, it may have been that our bonds with one another were so much stronger, and the pain when those bonds were broken was so much worse.

When we returned to our quarters, we didn't say a word to one another. I displayed the ship's vid feeds on my Infotab and listened to the vessel's ambient sounds. Little more than the steady thrumming of the mechanical systems could be heard. Almost all of the dialog was from the passageway outside of Ebo's quarters where Murph and Torm were treating his injuries. Ebo was talking, which I thought was a good sign that he would recover.

After a few minutes, Mec opened the door to our quarters. "Which one of you came to help me on Benzolar when we were under fire?" he asked. "Captain wants to see us in the hangar to ask what happened."

"That was me," Keeto said, leaving with Mec.

207

Once again, I pulled out my Infotab to watch the vid feed and tapped the tile that provided a full-screen view of the hangar. There was no sign of the captain. Only Bazz and Tank were there. I went back to the tiled view and saw Captain Skully step from the bridge onto his cabin.

I switched back to the hangar view and saw Mec entering with Keeto. Tank grabbed Keeto and then slammed Keeto into a wall. I alerted my fellow kloormari, who brought up the same view on their Infotabs.

While Tank kept Keeto pinned to the wall, Bazz put his face right up to Keeto's eye. "Well, well, now we finally know what you kloomer bastards are really about!"

"I do not understand," Keeto replied.

"We were being fired upon, and you did nothing to defend us! Nothing!"

"You were asking me to do something I wasn't capable of!" Keeto retorted, clearly frightened.

"Yeah, and I know why!" Mec shouted. "Because you and your freak species are cowards! Yellow-bellied, slime-sucking, worthless cowards!"

In our quarters, my fellow kloormari and I watched the scene unfold in horror. "We should go up there and stop this!" Kroz said.

"But if we do, it could give away the fact that we have the vessel under surveillance," K'raftan said.

Bazz held his blaster up to Keeto's eye. "I should just blast its worthless brains out right now!"

"You are not aiming at the correct place for that," Keeto said.

"Shut up!" Bazz shouted as he kicked Keeto in the mid-abdominal area.

"Look, we need to do something," Mec said to Bazz. "I wish we could just kill the whole lot of these kloomers and be done with it, but the captain's going to have a problem with that."

"You know, I've heard that if one of these kloomers loses an arm or a leg, it'll grow back," Tank said.

Bazz smiled wickedly. "Well, let's find out, shall we?"

Mec helped Tank pin Keeto down. Bazz grabbed one of Keeto's topmost claspers and tugged violently. Keeto began to scream from all eight vocal outlets in a horrifying, discordant blend of noises.

Kroz left our quarters. "I can't let this happen."

Bazz's tugging wasn't working, so he started twisting Keeto's limb. Keeto's shrieks became so loud that the three humans winced in pain at the assault on their ears. Bazz finally managed to separate the limb from Keeto's body. Connective tissue bridged the gap between Keeto's limb and body before snapping. Milky bluish bodily fluid spilled from the hole left in Keeto's side and from the limb itself.

Keeto's body slumped to the deck and started shaking with violent shock-induced seizures. Bazz took the severed limb and started beating Keeto with it. As Bazz swung the limb up to take another blow, a chunk of "meat" flew out of the limb, leaving a hollow tube that Bazz used to land a couple of additional blows.

"You say a word about this, and we'll do even worse to the whole lot of you!" Bazz warned Keeto.

We could take no more. We all ran from our quarters to put a stop to the torture. By the time we arrived at the hangar—and even by the time that Kroz had arrived ahead of us—Mec, Tank, and Bazz were gone. I put the end of one of my hands into Keeto's wound to stem the flow of fluid, and then we all carried Keeto back to our quarters.

Keeto lapsed in and out of shock and unconsciousness.

"What happened down on the planet?" K'raftan asked.

"I crawled to Mec's position, and he pointed over to Ebo," Keeto explained between seizures. "The berm that Ebo was behind was hit by a blast wave from a mortar. Rocks were blasted from the top of the berm and hit Ebo in the head and chest. I dodged blaster fire to run across open ground to Ebo. Mec told me to grab Ebo's sidearm, so I did. He shouted, 'Lay down some covering fire, so I can get over there and help Ebo.' I said, 'I can't do that; I might kill someone.' Mec said, 'That's the whole idea!' Then he called me a kloomer idiot. In the end, I shot at the ground in front of a terrorist position, and Mec ran over. We grabbed Ebo and ran back to the transport with him."

Keeto had another bout of seizures before he continued. "I'm sorry; I just couldn't do it. I can't kill another being, no matter how bad they are!"

"None of us can," I assured Keeto.

"You need to rest now, Keeto," Kroz said. "Just close your eye and relax."

"There's just one more thing," Keeto stated before losing consciousness, turning to me. "Kelvoo, I think we need to take another look at your idea. I think you should have a baby."

# TWENTY-NINE: DEATH AND RENEWAL

It wasn't long after the horror in the hangar when we used our Infotabs to watch a group of crew members, including Tank, Mec, and Bazz, use their access cards to barge onto the bridge and demand to speak with Captain Skully.

"Look," Skully said, "we're getting prepped for the next jump. Can't this wait a few hours?" The trio assured him that it could not.

"Fine," he said, "we'll talk in the barroom, but make it quick. Go there now, and I'll be a couple of minutes behind you." We followed Skully on the vid feeds. We saw him go to Torm's quarters and ask him whether his sidearm had been stowed yet. Torm still had his blaster in his cabin. Skully asked him to put it in his holster and accompany him to the barroom "just in case."

We switched our view to the vid feed from the barroom and watched Skully and Torm join Tank, Mec, and Bazz. Tank didn't beat around the bush. "We've had it with those effing kloomers, Captain. We want 'em off this ship now!"

"And why exactly is that?" Skully asked in exasperation.

"Because we can't trust them!" Mec said. "Ebo was knocked out cold, and I was pinned down. I called for help, and some freaking kloomer crawled up to me like some kinda freaking lobster. I pointed to Ebo, and next thing you know, the kloomer was getting shot at while it sprinted over to Ebo. I told it to grab Ebo's blaster and start shooting to give me cover, so I could get over there. But the bastard refused! Seriously! It said, 'Ooh, la-di-da, I can't do that. I might kill someone.'"

Skully's reply started off calmly, but it didn't stay that way. "So, let me get this straight. You're telling me that you were pinned down by enemy fire, your crewmate was lying on the ground injured, and you called for help. Next, a kloormar, whose only job was to offload cargo, risked his life by crossing dangerous ground to offer assistance. Next, that kloormar got shot at while crossing the battlefield to help your injured crewmate, and now you're complaining because he wouldn't shoot at the enemy? The way some of you buffoons—and yes, I'm looking at you, Bazz—the way you've been treating the kloormari, you should be grateful that the kloormar didn't shoot you and claim that the enemy did it! Of course, that wouldn't happen, because the kloormari are incapable of killing anything. That's why they don't carry weapons on missions. All three of you should be grateful for the help, and you, Mec, should be especially grateful that one brave kloormar came to your aid and helped save your crewmate's life!"

By then, Captain Skully was bellowing with rage. "Now, the three of you better get out of my sight. I should give that kloormar your pay for the mission, and I should get Torm here to rip each of you a new one—literally!" With that the meeting ended.

We watched the vid feed as the bridge crew prepared for a jump. While we waited, we discussed having a baby to get our hands on whatever we would need to take control of the ship. K'tatmal's death seemed to have completely changed my teammates' opinions. This made sense since the decision to add a new kloormar to a village would often be in response to another villager's death. The change of heart seemed to come about because K'tatmal's death provided the necessary rationale. We decided to "give it a go" once the jump and acceleration were complete.

After the jump and hyper-acceleration, and once the *Jezebel's Fury* had reached its target speed of about 998, we decided to "do the deed." I made myself comfortable in the alcove, out of sight of the camera. The team lined up so each could provide me with their genetic contribution. At the back of the line, Kroz and K'aablart were supporting Keeto who, despite severe injury, insisted on playing the appropriate role.

Just as we were about to consummate our action, Captain Skully opened the door and strode in. Any kloormar would have known what was about to take place, but to the captain, we must have formed a strange tableau.

"What are you lot up to?" he asked.

"Practicing the procedure for greeting a kloormari chieftain from a faraway village," I lied. I was quite astonished by my casual and almost instinctive ability to do so. A month earlier I wouldn't have been capable of such subterfuge.

Skully asked me to accompany him. We went to his table in the barroom, and he briefed me on his conversation with Mec, Tank, and Bazz. Since I had already seen and heard the conversation, I knew that he related it fairly accurately, though he did add a few embellishments.

"I'm worried," he said. "I'm worried that I'm losing the crew's support. So far, I'm just concerned about Mec and Tank and especially Bazz, but I know how well fear and ignorance spread, especially among ignorant people. They're trying to sow fear and doubt about your group, and it's just so stupidly destructive to the mission. These morons are actually attacking the same beings that are making their lives easier, and to be honest, more profitable!"

I took the opportunity to tell him what the three humans had done to Keeto. He shook his head. "Things have obviously deteriorated far more than

I'd imagined. I'd love nothing more than to have Torm go to town on them, but if I do that, I'd be seen as siding with you lads and selling out my own species. I can pretty much guarantee that the result would be a full-on mutiny, and that wouldn't end well for you or your friends.

"I don't see any choice but to calm things down by throwing a bone to my fellow humans. Please understand, Kelvoo, this is the last thing I want to do, but I think I'm going to have to lock you and your team in your quarters. I will only do so from 22:00 to 08:00 every night when we have minimal crew on duty. I hope you understand that this is mostly for your protection. I wouldn't want some idiots charging into your quarters in the middle of the night and attacking you. At the same time, I can present this plan to the crew to show that I'm taking their concerns into account and taking action, supposedly to protect them."

"I think you may find that we're more receptive to your idea than you thought we'd be," I replied. "I welcome your plan to restrict access to us, for our protection. Of course, we can express dismay at your decision so that the human crew thinks we are being punished, even though I don't know exactly what the human crew thinks we did wrong.

"Please do understand, Captain Skully, we can tolerate being confined for ten hours per day but not for any longer. If that happened, we would experience a deterioration in our mental health, which would render us highly unproductive to the mission. We need to keep busy and productive, which means we need to perform our cleaning duties from 10:00 to 18:00, as we do now."

"Thank you, Kelvoo," he said. "You know, I wish my entire crew was kloormari. What are the chances of you and your team, plus a few more kloormari, being my crew for my next mission?"

"I'm sorry, Captain, but I think the chances are zero. Please keep in mind that we are on this mission against our will. We are making the best of our situation, but we are entirely focused on returning to our homes when we're done."

"Oh, well, I figured it couldn't hurt to ask. By the way, there shouldn't be any drama or tragedy on our next stop."

"I'm glad to hear that. What will we be doing?"

"Just taking a bunch of kids to boarding school. Anyway, thanks again, Kelvoo."

With that, I made my way back to our quarters. I was puzzled by the captain's overt display of respect and kindness toward us—traits that would not be present in a narcissist. I couldn't help wondering whether he was trying to "play both sides."

"I have news," I said to my team when I returned, "but first, let's get on with the task at hand."

I took up my previous position in the alcove, and again my fellow kloormari formed a line. Kleloma's reproductive siphon extended toward me.

"Hope I'm not interrupting anything, my friends!" a familiar human voice said from the doorway. By that point, I was growing irritated.

Reverend Hol entered, saw the lineup, and asked what was going on. Once again, a lie came easily to me. "Just trying to sort ourselves in order of intelligence divided by weight," I said. Hol seemed nonplussed. As I stood up, Hol approached us. "I came by to express my deepest sympathies for the loss of your comrade. Please forgive me for asking, but what was his name?"

"K'tatmal," K'raftan replied.

"Oh, yes, yes, Katmal. It must be very difficult for you to be feeling this loss, especially when you believe that someone's death is the end for them, and there is nothing beyond."

Hol paused as if waiting for a response. When he got none, he continued. "What if I were to tell you that it doesn't have to be that way? What would you say if I told you that you have a chance for eternal life in a perfect paradise after you die?"

"If I wasn't already familiar with human superstitions," I replied, "I would say that you should receive a psychiatric assessment."

"Please, my friends, just listen to me. Imagine that, the moment he passed away, Katmal's soul—his mind and the essence of his being—left his body and shot, like a rocket, up beyond the sky. Please try to imagine that."

"We are kloormari," I said. "We aren't capable of imagination."

"Then don't *imagine* it," Hol said. "Instead, take my word when I tell you that, when believers die, their souls are taken to a place where they are reunited with loved ones who had died before. The souls of the righteous are uplifted to a place with choirs of angels where they can eternally bask in the pure and perfect love of the Almighty! Doesn't that sound so much better than just ceasing to exist?"

"If your mythology is truly fact," I retorted, "then K'tatmal is suffering unspeakable pain, burning in fire for all eternity, existing in misery and damnation forevermore."

"I believe," the reverend said, "that at our moment of death, Almighty God comes to us and gives us the opportunity to confess our sins and accept his love. If Katmal accepted God into his heart, then he is enjoying paradise."

"So, your god keeps himself hidden from us in this universe, but when we die, he gives us one last chance? That seems rather convenient, doesn't it? We might as well just wait for God's wonderful invitation at the moment we die!"

"No, that was speculation on my part. God's ways are a mystery, so we must have faith that he will guide us. Why not just accept God now instead of risking your immortal soul? Let him into your heart now so that you can have eternal life. Just repeat after me: I bear witness that there is no god but—"

"No thank you," I interjected, "but I do have questions."

"Yes, my friend."

"When you are trying to win converts to your church, do you find it easier when your prospect is suffering a loss or is in crisis? Is an individual more susceptible to your influence when they are vulnerable? How do you rationalize such actions?"

"I appreciate your skepticism, my friend, but it will only make me redouble my efforts to save your souls." Hol's voice took on a testy tone. "Since none of you are willing to pray for the soul of your fallen comrade, I will do so. I shall also pray for each and every one of you." With that, he left.

I turned to my teammates. "So, shall we get this thing done?"

Once again, I took my position in the alcove. This time while they lined up to impregnate me, my fellow kloormari watched the passageway on their Infotabs to warn of any further possibilities of coitus interruptus.

I opened my reproductive pouch, and each kloormar, in turn, deposited their genetic material into me.

Humans seem to have a fascination with acts that may lead to pregnancy. If asked by a human to describe what it felt like to be impregnated by seven kloormari, I would reply, "Squishy."

# THIRTY: SCHOOL BUS

After our group intercourse, we watched our Infotabs to see Captain Skully make the rounds to Bazz, Mec, and Tank as well as several other crew members. He let them know that, "upon further reflection," he was ordering the kloormari to be under lockdown in their quarters for ten hours per night. This seemed to placate the crew for the time being, though some expressed surprise and regret.

We continued to perform our routine cleaning duties, but we stayed clear of Bazz, Tank, and Mec's quarters. Ebo, Murph, and Spaggy were among those who chatted with us in the passageways or their quarters and privately expressed sympathy toward us. They let us know that they thought the lockdown was unfair.

For the next twenty-one days, we fell into a mostly uneventful routine. Brenna and May were starting to hone their reading skills. May could sound out simple words phonetically while Brenna had memorized some words with sounds that didn't match their spelling, like *cough, right,* and *two.*

Each girl had an Infotab, but the only stories that had been loaded on them were religious parables that didn't provide a step-by-step approach to learning how to read. My teammates and I found a wide variety of early reader children's books on our InfoServer, so we copied them over to the girls' devices.

Picture books seemed to result in faster learning. This puzzled me at first, since I thought that the images would just be a distraction and wouldn't interest a child. It turned out that the girls were able to associate unknown words with parts of the corresponding pictures, which helped them widen their vocabulary of written words. The books included *The Higgledy-Piggledy Sarayan Barnyard, I Want to Be in Zero G,* and *Why are Human Parents so Weird?*

By the time we arrived at our next stop, Brenna could read children's books up to the six-year-old level, and May could get through simpler books with a little bit of help along the way. Often, Brenna would assist May. While I observed that human children learn at a far slower pace than kloormari infants, I took considerable interest in the girls' learning process, probably because I was carrying an offspring whose education might just be our salvation.

215

During the journey to our next stop, Keeto started to recover from the dismemberment. Keeto was in too much pain and lacked the energy to help with any of our chores, but after a few days, the wound had closed over and stopped weeping, and then the small bud of a new clasper limb began to form.

We spent a lot of our time refining our plan. We were going to need a camera and a blank access card. We could convert the access card to a command card by copying the data from the captain's command card, if we could just get hold of it.

Obtaining a camera was easy. There were many cameras throughout the vessel that had never been activated because, according to Kroz, the ship had a cheap surveillance processor that didn't have the bandwidth for all of the cameras on board. There was actually a second camera in our room. If it had been activated, there would have been no blind spots in our quarters. I let Kroz crawl up onto my shoulders to reach the unused camera, which was nothing more than a glassy dome about four millimeters across with a magnetic mount on the back.

A simple close-proximity device scan on Kroz's Infotab provided the camera's ID. When Kroz activated the camera from the Infotab and added a link to the InfoServer, we could see the feed from the camera on our devices.

We obtained a couple of blank access cards by dumb luck. Snowy had been trying to find a pair of socks to replace ones that he had worn out by searching through an extremely messy crew-only storeroom. He had Keesooni come in and assist him in tidying and reorganizing the room. He asked Keesooni to take blank access cards that were scattered in a box and stack them neatly. He probably thought we would have no interest in non-activated cards since we wouldn't have access to the data to save onto the cards. Of course, Keesooni was sure to slip two of the cards into the Infotab pouch.

About ten days after we left the horror of Benzolar 3, four of us were assigned to help unload provisions from a freezer to a refrigerator behind the galley. Each cooler was a metal room that was five meters square. The door to the freezer and the door to the refrigerator were just a few paces apart, so we formed a chain to pass boxes of frozen food to the refrigeration room.

K'aablart was farthest inside the freezer. From K'aablart, the boxes were passed to Spaggy, then to me, then to K'raftan, Kleloma, Wanky, and finally Mec. When the final box had left the freezer, we walked into the fridge and stowed the remaining boxes neatly.

In the last stage of our task, K'raftan, Kleloma, and I noticed that our limbs didn't respond to our intended actions as quickly as normal and were aching slightly. I also noticed condensation when we exhaled through our vocal outlets, and I recalled the hypothermia incident at the high commissioner's residence on Saraya.

"Where's K'aablart?" I exclaimed suddenly.

We stepped over to the freezer and saw K'aablart squatting on the floor, motionless. We moved K'aablart into the galley as quickly as possible. I placed an ear next to K'aablart's vocal outlets and could barely hear K'aablart exhaling.

"What's the matter with him?" Wanky asked.

"I experienced this once before with a group of other kloormari on a cool evening on Saraya," I explained. "It seems that we kloormari go into some kind of hibernation when we are exposed to cold temperatures."

"How long can you stay in hibernation?" Mec asked.

"I don't know," I replied. "When it happened before, it was four or five hours before we were brought in out of the cold. Nobody knows how harmful this is or how long we can survive being cold."

"Is he going to be okay?" Spaggy asked.

"I think so. K'aablart is breathing—just very slowly. When K'aablart warms up a bit, consciousness will come back, but there will be a lot of pain while the joints and muscles start to loosen up.

Spaggy and Wanky offered to help us carry K'aablart to our quarters, but Mec left, wanting nothing to do with us. We assured the remaining humans that we would take care of K'aablart. We stayed in the galley until K'aablart was ready for a slow and painful walk back to our quarters.

When we returned to the group, they reported that they had been watching the incident. They couldn't see the coolers behind the galley, but when we brought K'aablart out, they could see and hear everything. They wanted to come and help but were worried that their actions would indicate that we had surveillance capabilities. When Mec left, they followed him on the vid cameras and watched him tell several other crew members about our reaction to cold. I was very concerned about how this revelation might be used against us.

Two weeks after I was impregnated, I could feel movement inside my reproductive pouch. I went to a well-lit area of our quarters and pulled my pouch open a little bit. It was fascinating to see a tiny creature there. It was bluish-grey and covered with pink slime.

A cord consisting of four milky pink-and-blue tubes, twisted together, ran from the anterior side of the pouch to four locations on the creature's body. Unlike a human umbilical cord that provides oxygenated blood, the four kloormari cords lead to the baby's four brain centers. According to a biologist on the *Pacifica Spirit*, the cords provide hormones that stimulate neural development along with information that is transmitted via electro-chemical signals, providing the body with basic data on how to function.

I found the eye of the fetus to be the most interesting. It was a perfectly formed, miniature eye with tiny triangular segments. Through a thin layer of pink slime, I saw that each segment was white. The segments would obtain their characteristic amber color closer to the creature's birthdate. The fetus blinked a couple of times, then stretched its limbs before curling into a ball. I decided not to disturb the creature's development any further and let my pouch close.

Captain Skully held the pre-mission briefing the day before our arrival so that C-12 could be converted into a dormitory. "You kloormari fellas don't seem to be using the lovely bunks that we provided for you, so I hope you don't mind giving them up for our passengers." He told us that we would be landing on XR-318, a barren, rocky planet with minimal water and vegetation and a place so unremarkable that nobody had bothered to give it an official name. The planet was only of value as a treasure trove of precious metals and rare-earth elements that were being mined as rapidly as possible.

Some of the children from the mining colony were to be transported to a boarding school on a planet named Sirenar. In addition to taking on passengers, we were to take on a load of the precious element palladium as payment. The humans were to accompany the passengers, and the kloormari were charged with loading and unloading payment, as we had done at Friendship Colony.

After the briefing, we moved our little-used beds from our quarters and across the hallway into C-12. Spaggy showed us where to find floor mats, sleeping sacks, and pillows to be used as additional beds to accommodate the large number of passengers. Due to our previous explorations of the ship, we knew where these items were stored, but we weren't going to let that information slip out. Within forty minutes, a new human-ready dormitory was created. A washroom with showers was located at the end of the passageway for the comfort of our guests.

When we had decelerated to a normal orbital velocity, Captain Skully and a contingent of human crew boarded the transport while the kloormari got aboard the cargo shuttle with Pilo at the helm. We touched down on a dusty brown plain surrounded by mountains. The main transport had landed about half a kilometer away from our shuttle.

We stepped outside into a windy atmosphere laden with gritty dust that made each of us squint and blink frequently. In the distance, I saw a line of nearly grown children, each wearing a backpack. They were followed by a hoverlift laden with suitcases and duffel bags, all heading toward the transport. A line of crew members, led (I assumed) by Captain Skully, was walking across the plain to greet the group.

I took considerable interest in the huge yellow vehicles carrying ore across the plain between the mountains and a large metal structure, which I assumed was a refinery. I had never seen a wheeled vehicle before. I had read that they are used in some industries, such as mining and construction, where the loads were too heavy for hover transportation. The ore carriers must have been fifteen meters high.

A large, wheeled vehicle with a long flat deck approached us directly from the refinery. Pilo ordered us to take the hoverlift out. Two hundred palladium ingots were strapped down to the middle of the vehicle's deck, surrounded by twelve armed guards. The guards jumped down from the deck and formed a perimeter while we kloormari transferred the palladium to the hoverlift and into the cargo hold.

The guards jumped back onto the vehicle's cargo deck, and the vehicle drove directly to the refinery, leaving billowing clouds of choking dust in its wake. We were ordered back on board and then lifted off while passengers were still boarding the main transport. The trip back to the *Jezebel's Fury* was quick, and we were able to unload and stow the ingots in about ten minutes, well before the main transport arrived. The entire mission was uneventful— wonderfully and refreshingly uneventful!

About half an hour after settling back into our quarters, we heard a cacophony of voices coming down the passageway. Twenty-eight young female humans walked into room C-12 across the hall from us, followed by Captain Skully. He opened our door and asked us to accompany him.

"Ladies," he said, addressing the newcomers, "I'd like you to meet these crew members. Their species is called kloormari, and they're from the planet Kuw'baal. They'll be keeping you entertained on your voyage to school," he added, to my surprise.

My teammates and I greeted them. Some of the young humans looked despondent and stared at the floor. Others replied with various levels of enthusiasm. Many seemed to be frightened by our appearance.

Captain Skully took me aside. "I need you and your boys to take care of these girls. They need to get to school with their virtue intact, if you know what I mean."

I indicated that I didn't, so he continued. "I can't trust some of my human crew with these girls, and I've told them all to stay the hell away from this entire section of the ship. These girls are too young, but that wouldn't stop some of the perverts we have aboard. If you see any male crew member so much as set foot in the passageway, hit the button on the wall in here and report it. I'll have Torm drag them away and deal with them. By the way, Torm's allowed in here only for the purpose of dragging crew members out!"

I assured him that we would be vigilant.

"These girls are going to be bored a lot of the time, so try to keep them entertained," he continued. I had no idea how we would accomplish that. "We're going to jump in a couple of hours. Some of these girls have never been off XR-318, so they've never experienced a jump. Others may have jumped but only in a way like you experienced on the *Pacifica*, so you can start by preparing them for what to expect. The last thing we need is a bunch of terrified schoolgirls running amok!" he said with a grin as he left us alone with the twenty-eight human girls.

"Let's introduce ourselves," Kleloma suggested. We made the rounds. I stopped at each girl and introduced myself. I asked for their names and ages. Each girl had a fairly typical female human name like Melissa, Janet, Sandra, Andrea, Michelle, and so on. Every girl's age was between twelve and fourteen.

I asked Sandra where they were going to school. "On Sirenar," she said.

"Are the boys traveling to your school separately?"

"Why would boys be going to our school?" Michelle asked. About a dozen girls giggled nervously, some of them trying to hide their laughter by putting their hands over their mouths.

"We're going to the Horse Academy!" Melissa said.

"Shh! We're not s'posed to talk about it!" Michelle admonished.

I decided not to pry any further.

Some of the girls were sad. Janet had tears rolling down her cheeks. "What's the matter?" I asked.

"I don't wanna go to school," she sobbed. "I miss my ma and my little brother and sister."

"You shoulda seen her ma," Andrea said. "She was screamin' and wailin', 'Don't take my baby!' They had to hold her back and take Janet away, quick as can be!" With that, Janet started crying in earnest, followed by several of the other girls.

The rest of the girls just stared, looked at vids on their Infotabs, or chatted with one another and giggled. From what I knew about human homesickness and the strength of the attachment between offspring and parents, I figured that the girls who appeared unfazed were putting on a brave front.

When Captain Skully made a ship-wide thirty-minute jump warning, I stood in front of the group and explained what they could expect. "Some of you might have jumped before, but probably not like this," I said. I went on to explain that they would feel like they were in outer space with no body and no feeling. This information seemed to panic most of the girls. They frequently asked how much longer until the jump. The closer we got to the time, the more frightened they were. This left me wondering whether it would have been better to say nothing and let them endure the shock, unprepared.

When the thirty-second warning sounded, the girls gathered in the middle of the floor and clasped hands. Some were sitting while others were kneeling and whispering prayers.

When we exited from the jump, the girls had clearly been traumatized by their experience. They were oddly quiet. Some were curled into a ball or sitting up, hugging their knees to their chests and rocking gently. Michelle and Andrea were sitting on their bunks, trying with limited success to look casual. When our hyper-acceleration started with all of its back-and-forth forces and bouncing, the girls snapped out of their stunned silence, and many started screaming.

Once the *Jezebel's Fury* was up to speed, the three concubines entered the room wearing their uniforms. Their presence seemed to calm the passengers, perhaps because they were just a few years older than the girls, but the girls also seemed to have a reverence for the young women.

The visible wounds had mostly healed on the concubine that Brawn had assaulted. Her broken leg was supported by a lighter-weight splint, and she moved with the aid of a crutch that a crew member had probably welded together.

The concubines' faces showed little emotion at first, but that changed when the girls gathered around them. Some of the girls introduced themselves to the concubines. Some said things like, "I think you're real pretty," "I like your dress," "Your shoes are so beautiful," and "What's your name?"

We learned that the ship's concubines' names were Lisa and Zoe, and the injured one was Sandra. "Just like me!" said a younger passenger with the same name. The crew, however, called them Trixie, Pixie, and Candy. We also learned that Lisa was twenty years old, and the other two were eighteen. The girls asked questions about what to expect from school.

"It's hard at first," Lisa said, "but you just learn to cope."

"How do we do that?" Janet asked.

"Well," Sandra replied, "when we jumped, remember how it felt like you were separated from your body?"

"Yeah, that was so scary!" Janet exclaimed.

"Yeah, it's scary at first, but when you take some of your lessons at school, you just have to *imagine* that your mind and your body are not connected," Sandra said. "Here on the ship, I just *imagine* that I'm a different person named Candy, and the Sandra part of me is living a regular life."

I didn't understand what Sandra was talking about, probably because it involved imagination. The group was much calmer now, so I didn't want to intrude by asking questions. I was surprised that the concubines had been to school, though I supposed they needed to be able to have intelligent conversations with their clients.

After a while, Lisa and Zoe excused themselves, telling the girls that they had to return to work. Sandra said she would stay a while longer and that Captain Skully had ordered the concubines to take turns so that one of them would be there to keep the girls company until they completed the journey to school.

That night, we kloormari were no longer locked inside our quarters. Instead, the doors at each end of the passageway were locked, so we could move between our quarters and the girls' dormitory.

The next morning, it was my turn to give Brenna and May their reading lesson. When I got to their quarters, Murph was about to leave for his shift. I suggested that his daughters might want to visit the schoolgirls in C-12.

Murph agreed that it would be nice for his girls to meet some other young ladies.

The passengers enjoyed having visitors, and many thought that little May was especially adorable or cute. I found it very interesting to see a ten-year-old and even a four-year-old reading stories to twelve-, thirteen-, and fourteen-year-olds and showing them how to read and sound out words.

Seven days after the girls boarded, I felt some unusual movement in my reproductive pouch. I found a quiet place at the end of a passageway to peek into it. When I looked down, I was shocked to see that my pouch had opened part of the way. A tiny eyestalk was extending out of the opening, and a light-yellow eye was swiveling around, taking in the surroundings.

Not wanting my pregnancy to be discovered, I wanted to push the fetus back inside me. To avoid pushing on the creature's delicate eye dome, I pulled my pouch flap out to widen the opening. Then I used two of my claspers to grasp the creature's body and ease it deeper inside. As I cradled the tiny kloormar and shifted it farther down, it made a soft mewling sound. I cannot explain why, but I felt compelled to talk to it, though I was careful to speak in the ultrasonic range so that no humans would be alerted.

"Hush, little one," I said in kloormari. "Stay right where you are, nice and secure, until you're ready. It isn't safe out here."

# THIRTY-ONE: BIRTH DAY

The transport and the cargo shuttle touched down on an island, perhaps two square kilometers in size, in the middle of a clear azure ocean, far out of sight of any other land. The island held a collection of low buildings surrounded by manicured gardens. Our vessels were directed to land between the novices' campus and the seniors' campus. The vessels landed about one hundred meters from each other.

The kloormari on the cargo shuttle were directed to offload the palladium into the custody of the school's security force. At the same time, the transport was to offload the students into the custody of the school's chancellor. Next, the transport was to pick-up thirty new graduates from the school. The *Jezebel's Fury* would then take them to the mining colony.

For the trip, we took 135 of the 200 ingots that had been aboard the *Jezebel's Fury*. I assumed that the remaining sixty-five ingots were kept as the mission's "handling fees."

Earlier, back on the ship, when the call had come for the students to make their way to the transport, some of the girls were excited to find out what was in store while others were full of dread. All of the girls were quiet and introspective as we kloormari parted ways with them and headed to the hangar.

As we offloaded the ingots, the girls left the transport and were led by an imposing, robed woman along a path to the novices' campus. The girls waved at us across the lush lawn, and a couple of them shouted their thanks.

The novices' campus was surrounded by high grey walls with a tall set of metal gates and security people at the entrance. I wondered whether the school had problems with homesick runaway students. I thought that the security measures were excessive given the fact that we were on a tiny island in the middle of a vast ocean.

As the last of our passengers entered the campus and the gates swung shut, I realized how interesting it had been to get to know these young women. They reminded me of myself and my fellow kloormari, full of innocence and naïveté, being thrust into a new and strange situation. I was going to miss them.

As we finished up and were about to board the shuttle to leave, I saw about one hundred young women exit from the seniors' campus and head toward the transport. Before they got very far, a line of security personnel blocked their path and allowed the thirty designated graduates to proceed. As they departed, the graduates waved back at their schoolmates, and I heard occasional shouts of "Goodbye!", "Good luck!", and "We love you!"

When the thirty graduates got close to the transport, a terrible realization hit me like a sharp blow. The young graduating women were all wearing the same white dresses with gold trim and the same high-heeled strapped footwear as the concubines on the *Jezebel's Fury*!

On the ride back to the ship, I felt unbearably foolish. *How could you not have known that the girls were going to concubine school? When little Melissa said they were heading to the "Horse Academy," she obviously meant "Whore's Academy." When Sandra/Candy advised young Janet to detach her mind from her body during lessons, it's obvious that she was talking about performing sexual acts against their will! How incredibly stupid of me not to see it!* I wondered whether I had taken on the human trait of seeing only what I had wanted to see and ignoring the obvious tragedy of the situation.

In an act of psychological self-defence, I tried to rationalize the situation. *Why is this bothering me? These girls are learning a job that will earn them a living. Many jobs involve performing unpleasant tasks, so what's the difference with this line of work?*

I recalled information that I had read about prostitutes on modern-day Terra. Those were women who had selected prostitution from a variety of careers. They were licensed to practice their trade, they belonged to professional organizations that advocated for them, and they had strong protections under the law.

I realized that the difference was choice. What choice of career did a twelve-year-old girl from a mining colony have, especially in a society that frowned upon a normal education for girls? I also thought about the crew's attitude toward Lisa, Zoe, and poor, brutalized Sandra. These women weren't treated as humans; they were considered property to be used for the crew's pleasure. I contrasted that with the intelligent, successful women from the *Pacifica Spirit*, and I was struck by the gulf between the two cultures and their treatment of females.

*Why are the humans like this?* I wondered. *What's to be gained by subjugating one gender below the other? Wouldn't a man enjoy the close company of a woman if she was actually interested in enjoying the experience?* I could make no sense of any of it.

Like the girls before them, the new women stayed in room C-12, and we were assigned to "guard" them. The previous passengers had spent their nights sleeping in C-12 but had spent their days between their room and our quarters. With the likelihood that I would be hatching a baby in the coming days, we decided not to invite the women to visit our quarters in the interest of "giving them privacy."

We discussed how our baby would be attended to. We decided to take turns in the alcove, attending to the baby and providing it with algel, education, and any other needs. If we all had to be somewhere, or if any crew members arrived unexpectedly, we would leave the baby in the alcove and close the doors. We would teach the baby to speak kloormari by talking to it in the ultrasonic frequencies in the hope that it would only vocalize in a high register, and the humans wouldn't hear it.

Kroz came up with a clever solution to be used in an emergency. If we needed to conceal our activities, Kroz could replace the live vid feed from our quarters with recorded vid from the pre-baby days. To deal with the "jump" in the vid feed, Kroz created a pixelated, blurred transition that we hoped would be perceived as a "glitch" in the feed. We didn't know how well the crew monitored the vid feeds from around the ship. Since we had never been questioned about our previous activities, we figured that either the feeds were just shown on panels that weren't actively monitored, or the captain and crew were doing an excellent job of keeping secret the fact that we were under constant surveillance.

"Since you're hosting our offspring, and you have naming rights," Ksoomu said, "have you thought about the name that you want to give the baby?"

Before I could answer, five of my teammates threw suggestions at me: K'tama, Krerku, Kooaukulu, K'peetru, and K'terra.

"I like K'terra," Ksoomu said, "because it includes the name of the planet where the good humans live." I thanked my teammates for their suggestions and told them that I would consider them all. It might have been the first time that I knowingly lied to my fellow kloormari.

For the first three days of the trip back to XR-318, we only got to learn a little bit about our new passengers. As before, Lisa, Zoe, and Sandra kept them company. We were surprised that our passengers were quite unfazed by our strange appearance. While the jump from Sirenar made them nervous, they didn't display the terror that their predecessors had exhibited. I asked one of the women, Tracey (now called "Lura"), about that. She said that the school had taught them to expect stressful circumstances and had subjected them to many. They were taught how to numb themselves to frightening situations.

None of the graduates had enjoyed school. "That wasn't the point," said Marta (now Desiree). "The point is to look forward to using our skills after school to get a good man and a good life."

Desiree's comment got the young women chatting and giggling about what kind of man they were going to snag. They teased one another about who would get a nice, kind, "hunk" of a man and who would get a mean, old, ugly one. They seemed oblivious to the plight of the ship's own "concs" and their life of servitude to an agglomeration of men whom the captain had told me were "subhuman" and "mouth-breathing morons." Overall, our passengers kept to themselves and seemed to be emotionally detached.

Early on the fourth day of the trip back to the mining colony, I was in C-12 having a pleasant conversation with Marta when I felt something peculiar in my reproductive pouch. I looked down and saw that the baby had crawled halfway out. I placed an arm over it. "I'm so sorry to interrupt, Marta, but I'm not feeling well. I need to go back to my quarters for some food and rest."

I ran back across the passageway and into the alcove. On my way, I shouted to my comrades in ultrasonic kloormari. "It's here! The baby! It's here! Don't panic! Stay calm! The baby's here!" I didn't have the presence of mind to realize that I was in full panic mode and was anything but calm!

Fortunately, my teammates did stay calm. The ones who had also been in C-12 excused themselves and made their way to our quarters. The last kloormar closed the door. Three kloormari gathered close to me. The rest stayed farther away so that half of us were in view of our room's surveillance camera. If we had all been crowded into the camera's blind spot, it may have raised the suspicion of anybody who was monitoring us.

The baby crawled the rest of the way out of me, leaving a slime trail as it climbed up my abdomen, dragging its "umbilical" cords behind it. K'raftan fetched a fresh cup of algel from the incubation vat. When the baby reached the end of the cords and could climb no further, it reached down, and one by one, gave a pinch and a quick pull on each cord where it was attached to the body. As each cord detached, fluid leaked from the "navel" for a moment, then an epidermal flap closed over the opening to seal it.

As per kloormari custom, when the fourth cord fell away, the new kloormar was officially acknowledged as being born. With its naming, the new creature would be recognized as a sentient being.

I had chosen the baby's name from the moment I'd concocted the notion to produce a child. In the closest thing to any form of ceremony used by the kloormari, I held the baby aloft. "My fellow kloormari, I present our offspring to you. Forthwith, this kloormar shall be known as 'Sam.'"

"Welcome, Sam," I said in unison with the rest of Sam's parents.

# THIRTY-TWO: CATTLE AUCTION

Every member of our team except for the youngest, K'raftan, had contributed genetic material to a pregnancy at least once before, but I was the first member of our group to actually host a developing fetus.

My teammates were surprised but also pleased that I'd dispensed with the tradition of having the baby's name start with a "K" (a "click") sound. Everything we'd been through, for better or worse, had come about because of our contact with Sam Buchanan and his teachings, so providing the same given name to our child made sense. There was also the profound realization that our child would be the first kloormar ever born somewhere other than our home world, which was significant enough to change the naming convention.

Caring for a child proved to be more of a challenge than any of us had anticipated. On Kuw'baal, infants ran free. They tended to associate themselves with all of their parents and sometimes one or two additional kloormari. In most cases, one of those kloormari provided the beginning of an education. In our case, we would take turns educating Sam in order to provide the necessary skills as rapidly as possible.

Sam couldn't be allowed to roam free for fear of being discovered by a human. As such, Baby Sam was restricted to the alcove and a small area just outside of it. Sam was able to crawl on all twelve appendages within a few hours after birth. By the second day, Sam could walk upright for short distances. Sam didn't understand having to remain in a small area, so constant supervision was necessary. Sam kept trying to wander away.

By the end of the second day, Sam could identify and speak the name of each kloormar on the ship as well as self-identify.

Baby kloormari don't know how to meditate, probably because their brains are mostly empty and don't need to cross-reference and catalog much information. They remember every sight, sound, touch, taste, and smell. In my case, I remember everything from the first moment I peered outside of my host's pouch, but it was a few weeks until I organized my memories for faster retrieval. Instead of meditating, babies have bursts of physical energy and intellectual curiosity, followed by a recovery time that resembles human sleep. Upon waking, they gulp down a bolus of algel, and the burst of energy repeats. This cycle made life difficult for us as Sam's caregivers, since we needed approximately eight solid hours of meditation per day to function optimally.

On the third day, during each burst of energy, the baby decided that jumping was a worthwhile activity. With each jumping session, Sam was able to reach a greater height.

K'raftan was watching and teaching Sam in the alcove early in the evening. K'raftan was seated, legs stretched out to partly block the exit into our main quarters. When K'raftan wasn't watching, Sam leapt over K'raftan's legs and ran into our quarters. K'raftan raised the alarm, and Kroz immediately switched the vid feed to show a previous recording from our quarters. Since the infant was not highly coordinated at such an early stage, Sam fell but continued to scurry along on all twelve limbs.

The seven of us who were in the room scrambled to corral Baby Sam. The scene was reminiscent of early Terran slapstick comedy vids as we tripped over one another trying to catch our baby while trying to avoid kicking or tripping over Sam.

K'aablart had been visiting the humans in C-12 and heard a high-pitched commotion as we shouted to one another in ultrasonic kloormari while trying to capture Sam. When K'aablart opened the door to our quarters to investigate, the baby just happened to be running past the doorway. Sam veered sharply to the right, scuttled between K'aablart's legs, and zoomed through the open door into C-12.

Startled shrieks erupted from the young women as a miniature kloormar zigged and zagged between their bunks. K'aablart ran back toward C-12 while Kroz used an Infotab to kill the vid feed from C-12. Unfortunately, Kroz hadn't set up the ability to replay old vid from C-12, so we hoped the bridge crew wouldn't notice that the feed from ladies' dorm had gone blank.

Six of us tried to exit from our quarters at the same time. We jammed into the exit, forming a writhing morass of bodies, limbs, and eye domes that human viewers would have found uproariously funny. When the logjam broke, we fell into the passageway, forming a kloormari dogpile.

In Room C-12, some of the women were standing on their beds, and others were backing away from Sam, who was running back and forth along the far wall.

"Help us catch that baby!" I shouted to the humans as I entered the room. "Don't worry; it's harmless!" It took me a moment to realize I was shouting in Terran but in a higher pitch than any human could hear.

I repeated my urgent instructions in a lower register. Having recovered from their initial shock, twelve of the young women helped form a human cordon around Sam, who was in a corner of the room, squealing with primal terror. The humans must have seemed strange and menacing. I made my way through the line of women and scooped up the baby. I took Sam to a corner where there was a tiny area out of the camera's view. On my way, I took a sheet off one of the bunks and wrapped baby Sam in it for concealment. Once I was in the corner, I asked Kroz to restore the vid feed from C-12.

"What the hell is going on?" one of the women asked.

I asked them to back away, so I could explain. "As you are probably aware, this room is under vid surveillance by the captain and crew. Please don't gather 'round, or you'll draw attention to what is happening, and that won't be good for any of us!

"What I have here is a baby kloormar named Sam. Sam was born three days ago. We've kept Sam a secret, because if the crew found out, this baby and all of us would be killed. I hope you're kind enough that you don't want to see this innocent child destroyed. I'm asking all of you to keep this situation and this baby a secret."

"You don't have to worry about that!" Tracey (a.k.a. Lura) said. "Discretion was the most important thing we learned at school. We promise we're not going to tell. Keeping secrets is a skill that'll keep us alive!" Tracey's companions all nodded or otherwise affirmed her promise.

"What's its name?" one of the women asked.

"Sam," I replied.

"So, it's a boy then? He's so adorable!"

"It's not a boy or a girl. We kloormari are neither male nor female."

"But who's its mom then?"

"All eight of us are Sam's mom *and* dad. If you are asking whose body hosted Sam, that would be me."

"Can we hold Sam? It's so cute!"

"If you want to have a closer look, you can come up to the baby one at a time, but please don't touch or hold Sam. If there's one thing that's going to keep this baby alive, it's a healthy fear of humans!"

The women were very respectful of my request. Some took a close look at Sam, but they helped to avoid drawing attention by ensuring that the baby was not the center of the group's focus. We were all grateful to the young women. A few minutes later, I wrapped Sam up and returned to the alcove in the kloormari quarters.

The introduction of Sam helped break the ice in our relations with the passengers. They became less withdrawn, and we spent more time talking with each of them. Each woman had her own interesting and often tragic story, and we grew to appreciate the women much more during the remainder of the trip.

A few days later, we arrived back in orbit around XR-318. There were to be no visits to the surface. Instead, workers and management from the colony were to take a company shuttle to the *Jezebel's Fury* to conduct business on the ship.

Sam's Team was ordered into our quarters, and we were locked inside for a few hours before the guests were due to arrive. On our Infotabs, we watched the vid feed of the arrival of a shuttle emblazoned with a mining company's logo. A group of crew members escorted thirty-two men from the main hold. When we saw them approaching our part of the ship, Keeto, who was watching Sam, made sure that Sam was shut in the alcove. We heard the men in the corridor as they were ushered into room C-12.

It was fortunate that Baby Sam was concealed when Captain Skully opened our door. "Kelvoo, might I see you for a moment or two?"

When I stepped into the passageway, he slapped my shoulder in a friendly fashion. "You know, Kelvoo, it's been so long since we had one of our nice chats, I thought we should take the opportunity to catch up. Besides, you might be interested in watching something that's about to start."

In C-12, the visiting colonists were seated in rows of chairs, laughing and chatting loudly with one another. The young women were sitting on a row of chairs that lined one side of the room. Front and center was a raised platform.

"So, what's new, Kelvoo?" Skully asked.

"Nothing really. Not much at all has happened since Benzolar 3."

"I'm glad to hear it. I'm sorry we're having to lock your section at night, but it seems to have calmed the crew. I'm afraid that the lockdowns will have to continue, but if you keep your heads down and your noses clean—if you had heads, that is—and if you don't rile the crew up again, then we all might just survive this mission!"

After a minute or two, the crowd started to settle down.

"Alright, Reverend Hol," Captain Skully said. "Let's get things underway."

The reverend stood on the stage and faced the crowd. "It is my honor to introduce this new batch of lovely concubines to you." The crowd applauded and roared their approval. "Did you know that the use of concubines goes back many thousands of years? The scriptures speak of great kings with many wives and women to attend to them, so it's good to see you men continuing that sacred custom!"

"Shut up, Rev, and bring out the tarts!" a miner shouted. Whoops of approval came from the crowd.

"Alright, alright," Hol said. "All I want to say is that some of you may practice a form of our religion that says it's a sin to lie with a woman outside of marriage, so for those of you that feel that way, I am here to conduct nice, quick ceremonies, including official marriage certificates for a reasonable fee, right after the auction has concluded. With that, I shall let these charming young women present themselves to you."

As the reverend left the stage, Skully nodded in his direction while muttering under his breath. "What a schmuck!"

Loud music started playing with a heavy bass beat, and one by one, the young women took to the stage, stated their new "conc" name, and described the sex acts that they ostensibly specialized in. Each pranced back and forth and smiled at the men as they jiggled and shook various parts of their anatomy. Each performance lasted for about one minute. Each move seemed to be precisely choreographed, leading me to conclude that each woman's routine had been practiced and perfected at the school. The men responded with cheers, whistles, and hoots, along with comments that ranged from suggestive to extremely vulgar, in my view.

While the performances were taking place, Captain Skully leaned over to me. "When you and your boys offloaded payment at the school, what did you think the payment was in exchange for?"

"I assumed that the parents of the new students were paying for their daughters' tuition."

He chuckled. "I thought that might've been your impression, but I'm afraid you're way off! Parents don't pay for their children to attend the academy; the academy pays parents handsomely for their daughters! Parents submit photos to the academy, and if the academy thinks a girl is pretty enough, they make the parents an offer. It's not like parents aspire to turn their children into prostitutes, and they sure as hell wouldn't pay for the 'privilege.' I mean, there are lots of dads who like the company of harlots, but that doesn't mean they want their own daughter to be one. That takes money and lots of it!

"No, Kelvoo, the palladium ingots we dropped off were advance payments for some of the girls who are shaking their thing on the stage right now. Ten of the men here have paid in advance for first choice of these ladies. Once they've made their selections, the rest of these women will be auctioned off, one by one."

All of this information was deeply troubling. If I had a human's physiology, I believe I would have felt sickened by what I was witnessing.

When the last woman completed her performance, Captain Skully took the stage and pulled up a list on his Infotab. "Alright," he said, "which one of you is William Guzman?"

A short, stocky, balding man stood. He had a fringe of brown-and-grey hair and a bushy beard.

"As the top advance bidder, you get first selection!" Skully said. "Which of these gorgeous girls are you going to take home with you?"

"Zedna!" the man exclaimed.

The young woman with that name strode across the stage with a smile, which I saw quickly fade when she passed the successful bidder and was no longer in his range of vision. I watched her closely as she took a seat along the opposite wall of the room, and I'm quite sure that I saw a tear glistening on one of her lower eyelids.

"C'mon, Bill, that's the one I wanted!" a man shouted.

"I'll see you at poker night on Saturday," Bill called back. "If you win, I might just let you have a ride or two!" That elicited many chuckles from the other guests.

When the advance payers had made their selections, a traditional auction took place, with Hol serving as auctioneer. It reminded me of a cattle auction vid that I had seen when I was studying Terran agriculture.

The auction concluded with four of the women remaining unsold since there were no buyers willing to come up to the reserve price. They were Tracey, Hilda, Yana, and Nancy. They remained in their original seats across the room from the women who had been sold. All four of them were crying and looking utterly humiliated. The men who had purchased a woman (some of them bought two), were permitted to go to their new prizes. While I went to the four "leftovers," as they called themselves, to console them, Hol was performing "quickie" marriages for the four men who wanted them, charging each of them 500,000 SimCash units to "legitimize" their relationships "in the eyes of the Almighty."

Most of the purchased women put on a brave face and did their best to smile for their new owners. By that time, I was able to read human facial expressions and body language well enough to know that not one of the young women was truly happy.

I thought back to the conversations that the women had had with one another shortly after we picked them up from the academy. They had been talking about being paired with a nice, kind, and preferably wealthy man who would take good care of them. I was certain that none of these sad women were going to end up anywhere near what their daydreams, fantasies, or their school had suggested.

As the men left for the shuttle trip back home, the auction winners took their females by the hand, or more nastily, with a firm grip on an upper arm or the back of the neck. Some of the women looked back at the four friends they were leaving behind, shouting things like "Sorry!" or "You'll get a good guy! Just wait, you'll see!"

The whole scene made me sadder than I had ever felt up to that point.

# THIRTY-THREE: PREPARATION

We made our way to an Outlier freighter named *Bountiful*. Along the way, Kroz recorded moving and still images from all active surveillance cameras and programmed a system to switch the live feed on any camera with pre-recorded content.

By this time, Baby Sam could have basic conversations with us. We found Infotabs to be very helpful in Sam's education and thought that they could forever change the future education of Kloormari infants and children. For example, we could display a schematic of our quarters and identify parts of the room. When Sam grasped the spatial concepts of plans and maps, we moved on to the schematic of the entire vessel. We showed Sam the ventilation ducts and pointed to a louvered vent cover in our quarters. We said that we intended for Sam to use the ducts in the future to travel around the vessel. This made Sam nervous but excited, because Sam sensed an opportunity to make a valuable contribution to our team.

Now that we were training Baby Sam to carry out a mission, the team discussed a variety of plans and scenarios. I pointed out that there were twenty blaster rifles in the hold that we had been unable to deliver on the previous mission to Benzolar 3. I suggested that the rifles might be useful when seizing control of the ship.

"What good are rifles when none of us are capable of killing another being?" Keesooni asked. "Kelvoo, would you be willing to kill a human?"

"No, Keesooni, I don't think I could, even if my life was in immediate danger, but the humans don't need to know that. We can still use the weapons to threaten the crew into surrendering. I don't think there would be any harm in taking a look at the rifles and maybe learning how to use them. You never know. Maybe we can force ourselves to use them in the most dire situation."

We could see the two crates of rifles via a camera in the main hold. Since crew members rarely ventured to the hold during the day, and since no movement could be expected there, Kroz was able to substitute a still image of the hold in the feed from the camera. Keesooni, K'raftan, and I made our way to the hold.

We opened a rifle crate, and we each pulled the wrapping off a rifle. Each rifle came with a manual, written in standard Terran, titled, "How to Use and Care for Your Widowmaker MK-4." We read that the rifles had three settings—Practice, Slice, and Kill—which could be selected using the touch panel above the stock. The rifles had been shipped with empty power magazines. We read that a magazine could be charged from a standard DL-32 power outlet in thirty minutes and could store its energy for several months if unused.

The three of us pulled the twenty magazines and one charger out of the rifle crates and stashed them in the cleaning cart under a stack of rags and other supplies. We performed our regular cleaning duties around the ship. When done, we returned to our quarters and placed the items around the corner of the alcove. We plugged the charger in behind our algel incubation vat, and over the next several hours, swapped in each magazine until they were fully charged.

The next day, Kroz, Keeto, and Ksoomu took the cleaning cart and returned the charger and magazines to the main hold while K'raftan switched the hold's vid feed back to the still image. While in the hold, the trio each took a rifle, set it to practice mode, and tried aiming and shooting at various targets. In practice mode, each rifle would fire a bright but harmless ball of green plasma.

From that moment forward, groups of three kloormari would take turns practicing in the main hold. Learning to hit targets was interesting and challenging. We also used ourselves as targets, running between large crates for cover and dodging as one of our comrades took shots at us. Being hit by a plasma ball in practice mode felt like a slight static electrical shock. After each practice, we were careful to re-pack the weapons and their accessories in the crates.

When the *Jezebel's Fury* arrived at the freighter, we were locked in our quarters. From the external vid feed, we saw that the *Bountiful* had the same configuration as the *Orion Provider* but was only about half its size and rather decrepit looking. We saw several other vessels in the vicinity of the *Bountiful*, informing us that the area was a hotbed of Outlier activity.

The feeds from the cargo hold showed us that the gold and palladium were transferred to the freighter using the large transport. The four unsold concubines were also taken to the *Bountiful*, and we never saw them again. When the transport returned, it included a new supply of Vinamibefentyn, which appeared to be about the same quantity that we had previously supplied to Friendship Colony.

When the transfer of goods was complete, the crew was given two days of shore leave. Only three crew members rotated through the *Jezebel's Fury* at any given time during shore leave. We kloormari, however, remained behind. Despite their status as mere chattel, even the ship's three concubines, Lisa, Zoe, and Sandra, visited the *Bountiful*. We hoped they were given shore leave rather than having to ply their trade on the freighter. Just before he left, Captain Skully said he was sorry that we couldn't go, but he figured that some of the crew and visitors on the *Bountiful* wouldn't welcome a new and unfamiliar species. We were actually pleased to remain behind, thinking he was probably correct.

We took full advantage of the crew's shore leave. With only three crew members on board, we could monitor their movements almost all the time. We were able to locate some sections of ventilation duct that extended to little-used parts of the vessel. We took Sam to a short flow-through duct with no forced air that extended between the top catwalk in the main hangar and two smaller adjoining storage spaces.

We showed Sam how the slatted duct covers could be removed and latched back into place. Keesooni stood on the catwalk, opened a duct cover, and asked our baby to crawl through. I stood at the other end of the duct in one of the storage rooms and called Sam. Our baby was reluctant to enter the duct but bravely went ahead. Upon emerging on my side, Sam was coated in a fine layer of dust and grime and ejected clouds of dust via the vocal outlets, the kloormari equivalent of coughing. Sam emerged scared but triumphant, and I was sure to praise Sam's efforts and emphasize the importance of being able to navigate the ship's ventilation system.

Sam's transit of the metal ducts was loud. Each step made a noise that reverberated along the duct. We searched some of the storage rooms and closets adjoining the catwalks and found some adhesive tape. We used it along with cleaning rags to fashion pads for Sam's limbs. On the second day of the crew's leave, we returned to the cargo hold catwalk and let Sam explore the ducts between the three outlets. Sam enjoyed exploring and learned to crawl more quietly while stirring up much less dust.

When shore leave was over, the *Jezebel's Fury* set out for its next destination. I saw Captain Skully during my cleaning rounds and asked him where we were heading.

"Back to Friendship Colony for another vina delivery," he said.

"Isn't that rather soon?" I asked, "Didn't we deliver a year's supply only a couple of months ago?"

"I think they just want to secure a good supply into the future, so they've ordered more. This time you won't have to worry about being rushed by desperate colonists since they haven't gone through all of their previous supply yet."

Another jump and a few days later, we arrived at Friendship. Skully was correct. We landed on the pad atop the colony's main health center without the previous trip's last-minute diversions. We loaded payment while the human crew offloaded the vina. Since each trip was safe, and the cargo wasn't at risk, we completed the mission in two trips instead of spreading it out over ten.

\*\*\*

For the several weeks that followed our second trip to Friendship Colony, we settled into a routine. Most of our missions involved the delivery of mysterious cargo from one location to another in exchange for SimCash or precious metals and other goods. This included a mission to pick up and deliver weapons. Fortunately, these weapons were far more advanced than the twenty blaster rifles in the hold, so we still had access to the rifles if our situation ever warranted their use.

Our baby's education continued, and Sam was able to grasp more complicated concepts. Sam learned about our experiences since our first human contact and fully appreciated our wish to escape.

In the meantime, we continued to improve Brenna and May's reading comprehension, vocabulary, and speed. Both girls learned to read books that were suited to their respective ages. Brenna started to take an interest in the universe around her and began to read articles on subjects including planets, species, history, technology, and famous humans.

We also continued to monitor crew conversations. Over time, discussions about the kloormari gradually diminished. Bazz was still advocating for our elimination. Mec and Tank shared Bazz's opinion but only talked about us when Bazz raised the subject.

We were pleasantly surprised that Reverend Hol was a voice of reason. He tended to defend us in conversations, suggesting that his crewmates treat us with kindness and to have some tolerance for our differences. He reasoned that he still held out hope that at least one of us would "see the light," which could possibly lead to the conversion of our species.

We reached a point where we wondered whether we would ever need to take control of the *Jezebel's Fury*. Worry for our safety with each risky jump became our main concern, eclipsing our previous stress that we would be murdered by members of the crew. We thought about what would happen at the end of the six-month mission if Captain Skully actually returned us to Kuw'baal, and we wondered how we might take the baby home with us undetected. Maybe we would just tell the captain that one of us happened to get pregnant and give birth. He would understand, since he knew that kloormari are non-gender, or both genders depending upon one's perspective. We just weren't sure how accepting the rest of the crew would be.

And so, things started to fall into place and run smoothly—right up until the day that it started to fall apart.

# THIRTY-FOUR: HERETICS

One day, it was my turn to give Brenna and May a reading lesson. Before the lesson could start, Brenna asked me a question.

"Mr. Kloormar, is God real?"

I was taken aback, because I had never broached the subject of religion with the girls. I knew I needed to tread carefully because a major trait of superstitious humans was to cling to their beliefs and to reject and fear anything that could potentially weaken their faith. I had to balance my response by avoiding criticism of religion while speaking the truth to the best of my ability. I had developed a talent for lying to humans, so I certainly could have said, "Of course, God is real," but I wanted to reserve my lies for times when they could serve to avoid suffering or death.

"God is something that many humans and lots of other species have believed in throughout history," I said. "To humans, 'god' could mean anything from nature and the universe to a whole lot of gods who are responsible for different parts of life to the life force inside every person to the god that Reverend Hol talks about. You are real, Brenna, so the thoughts in your brain are real. Inside your mind, if you believe that God is real, then in that way, God is real."

"Okay, but do *you* believe in God?"

"Well, I wasn't raised by people who taught me about God, so I never learned about God or Allah or Yahweh or any of the other gods that humans have believed in, like Vishnu, Krishna, Zeus, Thor, Osiris, Tangaroa, or any of the other thousands of gods from human history. As a kloormar, I am limited to believing in things that I have proof of. For that reason, I don't personally believe in God, but I could be wrong. If *you* believe, then that's totally okay with me."

"But Reverend Hol says that, if you don't believe in God, you're going to hell and will get all burned up forever and ever!" May said.

"May, you shouldn't be worrying about stuff like that. I'll be okay."

"Please don't go to hell, Mistoo Koomah," May pleaded, her voice catching with emotion. "We love you."

I assured May that she didn't have to worry about me and that she and Brenna would understand better as they grew older and learned more. With that, we started the lesson as planned. Each girl read parts of their assigned books with my assistance, and then I asked them questions to assess their comprehension.

That evening, I updated my fellow kloormari on Brenna and May's progress and mentioned the conversation about religion. Sam took in the information and started asking about the concepts of god and religion, so we had a conversation about the subject. Sam found the whole thing to be bizarre and fascinating.

Over the following three days, other kloormari mentioned questions and conversations that they had with the girls concerning religion. I supposed that Brenna in particular had been reading diverse material that may have prompted her to question some of the things that they were being told. I saw this as a positive step in their development as humans.

Four days after Brenna raised questions about religion, K'aablart was allowing Sam to run back and forth along the wall that was in the surveillance blind spot while Keeto took a turn watching the vid feeds.

"Hide Sam!" Keeto shouted suddenly. "Hol is coming—fast!"

Baby Sam dove into the alcove and burrowed under a pile of blankets as the furious, red-faced holy man stormed into our quarters.

"How dare you?" Hol roared. "Filling the heads of two innocent little girls with your blasphemous filth!"

I stepped forward to confront him. "What blasphemous filth are you referring to?"

"Telling Murph's girls that you don't believe in Almighty God! Telling them about humans who have worshipped other gods and invoking the unholy names of other deities! False gods that are nothing more than manifestations of Satan! How dare you? You vile heretics!"

"Perhaps there has been a misunderstanding, Reverend," I said calmly. "None of us has ever raised the issue of religion with Murph's girls. They have simply asked questions out of curiosity. For example, they asked me whether I believe in God. I answered honestly that I do not, but I was sure to add that I have no issue with their belief. Are you suggesting that I should have lied to the girls?"

"You should have told them the truth! That there is only one god, and his name is Yahweh-Allah. His son is Yeshua, and his prophet is Mohammad! You should have respected their beliefs by saying so! Now you have corrupted their innocent minds!"

"Reverend, are your beliefs so fragile that they can be threatened by 'aliens' like us answering the questions of little girls with honesty? And while we're on the subject of innocent minds, what makes you think that it's alright to preach to those girls a gospel that calls for peace, kindness, and goodwill while serving on a mission of criminal activity? What makes it alright for you to frighten these children with tales of hell and eternal damnation for anyone that doesn't follow you? Who appointed you as God? You should have seen little May sobbing with worry that her teachers would be burning in hell for not believing in your 'ever merciful' god.

"In the brief time that we have spent in the company of humans, I have encountered intelligent people who espouse your religion's ideals of kindness and compassion while being atheists. I have also encountered people who claim to follow religion who have been abusive to those who are different. Do you see Keeto here? Do you see Keeto's partly regrown clasper limb? One of your wonderful followers twisted and tore it off and then proceeded to beat Keeto with it! Perhaps, Hol, you are nothing but a third-rate preacher who is only capable of spreading a gospel of hate and ignorance!"

Hol's face turned a deep red. He clenched his fists as he shook with rage. Hol could only sputter for a moment as he tried to find his words. "I gave you every chance to save your souls! I told you to open your hearts to God's truth, and you refused! Now you can all be damned to the fires of hell for all I care!"

"Will that be all?" I asked.

"No! I also forbid you from speaking to those girls ever again!"

"You have no authority over us or those children," I replied as calmly as possible. "Only their father, Murph, can tell us to stay away."

"Heretical demon spawn!" Hol blustered. "I cast you out! Out, I say!"

"No, Hol. These are our quarters. We are casting you out! Be gone, and never again barge in here uninvited!"

Sam had heard everything from the alcove and found the whole exchange to be quite traumatic.

We watched the vid feeds as the holy man stormed away along the passageway, ranting to whoever would listen. He gathered together Tank, Mec, Bazz (of course), and several other members of the crew.

Captain Skully was sitting in the barroom having a conversation with Spaggy when Hol's posse burst in, riled up and shouting with outrage. Hol raved about how the "effing kloomers" had undermined the faith of Murph's children. He spouted off with much hyperbole, a great deal of embellishment, and many outright falsehoods.

"In the name of Almighty God, we demand that you rid us of these demonic creatures!" Hol screamed.

The captain threw his hands up. "You win, Hol."

Hol's mob fell silent. "Really?" Hol asked.

"Did you for a moment think I had any intention of returning the kloormari to their planet where they could tell the Alliance about all the things we've been getting up to? How stupid do you think I am?

"I had hoped that I could convince them to become permanent crew members because their work ethic and intelligence put all of you to shame! Obviously, that isn't going to happen, so what choice do I have but to terminate them? I'm not going to do it now with all of you in a flap, boiling over with rage. I still have use for them. We have just two more tasks to complete before the mission is over. When those tasks are done, so are our guests. Is that good enough for you lot?"

"Fine!" Hol spat. The rest of his group, looking rather chastened, muttered their agreement.

"Since all of you are so hell-bent on being rid of our guests, I'm not going to do your dirty work. Hol, if I told you to take a blaster and murder one of our guests, could you do it?"

"It isn't murder, Captain, especially when you're dealing with evil beings. It's called righteous justice. Give me a blaster, and I'll be first in line to send a kloomer to hell!"

"Get out, Hol! The rest of you too. Get out of my sight!"

As they got up to leave, Hol turned to his co-conspirators. "Let's not go telling the rest of the crew about this unless we're sure they're on our side. The last thing we need is to have someone blabbing to the kloomers."

When the last of Hol's posse left, Captain Skully put his head in his hands.

"That's real sad, Cap'n," Spaggy said. "None of those kloormari boys ever bothered me. I kind of got to like them."

Skully nodded, his head still in his hands. "Me too."

While we kloormari watched the scene unfold, we were nearly in a state of panic. We were going to have to put our plan into action immediately.

After the mob broke up, we saw Hol visit Murph's quarters. Murph let him in and closed the door, so we couldn't tell what was happening. A few minutes later, Hol left. Then we saw Murph walking down the corridor with May clutching one of his hands and Brenna holding the other.

"They're heading this way," Kroz reported as Sam went back into hiding.

Murph was polite enough to knock on our door. K'raftan opened it and invited the family in. Both of the girls were crying, and their father was visibly shaken, his eyes on the floor. "My girls aren't s'posed to see you anymore," he said.

Brenna sobbed, her face contorted with pain. "I'm so sorry. I shouldn't have told anyone what we were talking about. Reverend Hol asked us how things were going, and . . . and I didn't think he was going to mind. I feel so bad. It's all my fault!"

May had been crying so hard that she gave herself the hiccups. "We're sorry, we're sorry, we're so sorry, Mistoo Koomahs!" she said between spasms. "Now we can't read, an' we're gonna be dumb and stupid!"

"None of this is your fault," K'raftan said in a soothing, gentle tone. "You're both growing up in a time when some people don't understand the *real* differences between right and wrong. You mustn't blame yourselves for that."

I knelt down in front of the girls. "You're not going to be dumb and stupid," I added softly. "Both of you have learned so much, and we know how smart you really are. All we did was help get you started. Now that you know how to read, there's no limit to your learning. We're already so proud of you.

"We have been lucky enough to work with some very smart and talented women, and we're all sure that you're both going to be just like them. There's just one thing that you need to believe in, and that's *yourselves*. Don't ever think that you're dumb or stupid, and don't ever let anyone tell you that."

I turned to face Murph. "I'm sure your dad here is going to make sure that you have lots to read. I'm sure that, when this mission is over and he takes you back home, he'll use the SimCash that he's earning to continue your education. Perhaps, when you're older, you can go to school on Earth, and you can be the wonderful, successful young women that we already see inside of you."

I turned back to Brenna and May. "Please take care of yourselves and your dad here. He's a good man, and we can see how much he cares about you. We all love you very, very much."

"Thank you," Murph said gently. He looked up, and we could see tears glistening on his cheeks. "I'm real sorry too."

We watched Brenna and May cling to their father as they walked away down the corridor.

# THIRTY-FIVE: THE HEIST

The next morning, we started cleaning as soon as our door was unlocked at 08:00. In recent weeks, the crew had decided that 08:00 was too early to start their morning shift, so most didn't leave their quarters before 09:00. We surmised that, since the mission was in its final weeks, and since we took care of the more mundane housekeeping tasks, the crew were apt to just coast along. Only Captain Skully had the discipline to maintain his previous schedule. Each morning, the bridge vid feed showed him arriving a 07:00, give or take a few minutes.

The vessel's schematics showed a forced-air ventilation duct that pushed warm or cool air into a conduit that ran between the barroom and the bridge with a fork to the right that led to Skully's quarters.

We dressed Sam in padding to allow for a quiet transit through the ducts. We also placed a metal band around Sam's eyestalk. A magnet-backed surveillance camera was attached to the front of the band. Kroz had linked the camera's feed to our Infotabs, so we could monitor Sam's movements. We saw Captain Skully on the bridge wearing the lanyard that was clipped to his command card. Kroz and I made our way to the barroom with Sam hidden in our cleaning supply cart.

We had reviewed the plan with Sam hundreds of times. When we arrived at the barroom, it was empty as we had hoped. We went to the raised platform where the captain's table was located. The vent cover was in the forward wall, just below the ceiling. Kroz checked the vid feed for any approaching humans and to see whether any bridge crew were looking at the surveillance monitors. Kroz gave the all-clear, so I removed the cover, and we each grabbed a duster, so we could appear to be cleaning dust from the duct if anyone walked in at an inopportune moment.

As I lifted Sam out of the cart, doubts flooded my mind. *Is this really our best option? If Sam gets caught, they'll kill all of us! Was it wrong to create an innocent new life and then exploit that life to save our skins?*

"What's wrong?" Sam asked, sensing my hesitation. "Shouldn't we get going?"

I snapped out of my mental paralysis, then lifted Sam up to the conduit. As soon as I replaced the cover, Sam called back to me in an ultrasonic pitch. "Don't be so worried. You trained me well. This is going to be easy!"

Kroz and I placed our Infotabs on top of the cart, so we could see a "Sam's-eye view" while we were wiping down surfaces. It turned out that we couldn't see anything in the blackness of the duct's interior. This made my respiration rate quicken and my extremities shake. "Can you see anything, Sam?" I asked.

"Not a thing," Sam replied faintly, "but don't worry, I'm just going to feel for the duct that branches off to the right."

After what seemed like hours, we saw a faint glow from the bottom of the duct in front of Sam. When Sam arrived at the light, we saw that its source was from the duct cover in the ceiling of Skully's quarters. We could also see that the duct was much narrower than the feeder conduit that it branched from. Sam was not going to be able to turn around without first backing up to the feeder conduit.

We could tell when Sam removed the metal band and peeled off the camera. Due to the small size of Sam's limbs, Sam was able to reach through the grill and place the camera on the outside of one of the slats, so it was perfectly angled to cover as much of the cabin as possible. We could see the captain's bed with two nightstands. A desk and chair were positioned against the far wall. A lockbox was placed on the far nightstand with a simple, old-style numeric keypad on its door.

Now that the camera wasn't mounted to Sam, we had no idea of Sam's progress until we heard Sam's voice from the conduit. "I'm back in the main duct. I've turned around, and I'm heading back to you." A few minutes later, we saw Sam nearing the vent cover. At the same time, Kroz saw two crew members entering the corridor outside the barroom.

"Sam, Hold!" Kroz warned.

My anxiety spiked when I saw that one of the crew was Bazz. He stepped halfway into the barroom, stabbed two fingers in our direction, and smirked. "Won't be long till yer all dead meat!"

"Thank you for the warning, Bazz. We really appreciate it," I replied, somehow maintaining my composure.

Bazz shot an obscene gesture our way and continued toward the bridge for his shift.

"Sam, continue," Kroz said.

When we could see Sam through the slats, we made a final check of the surrounding area. Then we removed the vent cover, and I stretched a sheet of cloth between my arms and let Sam fall into it. I wrapped Sam in the cloth and placed it in the bottom of the cart. When Sam jumped from the vent, clumps of dust fell to the floor and billowed into the air.

I slapped the vent cover back into place and swept a pile of dust from the floor. At the same time, Sam started coughing, so we covered Sam with cloths and supplies to try to muffle the sound. Then we beat a hasty retreat back to our quarters.

We moved the cart outside of the alcove, and Sam jumped out. As relieved as we were, Sam was starting to realize the gravity of the situation and the risks that we were all taking. I told Sam that meditation could be very helpful for sorting thoughts and dealing with high stress. "I think you're old enough to try to meditate now," I said.

I asked Sam to get comfortable in the alcove. "Close your eye, relax, and listen to my voice," I instructed. I suggested things for Sam to think about and techniques for clearing the mind. Within five minutes, Sam was in a deep state of meditation and stayed in that state for six hours. When Sam regained consciousness, Sam told us how wonderful the experience had been. "I have way more energy now, and my mind is so much sharper! I was scared of going back into the vents, but I'm a lot more confident now!"

"There's nothing wrong with being scared, Sam," I replied. "It can be useful for staying alive!"

"I know I might not stay alive," Sam said, "but it is very important for me to try to help. That was why you made me."

At that moment, the thought of losing Sam was unbearable.

From the moment Sam had placed the camera in the captain's quarters, my teammates had viewed the feed intently. For the next three days, we followed Skully's activities in his quarters. He was a man of habit. He entered his quarters at about 22:00 each evening, took out his night clothes—shorts and a T-shirt—and then he opened the lockbox and put his command card inside. He spent 20–30 minutes in his adjoining washroom, showering and performing other ablutions, we assumed. After that, he read his Infotab for a few minutes before falling asleep.

The most important information that we gleaned was the combination that Skully entered to open the lockbox. We couldn't see it the first night because he was sitting on his bed with his body blocking our view. That wasn't the case the next morning. He had an alarm set for 05:30. After getting out of bed and dressing, he went to the galley. At 06:30, he returned to his quarters and used the washroom. At 06:55, he retrieved his card before stepping onto the bridge. We could clearly see the combination that he had entered, and we were surprised that he used only a four-digit combination that lacked originality: 4-3-2-1!

Phase one of our plan was accomplished, but his routine presented us with a roadblock. Our quarters were unlocked from 08:00 through 20:00 daily, and Skully was in possession of his command card during the entire time.

To prepare for phase two, Kroz had written software and installed it on each of our Infotabs. As soon as a command card touched the Infotab screen, its contents would be copied to the device. Since an Infotab was almost as large as Sam's torso, we had rigged a harness so that Sam could wear the device on the chest or back, depending on the direction in which Sam was moving. We also had a cord with large knots tied at regular intervals that Sam could use to climb down from the ceiling vent in the captain's cabin and then back up again when the information had been obtained. Sam had practiced climbing the rope a great many times and was able to scrabble up it with ease.

We kept waiting for an opening to send Sam into the captain's quarters while the card was in the lockbox, but no opportunities arose. We were becoming concerned as the ship was only ten days from its next destination.

One morning at 05:03, we heard Sam's voice calling to us, seemingly from inside a wall behind the algel incubator. We rushed to the wall. Sam was inside the ventilation system, having entered a vent cover just above the floor!

"I'm going to try to get the command card!" Sam said.

"No, Sam!" Kroz shouted. "It's too complicated to try to navigate the ventilation system from here. We don't know what obstacles you're going to run into!"

"It's too dangerous, Sam!" I pleaded. "Come back right now! I forbid you from doing this!"

"Watch all of the monitors," Sam said. "If you see me on one, switch out the feed that goes to the bridge monitors."

At that moment, K'raftan shouted something quite remarkable: "We love you, Sam!"

Sam didn't reply. We figured that Sam was already on the way, hopefully not about to get lost somewhere in the ship's environmental systems.

I thought about what K'raftan had said and realized it was true. The eight of us had made Sam, so Sam was the living embodiment of our team. Instead of running loose around a kloormari village, Sam's entire life had been spent in close quarters with us. As a result, we noticed some of the things that made Sam unique: Sam's pattern of speckles, Sam's manner of speaking, and even the way Sam smelled. As I pondered these things, I realized we had a deep personal bond with Sam unlike anything we had ever experienced. We loved Sam very much indeed.

I felt as though my life would be over if Sam died. I cared about Sam's well-being far more than my own. I felt that I understood what Samuel Buchanan had said to me about the parent-child bond when we had climbed the hill to the lake, and Sam had spread the ashes of his mother.

Right at that moment, our beloved baby Sam was somewhere in the inner workings of an Outlier vessel surrounded by a hostile crew of criminals. I thought I couldn't cope with the helplessness, and yet I had no choice but to wait and see what was going to happen.

At 05:32, Kroz spotted Sam exiting from a floor-level duct in a passageway lined with crew quarters. Kroz was about to replace the feed from the passageway, but before Kroz could respond, Sam dashed across the passageway, and to my abject horror, leapt through the open door into Bazz's quarters!

Fortunately, we could see that Bazz was in the galley. Unfortunately, we had no visibility into Bazz's quarters. We pulled up the vessel schematic and examined the ventilation duct that led to Bazz's cabin. We could see a route to the captain's quarters, but it was circuitous.

A wave of panic broke over me as Bazz returned to his quarters with a plateful of breakfast. I held my breath, listening for a terrible commotion. When one wasn't forthcoming, I surmised that Sam was back in the ductwork.

At 05:47, we saw the captain leave his quarters. The whole scene moved as Sam removed the vent cover with the camera attached to it. Sam had the good sense to lay the cover down partly inside the vent, so the camera was still pointing into the room. We watched the rope drop onto the captain's bed.

A jolt of terror gripped us when we heard Skully on the bridge. "Excuse me a moment," he said, "I forgot my Infotab. Be right back."

"Sam, hold!" three of us shouted in unison even though there was no possibility that Sam would hear.

Sam had a leg hanging down outside of the vent and was about to descend the rope when Sam must have heard the captain turning the handle of the cabin door. Sam yanked the rope back into the duct and was just starting to move the vent cover back into place when we saw the captain below. *Don't look up . . . Don't look up*, I said in my mind as if my thoughts could have prevented Skully from seeing that the vent cover was completely out of place.

Skully took his Infotab, which was resting on top of the lockbox. After he returned to the bridge, little Sam threw the rope down, scrambled to the bottom, and entered the combination. The lockbox opened. Sam took the command card and tapped it on the Infotab's screen, then turned toward the camera and leaned back so we could see a green box on the screen, indicating a successful read. Sam closed the lockbox, shot back up the rope, reeled it in, and replaced the vent cover.

Only 11.7 seconds elapsed from the moment that Sam started to descend the rope until the vent cover was back in place. Seconds after that, our Infotabs received a message from Sam's device with the information from the command card.

The third phase of our plan was to get the captain's command access code. Kroz could have started working on that, but none of us could even think clearly until Sam was safely back in our quarters.

There was no sign of Sam as the minutes ticked by with slow, sustained agony. After an hour, we started to fear the worst. After two hours, we were in a state of abject despair. We couldn't eat our morning algel, and we couldn't think of performing our cleaning rounds.

Almost four hours after Sam transmitted the command card information to us, we heard a rustling sound and a faint "Hello" from behind the algel vat.

We rushed over, removed the vent cover, and a little ball of dust with Sam in the middle of it spilled out onto the floor.

We moved the little dust ball to the alcove, wrapped Sam in a sheet, and went to the washroom where we put Sam under a flow of warm water in the shower. Sam's tiny body had the consistency of a soaked rag. I brought our baby a handful of algel, which took every scrap of Sam's remaining energy to consume. We wrapped Sam in a clean sheet and then moved Sam to the alcove, where Sam entered a deep meditative state.

By the time that we had secured Baby Sam, our cleaning shift was scheduled to begin. Kroz stayed behind while I set out to perform the next step in our plan. I took the cleaning cart to a service panel located at the end of a corridor one deck below the bridge. That location was not monitored by a camera. I opened the panel cover and saw exactly what Kroz had described: a set of seven photonic processor cards plugged into a junction panel.

As Kroz had instructed, I jiggled one of the cards loose, then plugged it back in. I was to perform this with each card until a yellow warning light lit up on top of the junction panel. Kroz had said that the light would turn on, and an alarm would sound on the bridge when a crucial system had been disrupted. Captain Skully would have to enter his command access code to silence the alarm.

I pushed the card back into place, closed the panel cover, and gave it a quick wipe. As I started pushing the cart back along the passageway, the captain made a ship-wide announcement ordering Mec to report to the bridge immediately. As I reached the end of the corridor, I stopped short, narrowly avoiding a collision with Mec as he ran to a stairway and up to the deck where the bridge was located.

I made my way back to our quarters as quickly as I could without raising undue suspicion. As I entered, I heard the high-pitched alarm from the bridge, converted to an ultrasonic frequency, coming from Kroz's Infotab. Then the alarm fell silent.

"We have the command code!" Kroz announced.

Kroz started rapidly entering commands on the Infotab. "I've just covered our tracks. Now we can not only access but also control every system on this vessel!"

I stayed while Kroz continued to work and keep me informed. "Unfortunately," Kroz said, "this will take longer than I had hoped. In a proper control system, functionality is organized into levels. At the highest level, we would expect to have a module for engines, environmental controls, air and water, and so on. Below that we would have lower-level functions.

"As we've all observed, *Jezebel's Fury* seems to have been cobbled together from a collection of vessels and parts. The control system also appears to have been thrown together. There is no hierarchy, just a jumble of

247

functions and procedures without any uniform standards. I'm going to have to build my interface one function at a time with plenty of trial and error."

In the meantime, I watched the bridge vid feed. Captain Skully pointed to the control panel where the alarm indicator had been flashing. Mec tapped various commands into a side panel and his Infotab. He must have tracked down the source of the alarm, since he walked down to the service panel where I had caused the disruption. After examining the service panel closely, Mec left.

For several hours, I waited for the baby to regain consciousness, obsessively checking on Sam every few minutes. Sam didn't wake until our entire team had returned and were ready for our evening feeding. Each of us spent time with Sam. When my turn came up, I talked about how panicked I was during Sam's mission and the lengthy absence after the command card data was transmitted.

"Once I sent the information," Sam said, "I was able to take my time and figure out how to get back here without being in any rooms or passageways. I was able to follow the map on the Infotab, and I used the screen to shine some light inside the vents. It took a long time, but it was much safer." Sam looked at me. "Did I do a good job?"

I thought about Sam's question. In most circumstances, a kloormar would say that Sam had followed the training and instructions and did a satisfactory job, but the word, "satisfactory" didn't match the joy that was flowing inside me.

"Sam, you were amazing!" I said. "You are so brave and so smart. We are all so proud of you."

"What does 'proud' mean?" Sam asked.

"It means that we feel great pleasure simply to know someone as wonderful as you. It means you are a great kloormar, and we are all very fortunate to have you as part of our team."

I went on to say that Sam's actions would be recorded in the history of our species as one of the greatest deeds ever performed by a kloormar. "Our history will tell the kloormari and many other species how you risked your safety to save your fellow kloormari. You will be a hero!"

"I am pleased to know that," Sam said. "If I die before you go back to Kuw'baal, at least I did what I was born for."

Sam's statement jolted me.

"Sam," I said, "please don't talk about dying. Just the thought is so terrible. You are going to be fine. Do you understand? We are all going to go home very soon."

Of course, I had no basis to assume that any of us would return home safely, and before that moment, I would never have considered lying to another kloormar. In this case, however, it just felt right.

# THIRTY-SIX: UNTHINKABLE

We were all relying on Kroz to build an Infotab interface to the ship's systems. Meanwhile, we listened to Sam recount the trip through the vessel's ventilation conduits and the various narrow escapes and impediments that Sam encountered along the way.

While listening to Sam, I monitored Skully's movements on the ship's surveillance system. He walked through his quarters and moved out of the camera's line of sight toward his washroom. Seven minutes later, he emerged. He was heading back to the bridge when he glanced up for a moment.

Skully went back to the washroom and retrieved a small rectangular mirror, then sat at his desk with his back to the camera. I looked very closely and saw his right eye reflected in the mirror. He was angling the mirror to look up and behind him.

"I think the captain may have noticed the camera in his room," I announced.

"Well, at least he doesn't know who placed it there," Kleloma said.

Skully returned to the bridge where Pilo was the only other occupant. "I need you to round up ten crew, including yourself," Skully said. "Code delta."

"I think the captain's forming an investigation team," I said.

"Luckily, there's nothing to tie the camera back to us," K'raftan replied, "especially since the bridge has been constantly locked. The captain's going to assume it was one of the crew who had regular access."

A few minutes later, Pilo returned with nine crew members. Each one was wearing a sidearm. "Let's all listen to some music, shall we?" Skully said.

He pulled up some loud, grating music on his Infotab and routed it through the speakers on the bridge. The group huddled close together and talked. We could hear none of the conversation over the din. Mec said something that seemed to pique Skully's interest.

The crowd dispersed, heading for different parts of the vessel at an unusually slow pace, though Skully moved swiftly. When it was clear that he was making his way to the passageway outside our quarters, I sounded the alarm. Kroz issued the command to clear our Infotab screens, and we put our devices down while Sam dived below the bedding in the alcove. I wondered what the other crew members were up to, but we couldn't look at our devices if Skully came in.

Moments later, he burst into our room. We feigned mild surprise and casually welcomed him with perfunctory greetings.

"How can we help you today, Captain?" I asked.

"Oh, just a friendly visit," he assured us while closing the door. "We're getting near the end of our mission, and you must be getting excited to return to your home world."

We assured him that he was correct.

"There's one thing that you can help me with, actually. It seems that someone's very interested in all of the goings-on inside my cabin. Would any of you happen to know what I'm talking about?"

"What kinds of things would be going on that would interest someone?" I asked.

"Nothing in particular, but for some reason, a vid camera seems to have appeared in my quarters. I'm just here to ask you fellas to keep your lovely yellow eyes peeled for any suspicious activity, okay?"

We assured him that we'd be vigilant, and we felt relieved when he reached for the door.

Skully paused and turned back toward us. "Just one more thing. We had a mysterious alarm go off on the bridge. Mec was able to trace it to a service panel on the deck below. He happened to remember seeing one of you leaving the same area right after the alarm started." He paused and rubbed his chin. "How curious!"

With that, he flung the door open, and ten crew burst in, weapons drawn. We were terrified. I could hardly maintain control over my faculties.

"Now, if you fellas don't mind, I need you to step over there." Skully motioned to an empty corner of the room opposite the algel vat and the alcove.

"Well, we do mind, Captain!" I said. "Why would you burst in here and start making accusations? Do you have any specific allegations or proof?"

"C'mon, Captain!" Bazz shouted. "Let me blast the hell out of 'em!"

"If you don't get over there in one second, we start shooting!" Skully yelled.

We had no choice but to move. We were ordered to squeeze together in a tight group. Skully ordered Brawn, Hol, and Tank to keep their blasters trained on us. "Tear this place apart!" he shouted. "Search every nook and cranny!"

The intruders looked under the algel incubator. They removed the vent cover behind it and looked inside. Worst of all, Bazz and Pilo entered the alcove and started throwing its contents out.

"Get out of there!" I shouted in an absolute panic. "Those are our personal possessions!"

"What in bloody God's name is that?" Bazz exclaimed suddenly.

Bazz hoisted Sam up by the eyestalk and dangled our baby in front of us. "What the hell have we got here?" Bazz un-holstered his blaster and pressed it into Sam's midriff. Sam was screeching with terror, both ultrasonically and in a range that humans could hear.

Every kloormar in the room cried out in panic. "No!" I screamed. "It's just a baby!"

Skully was astonished. He pointed his blaster directly at the center of my body. All of the humans except for Bazz gathered around my group, aiming their blasters at us. Bazz kept his blaster against Sam, who continued screeching. "Start explaining, now!" Skully roared.

I was breathing so fast that I could hardly speak. I had to close my eyelid and concentrate to get the words out. "The baby's name is Sam," I gasped.

"And how did you manage to smuggle a baby kloormar onto my ship?"

"We didn't. Honestly, Captain! Sam was born just a week ago!" Yet another lie.

"Liars!" Reverend Hol roared. "You're all males! Where are you hiding a female?"

Despite my horror, I managed to speak. "Reverend, hasn't it occurred to you that other species may have a different concept of gender? Maybe they don't even have a concept of gender at all! Maybe other species reproduce differently than you're used to."

"You perverted scum!" Hol spat. He turned and pointed at our terrified baby. "This abomination is the result of homosexual fornication! This is a blasphemous affront to our Lord and Creator."

"Calm yourself, Hol!" Skully ordered.

"Don't you see, Captain?" Hol blustered. "They've started breeding! It's part of their plan! They're going to take over the ship! They're going to put us in the minority, and they aren't going to stop there! Oh no! They're going to spread to other planets and breed like a demon plague until our species has been replaced across the whole galaxy!"

The captain leaned close to Hol's face. "Shut the hell up, you ranting, frothing, delusional lunatic!" He turned back to me. "Which of you lying creeps is the mom, and who's the dad?"

"It's not like that, Captain," I said. "Sam grew from a fetus in my reproductive pouch. Each of the other kloormari contributed their genetic material. Sam carries the genes of all my kloormari comrades. Sam is the true child of each and every one of us."

Once again, the holy man couldn't restrain himself. "This creature is . . . is the result of homosexual *group* fornication? In the name of God, I demand that we kill each and every one of them. Now!"

The mob had been whipped into a frenzy. Their faces were red, and their fingers moved back and forth over their blaster triggers as if they were literally itching to open fire.

"We will do no such thing!" Skully shouted. Then he attempted to calm himself. "We're going to calmly walk out of here, and we are going to lock these creatures in here. Brawn and Tank, you will stand guard outside the door until I figure out what we're going to do." He looked directly at me. "I had really started to think I could trust you," he said in a voice that seemed to be filled with genuine emotion. "Most of the men here thought I was crazy, but I stuck my neck out and defended all of you! How could you do this to me? I actually believed we were friends. You have betrayed me and all of these good men!"

At that moment, I realized Skully had been granted a perfect excuse for making good on his promise to kill us all. Secretly giving birth to a new kloormar had given him a rationale for murder, with little or no personal guilt.

He held the door open as the humans started to leave the room. Bazz remained, continuing to hold the blaster on Sam.

"Please give us our baby back," Keeto implored. "Captain, please, sir, give us our baby back!"

"Put the baby down, Bazz," Skully ordered.

"Gladly," Bazz said. He holstered his weapon, then held Sam out at arm's length and shoulder height. He stepped back, putting one foot behind him. When Bazz started to move forward, he released his grip on Sam's eyestalk. As Sam started to drop to the floor, Bazz stepped forward and kicked our baby with his heavily booted foot.

Sam cried out in shock and agony as the baby's tiny body flew up and toward us. Sam struck the edge of a structural metal beam that ran along the ceiling and plummeted to the deck directly in front of us. Sam lay there, limbs twitching, the baby's breathing shallow and raspy.

Skully pointed his blaster at Bazz's head. "You bloody idiot! What the hell did you do that for? Get the goddamn hell out of here!" As Bazz walked through the door, Skully booted him in the buttocks.

We gathered around the child. We didn't want to move Sam until we knew that doing so wouldn't make Sam's injuries worse.

"I feel wet," Sam said. Sam rolled slightly, and we saw a pool of milky blue circulatory fluid beneath Sam's body. When Sam moved, more fluid leaked from the torso and the base of the optical dome.

I couldn't just let Sam lie on the hard metal deck. I picked Sam up and cradled my baby. "It's okay, Sam," I said, trying but failing to sound soothing. "You're going to be okay. Just stay calm."

"It *is* going to be okay," Sam replied. "You have all worked so hard and been in so much danger to make me. You taught me well, and I was able to help. I am glad for that. I love all of you, but I have to go now."

"No, Sam!" I cried, "You mustn't say that. You can't go! Oh no Sam, you can't die. You must live forever! You have to!"

"Sorry," Sam gasped, "but I am dying now."

Sam's eyelid closed for the last time. I held our precious baby close as Sam's life slipped away.

# THIRTY-SEVEN: UNIMAGINABLE

Humans have an expression that I have heard or read on various occasions: "Something snapped." The expression is used to describe the moment when a mental breakdown occurs. For example, "I couldn't take it anymore, and in my mind, *something snapped*." Or "*Something snapped*, and Jack went on a murderous rampage!"

I wouldn't use "something snapped" to describe the moment of my breakdown. It was more like *something connected* or *something opened* or something deep within me was *awakened*.

At the moment when my child died in my arms, I did something that my mentor, Samuel Buchanan, had encouraged me and my teammates to do, something that I believed a kloormar was totally incapable of.

I imagined.

I imagined punching Bazz in his vile face and seeing him fall to the floor, unconscious and bleeding from his nose.

I imagined using the electric whip that Torm had wielded against Brawn and beating Bazz until his burning skin was flayed clean off! I imagined the feeling of the whip's handle in my hand and the spray of blood and the smell of burning flesh and the sound of electric buzzing and snapping and the screams of agony and the sight of the skin parting, the blood flowing, and the smoke rising.

I imagined putting Bazz in an airlock, subjecting him to decompression, and then pumping the air back in, over and over again. I imagined hearing his screams and gasps slowly fade as the air thinned, then replacing the air until he regained consciousness. I imagined making him plead for his life and then repeating the process over and over and over again.

I imagined Bazz tied down, eyes wide with horror, pleading with me, begging for mercy as I used a knife to slowly and methodically mutilate his face and body and then cut away minor appendages and then his male parts, then disarticulate each of his limbs, then open his chest and abdomen, pull out his large intestine, and wrap it around his neck to throttle him and watch his beady human eyes bug out, and finally, pull out his still-beating heart and stab it again and again and again.

Concurrent with these imaginings, I imagined how satisfying it would feel, how pleasurable it would be, how gratifying and gleeful to cause the greatest possible suffering to a being who had brought such suffering to me and my friends and poor, poor Sam.

K'raftan pulled me out of my altered mental state by jostling me. "Kelvoo, Kelvoo, are you alright?"

"Yes, I'm fine."

"You were shaking and unresponsive."

"I'm sorry. I am having a very hard time dealing with what has just happened."

"We all are, Kelvoo. We all are."

I didn't want to tell K'raftan or any of the other kloormari what I had just experienced because I was ashamed. *What is wrong with my brains?* I wondered. *Why would I be thinking about things that haven't happened and might not even be possible? Why would I be thinking about taking pleasure in destroying another being, even if that other being is cruel and dangerous? What am I becoming? Why would Sam Buchanan ever have encouraged us to imagine? What good can possibly come of this?*

I resolved never to let myself imagine again.

In normal circumstances, kloormari think pretty much alike and will react to a situation in similar ways. This is one of the reasons why it is fast and easy to come up with a consensus when everyday decisions must be made in normal kloormari society. In our case, we did not react to our baby's death in similar ways. We each experienced grief, but we didn't process it in the same way. Regardless of how we were reacting, one thing was clear: The intensity of our despair was beyond what we ever could have conceived.

After my revenge fantasy, I turned inward. I stared blankly and stayed silent. Ksoomu, Keesooni, and K'aablart were the same. Keeto, K'raftan, and Kleloma were more agitated—pacing or mindlessly looking at their Infotabs. Kroz was trying to cope by working obsessively on gaining control of the ship.

"The captain is directing Mec to do something with the ventilation system under the galley," Kroz reported. "Mec seems to be bypassing some conduits and opening and closing valves."

"We don't care, Kroz," Kleloma exclaimed. "How can you be thinking about the mission now? Don't you understand what we've all just lost?"

"I understand all too well, Kleloma. I don't want to think about what just happened. If I can concentrate on the mission, I won't think about the other things."

After a while, I noticed that my body was aching. I had read about humans experiencing depression or grief and how these emotions could produce physical pain, sometimes referred to as "heartache." I thought about it further and wondered why much of the aching was in my joints. I took a deep breath and exhaled forcefully in much the same way as a human sighing. When I did that, I noticed a fine mist forming in the air that was exiting through my vocal outlets.

"I know why Mec was working on the ducting," I said. "We're being refrigerated."

At that moment, Skully made an announcement, calling the ten members of the murdering group to a meeting in the barroom, including the guards outside our quarters.

"I'm trying to find a pathway through the ship's systems to the environmental and security controls," Kroz said.

"What's the point?" I asked in my despair. "Even if we get control, there's no guarantee that we're going to win. We're up against a ruthless enemy, and we're no match for them."

"Do you think Sam would have been pleased to see us give up?" Kroz replied, working feverishly. "Do you want Sam's death to have meant nothing? Aren't you interested in getting back home so that we can honor our memories of Sam by telling Sam's story and adding it to the historical texts? If we do manage to survive, we need to tell the story of the newborn infant whose life was given so that we could all receive salvation. I know that it all seems hopeless, and I agree that our chances of success are minimal, but the point is that we are *trying*. If we die trying, at least we will die with some honor."

Kroz's words brought me to shame. "I'm sorry, Kroz. You're right."

I pulled up the ship's surveillance on my Infotab. Captain Skully was addressing the group in the barroom.

"Here's the plan," he said, "I'm putting those lying kloomer bastards on ice. I don't know whether they bugged my cabin or caused the alarm, but we know they've kept important information from us."

"But what if they're watching and listening to us right now, Captain?" Wanky asked.

"I don't give a damn if they are. In fact, I'm happy if they are! Let them know exactly what's in store for them!" he looked toward the surveillance camera. "You hear that, you goddamn kloomer scum?"

He turned back to his men. "I'm chilling the bastards until the final stop of our mission, back at the *Bountiful*, to offload and sell everything we have onboard. We don't know how long they can last in a fridge, but if they make it, they can do all of the heavy lifting, at the point of our blasters, and get that transport loaded.

"I don't want to make a mess, so when we're done at the *Bountiful*, we'll lock them back in their quarters, get them nice and cooled off again, and then we'll get in some good blaster practice at point-blank range. Then we can all go back to our homes and families and live our lives as happy, wealthy men!"

The captain's gang was greatly cheered by his remarks.

Meanwhile, our quarters were getting colder. I tried blocking the vent behind the algel vat, but cold air must have been pouring through another vent that was in place two levels up in the ceiling.

Back on Saraya, when cold had rendered us unconscious, it had sneaked up, and we hadn't noticed a change in our bodies. It was different this time. The stiffness and pain grew until it was almost unbearable. I didn't know whether the cause was that we were being chilled faster or whether it was simply the knowledge of what was happening that made the experience so much worse.

I went to the alcove and removed every sheet and blanket except for the sheet that I had wrapped Sam's body in. I placed the bedding around Kroz to help extend the time that could be spent trying to take control.

"I'm nearly there," Kroz said.

A few minutes later, as my teammates and I became unable to move, Kroz slurred, "I'm sorry. I tried." Kroz slumped over. Losing consciousness was painful, but it was also a merciful respite from our emotional agony.

257

# THIRTY-EIGHT: CHILL AND KILL

If I'd had a head, it would have been splitting. Every part of me hurt. I forced my eyelid to open, and I could only see blurry blobs. Just the thought of moving made the pain worse. I lapsed back into oblivion.

I don't know whether it was days, hours, or minutes later, but I woke again in much the same state. My legs were locked in my usual squatting position for meditation. I saw the blurry outlines of my teammates. Some were stuck in a kneeling or squatting position. Others were lying on the deck, including Kroz, who was lying on one side, slumped under sheets and blankets.

I managed to crawl over to try to rouse Kroz. I was surprised to find that, despite being prone, Kroz was conscious and frantically entering commands into the Infotab.

"How's the algel doing?" Kroz slurred.

I looked up at the incubation vat. "Not well." I crawled over to the vat. Since it had been unattended for a week, and no algel had been removed, the vat was overflowing. Algel was flowing down the outside of the vat, and some was piled on the floor. Much of the overflowing algel had turned brown as it started to rot and release a rank odor.

I took a large handful of the fresher algel and stuffed it into my food pouch. My body suddenly cramped up as it went into shock at the sudden introduction of food into my dormant digestive system. When the shock passed, I felt slightly better. I looked at the chronometer on my Infotab and saw that seven days and two hours had passed since the chilling had begun.

I took another handful of algel and managed to walk back to place a small quantity into Kroz's pouch. Over the next twenty-seven minutes, I fed Kroz a small amount at a time. By then all of the other kloormari were trying to move and were in varying states of consciousness.

Captain Skully and his crew must have seen us moving because soon Skully and his gang of ten stepped into our quarters with their weapons drawn.

Kroz remained under the blankets and put down the Infotab. I stayed kneeling next to Kroz and turned toward the captain, slowly and stiffly, to ensure he saw the pain that I was in. He walked over to me and knelt on one knee to address me at my level. He gently placed a hand on one of my shoulders and asked how I was doing. His disingenuous concern disgusted me.

"How do you think I'm doing, Captain? Your thugs killed our baby. Then you and your crew refrigerated us for a week. My kloormari companions and I are in intense pain. Nobody knows the longer-term health effects on our species."

"I feel bad for all of you," he said, "but why did you conceal your baby from us?"

"Do you honestly think, Captain, that your charming crew—including the likes of Bazz, Hol, Mec, and Tank—would have embraced little Sam? Do you think they would have welcomed our new addition with acceptance and love?"

Skully had no answer. He stood and looked down at me. "We are twenty-four hours out from the *Bountiful*, and we would very much appreciate your help with the offload."

"Do you not see our condition, Captain?" I asked wearily. "We will be in no shape to be put to work in twenty-four hours. We need more time to recover."

He took a step back and smiled sarcastically. "Oh dear! Well, of course we would never impose on you by making you work when you aren't in tip-top shape, so let's give you an extension." He pulled out his Infotab to check its chronometer. "Let's give you . . . twenty-four hours and ten minutes!"

His snide remark elicited chuckles from his gang of thugs.

"Of course, you have every right to refuse," Skully added, "if you would prefer more time to chill in your quarters." Then he softened his tone. "Just remember, this is the end of a long, hard road for all of you. When this task is over, so is our mission. You will all be returned to your homes, and we can all put any past unpleasantries behind us."

Behind Skully, I saw Bazz and Hol exchanged a glance and a smirk.

With that, Skully and his crew departed. "See you tomorrow!" Skully called back through the door with mock cheerfulness.

By then, Kroz was able to kneel, and after several minutes, stand. Kroz moved closer to the wall that wasn't visible to the camera and kept working on a control interface. All of us began eating, flexing our joints, and stretching our limbs, working through the intense pain to regain some control over our exhausted bodies. We collected the algel that was decaying, along with excess algel that could have clogged the incubation vat, and flushed it down the toilet. We also asked Kroz to keep us informed. We couldn't deal with baby Sam's body, so we left it in the alcove, securely wrapped in a sheet.

"I have mapped out access to each control system," Kroz said, "but the greatest challenge now is issuing commands without triggering an alarm or having a console on the bridge showing the crew exactly what's happening."

259

Six hours after Skully's gang had left, Kroz updated us. "I'm ready to perform a simple test. If you could all remain motionless for a few seconds, I will take a still image and replace the vid feed from our quarters." We hadn't been moving much anyway, so it was easy for us to pause. "Okay, hold," Kroz said. A second later, we heard the mechanism inside our door unlock, and then the door slid open! Another second later, the door shut itself and relocked. Kroz restored the vid feed to the live image. "We can move again. It is done. We have control of *Jezebel's Fury*. We can control the ship's systems undetected!"

When kloormari receive good news, it would never occur to them to whoop, holler, or cheer, so our reaction to Kroz's news was intense but silent relief.

Then K'aablart brought up the next daunting challenge in our path. Our plan required the use of the blaster rifles sitting in the main hold. Since it was the captain's intention to unload and sell all of the cargo, we had to obtain the rifles as soon as possible.

As we were formulating our plans and discussing our options, I realized we were all behaving as we would have just over a week ago. *Why are we acting as if this is just another crisis to overcome?* I wondered. *Sam is gone forever, and our entire reality has been shattered! Doesn't that matter to us? Why are we behaving so damned normally?*

My thoughts led me to recall and mentally relive the inconceivable horror of Sam's death. Next, I recalled Kroz's impassioned plea that we must carry on in order to give Sam's short life some meaning and to spread word of Sam's story as an example to others. That thought brought me back to the urgency of our escape plan.

We agreed on the plan to fetch the rifles. We had all recovered mentally, but we continued to experience severe stiffness and pain. We decided to implement the plan immediately instead of waiting until the last minute and increasing our risk of failure.

K'raftan, K'aablart, Kleloma, and I were to take the "back way" to the main hold by moving up to the top deck and accessing the hold via the hangar. Since this route would take us through some rarely visited parts of the ship, Kroz could freeze the vid images from each section as we went. Ksoomu, Keeto, and Keesooni would stay with Kroz in our quarters. They would monitor the human crew's movements. While we raided the hold, Kroz's team could communicate by making a vessel-wide announcement but speaking in an ultrasonic register. We could communicate back to them in a similar register over the communication system that was already broadcasting from most of the vessel.

Kroz found a previous recording of us relaxing and reading our Infotabs in our quarters. Kroz froze the vid on its first frame and asked us to assume the exact placement and poses shown in the vid. When we were there, Kroz switched the feed to the previous vid and told us that we had one hour and fourteen minutes before the vid showed some of us leaving our quarters, which would have raised suspicion since our door was supposed to be locked.

Kroz unlocked the door to our quarters, and our foursome slipped out into the passageway. We turned toward the aft of the vessel and climbed two stairwells. Along the way, Kroz's reassuring high-pitched voice would say, "All clear, proceed," and we would enter the next section. We made our way through the hangar, onto the top catwalk in the hold, and down to the main hold deck without incident.

The rifle crates were exactly where we had left them. Kleloma and K'aablart fetched the closest hoverlift, stopping along the way to collect two bundles of scaffolding poles that were stacked by the starboard bulkhead. For the sake of speed, we upended each crate to dump the rifles, magazines, and chargers onto the hoverlift's deck. We clipped a power magazine to each rifle.

We took the padded packing material, placed it around the scaffold poles, and packed the poles into the crates to simulate the weight of the rifles. We closed and latched the crates and then put them back into their original positions.

The four of us jumped onto the hoverlift. As we started to move, we heard Kroz's alarmed voice. "Hold! Hold! Hold! One concubine and one crew member heading at high speed toward the main hold. Aft entrance at main deck level!"

We halted the hoverlift and started moving it to a place behind the transport. We heard Lisa giggling and shouting in a sing-song voice "Catch me if you can!" she said as she ran into the hold. When Lisa caught sight of us directly in front of her, she stopped cold and gaped at us.

Lisa snapped out of her shock as soon as we heard loud, rapid footsteps coming up behind her. A laughing male voice called out to her. "I'm going to catch you, Trixie, you little scamp!" Lisa ran away from us, toward the port bulkhead, calling back with the same giggling voice as before. "Over here, big boy! Come and get it!"

By that time, we were concealed in a shadowy area behind the transport. Peering under the transport, we saw Lisa's pursuer coming into view. It was none other than the holy man himself, Reverend Hol. Lisa positioned herself behind two pallets of drums containing hydraulic fluid. Hol positioned himself opposite Lisa. As he moved in one direction, Lisa moved the other way. Twice, Hol chased Lisa around the drums.

Finally, Lisa somehow sprinted to the port bulkhead in her ridiculously high heels. She leaned back against a section of the wall that sloped back, so she was partly prone. "You win, Reverend!" she exclaimed, smiling. "I'm ready to confess my sins to you!"

Hol grabbed Lisa's wrists and held them to the wall. Then the two of them had a conversation that seemed to be rather well rehearsed.

"Trixie of *Jezebel's Fury*, confess your sins to me!"

"I have sinned through my wicked, wicked thoughts!"

"And what, exactly, have these thoughts been about?"

"You, oh mighty Reverend! You, you irresistible, sexy man! My wicked mind wants to know the holy bliss of your blessing! Ravish me, oh great one! Please!"

"Oh, you wicked temptress! I see only one path to redemption. I must fill you with the glory of the Lord!"

With that the reverend dropped his trousers, hiked up Lisa's short skirt, and started vigorously copulating with her.

Lisa put her arms around Hol's back and then waved at us to indicate, we assumed, that this was our chance to make a move. We piloted the hoverlift straight up five levels to the ceiling and then flew behind the thoroughly occupied reverend, all the way to the doors into the hangar. We were worried that the sound of the doors opening would catch Hol's attention, but Lisa prevented that by screaming. "Oh yes, Reverend! I can feel your power! Give me your blessings, give it to meeeeee!"

Kroz remotely opened the doors for us during Lisa's command performance. As we glided into the hangar, I looked back and saw Lisa extend an arm toward us behind the reverend's back and make a clear thumbs-up gesture. As the doors closed behind us, Hol added to the chorus. "Oh, glory! Oh, glory! Oh, glory beeeeee!"

We rode the hoverlift to the aft end of the hangar. From that point, the passageways were too narrow to accommodate the width of the lift. Each of us slung two rifles over our shoulders and carried a third. In all of the excitement, we had managed to ignore our continuing pain, but the weapons were heavy, and we felt all of the previous pain and then some as we lugged the rifles into our quarters.

When we returned to collect the remaining eight rifles, we took two blankets with us. We were joined by Ksoomu and Keesooni. On our way to the hangar, Kroz told us to hold twice when human crew members were spotted close by.

When we got to the hangar, we wrapped the chargers in the blankets. Kroz reported that Lisa and Hol had left the main hold, so Kleloma and K'aablart piloted the hoverlift back to its previous position. K'raftan and I each took a rifle and a blanket full of chargers. Having come from our quarters and being better rested, Ksoomu and Keesooni each took three rifles.

Shortly after arriving back at our quarters with the last of the weaponry, Kleloma and K'aablart returned to us from the hold. We stowed the weapons in the alcove. Kroz closed the alcove door, locked it, and revoked the ability of the human crew to unlock it.

The vid clip that Kroz had been using to replace the live feed was almost at its end. Kroz showed us a still image from the vid, a minute or two after what was currently playing. We assumed the depicted positions. As that frame came up in the recorded vid, Kroz said, "Switching to live in three, two, one, now." We could then start moving and resting for the ordeal that awaited us in just over fifteen hours.

At that moment, my entire body started cramping up. I curled into a ball of pain, as did the other kloormari who had retrieved the rifles. The effort of loading the weapons onto the hoverlift and lugging them to our quarters had compounded with our existing injuries from being chilled into unconsciousness.

As we writhed in pain, Kroz and Keeto came up with an idea. They took some sheets into the washroom, soaked them in hot water, and used them to warm our limbs. They followed that by gently stretching and massaging our limbs. We did notice some improvement, but it was minimal. A little after two hours later, we started to un-cramp, but we were still very sore and stiff.

I asked my teammates whether we should go over our final plan or think about contingencies, but we couldn't think of anything to add to our already thorough plan. Kroz suggested that we spend the remaining time deep in meditation with a focus on healing our bodies and clearing our minds.

I had a fitful meditation—periods of deep concentration interspersed with replays of the stress and tragedies of the past days.

We were jolted into consciousness when the *Jezebel's Fury* started vibrating and pushing us back and forth as the ship decelerated from a velocity of 998 to nearly zero. We were still three hours away from the time that Skully said we were due to arrive, so we managed to meditate for two more hours. When we woke again, our minds were much clearer, but due to our lack of motion, our bodies were as stiff as ever. We spent the final hour stretching our limbs.

Skully and his gang entered our quarters seventeen minutes later than he had predicted. All eleven men had blasters in their hands. "This way," Skully said, leading the way to the main cargo hold. "If any of these kloomers decides to make a run for it, shoot it. Actually, if that happens, just shoot any of them."

Making a run for it wasn't part of our plan. We were limping or walking, or we had one shoulder slumped down, or our bodies were bent due to our lingering pain and soreness. "What a sorry lot you are," Skully remarked as we entered the main hold with him leading and ten blasters pointed at us from behind.

The rest of the human crew were waiting for us beside the transport's open rear hatch. Each crew member had a sidearm, but only the gang of ten had theirs drawn. Spaggy, Snowy, Ebo, Brawn, and Torm seemed to be in a very sad state and avoided looking at us. Murph had tears on his cheeks. He looked toward me, put his palm over his chest, and mouthed, "I'm sorry."

"Load it up, fellas!" Skully shouted. We started with the two crates that used to hold rifles. We were glad to get them stowed before any humans decided to inspect the contents. The rest of the work involved loading ingots of precious metals. We struggled to lift each ingot through the pain, and we frequently dropped them.

Bazz wasn't satisfied with our performance. He gave Keeto a kick. "Hurry up!" he shouted. Keeto was sent sprawling onto the deck. Keeto turned to Bazz. "I assume that you're in no hurry to get this mission finished and return back home. If that's true, just keep on injuring us." Bazz pulled a foot back to deliver another kick, but the captain stopped him.

"Stow the attitude, Bazz, unless you'd like to pitch in and hoist a few tons of cargo yourself!"

Bazz clenched his fists and backed away.

For two hours, the crew stood by and watched us struggle until all of the remaining contents of the cargo bay had been loaded. At that moment, Skully led us back to our quarters with the ten thugs following behind.

"Sleep tight, kloomers!" Bazz called out as Skully used his Infotab to close and lock our door.

We watched as the crew returned to the cargo hold. Most piled onto the transport while a few others got onto the smaller shuttle in the hangar. Spaggy, Ebo, Snowy, Brawn, Torm, and Murph declined the opportunity to visit the *Bountiful*.

"Too bad for you," Skully said. "You're going to miss a great party!"

Pilo and Mec were ordered to stay on the bridge to provide security. "Don't worry," Skully told them. "I'll make sure you get a bonus for the inconvenience."

We watched on the external vid feed as the vessels crossed the short distance to the *Bountiful*. We also watched the remaining crew proceed to the barroom, except for Pilo and Mec, who took their stations on the bridge. We watched and listened to the barroom. The six crew members shared stories about the kloormari team and their sadness that we were no longer going to be around.

"Isn't there anything we can do to help?" Murph asked. "My little girls love those guys. They taught 'em how to read, you know!"

"I wish there was," Ebo replied, "but if we help them, where are we going to run? The captain would kill us. If we grabbed the shuttle and ran, we'd be wanted by the Brotherhood or caught by the Planetary Alliance and locked up forever."

That was the first time we had heard of something called the "Brotherhood."

"This isn't my first mission," Spaggy added. "Unfortunately, a lot of beings lose their lives on many of these trips. After all, we *are* working for a criminal organization. It's just extra sad this time because I really love those guys!"

We also listened to Pilo and Mec on the bridge. They didn't have anything interesting to say. They just talked about what they would do and how they would spend all of their SimCash when they got home.

Eight hours and seven minutes after most of the crew left for the *Bountiful*, they returned. Many of them staggered off the transport or the shuttle in an apparent state of intoxication.

Skully marched soberly to the bridge. "Start the chill," he told Mec.

Less than a minute later, we felt a stronger flow of air coming from the vent behind the algel vat. No doubt, the same was true for the vent in the ceiling.

"I'm leaving the air flow on," Kroz said, "but I'm switching the temperature control to keep us at a comfortable twenty degrees Celsius. The bridge has the ability to read the temperature in each room, so I'm setting their readout to show a drop of one degree every three minutes, holding steady when it shows that we're at four degrees."

Twenty minutes later, Kroz gave us another update. "Okay, now we're supposed to start feeling the effects. Let's gradually start moving more slowly. Let's touch our joints as if we're wondering why they're so stiff."

Ten minutes after that, Kroz opened the door to the alcove. "Now, let's say we've figured out what's happening. Let's each take a blanket from the alcove, then find a spot on the deck and position yourself comfortably in a pose that you can hold for a while. Some of you may want to fall onto your side in a few minutes."

Five minutes passed. "Let's close our eyes now and hold for five more minutes," Kroz said. "Alright, I've frozen the image where we're at right now. Let's each leave our blankets on the deck in their current position and take a weapon and put it under our blanket." We did so, and then Kroz closed and locked the alcove door.

"Now we wait until the captain decides to bring his gang in here and murder us. Let's monitor the captain and the general whereabouts of the crew. When they're heading this way, go back to your positions, grab your weapons, and prepare for 'Operation Sam.'"

There was nothing left to do but wait and hope we would bring honor to the memory of our little Baby Sam.

# THIRTY-NINE: OPERATION SAM

Captain Skully kept us waiting until well into the next morning. The ship had left the *Bountiful* a few hours earlier and was underway. It hadn't jumped yet and was moving at a slow, steady pace. I figured that the captain wanted to take care of his problem with us before jumping toward home.

Finally, he assembled his gang of thugs in the barroom.

"What's the plan, Captain?" Wanky asked.

"We walk into their quarters and shoot their chilly, unconscious bodies," Skully replied. "I hope that's not too risky or complicated for you."

His gang tittered at his remark.

"Alright, let's get this over with," Skully said as the group left the barroom and headed down toward us.

"Assume positions," Kroz said. We crawled under our blankets and assumed positions that matched the still image from our quarters.

"Weapons powered up, safeties off, firing mode set to 'kill,'" I added.

Kroz was positioned with half an eye watching the door while the other half was under the blanket watching the Infotab.

Skully entered first, followed by his gangsters.

"Shouldn't it be cold in here?" Tank asked.

"Better do this now!" Skully barked.

As the men raised their weapons, Kroz tapped an icon on the Infotab. The men jumped as the door to our quarters slammed shut, locking us all in.

"Shoot 'em all! Now!" Skully shouted.

The gangsters squeezed their triggers, but nothing happened. They looked at their weapons, stunned.

"Now," I said urgently but calmly. As we jumped up and aimed our rifles at the men's chests, some of them kept squeezing their triggers or hitting their weapons as if to jostle a faulty connection back into place.

"Put your hands behind your heads, back up to the wall behind you, and kneel, facing the wall," Kleloma said.

The men started to move back, but they stopped when Skully stood his ground. "We will do no such thing!" His voice was calm and clear despite the slight shaking in his hands. "Do you have any idea what you're getting yourselves into? Do you have any idea who we are and what we're capable of?"

"We have a far better idea than you can imagine!" K'raftan replied.

It seemed as though Skully was stalling for time. He turned to me. "What the hell have you done to our weapons?"

His question took me back to my first private conversation with him, when he boasted about how he had tricked us into boarding the *Jezebel's Fury*. I had wondered why he would give away information when he didn't have to. Now I understood. The idea of explaining how we outsmarted him and his crew held great emotional appeal to me. I also thought that it might make the men realize they had no options but to comply with our commands. I asked Kroz to answer the captain's question.

"Well, you see, Captain, while your weapons are aboard this vessel, they're connected to the ship's network. If you had bothered to look at any documentation regarding the network's special features and their interface to the weapons, you would have seen mention of a 'lockout' feature. It lets you render your weapons useless if a hostile force has taken your vessel. Fortunately for us, our rifles can't connect to networks."

"Now," I said, "as pleasant as this conversation has been, I order all of you to back up to the wall."

"What's the point, Kelvoo?" Skully asked. "You have the weapons, so why not just shoot us right here in cold blood?"

His question made some of his gang visibly nervous.

"We are kloormari," I stated. "We never kill unless necessary, but we will have no choice if you don't comply immediately!"

Bazz stepped past the captain. "They're not going to kill us. They don't have it in them." He looked directly at Keeto. "I can't tell any of you kloomers apart, but I sure recognize you with your stumpy little baby arm! Now, if you don't want me to tear it off again, you'll hand your rifle to me."

"No!" Keeto shouted, shoving the end of the barrel toward Bazz's chest as Bazz took another step forward. "I'll shoot . . . I really will!"

Bazz's crewmates and the captain stared with rapt attention and in total silence.

"My friend," Bazz said with a smile, "I don't want you to have to do anything that you think is wrong. Do you really want to be a killer? Wouldn't that go against everything you stand for?"

When Bazz took another step forward, Keeto spoke to me ultrasonically. "I can't do it, Kelvoo! I just can't!" Keeto said with utter terror.

"Yes, you can, Keeto," I replied. "Just pull the trigger!" As I said the words, I realized that none of us wanted to shoot. I cursed myself and my weakness. I couldn't believe that I had gleefully imagined all of the terrible things that I would to Bazz if I had the chance, and now that the opportunity presented itself, I was paralyzed!

Bazz stepped right in front of the barrel of Keeto's rifle, his chest almost touching it. "Come on," he said gently. "Just give the rifle to your old friend, Uncle Bazzy."

Bazz slowly made a fist, placed it under the end of the barrel, and gradually lifted it. "There we go," he said softly. "Nice and easy."

When the barrel was pointing to the ceiling, Bazz snatched the rifle away from Keeto and took two steps back.

"I'm sorry!" Keeto exclaimed in a register that was clearly heard by human and kloormar alike.

"You should be sorry, you pathetic losers!" Bazz said with a smile as he started lowering the barrel toward Keeto.

At the moment when the rifle's line of fire was going to intersect Keeto's eye dome, something inside me twitched.

A brilliant ball of plasma left my rifle's barrel and struck Bazz in the shoulder, knocking him flat on his back and sending Keeto's rifle sliding in front of my teammates. Bazz's jacket had a hole in the shoulder that was the size of a human hand. The edges were black and smoldering. A cauterized gash had penetrated Bazz's shoulder to the bone, exposing meat that was brown and cooked on the outside and pink in the middle.

My fellow kloormari snapped upright and pointed their rifles at the men with great intensity. I instructed Keeto to retrieve the rifle.

Bazz screamed at me with rage through his tightly clenched teeth. "Bastard! We should have killed you from the start!"

I'd had enough. I switched my rifle's firing mode to "slice" and pointed it at the deck beside Bazz's ankles. I held the trigger down and slashed the steady beam across Bazz. He cried out in agony as the beam burned a swath through his trousers and ankles. Bazz, on his back, put his hands on the deck, lifted his torso, and dragged his legs and feet a short distance from me. "Scum! Kloomer filth!"

Before Bazz could continue, I made another slash across his thighs. He screamed in agony, then collapsed and was flat on his back again. Defeated, Bazz shook his head, then looked directly at me. "What did I ever do to you?"

It took me less than a second to respond, but before I did, something happened that was almost magical. It was as if time had slowed, giving me the luxury of deciding exactly what to do next.

I reviewed my choices: I could say nothing and just kill Bazz. I could list any number of verbal or physical assaults that he had committed against me or any of my teammates—the idiot wouldn't be able to distinguish between us anyway. Finally, I could choose one single example. For reasons I can't adequately explain, I wanted to say something to invoke an expression of utter terror on that despicable face. I wanted him to know exactly what was going to happen next.

I knew precisely what to say.

I pointed the barrel of my rifle directly between Bazz's beady human eyes and leaned down toward him. Then I used all of my vocal outlets to produce the loudest, most discordant, and most demonic-sounding voice that I could produce. "YOU . . . MURDERED . . . MY . . . BABY!"

Bazz's red, sweat-beaded face took on a terrified appearance. His eyes opened wide at first and then squeezed shut. "No! No! Please, no!" he begged. That was good enough for me.

Bazz was dead the moment I fired the plasma beam into his head, but *that* was *not* good enough for me! I continued to pull the trigger, discharging the magazine directly into the center of his face, which became obscured by flame and smoke. Still, I held the trigger until the steam produced from the boiling fluids in Bazz's skull became too much.

With a loud pop, Bazz's skull split open. Fried brains and blood shot out as half of his skull, with burning hair attached, skittered across the deck and bounced off a wall.

When I released the trigger, the deck plating was glowing with white incandescence where Bazz's head used to be. Smoke billowed from pieces of blackened bone and tissue.

I snapped the rifle up and pointed it at the group of panicked humans. "WHO'S NEXT?" I yelled, using the voice that I had used to send Bazz to his just reward.

Skully and his terrified gangsters moved straight to the wall and knelt down. They faced the wall and placed their hands behind their heads. They were shaking. A puddle of urine spread under Pilo.

In a desperate move, Skully slapped the button on a communications unit above his head. "Mutiny in the kloomer quarters! All hands, defend the ship!"

He cowered, expecting to be shot for his heroics, but his efforts were for naught.

"I didn't hear your voice over the ship's speakers," Pilo said.

"If you don't think that we considered every contingency in our plan, you seriously underestimated our intelligence," Kroz said.

"Let us show you how a ship-wide announcement is made," I added. "K'raftan . . ."

Kroz used an Infotab to open the door for K'raftan and activate the comm unit in C-12. K'raftan crossed the passageway into C-12 and made a ship-wide announcement in a voice that perfectly matched the captain's in tone, rhythm, accent, and every other perceptible way, "All crew. Emergency! Code red! Code red! Code red! Proceed immediately to C-12. All of you! Bridge crew included! Gather in C-12 and don't move! The rest of us will join you shortly with further instructions."

K'raftan dashed back across into our quarters, and Kroz locked the door.

"Lying bastards!" Skully said. "Why did I ever trust you?"

"You're only in this predicament because *we* trusted *you!*" I retorted.

We kept our rifles leveled at Skully and his men. Kroz kept half of an eye on the men and half on an Infotab while narrating the whereabouts of the remaining crew. "They're all running into C-12 just like good crew members," Kroz reported.

We could hear some of the conversations between the crew, converted to ultrasonic so only we could detect them. "What do you figure is going on?" Snowy asked.

"Maybe our kloormari friends aren't making things easy for the captain's group," Spaggy replied.

"I'm counting twenty crew in C-12," Kroz said in kloormari. "When we add the humans we're holding here, we're one short."

"This isn't right," a crew member in C-12 said. "Why aren't we hearing from the captain?"

"Let's give it two minutes," another crew member replied. "Then I say we go find our buddies."

We had no choice but to make our next move, even if one crew member was still roaming free. Kroz slammed and locked the door to C-12 along with the door at each end of the passageway while opening our door. Ksoomu and K'raftan exited into the passage and positioned themselves at the forward end. Keeto and Kleloma took the aft end of the passage.

K'aablart, Keesooni, Kroz, and I ordered the thugs to stand. "To C-12! All of you!" I shouted. The humans filed out into the passageway with our four rifles urging them forward. Ksoomu, K'raftan, Keeto, and Kleloma had them covered from each end of the passageway. When the men were outside of C-12, Kroz opened the door. We ordered them in and then locked the door behind them.

There was a viewing window in the door at each end of the passageway. Through the window we saw Mec exiting from a washroom in a hurry, no doubt to comply with the order to proceed to C-12. As Mec approached the glass, he saw us and our rifles, then sprinted away.

Sticking with our plan, we proceeded up a level and entered C-12 on the catwalk that circled the room. From our perch we could keep the humans guarded until we could turn them over to the appropriate authorities.

"Okay, wise guys!" Skully shouted. "You've murdered Bazz, taken us prisoner, and taken our ship. Now what? What in the hell are you going to do? Pilot it back home?"

This was the first time that the crew, outside of Skully's gang, had heard about Bazz's death. They reacted with surprise and alarm.

"No, we're just going to the nearest Planetary Alliance planet or facility," Kroz replied. "After all, we've had six months to figure out how to operate this cobbled-together monstrosity."

"Hey, where's Mec?" Tank asked.

Skully made a slashing motion across his throat, trying to tell Tank to keep his mouth shut. "Don't worry, Captain," I said. "We know Mec's running around out there. He'll be joining you soon enough."

"You kloomers are so screwed! Mec knows every bolt of *Jezebel's Fury*. The eight of you are no match for him!"

We turned our attention to our Infotabs. The men tried to do the same, but Kroz had deactivated their devices.

The vid feed showed Mec on the main deck of the cargo hold. He was using a hoverlift to move a large piece of equipment, uncovering a hatch in the deck. Then he lowered himself down the hatch.

"Our trajectory is being changed," Kroz said a moment later. "We're slowing down relative to the *Bountiful*. Now we're stationary relative to the *Bountiful*."

"Let's get back underway," I said.

"I'm trying, but the vessel isn't responding! There must be some kind of manual override and control panel below the cargo hold!"

The next time we saw Mec on the vid feed, he was running onto the bridge. We had no idea how he'd got there without us spotting him first. There must have been hidden passageways that weren't included on our less detailed schematic. On his way, Mec laid a pole in the lower track of the door. Kroz tried to close the door to trap Mec on the bridge, but Mec had successfully jammed it.

Mec was carrying a large power tool as well as a piece of equipment, about a meter long, which he dropped onto the deck of the bridge. It appeared to have been mangled. Next, we saw Mec using the main control panel.

"He just transmitted an encoded message!" Kroz reported. "I'm shutting down external communication now."

"What's the message?" I asked.

"I'm applying the ship's hash key to it now. Just a moment . . . it's decrypting . . . it's a distress call. He said the ship has been taken over by aliens. He asked all Brotherhood vessels to respond. He transmitted our coordinates and . . . he's offering one billion SimCash units to the ship that rescues them!"

Our hope started fading. Fast.

Mec ran back through the jammed door, turned to the port side of the vessel into an area without vid coverage, and disappeared again. From our cleaning duty days, we recalled that there were two hatches in that particular blind spot that had been bolted shut. We heard Mec using the power tool, which we assumed he was using to open a hatch.

Several minutes passed. Our overall audio monitoring of the comm units picked up Mec shouting, "Can you kloomers hear me? You might want to take a look in your quarters!"

271

We didn't know whether Mec realized we had access to the feed from the cameras or whether he was trying to lure some of us into our quarters. We didn't want to give away any information, so we stayed silent. One minute later, the vid feed showed an oval hatch fall from the ceiling of our quarters. A man's arm extended down through the hatch holding a black capsule-shaped object. The arm tossed the object down onto the deck and then withdrew quickly. The capsule hit the deck, bounced once, and rolled under the algel incubation vat.

A blast went off, which showed as a flash on the screen, followed by flying debris from the shattered algel vat and then blackness as thick smoke billowed out. The blast reverberated throughout the vessel. This elicited a cheer from about half of the human crew. Skully laughed. "I'll say it again: You kloomers are so screwed!"

After the blast, we saw the concubines, Murph's daughters, and Hol's wife exit from their quarters and look around. I used the comm unit on the catwalk to broadcast in Skully's voice. "All civilians please stay calm. The situation is under control, but you must return to your quarters and stay there until I give you the all-clear. That includes you, May and Brenna." The civilians all did as they were told.

The next time we saw Mec, he was standing on the deck in the center of the main hold, looking up toward one of the cameras on an aft catwalk. Mec raised his arms and made fists as if flexing his muscles. "So, kloomers, let's take a look at the situation, shall we? Number one, *Jezebel's Fury* isn't going anywhere! Can you see me, kloomers? Maybe you saw me dump the ship's flow control unit onto the bridge, all busted up beyond repair! Ha-ha! I put its tiny control processors into the waste disposal and purged them into space! You're screwed!

"Number two, we're nice and close to the *Bountiful* and at least half a dozen Brotherhood ships as big as this one! I've sent a distress call, and they're on the way right now! You're *royally* screwed!

"Number three, your food supply is toast—burned toast! How long can you live without your precious algel, kloomers? Ha-ha-ha! You're *totally, royally* screwed!"

Mec started dancing and shouting out the *Jezebel's Fury* song.

We're the boys of *Jezebel's Fury*.
We're rotten, low life scum!
We're dirty sons of dirty whores.
Riled up and full of rum!

Kroz worked on the Infotab. "I'm overriding a couple of safety protocols. . ."

Full of rum, we're full of rum!
Hide your women, here we come!
Join with us; we'll have some fun!
If you won't, you'd better run!

We saw evidence of a breeze in the hold. A few lightweight pieces of packaging material started to become airborne behind Mec.

We're the boys of *Jezebel's Fury*.
We'll kill you while we smile—

"What the hell?" he shouted.

We saw the huge outer doors slowly opening behind Mec as the breeze rapidly transformed into a gale. Equipment and empty crates started sliding and hitting the transport. Drums of fluid tipped and began rolling. The transport, parked just inside the doors, started sliding. It partly tipped over before being blocked by the doors, which were still slowly rolling open.

By this time, Mec was crawling along the deck against a hurricane. Somehow, he was making headway toward the hatch that he'd previously disappeared into. As Mec reached for the edge of the opening, a hoverlift broke loose and smashed into his shoulder. Mec slid and tumbled toward the outer doors. He collided with the transport, his midsection wrapping around a landing-skid support strut.

As the outer doors continued to move, the starboard door cleared the edge of the transport, which went spinning into the void along with thousands of debris fragments and clouds of ice vapor, instantly forming as the hold's air escaped. I switched my Infotab to show the feed from the external camera above the bow doors. I could just barely discern Mec's form tumbling away into the distance.

The problem of Mec had been solved, but that didn't make him any less correct.

We were totally, royally screwed!

# FORTY: BOARDING PARTY

All we could do was wait. We discussed whether to surrender to the inevitable Outlier boarding party or stand our ground. We decided to fight out of respect for Baby Sam's sacrifice.

While we waited, we recorded personal messages and our thoughts on our Infotabs. We spoke in audible Terran in the hope that someone would hear at least one of our stories, and word of our struggles would find their way back to our species, perhaps via the Planetary Alliance.

While we recorded our messages on the catwalk, Skully and much of the crew smirked. They made no effort to escape; they just lazed around, waiting to be rescued.

Three hours and twenty-seven minutes after Mec sent the distress call, we saw a rapidly approaching object on the external vid feeds. Within a few seconds, the ship's immense size became obvious. It was shaped like a sharp-edged wedge. Its external surfaces ranged from deep green to black and bristled with weapons. We'd had no idea that the Outliers had such a vessel. Perhaps they had a very powerful ally.

The warship positioned itself directly over top of the *Jezebel's Fury*, blocking our view of the stars above. We got the best view from an external camera on top of the *Jezebel's Fury* at the stern, facing along the length of our vessel.

From the belly of the warship, two flexible straps shot out to each side. The straps had thrusters on their tips, which fired to make them wrap under the *Jezebel's Fury* and join together below. The warship started reeling in the straps, pulling us closer to its underside. Spring-loaded struts extended from beneath the warship. The struts compressed against the *Jezebel's Fury's* upper hull, ensuring we were held firmly in place.

While we were being pulled to the warship, the hull of the *Jezebel's Fury* flexed slightly, producing creaking and groaning noises. The human crew knew what those sounds meant and cheered with delight.

A flexible tube, about one and a half meters wide, extended out of the warship. It appeared to end with a soft, flexible ring that sealed to the smooth surface of the *Jezebel's Fury*, just behind the bridge.

"I'm going to be the first to greet our guests," I said to my kloormari comrades. "It's been a great adventure, and I cherish every moment that we've spent together."

I exited from C-12 and descended a level. From the passageway, I asked Kroz to open the door to our former quarters and the alcove inside. Smoke poured from the top of the doorway. As I entered, I was able to avoid the worst of the smoke by crawling below it. Algel was sprayed everywhere. Most of it had turned an opaque white from shock and heat, rendering it completely indigestible.

I took a fresh power magazine from the alcove, since I had drained more than half the energy in the previous clip into Bazz's face. I clipped the new magazine to the rifle and asked Kroz to provide me with a clear path to the bridge. As I walked, doors opened in front of me and slammed shut behind.

From the short passageway that led to the bridge, I saw a circular cut being made in the bridge's ceiling where the tube from the warship joined onto the *Jezebel's Fury*. Sparks and drops of molten metal fell to the deck. I positioned my body around the corner with part of my eye and my rifle pointing down the passageway, ready to shoot the first Outlier to drop down.

A circle of hull plating crashed down onto the bridge deck, followed by a white spray of heat-dispersing fire-retardant foam. I jumped with alarm at the noise, my breathing rate increased, and I had to tense my limbs to stop them from shaking.

"Stay where you are, or I'll shoot!" I shouted when I heard movement in the tube.

"Identify yourself," an amplified voice said from the tube.

"I am Kelvoo of the planet Kuw'baal. My people have taken control of this vessel. If you try to take this vessel from us, you will be destroyed! I demand that you withdraw immediately!"

The absurdity of my statement wasn't lost on me.

A thin pole poked down from the hole in the ceiling. A small sphere rotated at the end of the pole.

"Kelvoo of Kuw'baal," a much calmer voice replied, "we need to verify that you are speaking the truth. I have lowered a camera into the bridge. Please step into view."

I felt oddly reassured by the calm voice, but I didn't want to take any chances, so I dashed across the passageway in less than half a second and took up a position on the other side. The pole retracted.

"Alright, Kelvoo," the voice said, "I am going to lower my head through the hole, so you can see my face. If you don't shoot me, I will descend onto the bridge. Just me and nobody else. I will show you my hands, so you can see I'm unarmed. You may keep your weapon pointed at me if you wish."

I watched with great anxiety, followed by confusion, as a large grey head with small facial features emerged. The head descended on a long neck that stretched well below the ceiling.

"I am Sub-Commander Trexelan of the Sarayan Security Forces vessel *Natami*. We acknowledge you, Kelvoo of Kuw'baal. We have been searching for your group for a very long time."

The sub-commander's head rotated up, her feet rotated down, and she gracefully lowered herself to a standing position directly in front of me. I lowered my rifle.

"Are all eight of you alive and well?" Trexelan asked.

I snapped my rifle straight up and aimed it at her. "Why has your species aligned itself with the human Outliers?" I shouted.

"What are you talking about, Kelvoo?" she asked calmly as she raised her hands higher.

"How could you possibly know there are eight of us if you haven't been communicating with the human crew of this vessel?"

"Alright, Kelvoo. Please calm down and listen to me. First, we know that nine kloormari left Kuw'baal with a human claiming to be Captain Roger Smith. Second, we know that your comrade, K'tatmal, was left behind on Benzolar 3. That leaves eight of you."

"How did you find out about K'tatmal's death?"

"Death?" the sub-commander asked. "Kelvoo, I can assure you that K'tatmal is very much alive! In fact, the only reason we were able to track you down was because of K'tatmal's cooperation and detailed information! I am standing before you as a representative of the Planetary Alliance. We are here to rescue you from your kidnappers. If you wish to return to Kuw'baal, we are here to take you home. It's over, Kelvoo."

"Please forgive me," I said as I dropped my rifle. Both sets of my knees collapsed beneath me, and I bowed down before Trexelan. Emotions that I could never have conceived of flooded every part of my mind and my body as the words "It's over" reverberated through me.

She bent down and touched my shoulder. "Everything is going to be alright. All we need to do now is secure this vessel. I know there must be so much going through your mind right now, but if you can, would you please stand up?"

I did as she requested.

"When did you gain control of this ship?"

"About three hours ago."

"Only three hours? How many human crew are there? Did you kill them all when you took the vessel? How many are still at large?"

"There were thirty-two crew in all. Unfortunately, two were killed in the struggle. We are holding the others captive."

She stared at me in astonishment. "Are you telling me that a group of eight untrained kloormari overpowered thirty-two human members of a notorious criminal gang?"

"Well . . . yes, I suppose I am."

"Do you have any idea how incredible that is? I've seen plenty of action with the Sarayan Forces, and I've seen great acts of heroism, but I have never even heard of an accomplishment like yours! I will personally see to it that each and every one of you receives a medal and the highest civilian honors."

"But we don't deserve to be honored."

"Why not?"

"Because we took the lives of two humans, one of whom died at my own hand!"

"Kelvoo, there is nothing wrong with using lethal force to escape a criminal captor. You will suffer no negative consequences for your actions. There is one thing we have to take care of immediately though. With your permission, I would like a platoon of my soldiers to come aboard so we can remove your prisoners and secure them on our vessel."

"Yes, please!" I replied.

Trexelan spoke into a comm unit to summon the platoon. Moments later, thirty-eight heavily armed soldiers and their leader, Lieutenant Voxtol, descended onto the bridge.

"Would you mind directing us to the prisoners?" Trexelan asked politely. I replied that I would prefer to lead the Sarayans there.

"Lead the way then!" Trexelan said.

"Kroz, are you getting all of this?" I shouted in kloormari as we made our way through the vessel.

"Oh, yes! And we are greatly pleased!" Kroz exclaimed via a ship-wide kloormari language announcement. "Our human guests think that something quite different is about to happen. They can hear the footsteps of the soldiers approaching, and they think that their rescue is imminent!"

I asked Trexelan whether her soldiers would do me a favor when they entered room C-12. She replied that under most circumstances she wouldn't, but in this case, she thought the powers-that-be would probably be inclined to give her some leeway. I advised Kroz of my plan.

We stood outside the door to the catwalk above C-12. As the door slid open, I stepped through with my arms raised high in the air, followed by the business end of a rifle barrel.

Skully and half of the crew cheered wildly to see me at gunpoint. They jeered at us, and at me in particular. I stopped in the doorway so they could spew their venom.

"Kloomer scum! You're dead meat now!"

"Losers! Thought you could win, eh? You'll never beat us, you morons!"

"You're going to die even worse than that stupid kid of yours!"

That last comment crossed a line for me. I stepped to the side and rested my hands on the catwalk railing as a platoon of heavily armed Sarayan military personnel poured in, swarmed left and right, and trained their weapons on the humans below.

In that moment, I cherished the reactions of the hapless men. Slack-jawed astonishment, wide-eyed terror, dread, sadness, and hopelessness were painted on their faces. Some started to cry, others stared blankly, and many cowered and covered their heads as if expecting to be shot on the spot.

"On behalf of the Planetary Alliance," Trexelan said, "I place all humans present under arrest for kidnapping, with further charges to be announced later."

Most of the platoon exited and descended a level. Kroz opened the door into C-12. The human prisoners knelt and placed their hands behind their heads until the soldiers restrained their hands behind their backs and bound their ankles together with a short metal cord.

I followed as the prisoners were led, shuffling, to the bridge. A small circular hoverlift descended from the *Natami*. Three prisoners at a time were placed on the platform and ascended into the massive Sarayan vessel. I watched with intense relief as the last of them disappeared.

I told Trexelan that six civilians were also on board, including two children. She used her comm unit to ask a counselor to board the *Jezebel's Fury*. When the counselor arrived, I gave her directions to Hol's quarters, Murph's cabin, and the concubines' quarters so that Mary, May, Brenna, Lisa, Zoe, and Sandra's needs could be attended to. The counselor assured me that they would be treated with compassion and kindness on the *Natami*.

My pleasure was tempered by our food situation. Trexelan accompanied me to our former quarters, where we met up with the rest of the kloormari. The smoke had cleared, and we could survey the damage.

Almost all of the algel was inedible. We took four buckets from the cleaning supplies closet and managed to scrape together enough living algel to mostly fill them. Without the nutrients in the incubation vat, no new algel would grow. I estimated that, if we kept the remaining algel wet and refrigerated, we might be able to make it last for three days, by which time we would have consumed it all anyway. Only our InfoServer seemed to be relatively unscathed.

"Sub-Commander Trexelan," I said, "if you look inside the alcove, you will find the remains of an infant kloormar. Please dispose of the remains as you see fit."

"An infant?" she asked. "Where would a kloormari infant have come from?"

"From me," I replied. "I gave birth to that baby. Baby Sam was murdered by the humans."

Trexelan went to the alcove and gently unwound part of the sheet containing Sam's body. I couldn't bring myself to look at Sam, but the distinctive odor indicated that our poor baby's body was decomposing. "I am so sorry, Kelvoo," she said softly. Then her face and her voice hardened with resolve. "The humans must pay a heavy price for this."

After a moment of pondering our tragedy, Trexelan asked us to assemble on the bridge with our personal belongings, so we could transfer to more comfortable quarters on the *Natami* as the Sarayans' special guests. She said we could take the InfoServer if we wanted to, but its information would be well out of date. She assured us that the *Natami's* information servers would contain data that was much more current. She also asked us to bring the buckets of algel for cold storage on her vessel and to allow their scientists to study the possibility of growing more algel.

On the *Natami*, we were given eight adjoining cabins. Each cabin was white and clean and had a window that spanned the width of the room, providing a panoramic view of the stars. Compared to the *Jezebel's Fury*, our new quarters were the epitome of luxury. Just standing in my assigned quarters made me feel far more relaxed and tranquil. I dimmed the lights and spent an hour just staring at the stars, feeling my anxiety drifting away into the void.

We were called to a meeting and escorted to a conference room by Trexelan. I was reminded of the room where I had been taken shortly after I was first carried aboard the *Pacifica Spirit*. I felt a wistful fondness for those days of friendship and discovery.

We were met by the commander of the *Natami*. Captain Vykrata welcomed us and introduced two other Sarayans at the table. "This is Investigator Naltrom. Once you have had some rest, she will ask you to relate all of the details of your captivity. Our first concern, however, is for your well-being. Sub-commander Trexelan tells me that your food supply has been destroyed. This is Dr. Lalinio, the biology specialist on our science team."

"How many days can you survive without algel?" Dr. Lalinio asked.

"No more than three," Kroz said.

"How far are we from Kuw'baal or an incubation vat?" I inquired.

"I am sorry to report that we are twelve days from a sanctioned jump point and then another three days from Kuw'baal," Captain Vykrata said. "The nearest planet or vessel that would have an incubation vat is ten days away."

"Forgive me, Captain," I said. "I hope I'm not speaking out of turn when I ask whether it would be possible to jump from an unsanctioned location, as we did many times on *Jezebel's Fury*."

Captain Vykrata shook his head. "Unsanctioned jumps are one of the most serious possible offences under the interstellar navigation laws of the Planetary Alliance, even if such a jump could save lives. With the size of this vessel, the odds of catastrophe are substantial, and we have over one thousand personnel on board. Besides, our navigation systems are programmed to prevent jumps from or to unmapped jump points."

Dr. Lalinio jumped in. "I want to assure you all that we will do everything in our power to find a way to grow more algel from the remaining quantity that you have or to try to find an alternative source of nourishment for you."

"Thank you, Doctor," the captain replied. "Investigator Naltrom, please provide our guests with an overview of your goals for dealing with the human kidnappers."

Naltrom nodded. "My mission is to build a case against the accused humans, so they will never cause problems to any species, including their fellow humans, again. Starting tomorrow morning, I would like to interview each of you, as well as the female civilians, to get your accounts of the events from the moment that the criminals' leader landed on Kuw'baal, claiming to be Captain Roger Smith. By the way, his real name is Myron Pringle.

"There is a Terran expression, 'justice delayed is justice denied.' We Sarayans have always believed in that sentiment. At this moment, we have sufficient evidence to turn the suspects over to the Planetary Alliance Department of Justice. If we do so, you can expect the process of convicting and sentencing the suspects to wind its way through the bureaucracy for several years.

"If, however, we can meet a high standard of clear and convincing evidence, deep-space law allows us to pass summary judgement and impose a suitable sentence. We would very much prefer to take care of this matter expeditiously. It is important to us, as Sarayans, that the victims of crime bear witness to justice being done."

"What sort of evidence would you need to meet a high standard?" Keeto asked.

"Well, ideally we would have documentation in the form of vid recordings. *Jezebel's Fury* has an adequate vid surveillance system, but nothing was recorded. I'm sure the captain and crew made sure of that just in case they ended up in the situation that's facing them now."

"I think that I can help with that," Kroz said.

"How so?" Naltrom asked.

"Early in our captivity, before our first off-vessel mission, I was able to tap into all of the vessel's vid feeds without any of the humans finding out. Doing so proved to be crucial to our survival. Anyway, I did happen to record all of the vid from that moment forward, both to the InfoServer and to all of our Infotabs, just in case it might be useful." While speaking, Kroz performed actions on the Infotab screen. "May I access your display panel?" Kroz asked, motioning to a large screen at the end of the room.

"By all means," Investigator Naltrom said.

"For example," Kroz said, "here is the moment when a crew member named Mec dropped an explosive device from a hatch and destroyed our food supply."

All of the Sarayans watched the vid clip with great satisfaction. Naltrom exuded relief. "You have just made our work so much easier! Now I have the utmost confidence that you will see justice served!"

When we left the conference room, Trexelan took us aside. "I'm so sorry for the loss of your baby. What would you like to do with the remains?"

"The kloormari have no special rituals or ceremonies for dealing with remains," I said. "In my village, we would often place the body in a stream to return its nutrients to our planet. Since that would not be practical here, you may cremate Sam's body, release the corpse into space, or do whatever else you see fit. Please do not ask us to participate in or witness the disposal. We are having a great deal of difficulty with the situation as it is."

# FORTY-ONE: DEEP-SPACE JUSTICE

On our first morning aboard the *Natami*, we each served ourselves a meager ration of algel from the cooler in the galley down the hall from our quarters. We had done the same thing the previous evening. We were keenly aware of our dwindling food supply, and we held out hope that Dr. Lalinio and the science team would come up with a solution.

Investigator Naltrom, along with two assistants and Sub-commander Trexelan, questioned Kroz first at 07:00. Kroz was interviewed for just over four hours. Next was Kleloma, whose session lasted two hours. Each subsequent kloormar was questioned for about one hour. I was the last witness to be questioned, by which time it was late in the evening.

As I knelt at the table with the seated Sarayans, Naltrom acknowledged the late hour and assured me that they only had a few questions. Trexelan explained that Kroz had provided a list of incidents, and with perfect kloormari memory, could lead them to each supporting vid with the precise date, time, and cameras that captured the incident. The kloormari who were questioned before me were simply required to corroborate their fellow kloormari's previous submissions. Naltrom was extremely pleased by how perfectly our recollections matched one another.

By the time that they got to me, Naltrom's investigation team only had a few perfunctory questions.

"Is there anything that you would like to say to us, and are there any questions that we might be able to answer?" Trexelan asked when they were finished.

"Yes," I replied. "If the suspects are found guilty, what type of sentence do you anticipate handing down?"

"Many of your fellow witnesses asked that same question," Naltrom replied. "It is against our policy to reveal possible sentences in case doing so would influence your testimony." Naltrom's reply made sense to me, so I didn't pursue it further.

"When judging each suspect, I hope you will take some things into account," I said. "At their core, I believe that some members of the crew are good people." I went on to cite examples of Spaggy, Ebo, Snowy, Brawn, and even Torm treating us with respect and declining to participate in our persecution. I gave a special mention of Murph, who cared deeply for his young daughters and trusted us to provide them with some education.

"Thank you for bringing this to our attention," Naltrom said. "These concerns of yours will be taken into account. At the same time, you must understand that every human member of *Jezebel's Fury's* crew served their captain through their own choice. Unlike you and your fellow kloormari, no human crew member was forced to participate. As such, they all aided and abetted in the commission of some truly terrible crimes in the service of the Brotherhood."

"This is the third time that I've heard of the Brotherhood. What exactly is that?"

Trexelan answered. "It's a term used by Outliers to describe a loose affiliation of criminal organizations. No matter what you may have heard about the Outlier colonies, the great majority of their citizens are peaceful humans who just want to have a good life. Keep in mind that criminals and 'undesirable' humans were cast out to the colonies or compelled to leave Terra a few generations ago. Their descendants bear little resemblance to their ancestors. The problem is that the Outlier planets, Perdition and Exile, are plagued by a small but powerful element of criminal gangs. Corruption is also rife within their political class.

"The captain and crew of *Jezebel's Fury* were a small gang with the fastest vessel known to exist. Their dangerous, unauthorized jumps, combined with their high velocity, is what allowed them to evade us for so long. You may have noticed that, when you went on a mission, the vessel would jump and then spend several days, heading to the next destination at high speed. Did you ever wonder why they didn't just jump to a spot close to their destination?"

"Yes, actually. I was curious about that," I replied.

"Well, when a jump occurs, it causes a disruption in the fabric of space-time. This allows us to instantly detect jumps within this sector of the galaxy and to locate the source immediately. We learned of the areas that *Jezebel's Fury* operated in—Friendship Colony, Benzolar, various mining operations, and so on—and we had our vessels stationed in these areas. The problem was, we didn't know exactly where the vessel would jump to, and when it completed a jump, *Jezebel's Fury* moved at such a high speed that we couldn't track it to its intended destination, and we certainly couldn't catch up to it."

Trexelan apologized for her rambling response to my question about the Brotherhood. I assured her that I really appreciated the information and that it helped to fill in a great deal of missing information.

"How long have you been trying to catch *Jezebel's Fury*?" I asked.

"From just a few days after you were taken from Kuw'baal," Trexelan said. "At that point, a follow-up Terran expedition arrived at your planet. The crew was extremely alarmed to learn that the former students of Samuel Buchanan, except Kwazka, had left.

"Kwazka gave a detailed description of your encounters with the so-called 'Captain Smith.' It didn't take long to determine that you had been duped onto *Jezebel's Fury*, and in effect, kidnapped.

"With the kloormari as potential allies and perhaps future members of the Planetary Alliance, your well-being was of extreme importance, and a highly sensitive matter. A fleet of Alliance vessels has been trying to track you down ever since. The entire Alliance will be so relieved by your safe return. We will share the news with them as soon as we are close to a communications relay. Is there anything else you would like to know?"

"I feel compelled to say that not all of our missions were for evil purposes," I replied. "For example, we went on two missions to deliver critical medicine to Friendship Colony. I know that the captain must have charged them an unreasonably high price, but you should have seen how grateful the colonists were!"

"You must be referring to Vinamibefentyn," Trexelan said. "Kelvoo, do you know which illness is treated with 'vina'?"

"No, I've been curious about that, but none of the crew mentioned it."

"Well, Kelvoo, the only thing that Vinamibefentyn treats is Vinamibefentyn addiction!"

"I don't understand."

"Vina was developed by a narcotics manufacturer, owned and operated by a consortium of Brotherhood gangs. They wanted to take the most powerful and addictive narcotics and develop a new drug based solely on the addictive qualities of previous drugs. The result was vina. It didn't provide any type of high. It also didn't induce any mood changes, at least not until it started wearing off. That's when it would result in the most awful illness and suffering, even after just one dose!

"Some purely evil Brotherhood members wanted to see what would happen if they placed the undetectable vina in the water supply of Friendship Colony. Sure enough, weeks later, the colonists became violently ill. That's when the Brotherhood had a captive market! They caused the disease, and then they held a monopoly on the cure!

"The residents of Friendship Colony are in a truly dire situation. We have tried to explain that to them, but most don't want to believe us. The Planetary Alliance is currently formulating plans to provide the colonists with the means to manufacture their own vina while we form a blockade against the Brotherhood. That's the short-term fix. In the meantime, we are frantically working on a treatment to cure vina addiction. I'm sorry to say that we have made little progress so far."

I told the investigative team how devastated I was to learn of the true purpose of the Friendship Colony missions and how sorry I was to have played a role. They assured me of their understanding that we hadn't known the truth, and we were only participating under duress.

"Was there nothing redeeming in anything we did?" I asked. "What about our mission to Benzolar 3? We were delivering weapons to the government to defend against bloodthirsty terrorists! I also want to know how K'tatmal escaped from them."

"Kelvoo, one person's 'terrorist' is another person's 'freedom fighter,'" Trexelan said. "From the Alliance's perspective, the rebels were trying to restore their democracy.

"There are two main political parties on Benzolar 3, the Freedom party and the Liberty party. Supporters of the Freedom party are staunch believers in arming the general population. They believe that not only do they have the right to own arms, they have a duty to obtain as many weapons as possible. Their philosophy is that the citizens must be armed so they have the ability to overthrow a corrupt government. Under the Freedom regime, the increase in availability of weapons led to a surge of deadly violence as a means of settling disputes.

"The Liberty party feels that weapons should only be in the hands of a small paramilitary force whose job is to enforce the planet's democratic constitution.

"A planetary election was held. Representatives from the Alliance were invited to observe. What we saw was a massively lopsided win in favor of the Liberty Party.

"The Freedom Party leaders cried foul, claiming, without evidence, that the election results were fraudulent and that they had won with a resounding majority. In an ironic twist of fate, the heavily armed civilians and their militias immediately came to the aid of an extremely corrupt government.

"The government declared martial law and cracked down on all opposition, committing untold atrocities in the process. Supporters of the Liberty Party went into hiding and launched guerilla attacks to overthrow the dictators. The Planetary Alliance established an embargo against the Benzolar system, and we have been providing material aid and defensive weapons to the rebels.

"Brotherhood gangs have long been in the business of selling weapons to the highest bidder, and the government of Benzolar 3 is willing to pay a premium. *Jezebel's Fury* used its great speed to circumvent our embargo. Of course, the rebels attacked your group to try to prevent delivery of the weapons."

"Are you saying that no good was served by any of the missions that we participated in?" I asked.

"Unfortunately, none that we are aware of," Investigator Naltrom replied.

"And what about K'tatmal? How did K'tatmal escape? And how did K'tatmal survive without algel?"

285

"The rebels learned that *Jezebel's Fury* was heading their way, and we had previously advised them that a group of your species had been kidnapped," Trexelan said. "During their attack on *Jezebel's Fury's* transport, they courageously rescued K'tatmal.

"The rebels took K'tatmal to one of their clandestine bases and explained the situation. K'tatmal was more than willing to provide the Alliance with any information that could ensure your safe return.

"There was only a day's worth of algel in K'tatmal's food container, and there was no way to procure more algel in time to save K'tatmal's life. Fortunately, Benzolar 3 has a large agricultural industry. The rebels put a team together, and with a great deal of bravery and loss of life, managed to raid an Agriculture Ministry research lab and take an incubation vat. K'tatmal nearly starved to death while the rebels took the small amount of algel and slowly grew more. It took two weeks before an Alliance vessel could meet up with the rebels and take K'tatmal and the algel vat back to Kuw'baal."

"What has happened since then?" I asked. "What is K'tatmal doing now?"

"It is my understanding that K'tatmal, who already had a deep interest in interstellar law, studied, passed the necessary exams, and is now representing the legal interests of the kloormari on Kuw'baal. It's quite a success story!"

I was very pleased to know that things had turned out well for K'tatmal. I was also astonished by the speed of K'tatmal's accomplishments.

Investigator Naltrom asked me whether I needed to know anything else. I assured the team that I did not. I also offered my deepest thanks for their patience with all of my questions. It was very late, and everyone in the room was thoroughly exhausted. I had a great deal of information to process, and I was looking forward to a long night of deep meditation to try to analyze and make sense of it all.

I took my small evening ration of algel, which did little to quell my strong sense of hunger, then I settled into my quarters to meditate.

The next morning, after a tiny breakfast, all of the kloormari, in addition to the three concubines, Lisa, Zoe, and Sandra, were called to a briefing held by the captain, who assured us that everything was being done to build a case against Myron Pringle and his crew.

Sandra clenched her teeth and her fists, the depth of her pain and rage coming through her voice. "I don't want any of those bastards to ever see the light of day!" Zoe rubbed her hand over Sandra's back, and Lisa held Sandra's forearm. Both nodded their support of Sandra's statement. I wondered whether my previous appeals for clemency had been misplaced.

Captain Vykrata informed us that the purpose of the briefing was to notify us of the charges being leveled against the suspects. They were as follows:

Aiding and abetting or committing acts of:
- Murder
- Kidnapping
- Assault
- Unlawful Confinement
- Extortion
- Slavery
- Sex Trafficking of Minors
- Human Trafficking
- Reckless Endangerment
- Purchase of a Banned Substance
- Transportation of a Banned Substance
- Trafficking of a Banned Substance
- Theft
- Failure to Provide the Necessities of Life
- Support of a Criminal Organization
- Support of an Enemy Government
- Violating a Planetary Embargo
- Evading Arrest
- Unauthorized Space-Time Disruption
- Operation of a Vessel at Unauthorized Velocity
- Operation of a Vessel in an Unsafe Manner
- Causing Hazards to Navigation
- Failure to Comply with Vessel Safety Requirements
- Failure to Register an Interstellar Vessel
- Insufficient Recordkeeping on an Interstellar Voyage

Captain Vykrata said that the charges had been read to the prisoners and that the investigative team was assembling the supporting vid clips. The evidence would be shown to the accused, so they could mount a defence if they chose to do so.

When the criminal justice matters were concluded, Dr. Lalinio gave a presentation on the progress that had been made to grow algel or to find an alternative. He was sorry to report that the *Natami* lacked the supplies to force our already damaged algel to grow. He added that the science team was trying to come up with alternative foods. He said that, if it would be alright, they could visit us later in the day to test some alternatives. We accepted the offer without hesitation.

When the meeting ended, we were free to roam in authorized sections of the *Natami*. Sub-commander Trexelan offered to show us around, but we were all feeling lethargic due to our dwindling algel rations, and we just wanted to be left alone in our quarters.

At 15:00, Dr. Lalinio visited us with two assistants. We went to the galley where three concoctions were presented. Two were soupy, and one was syrupy. The doctor asked each of us to open our food pouches, and a few drops of the algel substitute were placed inside. In every case, the result was the same: forceful expulsion of the substance. Our bodies thoroughly rejected the foreign matter.

On the morning of our third full day on the *Natami*, we woke with the knowledge that our evening meal would result in our consumption of the last of the algel. Our reduced rations had already made our hunger difficult to bear.

We were invited to a meeting with Dr. Lalinio, Sub-commander Trexelan, and Investigator Naltrom. The doctor delivered the bad news that no new progress had been made.

"My friends," Trexelan said, "there is one final option for your survival that we should bring up. I'm reluctant to suggest it, because it's risky, and it may bring back disturbing memories for you."

"I know what you are going to suggest," I said. "You're giving us the option to be chilled into an unconscious state, aren't you, Sub-commander?"

She nodded. "As a last resort, yes."

"We know that this type of 'hibernation' has severe aftereffects and likely takes a physical and mental toll on you," Dr. Lalinio added. "For that reason, we think it is best to use this option tomorrow morning, instead of waiting until you are suffering from starvation and perhaps unable to recover from the cooling."

"While we suggest that you seriously consider the hibernation option, we do want you to understand that the process will be considered a medical treatment," Trexelan advised. "You have the right to refuse any medical treatment if you wish."

"We hope to wrap up our prosecution of the prisoners today," Naltrom added. "We would very much like to show you that justice was done before you enter a state of hibernation.

"We are going to have a hearing in twenty-five minutes, where the suspects will have an opportunity to refute the charges and evidence against them. I hope that you will all attend. It is possible that a judgement will be rendered immediately. On the other hand, if the suspects choose to mount a defence, it may take several days for arguments. That would be unfortunate because you would miss the judgement. I don't think that's going to happen, since the suspects have been nothing but belligerent and uncooperative so far."

Shortly after the meeting, we were invited to the hearing where we were joined by the three young concubines in the hearing-room gallery. The accused men stood before us.

Captain Vykrata presided over the hearing. He began by naming each suspect. "You have been presented with the evidence against you on the following charges," he said, then proceeded to read the charges. "Do you wish to refute the charges and/or the evidence against you?"

Captain Skully (whom the court referred to by his actual name, "Myron Pringle") stood with his hands and feet shackled to his waist by lengths of metal cord. "We refute the entire legitimacy of this court," he stated in a loud, clear voice. "We do not recognize your species' jurisdiction over humans. We do not recognize the Planetary Alliance as having the right to pass judgement on us. We demand trial by our fellow Outlier humans."

"Your objections have been noted by this court numerous times and once again are rejected," Captain Vykrata replied. "The deep-space laws that we operate under clearly endow us with jurisdiction in this matter. If you do not answer the question, the evidence will be used against you, and judgement will be passed. I will not ask this again: Do you wish to refute the charges and/or the evidence against you?"

Mr. Pringle stood again and repeated his previous statement verbatim.

"Very well," Captain Vykrata said. "This court deems the evidence against you to be valid and accurate. By the power granted to me by the Planetary Alliance, I hereby find all of the accused guilty on all charges. Sentencing will be conducted in the prisoner holding area at 14:00."

"Since this is a merciful court, we shall now invite the prisoners' available family members to address the prisoners and make a statement if they wish. Bailiff, please bring Mary Hashemi, the wife of Reverend Anil Hashemi, into the hearing room."

I had never known Reverend Hol's real name prior to that moment.

Mary entered the room and stood before the prisoners. Captain Vykrata asked her whether she had anything to say to her husband or the court. Mary had always struck me as a quiet, compliant, meek human woman. Clearly, a side of her had been hidden to me.

"You sick, disgusting hypocrite!" she screamed. I thought Captain Vykrata would have Mary escorted from the hearing room for contempt, but then I realized she was directly addressing her husband!

"Oh, you had to go and be the great holy man, didn't you?" Mary said. "Had to be the center of attention! 'Oh, look at me! Reverend High and Mighty'!"

Reverend Hol gaped in astonishment, then shook his head as if imploring his wife to stop.

"Meanwhile, you go taking off to visit these whores at every opportunity," Mary said, motioning to the three young women, "you dirty hypocrite!"

Mary turned to Captain Vykrata, shaking with rage. "You know what's worse, Captain? Sometimes this bastard brought a whore or two into our quarters and made me watch! A couple of times he even forced me to join in, and if I didn't, I'd get a slap or a punch or a kick from this lowlife!"

Mary turned back to her husband. "I hope they throw the book at the whole lot of you, and you all go straight to hell!" With that she turned and stormed out of the hearing room.

I found myself feeling great admiration for Mary, leading me to poignant recollections of Bertie, another strong human woman whom I had the pleasure of knowing during our adventures on the *Pacifica Spirit*.

Next, Captain Vykrata asked the bailiff to bring Brenna and May Murphy into the hearing room. I was filled with dread, wondering what these poor girls could possibly say now that they were faced with the prospect of long-term separation from their only remaining parent.

The bailiff gently guided the girls to their place and told them in soft tones that they could say something to their father and the captain. Both of the girls were crying, their little bodies shaking with each sob. When their father, William Murphy, saw the faces of his distraught daughters, his large, soft face scrunched up as he broke down and unabashedly cried.

May tried to speak, but her sobbing was so powerful that she couldn't get any words out between her spasmodic breaths. Brenna was able to find her voice though. "Why did you do this, Daddy? Why did you help these men? Mama said it was a bad idea! She said those men were trouble!" Brenna broke down for a moment and then continued. "And then Mama died, and we were all so sad, and then you joined the bad men, and you took us away from our town and our friends!"

Brenna broke down again, but May filled the terrible void with a wail. "We lost our mommy, and now our daddy is going away too!"

The whole scene was too much for me. I shut my eye tight, overwhelmed by a feeling that my body had been hollowed out, and a terrifying darkness was descending all around me. It got worse when Brenna concluded with, "Why, Daddy? Why?"

Murph could only croak out a response. "I'm sorry, girls. Oh God, I'm so, so sorry!" Tears poured from his reddened eyes. "I just wanted to take you on an adventure. I just wanted to do something that would give you a good life. I wanted to be a good dad! That's all I ever wanted!"

Murph looked up at the ceiling and cried out to his dead wife. "I'm sorry, Sally! You were right! You were so smart! You were such a good mama! You were always right, and I shoulda listened to you! It's all screwed up 'cause of me! It's all my fault! I'm sorry."

May turned to Captain Vykrata. "Mr. Captain, what are you going to do to us?"

"When we arrive back at the kloormari's planet," Captain Vykrata replied, "you will be turned over to a local human representative of Terra. It will be their decision. We will take good care of you both before we arrive at Kuw'baal."

With that, Murph turned to my group of kloormari and pleaded directly to us. "My kloormari friends, please, take care of my little girls! Please, make sure they're gonna be okay!"

I may have spoken out of turn, but I couldn't help myself. For the first time, I couldn't get a complete sentence out. For some reason, my vocal outlet hesitated as I replied. "We will . . . we will do whatever we can."

Captain Vykrata asked the bailiff to escort May and Brenna from the hearing room. The girls wouldn't budge. When the bailiff tried to take their hands, May screamed. "Don't touch me! I don't wanna go! I want my daddy!" May and Brenna both reached their hands out toward their father.

Captain Vykrata told the bailiff to stand down and let the girls stay. "This hearing is concluded," he said. "The prisoners are to be escorted back to their cells. This court will reconvene at 14:00 in the prisoner holding area for sentencing."

As he stood to be escorted from the court, Murph looked up at his daughters one last time. "I'm so sorry." I saw his burly form sobbing as he was taken away through the exit door to the cells.

Sub-commander Trexelan went to May and Brenna. She knelt in front of them, took their hands, and spoke gently to them. Then she led them from the hearing room. We kloormari filed out somberly. We just wanted to go back to our quarters and be left alone. That's exactly what we did until 13:45 when Trexelan knocked on each of our doors.

"Come in," I said when I heard the knock.

Trexelan opened my door and extended her neck inside. "It's time to go to the sentencing."

"What's the point?" I said, despondent. "Everything's wrong."

"I can see how hard the last hearing was on all of you," Trexelan said, entering the room. "We have seen situations before where captives become emotionally attached to their captors."

"Trexelan, that's not the issue. Didn't you notice those two little girls? What kind of life are they possibly going to have now? Did you see their father begging us to take care of them? I said that we'd try, but I lied, because those girls are never going to be placed in our care. We wouldn't know how to raise human children anyway!"

"I understand, Kelvoo, I really do, but their father knew what he was doing when he joined the crew of *Jezebel's Fury*. His children are just more of the victims left behind by these horrible criminals."

"I'm reluctant to go to the sentencing, Trexelan. I'm scared of what the sentence might be. Some of those men were evil. The most despicable one is already dead. Some of the men are less evil. Some of them showed compassion and kindness toward my friends and me. I'm hoping that some of them will receive a sentence that gives them a chance to be rehabilitated."

"That's entirely up to Captain Vykrata." Trexelan took my hands in hers. "Kelvoo, I need you to understand how important it is for us as Sarayans to ensure that the victims of crime are there to witness justice. If you miss the sentencing, you might always regret that you weren't there. We are your rescuers and your hosts. Please grant us the honor of following our traditions with your attendance at the sentencing. After that, this terrible chapter can be closed for you and your kloormari friends."

Trexelan showed us the way to the prisoner holding area. It was a metal box surrounded by a gallery one level up along three sides. The holding area was reminiscent of room C-12 on the *Jezebel's Fury*.

We stood along the gallery railing while the shackled, convicted men were led by their guards into the lower level. Trexelan stood with us. The three concubines were also seated in our section. Soldiers bearing rifles stood at the railing along either side of the gallery. I was relieved that the prisoners' family members were not in the room.

When all of the invited guests were present, the door was opened for Captain Vykrata, who was dressed in full Sarayan military regalia. He stood beside us and then addressed the prisoners. "Having been found guilty of all charges by this court, do the prisoners wish to make a statement prior to sentencing?"

Captain Skully, as he was once known, stepped forward and looked up to our section of the gallery. He started to sing a song that I had never heard before. After the first line, the rest of the prisoners joined in.

> At the end of the day, I'll be flying away,
> traveling through the great, vast abyss.
> I'll be missing you so, with a heart full of woe,
> when we're parted and I reminisce.

> If my ship's good and true, I shall fly back to you,
> to your love and your touch and your kiss.
> By your side I shall stay, until my dying day,
> with our lives full of heavenly bliss.

> But if I should die, I beg you to try
> to forgive me and know that I care.
> In the night sky afar, just spy a bright star,
> and trust that my spirit is there.

> I'll be twinkling, you'll see, with a love that's set free,
> as my spirit shines down upon thee.

With the song concluded, Captain Skully stepped back among his men.

Captain Vykrata pronounced his sentence in a strong, steady voice. "It is the judgement of this court that all convicted prisoners present be sentenced to death."

My mind couldn't immediately process his words. *What? No, this can't be right!*

"This sentence is to be carried out immediately."

Before I could scream for him to stop, Captain Vykrata ordered the soldiers to open fire.

The soldiers on either side of the gallery shouldered their rifles, and the room lit up with the glow of plasma as it ripped through the bodies of the men below.

I entered a catatonic state, feeling as though I was floating outside of my body, like a dispassionate observer. My vision was dark and blurred around the edges.

I saw soldiers enter the lower level. The cries of the men who were still alive came through muffled and echoing, along with the final plasma blasts to their heads.

After the shooting was over, my fellow kloormari and I couldn't move, unable to process what we had just witnessed. Trexelan came to each of us, one by one. She gently touched my arm. "It's time to go," she said. "Please come with me."

Like a mindless robot, I let Trexelan lead me to the conference room where we had met after we were assigned our quarters on the *Natami*.

When we were assembled, Captain Vykrata walked in. By then I was less catatonic, but I found it difficult to concentrate with the maelstrom of thoughts and images swirling through my brains.

"I deeply regret the traumatic effect that the sentencing and executions have had on all of you," Captain Vykrata said. "I want you to know that we appreciated your pleas for leniency, and we took your concerns into account, but in the end, the list of offenses, dating back well before your involvement, was so extensive that we could not reduce the sentence for any of the criminals. We were not expecting such a strong reaction from you. Our understanding of the kloormari is that your species does not experience strong emotions or personal attachment."

"That could certainly be said of all of us before we were taken from Kuw'baal," Kroz replied.

"We have experienced things beyond the scope of any kloormari before us," I added. "We have been changed in the most profound ways."

"What would you like to do next?" Trexelan asked gently. "Are you ready to enter hibernation tomorrow morning?"

"No," I replied.

"No?" she responded in surprise.

"No. Not tomorrow morning. Now! Chill us now, please. We need to escape from our thoughts. Please release us into the black emptiness where we won't keep seeing the things we have seen today."

# FORTY-TWO: HOME

A plain, featureless room had been set up in advance of our expected hibernation. Batts of insulation had been affixed to the walls, floor, and ceiling, and a flexible insulated duct had been run from a refrigeration unit to the room.

The Sarayans had built eight frames of tubular metal that would keep us upright in the positions we would assume for the long sleep. This would stop us from falling and possibly blocking our breathing inlets. It would also give their medical team access to our bodies if they thought of anything that they could do to help us.

Before we entered the chiller, Dr. Lalinio brought us eight containers containing equal portions of the remaining algel. The algel actually amounted to generous final portions, and we were able to eat our fill, hoping that a larger amount of nourishment in our systems would increase our chances of survival. I was grateful for all of the activity. While my kloormari mind was wired to retain every memory, I was learning that I could suppress the power of my horrific memories by keeping busy and thinking pleasant or even mundane thoughts.

The eight of us filed into the chill room. Trexelan and Dr. Lalinio were dressed for the cold, wearing thickly padded jumpsuits with hoods, gloves, and large boots over thick socks. They told us that they would spend every moment with us until we were unconscious. This was comforting to me.

I locked my knees for the position that I wanted to hibernate in. Dr. Lalinio and Trexelan moved the frames into place and strapped them to my upper torso just below my shoulders. They did the same for each of my companions.

Dr. Lalinio told us when the cold air started to flow. That's when I told Trexelan that I had something important to say to her. She moved closer to me.

"I know that this is a risky thing we're doing here. If we don't survive, promise that you will tell my species our story, especially the story of the birth, heroism, and death of our precious Baby Sam."

"Kelvoo, if you and your friends don't make it, I absolutely promise that I will share the story—Baby Sam's story and all of the stories you have told us. Of course, I think it would be best for you to tell the stories yourselves because they are *your* stories, after all. Let us think positively. As you drift off into hibernation, picture yourself back on Kuw'baal sharing your stories with all of your fellow kloormari."

I closed my eye, and Trexelan gave my shoulder a reassuring squeeze. My body and my joints started to ache, but the pain was nowhere near as intense as our previous chilling. I was comforted by the presence of Trexelan and the doctor as I drowned out the horror of the bad memories with thoughts of returning to a normal and wonderfully mundane life on my beautiful home planet. As my brains shut down, I was enveloped by a deep, soothing, mindless darkness.

***

It felt as though no time had passed when I slowly regained partial consciousness. Even though any attempt at movement resulted in agony, I was able to partly open my eye. Trexelan was there with me. I took a breath in preparation to speak, but I could only inhale a fraction of the normal quantity of air.

"Don't try to talk, Kelvoo," Trexelan said soothingly. "You and your friends are in a very weak state right now. Just listen while I let you know what's happening. We are aboard the Terran transport vessel, *Arcturus*. We rerouted the *Natami* to stop by a communications relay station on our way to Kuw'baal. We used the station to send word of our situation to the humans on Kuw'baal. We asked them to transport an incubation vat of algel to a rendezvous location close to their nearest jump point. Three days after that, we arrived at a safe jump point. We jumped to the vicinity of Kuw'baal and met the *Arcturus* there.

"Not only did the *Arcturus* bring you algel, their vessel had plenty of space for your group. We started warming you slowly and then we transferred you to the *Arcturus* before you regained consciousness. I have been assigned to accompany you to Kuw'baal and to assist however I can as you become reacquainted with your home world. The *Arcturus* also brought a human doctor who has been studying kloormari physiology on Kuw'baal. I'd like you to meet Dr. Tricia Sanchez."

My eyelid was open enough that I could see through a tiny slit as Dr. Sanchez leaned into my field of view. "Kelvoo, it's so good to meet you and to know that you and your friends have survived. If it's alright with you, I'm going to try putting a small spoonful of algel into your food pouch."

Parts of my body lacked feeling. I couldn't figure out how to open my pouch, but Dr. Sanchez pulled it open a tiny bit. I *could* feel the wonderful texture of the algel inside of me. I experienced a sudden burst of energy, and my breathing involuntarily became extremely rapid. "Okay, that might have been a bit too much," Dr. Sanchez said. "Just try to calm yourself and get some more rest. In three days' time, you and your friends will be back home. Just close your eye and let yourself drift off again."

Exhausted, I lapsed back into oblivion almost instantly.

The next day, I woke twice. Each time, I took another dose of algel, which made me feel stronger but without the energy overload that I had experienced the previous day. When I tried to move, the physical pain was still severe but not as bad as it had been.

When I would drift off, it wasn't back to the blackness. It was more like a limited state of meditation. In my subconscious mind, I started recalling some of the bad memories. I learned to control my negative thoughts by using my imagination just a tiny bit. I simply imagined there was a little void deep within my abdomen. I imagined taking the terrifying thoughts and compressing the feelings associated with them down into the void. I found that the bad feelings would stay there if I concentrated on pleasant thoughts.

I managed to recall many good memories. They all involved the sights, sounds, and smells of my home planet. These were things that I had never given any thought to from the moment of my birth until Captain Smith/Skully/Myron Pringle had taken me away.

I thought about the collection of homes on the sides and top of the hill, all of the simple little huts built from ksada with roofs made from the leaves of the k'k'mos plant. My lovely village.

I thought about the stream that flowed past my village, lined with life-sustaining algel growing wild. I thought about the falls that flowed just a short walk from one end of the village and the soothing sound of algel plopping to the rocks below. I concentrated on my memories of meditating by the falls and the deep relaxation that would ensue.

I thought about the mineral plain just across the stream, with the crystalized residue that formed when it was dry. I thought about the heavy, restorative rainfall and the drama of the lightning and thunder that sometimes accompanied it. I thought about the plain after it rained, when I could wade through the warm, shallow water and see my rippled reflection below.

I also thought about the lake in the alpine valley that Sam Buchanan and I had hiked to. That memory was more difficult for me because it involved Sam, the human who'd had to endure an inquiry because of an unfortunate incident on the *Orion Provider*. Sam, who told me the sad tale of the loss of his mother and his struggle with grief. Sam, who provided the inspiration for the name of a baby kloormar who died tragically.

I found that I was able to think about the lake by remembering brief, still images and excluding Sam from the memories. Sam ended up stuffed into the void in my belly. When I had first seen the lake and the vibrant colors surrounding it, I had thought nothing of it. Now I realized how stunningly beautiful it really was.

Overall, Kuw'baal was an unremarkable planet compared with the diversity of life and the sweeping vistas of a planet like Saraya, but Kuw'baal was my *home*. Kuw'baal was the place of my birth, the place of my simple past life of writing and studying, and the place where I would die and return nutrients to the soil. For me, that's what made Kuw'baal the most incredible, beautiful place in the entire universe.

On the final day of the trip, I was able to stay awake for up to an hour at a time, and I had about 20 percent of my normal mobility. I could open my eye fully, and I could speak clearly. My kloormari companions were in the room with me, and I could converse with the two or three kloormari who would usually be awake at the same time that I was. We were positioned in a line facing a row of large rectangular windows. While awake, I enjoyed staring through the windows at the stars.

Later that day, Dr. Sanchez decided we were well enough for her to remove the tubular frames that had been supporting us. We couldn't stand yet, but we stayed in place with our knees locked in their original position.

The *Arcturus's* captain, Sadie Dixon, paid us a visit. She was very relaxed and affable. I had noticed a row of vid panels above the windows. I asked whether the *Arcturus* had external vid cameras.

"Several," she replied.

"Could you please send the vid feed to these monitors when we descend to Kuw'baal?" I asked.

"I'll make sure it happens," Captain Dixon said. "I'm not sure how much you'll be able to see since we're on track to land at your village shortly after nightfall, but we'll give it a try and hope for the best."

After Captain Dixon left, I asked Trexelan to wake me just before re-entry. She assured me that she would. Then I fell back into a deep relaxing state of meditation.

I felt my shoulder being jostled. I opened my eye.

"We're on our final orbit around Kuw'baal," Trexelan said. "Captain Dixon has announced that she will be rotating the *Arcturus* so that you can see your planet through the windows."

As the ship gently rolled, the curve of Kuw'baal's horizon came into view. I saw the perfect curve of a perfect sphere of pure white gently coming into view, contrasting with the blackness of outer space. A tingling sensation, accompanied by a wave of warmth, flooded my body. *This must be what humans call "joy."*

As we rounded the planet, I saw the edge of night and day and the orange glow that Ryla cast on the upper atmosphere. As we passed the boundary of day and started crossing into the night, the *Arcturus* rolled its belly toward the planet, slowed down, and began its graceful fall toward home. The monitor panels switched on, but at that point, there was nothing to see but darkness.

After a few minutes, my fellow kloormari and I could discern four disks of light that flickered over a surface. Seconds later, we realized we were seeing the vessel's landing floodlights illuminating the top of the cloud layer.

We felt a slight jolt as the belly of the *Arcturus* plunged into the dense clouds. The floodlights cast shafts of light through the clouds. I watched with intense concentration, looking for the three sets of mast-mounted lights that the *Pacifica Spirit* had left for the village. A couple of times, I thought I could see lights down below, but I realized I had been mistaken. I wondered whether my newfound imagination was playing tricks on me.

Suddenly, the whiteness outside was gone, and I saw lights piercing the blackness below. I didn't see three sets of lights as I had expected. Instead, I saw a hundred or more lights in a roughly oval area. There was another area, separate from the first, that had at least as many lights. A black void separated the two illuminated areas.

I reasoned that changes must have taken place in our absence. I knew that humans had been back to Kuw'baal, and some humans were living there now. Perhaps the humans had brought more lights for us.

The *Arcturus* fired its landing engines and slowed sharply. The floodlights illuminated a circular landing pad directly below us. I saw pilings surrounding the edge of the landing pad. The ship's lights spilled over the pad, illuminating some of the ground around it. I saw the telltale reflection of white crystals, and I realized the new pad had been built above the mineral plain.

As the *Arcturus* completed its descent, the view from below was obscured by flame, smoke, and dust. The side-view vid feeds revealed many lights on either side of the vessel.

When I felt the landing struts touch the pad and heard the engines shutting down, I was again flooded with the utmost joy.

My mind and body were exhausted. With great contentment, I let my eyelid close and happily descended into what was perhaps the deepest meditative state that I had ever experienced.

My mind was filled with a single, wonderful word: *Home*.

# PART 3: REALIZATION

# FORTY-THREE: CHANGES

My companions and I remained in an unconscious state for the rest of the night and through all of daylight the following day.

I woke well after dark on the second night, feeling greatly restored both physically and mentally. I was inside a structure that wasn't like anything I had seen in the village before. Initially, this made me wonder whether I was in my village at all. I was in a large room with white metal walls and a hard, polished floor. To either side of me were the other members of Sam's Team, still unconscious. The ceiling sloped higher behind me and lower in front, indicating that the building was long and narrow, with a sloped roof. Carts loaded with equipment lined the wall in front of me.

I was unsteady, but I slowly reached a standing position and walked a few steps. A kloormar I didn't recognize came into the room and strode straight toward me.

"Are you alright?" the kloormar asked, extending upper limbs and claspers to catch me if necessary. "We do not want you to fall."

"I am feeling quite well—far better than I thought I would this soon," I said. "I don't recognize you. Who are you?"

"I am a resident intern, Dr. Krenan. You do not recognize me because my home village is 237.4 kilometers away. I am here studying to become a primary care physician, specializing in kloormari physiology, as you might expect. I am under the supervision of attending physician Dr. Tricia Sanchez."

"Where is Dr. Sanchez? Also, do you know where I might find Sub-commander Trexelan?"

"Both have retired for the night and will be joining us in the morning. If there is an emergency, I can summon Dr. Sanchez. She advised me that some of you might regain consciousness tonight. Dr. Sanchez suggested that, if you were mobile, you might want to position yourself in front of the windows, so you can see your surroundings as the new day arrives, and the sky brightens."

I slowly made my way around a corner and down a short ramp to the "front" of the building where the ceiling was highest. Dr. Krenan followed closely behind, despite my assurances that I was not going to fall. The entire front wall, from floor to ceiling, consisted of windows, forming an observation gallery. Curved sofas and low tables were positioned at either end of the gallery, clearly for human use.

I placed myself in front of the windows. The lighting in the room was dim, providing a clear view out into the night. Outside the building, lights illuminated the ground just beyond the windows. The ground sloped down, and I could tell that the building had been constructed on the slope from the village that extended down to the stream and the plain. I couldn't see most of the stream because other metal buildings below were partly blocking the view, but when I looked far to the left, I could see distant lights reflecting off the stream's rippling water.

Directly ahead, I saw the new landing pad, fringed by a circle of lights. A great many lights shone from the hills in the distance on the far side of the mineral plain. I wondered about the purpose of lights in such a wilderness area.

A curving and illuminated path with pilings on either side snaked over the dark plain from the village to the landing pad. A much longer path led away from the pad to the area of lights in the distant hills. When I looked toward the sky, I saw a slight glow directly above as the village lights illuminated the bottom of the cloud layer. I saw a similar glow in the sky over the hills.

A little more than thirty minutes after I started staring through the window, Dr. Krenan accompanied K'aablart, who had awakened and was eager to join me. I described my interpretation of the scene outside, and K'aablart concurred. One by one, over the next two hours, each member of Sam's Team joined me to stare. We were satisfied to wait and watch the coming light reveal our home to us, and I felt very tranquil and content.

As the early morning sky started to lighten, we saw more metal-sided buildings on either side. We also saw the outline of a large object in the exact place where the *Pacifica Spirit* had landed. In the gathering light, the outline revealed it to *be* the *Pacifica Spirit*, or at least a vessel with exactly the same appearance.

The mineral flats grew brighter and were every bit as lovely as I remembered.

There was something strange beyond the plain, something that looked like little boxes on the hillsides. White ones, green ones, and red, yellow, and blue ones. Kroz used an Infotab in image-capture mode to zoom in on the hills and magnify the view. "Those are more metal buildings!" Kroz exclaimed. "I can see forty-eight of them, but based on their positions, I would estimate that there could be many more on the back sides of the hills. It's as if there's another village on the other side of the plain!"

The next thing we saw were cars and a bus hovering over the plain, moving between our village and the hills.

Just as we were trying to decide whether to feel wonderment or confusion, Dr. Sanchez and Sub-commander Trexelan entered the gallery.

"How wonderful to see all of you up and about!" Trexelan said.

"I've brought a special guest for you!" Dr. Sanchez announced. A moment later, our long-lost friend K'tatmal strode in!

"It is so pleasant to see all of you again!" K'tatmal exclaimed.

I was more overwhelmed with joy than I had thought I would be. The only words I could get out were, "So wonderful to see you, my friend!"

"I cannot tell you how relieved I am to see all of you alive and functioning," K'tatmal said. "After my experiences with all of you, I thought I would never see any of you again! Sub-commander Trexelan has been telling me about your awful ordeal. She also told me of your loss. I know that your time on *Jezebel's Fury* has changed all of you. I also experienced emotional changes even though I was with you only briefly. I realize how terribly you must have been affected by Baby Sam's murder, and I want you to know that you have my deepest sympathies."

At that moment, as much as I had appreciated K'tatmal's sentiments, I wished that our loss had not been brought up again. To tamp my sadness back down, I changed the subject.

"So, K'tatmal, there seem to have been a lot of changes around here. When we look outside, so much is different!"

"Oh yes," K'tatmal replied. "Our human friends have taken a great deal of interest in our planet. Construction of new facilities has been happening very rapidly, including the medical research center that we're in now."

"What about the changes on the hills in the distance? Are those buildings over there?"

"Yes indeed. That's a new town with permanent buildings where the human residents live."

"Human residents? Humans have permanently relocated to Kuw'baal? And is that the *Pacifica Spirit* over there?"

"It certainly is. Well, sort of. The *Pacifica* was decommissioned some time ago. It has been placed in its original position as a memorial to the humans' discovery of Kuw'baal. It is being converted into a museum to tell our story of first contact."

"And you, K'tatmal? You're working as an attorney?"

"That's right. First, I acquired an undergraduate degree in political science before studying interplanetary and Planetary Alliance law. I wrote the bar exam, and now I'm representing kloormari individuals and our species in general."

"I'm amazed, and quite honestly, very confused," I said. "I simply cannot figure out how you accomplished so much and especially how much has changed on Kuw'baal. How can this be possible after only six months?"

Trexelan and Dr. Sanchez exchanged surprised looks.

"Six months?" K'tatmal said. "Did nobody tell you? Kelvoo . . . all of you . . . the day we left with the human who called himself Captain Roger Smith . . . that was almost seven *years* ago!"

# FORTY-FOUR: BACK IN THE VILLAGE

I was astonished, but almost immediately, all eight of us figured out what had happened.

*Nine nine eight. Nine hundred and ninety-eight.* That was a number that finally made sense—the number that the captain of the *Jezebel's Fury* gave as the ship's target velocity on long trips between jumps.

I believed the captain when he had said that the *Jezebel's Fury* was the "fastest ship in the scrapyard." The pulling and pushing forces that we felt as the *Jezebel's Fury* tried to compensate for intense acceleration told me that we were traveling extremely fast, but I had no idea that we were tearing through space at .998 times the speed of light!

I recalled the formula for calculating time dilation.

$\Delta t' = \gamma \Delta t = \Delta t / \sqrt{(1 - v^2/c^2)}$

When I took six months of perceived time and the velocity of light multiplied by .998 and then applied them to the formula, I came up with more than seven years and ten months that would have passed on Kuw'baal. Of course, we hadn't been traveling at that high a speed for the entire trip. When I used five months of high-speed travel, I got six years and seven months, which was almost the amount of time that we had been missing. Perhaps our true speed relative to Kuw'baal was slightly faster, or maybe we had been moving at .998 for a little longer than five months. Regardless, for all intents and purposes, the math worked!

In addition to explaining the amount of change on Kuw'baal, the time-dilation effect also explained why we had made our second trip to Friendship Colony long before we thought they would require more Vinamibefentyn.

I recalled seeing the vid feed from the bridge, and I had wondered why the windows were obscured by metal plating. Now I realized that, as the vessel's speed increased, only the stars straight ahead would be visible, and a viewer would see the color of the stars shift from white to blue and then violet as the Doppler effect would shorten the wavelengths of the light. After that, the light would become ultraviolet and then shift to wavelengths of deadly radiation. That's why shielding had been necessary.

As the eight of us discussed our realization, Trexelan apologized for not having told us that time dilation may have applied to our voyage. She had assumed that we would have known. We didn't blame her at all since her assumption had been reasonable.

We spent the rest of the day resting, stretching, and chatting with Dr. Sanchez and K'tatmal, who brought us up to date on the "what and when" of the changes that had swept across Kuw'baal. We also spent time on our Infotabs to review nearly seven years' worth of recent history. There were now several InfoServers within range that we could connect to at will.

I wanted to learn more about Outlier colonists and criminal organizations, and more specifically, the Brotherhood and the *Jezebel's Fury*. I found a trove of relevant information. Many of the fact lists and articles had been written well before our first contact with humans. I thought it was odd that I had seen no such information before our departure.

When darkness fell, K'tatmal joined us to spend the night meditating in the medical facility. Dr. Sanchez cleared us to leave the building the next morning to reacquaint ourselves with our village. My meditation was productive and restorative.

The next morning, K'tatmal led us out through the main doors and into the village. I took a deep breath of my home planet's air. Overall, it was soothingly familiar, but the air bore some vague scents that seemed new to me.

A group of fifteen humans were waiting as we approached. On each side of the group, two humans wore uniforms with "Security" emblazoned across the chest and the back. The remaining humans were carrying vid cameras and other recording equipment, which they pointed in our direction. A small bus was hovering behind the humans.

As we approached the group of humans, they began shouting questions.

"Are you the kloormari who were abducted by the Outliers?"

"How does it feel to return to your planet?"

"What changes have you noticed since you returned?"

"What crimes did you help the Outliers to commit?"

"Which one of you is Kelvoo? Do you regret leaking information on the *Orion Provider*?"

K'tatmal advanced to a point between Sam's Team and the press. K'tatmal's arms extended as if to symbolically ward off the group. "Yes, I can confirm that these kloormari were my companions when we were illegally taken by the captain and crew of the Outlier vessel, *Jezebel's Fury*. My companions and I will not be answering any questions at this time."

K'tatmal's statement did not deter the reporters, who continued shouting questions. Finally, K'tatmal interrupted them. "All of you know the arrangements that allowed you to be here. The agreement was to let you capture still and vid images without questions or statements. You have had your 'photo op,' and now I am politely asking you to leave."

The security people ushered the press onto the small bus, which headed back toward the human's town.

K'tatmal turned to us. "This is where I must leave you for the day, as I have a great deal of work to attend to. I recommend that you walk through the village to become acquainted with the many changes. The villagers know to give you space, but they will be pleased to converse with you if you initiate communication. You may return to the medical building at any time or you may stay elsewhere."

I realized that humans might have found K'tatmal's statement to be officious and impersonal, especially in light of our shared experiences. I, however, appreciated K'tatmal's words. I liked how they reminded me of the way that I used to communicate before my emotions and manner of speech had been influenced by my experiences with humans.

I told my companions that I wanted to wander at my own pace, so I walked off by myself. I recognized many kloormari from the "pre-Jezebel" days. When I would greet one of them, they would respond in kind and sometimes add that they were pleased that I had returned or that they were glad that I had survived my ordeal. There were also many kloormari that I didn't recognize. I surmised that they had relocated to my village like Dr. Krenan had done, or perhaps they were visiting. No doubt, inter-village transportation would be available now, perhaps to all corners of Kuw'baal.

Only the overall layout of the village was familiar. The paths were much wider, and I saw none of the original huts made from ksada. The personal huts were built with the same type of corrugated metal as the medical facility. Each hut had glass windows and closable doors. Some buildings appeared to be personal homes that were larger than the single-room huts. The buildings were of various colors, and each building used similar components. I thought that perhaps each structure must be made from pre-fabricated parts that could be assembled in different configurations.

As I walked, I spotted the village elder, Kahini, and we exchanged greetings.

"Kahini, as I'm sure you can understand, I am unfamiliar with the village since so much has changed during my absence. Would you mind joining me as I walk? I have many questions."

"I would be pleased to," Kahini replied.

"How are the other elders, K'losk'oon and Kwazka?"

"K'losk'oon died six hundred and thirty-two days ago. Kwazka remains alive."

"I hope that K'losk'oon's death did not result in a severe loss of knowledge for the village."

"No, there was no perceptible impact. Now the humans and the InfoServers provide all of the useful knowledge that we need."

I didn't like what Kahini had just said, but I needed to learn more before expressing further thoughts on the matter. I told Kahini that I wanted to see the dwelling that I had left behind, or at least whatever was in that location now.

As I had expected, my dwelling had been replaced with a different building. In fact, eleven other dwellings that once were close to mine had all been replaced by a single larger building. Big windows lined the side of the building facing the path. Objects were displayed on the other side of the windows. Glass double doors opened and closed automatically as various kloormari entered and exited. A big sign stretched across the façade of the building, spelling out "Kloor-Mart."

"What does 'Kloor-Mart' mean?" I asked.

"That is where we purchase things," Kahini said. "Building supplies, cleaning products, hoverlifts, decorative items, Infotabs, items for children . . . almost anything we may need or want."

We continued to the edge of the village. A low, sprawling building had been constructed with lots of open space around it. A buzzer sounded from the building. Less than a minute later, over 200 kloormari children swarmed out.

"What am I looking at?" I asked.

"A large number of kloormari children," Kahini replied unhelpfully.

"Please explain."

"The building is a school that kloormari children attend from the ages of three through thirty years. The humans built the school for the village, and the children are learning the skills that we kloormari will need in order to integrate into, and benefit from, the human presence."

"How can there be so many children? When Sam's Team left, there were nine children in that age group. I realize the village includes many kloormari newcomers, but it couldn't have grown twenty-fold!"

"Ah, yes," Kahini said. "Our rate of reproduction has greatly increased. We no longer reproduce based on the needs of the village or the availability of resources. Thanks to the humans, we have unlimited resources. What we need now are more kloormari so that Kuw'baal can be developed for the greater good of all! I have personally provided my genetic material to fifty-two of those children," Kahini added with a hint of what seemed like human pride.

Some of the children strayed close to where Kahini and I were standing. One child was holding a small replica of a spacecraft and was running with it and making sounds like those from a rocket engine as if simulating flight. Other children clutched miniature models of humans or small kloormari. *Are those toys?* I wondered incredulously.

I also realized the children were speaking to one another in Terran.

"Why are these children speaking Terran?" I asked.

"That is an interesting question, Kelvoo. In fact, I was thinking of asking you why we are speaking Kloormari. You must be extremely proficient in Terran by now. Terran is the new language in the village. Some kloormari are still transitioning and speak a hybrid of both languages, but all of the younger kloormari use Terran, and most of the time, so do I."

"But Kahini," I objected, "we are kloormari. We are defined by our language. Terran is such a limited, monophonic language. In kloormari, we can convey complicated ideas in a fraction of the time. The structure of our language develops our neural pathways in ways that are unique to us. Surely, if we lose our language, we are destined to lose our identity!"

"It is true, Kelvoo, that kloormari is a far more sophisticated language, but Terran is so much easier to learn, to speak, and to write. From a practical point of view, Terran is more useful. It is also a standard language of the Planetary Alliance worlds. We have had visitors from various planets, and Terran has allowed us to have all sorts of very interesting dialogs. I understand what a shock it must be for you to return home and find that so much has changed. You must understand that things are better now. The humans have expanded our universe and our minds. They are also promising wonderful things once we have elevated ourselves to their level!"

Kahini's last sentence hit me hard. I wanted to reply angrily, but to avoid alienating Kahini, I said, "Kahini, I have been unfortunate enough to witness and experience the worst of humanity. We do not need to 'elevate' ourselves to their level. We are superior in our ability to learn. Our memories are superior, and our respect and consideration for one another is something that every human should strive toward."

"I respect your opinion, Kelvoo. One of the most important things that I have learned from humans is that opinions are diverse, but we can make allowance for those with different viewpoints. I will consider what you have said."

"Thank you, Kahini. Please be especially cautious when humans make promises. What happened to us on *Jezebel's Fury* is a perfect example of what can go wrong when you take the word of a deceptive human. I have a lot of information to process. I would very much like to go to the falls for a brief meditation. Would you care to join me?"

We walked down a path to the falls. I saw right away that something else had changed. The water, which used to be clear, was now muddy with sediment. What used to be the algel falls were now simply waterfalls, with only the rush of water and no plopping of algel to be heard. Even more serious was the complete lack of algel on the banks as far as I could see both upstream and down. I asked about the stream and the algel situation.

"I first noticed a decline in the volume of algel three hundred and ninety-four days ago," Kahini said, "shortly after construction began on a new, full-service spaceport twenty-six kilometers upstream. Hills had to be leveled and valleys filled in. As a result, various minerals and silt leached into the stream. It didn't really matter though because we had stopped picking algel by the stream long before that."

"Where do you obtain algel now?"

"We purchase it. Follow me."

Kahini led me to the top of the falls and pointed to a group of large cylindrical structures at the end of the village. "That's where our algel is grown now. We can buy it right from the farm or from a store like Kloor-Mart."

"But why should you have to pay for something that was once growing wild? It's like paying to breathe the air!"

"Ah! I think you misunderstand," Kahini replied. "It isn't as if we are truly *paying* for our algel since the humans are actually paying us. Every fifteen days each kloormari receives a SimCash payment. The humans call it 'indigenous support' or 'IS.' It is to compensate us for the use of our planet and its resources. So, yes, we may have to buy our algel from human-owned corporations, but we receive regular payments that let us live in better homes and acquire goods.

"Some kloormari, like me, choose to earn more by working, but work is completely optional now. If any kloormari want to watch vids all day, they can do so, and indeed, some do exactly that. The kloormari who choose not to work live in the smallest dwellings and can only afford the bare necessities of life."

I didn't want to believe what Kahini was saying. It wasn't just the village, its buildings, and the surrounding environment that had changed. The entire mindset and identity of my species had been transformed! I felt completely lost.

"By the way," Kahini said, "you had said that you wanted to meditate. Shall we do so?"

"I'm sorry, Kahini. I just don't think I can do it right now."

"Would you like to come to my home, Kelvoo? You may find it more relaxing there."

I welcomed Kahini's invitation.

Kahini's dwelling was spacious. It was constructed on top of pilings. Like the medical facility, one side of the building consisted of windows, providing a view across the village and over the plain, toward the humans' settlement.

There was no furniture to speak of since kloormari don't use chairs or beds, but there was a single table that housed an ornate algel dispenser with built-in refrigeration. The home's lighting was not simply practical; it was stylized. One of the walls had shelves that bore ornamental objects. One of the objects was a replica of the *Pacifica Spirit*, approximately 1.2 meters in length. The replica was extremely detailed and accurate. I could tell that it had been assembled by hand in what must have been a rather painstaking process.

I asked Kahini about the objects and said I was surprised to see artistic items in a kloormar's home. Kahini told me of four years spent serving as an emissary to the Planetary Alliance. Kahini had been to many events for dignitaries and had received many gifts, which were now on the shelves. I asked where the model of the *Pacifica* came from. Kahini had purchased it from a human artisan.

"I like to look closely at it sometimes," Kahini said. "It reminds me of the early days."

"But we are kloormari," I said. "We remember everything."

"True," Kahini agreed, "but having an object like that replica adds a certain richness to the memory."

*Strange*, I thought, *but I do understand Kahini's sentiment. Perhaps Sam's Team are not the only kloormari that have been emotionally influenced by humans.*

Kahini and I talked well into the evening. After I felt more relaxed, my mind turned toward the painful memories of Baby Sam. I related a few parts of the story, and then I asked Kahini where I could find some parchment, ink, and an ink tray.

"I haven't seen anything like that in over three years!" Kahini exclaimed.

"I don't understand," I said. "How do you write?"

"Digitally, on an Infotab—in Terran, of course."

"Alright, what about the old texts? Where can I find those?"

"On any InfoServer on Kuw'baal," Kahini said. "They have all been scanned and digitized."

"But . . . where are the original parchments?" I asked in near disbelief.

"Most were ground up. Some of the human dwellings have collections of plants around them. These are called 'gardens.' Many of the ground-up documents were mixed with decaying plant matter to make 'compost,' which is used to make human gardens grow better."

"Kahini . . . that's terrible!"

"Oh, it's not so bad," Kahini replied. "The scientists who examined the documents saved some of the original parchments that they thought had the most historical significance. I was one of hundreds of kloormari who assisted in the selection process. Those documents are kept in very secure places where they will be preserved."

"What kind of places?"

"You know, museums. All kinds of museums in several locations on Terra."

My mind started swirling with thoughts. *Is nothing sacred? And why am I thinking using human notions like "sacred"? How can we have any history or*

313

*meaning or purpose with our historical records removed from our home planet?*

I was devastated. Sensing my distress, Kahini tried to segue to a different subject. "Speaking of museums, did you notice the *Pacifica Spirit* at its original landing site? It is being developed into a museum! It is a very interesting project. Visitors will be able to view holographic recreations of events based on the original onboard vids.

"For instance, I'm told that visitors will be able to see the event where each of you piloted the *Pacifica* through the drone course. Then the visitors can choose a kloormar, like you for instance. They can sit at a console and play your role in a simulation. If they select you, they will get a score that they can compare with the 'Kelvoo Score'!"

"What?" I blurted, incredulous.

"Yes, very interesting, isn't it? It makes me wonder, since you have turned out to be alive, perhaps you could request a licensing fee for use of your likeness and experiences. You should ask K'tatmal about the legal aspects. You could also work at the Pacifica Museum and interact with visitors!"

I knew I was going to do no such thing. I also knew I wanted to end the conversation.

"Well, Kahini," I said, "it is late, and I am sure you can appreciate that I have had many experiences today that are very strange to me. I hope you don't mind if I excuse myself to meditate."

"Of course, Kelvoo. Please feel free to stay in my home tonight if you wish. I have found our conversations to be quite fascinating, and I have appreciated your unique perspectives."

I was feeling too tired to go anywhere else, so Kahini and I each took some algel from the dispenser, assumed a relaxed position, and meditated.

My meditation was fitful and often disturbing. I kept recalling the worst of my experiences with the humans despite my efforts to keep them suppressed. These thoughts blended with the changes that I had seen and Kahini had described. I couldn't predict where the changes would lead my species, and I feared for the future of the kloormari.

I realized I was never going to truly feel that I had returned home. I was a strange being on a strange planet.

# FORTY-FIVE: HOMELANDS

I woke from my meditation early the next morning, served myself a breakfast of Kahini's algel, and wandered around the village as soon as it was light enough to see.

I saw K'tatmal walking briskly and asked whether we could talk for a while.

"I have to go to court in the humans' town," K'tatmal said, "but if you would like to accompany me, we can chat along the way."

K'tatmal opened a large metal door in a rectangular building. Vehicles were parked inside with "Kuw'baal Legal Services" printed across their sides. One of the vehicles had padded seats, suitable for humans, while the others had kneeling pads and metal frames better suited to kloormari anatomy. K'tatmal and I entered one of the kloormari vehicles.

"Destination, Newton courthouse," K'tatmal said. "Low speed." The vehicle responded accordingly.

"What is Newton?" I asked.

"It's the informal name for the humans' town. On official maps, it's just called 'AA-01,' until the bureaucrats can come up with a label. They can't seem to agree on anything, so the residents started calling the place 'New Town,' which got shortened to 'Newton.'"

The vehicle hovered and moved out of the garage, then rose above the village and proceeded slowly across the stream and the plain. "I'm running a bit early today," K'tatmal said, "so we can talk while this car takes its time."

Along the way, I unloaded my concerns onto K'tatmal. I bemoaned the kloormari's acceptance of human values, the environmental damage, the handout of payments, and the destruction of our treasured documents.

"Kelvoo, you and I have had the benefit, if you can call it that, of experiencing the worst of humanity," K'tatmal said. "It has given us insight into what can, and sooner or later, probably will go wrong. I returned to Kuw'baal well before the rest of you, so things hadn't changed as dramatically for me as they have for you. Our fellow kloormari were very interested in my story and my cautionary tales since more humans were arriving all the time.

"Unfortunately, our fellow kloormari also saw the humans as superior beings who had unlimited knowledge to share. As we gained more knowledge, we started wanting to acquire many of the material possessions that humans enjoyed. My story and my warnings gradually became less important to the other kloormari.

"Most of the humans were well intentioned. They said all of the right things about wanting us to preserve our culture, but many of our own species were more interested in being like the humans. I kept trying to warn the kloormari, but in the end, it was as though I was talking to thin air. As you know, when I was part of Sam's Team, I was interested in law."

"As far as Sam's Team is concerned, you are and always will be a core part of us," I replied.

"Thank you, Kelvoo, I appreciate that. As I was saying, I decided to study law. I thought that, if I couldn't convince our species to be wary of humans, at least I could try to represent our interests within the confines of human and Alliance law."

By this time, the car was approaching Newton. The human dwellings were enormous. Around some of the homes were assortments of plants that Kahini had called "gardens." Most gardens were largely carpeted by a flat layer of green vegetation. K'tatmal said the plant was called "grass." I had known that from my previous studies after first contact, but it was interesting to see it in real life. K'tatmal said that grass was becoming a potential problem, since it was starting to spread beyond Newton, and nobody had studied its effect on Kuw'baal's ecosystem.

The car landed next to the Newton courthouse where a kloormari child was waiting to see K'tatmal. I had met K'tolin in passing perhaps ten years before that, and I estimated that the child would be about thirty years old now. As we exchanged greetings, a human male and female were walking toward the building, and an older human male arrived in a personal vehicle.

"Good morning, Mr. K'tatmal, so we have two defendants this morning?" the older man asked.

"No, your honor," K'tatmal replied. "Only young K'tolin here. This other kloormar is Kelvoo, a personal friend of mine." K'tatmal turned to me. "Kelvoo, meet Judge Singh."

The judge's face lit up, "Kelvoo! Of course! You're one of the eight kloormari who were abducted by the gangsters from the Brotherhood! What a terrible ordeal that must have been."

"Yes, your honor, it was very difficult."

"I suppose a few changes must have happened around here during your absence."

"No, your honor. From my perspective, *everything* has changed. 'Here' used to be wilderness. Our lives have changed, our village has changed, our customs have changed, our environment has changed, our language is changing, and our very identity is barely recognizable to me."

"I would like to hear more about that, Kelvoo. Perhaps we should meet sometime and have a nice chat."

I doubted that Judge Singh really wanted to hear more from me, but I assured him that I would consider his suggestion.

Judge Singh escorted us into the single-room courthouse. K'tatmal asked me to watch from the "gallery" and then showed K'tolin where to stand. The judge took a robe from a hook on the wall beside his "bench" and put it on over his clothing. The human couple walked in. Judge Singh consulted his Infotab and addressed the couple. "You must be Mr. and Mrs. Peterson. Please take your place at the plaintiff's podium."

Judge Singh started the proceedings for Peterson vs. K'tolin. The case lacked the suspense of the courtroom drama vids that I had watched during my education, but it was still interesting. The Petersons were suing K'tolin for damage caused to their car when K'tolin was walking on a hill behind their home and accidentally dislodged a rock. The rock rolled downhill, bounced, and gouged the finish on the Petersons' vehicle. The Petersons claimed that K'tolin was trespassing and should be required to pay 400,000 SimCash units for the damage to their property.

K'tatmal argued that trespassing should not be considered in the decision since K'tolin was not familiar with the concept of privately owned land (I wasn't either). "My client would never trespass *inside* a dwelling because kloormari culture would never tolerate it. The idea of staying off a piece of land, however, is unfamiliar to most kloormari," K'tatmal said. "Furthermore, your honor, the Petersons' property is not clearly delineated, so K'tolin could not have known anyway."

"I'm not particularly interested in the trespassing aspect," Judge Singh said. "Let's just take a look at the alleged actions and the damage."

The story was that K'tolin had been curious about Newton and had taken a public bus across to the town to look around. While climbing a hill to get a better view, K'tolin had accidentally dislodged a loose rock, damaging the vehicle. Judge Singh asked K'tolin why the Petersons shouldn't be compensated.

"It was just an accident," K'tolin replied. "I had no intention of damaging anything. Also, your honor, the rock did not damage the car. It left a mark, but that did not affect how well the vehicle functioned, so I do not understand why there is a problem."

The judge asked Mrs. Peterson for her perspective.

"Your honor," the woman said with exasperation, "this child was in a place that he . . . or she . . . or whatever . . . shouldn't have been. I am the top-performing real-estate agent in Newton. I show executive properties to important potential clients. I can't show them around in a total wreck of a car!"

317

Mr. Peterson shifted his weight from one foot to the other as though he was feeling slightly embarrassed.

Judge Singh asked to see an image of the damage and said that 400,000 SimCash units seemed rather expensive to fix such a minor scrape. He asked the Petersons for a copy of three quotes that they would have requested prior to making the repairs. Mrs. Peterson argued that she didn't have time to get quotes. She said there was just one repair shop in town, and other shops were in villages at least an hour away. She said she only had four hours before a VIP would be arriving at the landing pad, so she had to get the work done right away and had to pay a premium for an immediate repair.

K'tatmal said that K'tolin had offered to pay 200,000 units at the time of the incident.

"Is that true, K'tolin?" Judge Singh asked. "Why two hundred thousand specifically?"

"It is true, your honor. I made the offer because I only had two hundred thousand units saved up. You see, I am a student, so I only get basic indigenous support payments. I spend almost all of that for algel and housing. I do not have time to work at a job, but I am studying spacecraft mechanics, and I hope to find work when the new spaceport is completed. When I visited Newton, it was only because school was closed due to a teachers' study retreat. I am very sorry for the damage that I accidentally caused. I have 220,000 SimCash Units saved up, and I can pay that amount."

Judge Singh turned to K'tatmal. "How would you feel about having your client pay two hundred and twenty thousand units, plus performing some landscaping or cleaning work for the Petersons, let's say for a total of twenty hours? Perhaps K'tolin can work a couple of hours at a time after school."

Before K'tatmal could answer, Mrs. Peterson interrupted. "That's ridiculous, your honor! Do you know who I am? This punk came onto my property and destroyed my car, and you're only going to make this . . . this *thing* pay half?"

Judge Singh turned to Mrs. Peterson and spoke in a calm voice. "You've just changed my mind, Mrs. Peterson. I'm lowering the amount to two hundred thousand, and for this kloormar's own protection, I'm suggesting that K'tolin stays away from you and never sees you again! If you complain one more time, I'm going to dismiss your case altogether!"

Mrs. Peterson's eyes grew wide, and her jaw tightened with anger. She turned to her husband. "Let's go. We're getting out of here." Both of the Petersons left with haste.

Judge Singh turned to K'tolin. "I want to advise you, K'tolin, that you do need to be more careful in human territory. I think you are a good kloormar, and I admire that you are studying to better yourself. I would advise that, in the future, you visit Newton only when you have official business here."

With that the case was concluded.

As we left the courthouse, K'tolin thanked K'tatmal and then wandered along the path that led downhill toward the plain.

"Have you been asked to register with Indigenous Services yet?" K'tatmal asked.

"What does that mean?" I replied.

"It's how you become legally recognized as a native inhabitant of Kuw'baal. It's what you need to do to receive basic indigenous support payments. After all, you're going to need to buy yourself some algel at some point. Registering also gets you a place in line for your own dwelling. Construction is about to start on a new subdivision just upstream from the falls, so it shouldn't be long before you can get a home.

"In fact, now that I think about it, I should represent all of the other members of Sam's Team. I can argue that, since your previous homes were demolished, you should all move to the front of the waiting list! In the meantime, Kelvoo, you're welcome to stay in my home. Anyway, you need to get registered. Trust me on that. The Indigenous Services office is just up the road, and it will only take a few minutes. Let's go."

I decided to trust K'tatmal's advice.

"Why was a kloormari child being tried in a human court by a human judge?" I asked as we walked to the IS office.

"There are two divisions of law on Kuw'baal: human law and indigenous law. Disputes or crimes committed on kloormari lands are dealt with by the kloormari, which essentially means they aren't dealt with. After all, we've never needed a justice system since we have never committed crimes. Disagreements occur over minor matters, and as before, any elder can make a decision. On the other hand, crimes and disputes that happen in human areas and on Kuw'baal at large are handled by the human justice system."

"But K'tatmal, kloormari and human values are not the same! K'tolin didn't understand that it was forbidden to be on a human's land. In fact, I don't understand the concept myself. Why is it that, in exchange for money, a being can have exclusive access to part of a planet? Beings can reproduce, but land cannot. What happens when all of the land is owned? What will be left for everyone else? Also, K'tolin and I don't understand why such offence would be taken when an object is scratched or dented or marred in some way. If the object can still be used just as effectively, who would care?"

"Well, Kelvoo," K'tatmal said, "I suppose that's why we have our territories, and the humans have theirs."

"So, just how much of Kuw'baal is human territory?"

"It's easier to tell you where *our* territories are. Those are defined by the areas that we have traditionally lived in or used. Our village is a kloormari 'homeland.' The stream that flows past the village is one of the boundaries. Our homeland extends for a few kilometers upstream, downstream, and away from the stream.

"Each of the other kloormari villages is a homeland where human laws do not apply. There are also travel corridors between villages—routes that we have taken when walking from one village to another. The travel corridors belong to us, but humans may use them. They just can't settle there."

"So, where exactly are the human lands?" I asked.

"Everywhere that isn't a kloormari homeland falls under human jurisdiction."

"How much of the planet is that?"

K'tatmal's answer was wrenching: 99.1 percent of Kuw'baal was now under human jurisdiction.

"K'tatmal, that's appalling! How did our species allow this to happen?"

"You are absolutely right," K'tatmal replied. "The situation is beyond appalling. As I said earlier, I tried to warn the other villagers about the dangers, but there was little interest. The assumption was that humans have similar values to our own and would not take advantage of us. I don't think that, as individuals, the humans have tried to take advantage, but we are inexorably losing control of our world because of the political, economic, and social systems that the humans have introduced.

"As I said, my interest in law began when we were students of Samuel Buchanan. Shortly after my rescue and return, I decided to formalize my studies in order to understand human society better and with the hope of changing their system from within.

"Because of my brief time on *Jezebel's Fury*, I saw how dark human behavior can be. I also saw tremendous compassion and kindness on the part of the rebels of Benzolar 3 who rescued me, so I know there is hope for humanity."

"Are you saying I am misjudging humans because I was subjected to their evil for longer?" I asked.

"Not at all, Kelvoo. Yours is a story that every kloormar needs to hear. For nearly seven years now, the rights of the kloormari on Kuw'baal have slowly been chipped away, and we have grown complacent."

By then we had arrived outside the Indigenous Services office in Newton. "Shall we go in?" K'tatmal asked.

"I don't think so, K'tatmal. I'm not sure I want to be part of the fabric of the human system."

"I understand, Kelvoo. There may come a time soon when you will have no choice but to register and take the funding that is available. If you need more time, you have my support."

We turned and walked back to the car. After a long silence, K'tatmal spoke. "The return of Sam's Team is a watershed event in our history. It would be wonderful if we could use this moment to generate some motivation in our species to take more interest in our rights as sentient beings."

"How do you propose we do that?" I asked.

"I do not know," K'tatmal replied, "but I hope we will think of something."

After the car took us back to the village, K'tatmal entered a building. "My office is inside, and I have to get back to work," he said. "Please do come to my home this evening and stay for as long as you need." After K'tatmal gave me directions to the dwelling, I decided to walk through the village some more.

I made my way down to the path along the bank of the stream. In several places, new buildings encroached on the path, making it much narrower than before. I arrived at the spot on the path where I had been walking at twilight when I first saw the *Pacifica Spirit* descending from the dark sky. This was the place where I had run through the stream, sprinted to the *Pacifica's* landing site, and was almost burned to a crisp or bashed to death by flying rocks. *So that was the first time I was almost killed by humans,* I thought.

I didn't hold my thought for long because I heard my name being called from the medical facility up the hill. It was Trexelan. "Kelvoo, could you please come up here? I need to talk with you."

Once we were in the observation gallery, Trexelan turned to me. "Are you alright, Kelvoo? We haven't seen you for a couple of days. What have you been doing?"

"I'm alright," I said, "I've just been wandering and wondering. That's all."

"I'm glad to hear that, Kelvoo. I wanted to see you because I've been contacted by the Sarayan delegation to the Planetary Alliance. With the exception of the human representatives, the Alliance is very interested in everything that happened to your group during your abduction.

"You see, the Alliance has been debating the membership of Terra for some time. On one hand, the Terran humans have brought incredible creativity and resourcefulness to the Alliance. Humans can take an existing technology and produce it very efficiently. They are wonderful at coming up with new uses for technology and improving upon it. They produce wonderful works of art and things of beauty.

"On the other hand, even with the best of intentions, we see many humans who are driven by greed. They expect altruism from others, but they seem to lose perspective when they have an opportunity, as individuals, to get ahead. We have seen unthinkable behavior from Outlier humans, especially the ones that caused your group so much suffering, but we wonder how much of that is due to them having been cast out and neglected by their Terran counterparts.

"Since you and your friends returned to Kuw'baal, I have heard your friends say how devastated they have been by the changes that have occurred here in less than seven years. All along, the Planetary Alliance has been monitoring the situation on this planet, and we are disturbed by the erosion of the power and the rights that you should have as the indigenous species. The

321

Planetary Alliance is planning to hold a 'grand inquiry' to re-evaluate Terran membership, or at least the scope of Terran participation. The inquiry will need evidence and testimony from a variety of sources.

"Kelvoo, the Planetary Alliance would like to invite you to document your story for possible submission to the inquiry. Your account will need to be written in Terran since that is one of the Alliance's common languages. The Alliance would like to know every detail from your first contact with the humans, right up to the present."

Suddenly, the prospect of documenting my experiences filled me with dread. To do so I would have to recall and analyze every painful memory from the *Orion Provider*, to being lured onto the *Jezebel's Fury*, to the bullying and violence from the Outlier crew, to aiding the commission of terrible crimes, to the gruesome execution of the Outliers. But far worse than that, I would have to recall the memories that I had been working so hard to stuff down inside of me—the murder of my precious baby and my monstrous enjoyment of killing the human Bazz.

"I don't know whether I can do it," I said. "There are parts of my ordeal that I don't want to think about. Besides, why me? Why not one of the other kloormari who had the same experiences?"

"Actually, Kelvoo, I have spoken with all seven of your friends who returned to Kuw'baal with you. Every one of them said that you were best qualified to speak for the group. They told me that you were the first to be taken aboard the *Pacifica*, you had the closest relationship with Sam Buchanan, you spent the most time with the captain of *Jezebel's Fury*, you—and I'm sorry if this is painful—you hosted the baby inside your body, and you had the courage to defend the group against the crew member Bazz."

I became angry that Trexelan had brought up the most painful subjects. "I won't do it, Trexelan! I can't!"

Trexelan gently touched my shoulder. "When we started putting you into hibernation on the *Natami*, there was something you really wanted me to know. Your words were very powerful. Sarayans don't have perfect memories like the kloormari, but I remember what you said word for word: 'If we don't survive, promise me that you will tell my species our story, and especially the story of the birth, heroism, and death of our precious Baby Sam.'"

I didn't want to hear Trexelan repeating my own words back to me. I tried my best to distract myself, but she continued.

"When we returned you to this planet, and you were up and about again, I thought that the first thing you would do would be to start writing and telling your story. I know it's much harder to think about than you had expected, but I'm advising you to make the effort. I realize that strong emotions are new to you, but you can't keep suppressing your experiences and feelings. Doing so will destroy you from the inside out. Come on, Kelvoo. You can do this. If you don't, then the words you said to me on the *Natami* will mean nothing, and any lessons that could come from your story may never be learned."

Of course, Trexelan was right. My suppressed sadness and rage were already tearing me apart. It was time for me to, as a human might say, "grow a spine." At the same time, the words that K'tatmal had spoken less than an hour earlier came back to me: *"The return of Sam's Team is a watershed event in our history. It would be wonderful if we could use this moment to generate some motivation in our species to take more interest in our rights as sentient beings."*

I started to feel an emotional burden lifting. "Alright, Trexelan," I said. "I'll do it."

Trexelan thanked me, then asked me to stay in touch and to keep her updated on my progress. With that in mind, she transferred an unlock code from her Infotab to mine to allow my device to communicate with her and others on Kuw'baal via voice or data. "There you go, Kelvoo," she said. "A communications package, courtesy of the Sarayan delegation."

Now that I had a mission, there was more of a spring in my step as I returned to the path along the stream and continued walking. I started allowing myself to think about the one human whom I trusted implicitly: Samuel Buchanan. I wondered what had become of him and what he was doing now. I also wondered about Kwazka—the elder who hadn't joined us on the *Jezebel's Fury*. Just before we left with Captain Smith, Kwazka had said, "One member of Sam's Team must remain here to try to maintain and promote the practice of studying the ancient texts and creating new ones." Clearly, Kwazka had not succeeded, and I wondered about the sequence of events that had led to failure.

As I approached the downstream end of the village, I recognized K'pai. The young kloormar had been five years old when the *Pacifica Spirit* had arrived and would now be at least twelve. K'pai was using an Infotab very intently.

"Greetings, K'pai," I said.

"Hang on . . . just a tok," K'pai replied in Terran. "I'm gonna to pause this . . ." He finally looked up. "Oh, hey there, Kelvoo!"

"Would you mind speaking to me in kloormari?" I asked.

K'pai obliged and responded in kloormari. "Is this better? Sorry, Kelvoo. I was told how you were treated by the Outliers, so I suppose that's why you don't want me to you use their language."

"Thank you, K'pai. I think the main reason why I prefer to speak in our language is to try to preserve some of our culture. I notice, however, that your manner of speech has changed. You seem to have some type of accent when you speak kloormari."

"Sorry, Kelvoo, it's just that I haven't spoken kloormari in over four years. It's a complicated language to speak. My memory of our language is perfect, of course, but the muscles in my vocal outlets are out of practice, so some kloormari words are hard for me to pronounce. Terran is much easier for me."

It pained me to realize that this young kloormar was willfully abandoning a rich historical identity. "Alright, K'pai," I said in the interest of expediting a conversation, "if it's easier for you, let's speak Terran."

"Thanks, Kelvoo. That'd be koofi!"

"I notice you're using some words that I don't recognize. You said, 'Hang on a 'tok' and 'that'd be 'koofi.' Are these slang expressions?"

"Yeah, sorta. That's just the way kloom kids like me talk. I dunno where it came from. It's kinda like our own lang, ya know? It's koofi!"

I was curious about the possibility of a new subculture forming, so I thought I might find out more by trying to strike up a casual conversation.

"So, K'pai, you looked really interested in whatever was on your Infotab."

"Oh yeah, check this out," K'pai said, holding up the Infotab. "It's called 'Outlier Invasion.' It's the latest from K'Pow! Games."

K'pai un-paused the game and showed me how the screen could be touched to control a human character. "This duder's name is Commander Steele," K'pai said. The character was running through the corridors of a spaceship. The game showed glimpses of disfigured, disheveled human-shaped beings dressed in ragged, dirty clothing making grunting sounds and wielding weapons.

"What are those creatures?" I asked.

"Outlier humans, of course," K'pai replied. "Watch this."

K'pai had Commander Steele jump through a doorway and open fire on multiple Outliers. As each shot of plasma hit an Outlier, a spray of blood erupted and pooled on the floor under the fallen body. As each body fell, a score increased in the corner of the screen.

"I don't want to see any more!" I exclaimed as I put my hand up between the screen and my eye. K'pai paused the game again and put the Infotab in its holster.

"K'pai, that was very upsetting for me to see. First off, Outliers don't look like that. They look like any other human being. Yes, some of them are prone to violence and other crimes, but most of them are decent beings who just want a peaceful life. Second, the game does not accurately show the reality of killing another living being. I would know. I personally shot and killed an Outlier human with a blaster rifle."

"Duder!" K'pai exclaimed. "For real?"

"Yeah, 'Duder,' for real," I said solemnly, "and the memory tears me apart inside every day."

I proceeded to talk for over an hour, spilling my proverbial guts, telling young K'pai about the horrors I had seen, the crimes that I was forced to participate in, and the emotional impact on me and my companions. While I verbally unloaded, I thought it was strange to be telling my story, in Terran, to a child who had barely experienced life before first contact. At the same time, K'pai listened to every word with rapt fascination. I felt comfortable knowing that K'pai was an open book who wasn't going to judge me. I was almost overcome with all manner of emotions as I told my story.

"I guess everything's changed since you got back . . . big time!" K'pai remarked when I had covered the main events of my tale.

"Everything, K'pai. Absolutely everything . . . including me."

"But when the *Pacifica* came, you were totally into it! All of us were! You even got to go to school and get learned from Sam! Sam and you were like real buds!"

"Ah, Sam," I said. "I wonder what became of Sam Buchanan."

"What do you mean?"

"I wonder how he did when he got back to Terra, and I wonder where he is now."

K'pai pointed across the mineral plain. "He's about two clicks that way."

I felt a jolt through my body, and my respiration rate skyrocketed. "K'pai, are you saying that Sam Buchanan is right here on Kuw'baal?"

"Yeah! You didn't know?"

"I've got to go and see him!"

"Whoa, Duder! I don't think you wanna."

"Why not?"

"'Cause he's doofers! He's totally kloofed!"

"Pardon me?"

"He's insane, Duder! Nutso!"

"Why? What happened?"

"He kept coming to the village, ranting about how we had to stop the humans, going on about us losing who we are, telling us to say no to all the koofi new stuff that the humans were bringing. When he wasn't going all ranty on us, he was over in Newton shouting at the humans to go back home! Anyway, it's pretty obvs that he was way wrong. I mean, just look at how much better we're doing now!"

After listening to K'pai, my admiration for Sam soared. "Has Sam been here recently?" I asked.

"Nah, he just keeps to himself now. The humans in Newton don't like him, and he thinks we rejecto'd him, so he just lives in his little shack. 'Sam the Hermit,' that's what the humans and us klooms call him now."

"Where is Sam's shack?" I asked.

K'pai pointed to the hills across the plain, to the left of Newton. "See that hill with the flat top and the kinda round boulder at the bottom of it? Kwazka told me it's right around there."

"Kwazka? Please, K'pai, tell me about Kwazka. When I left Kuw'baal, Kwazka was going to make sure that we kept reading and writing. What happened?"

"I dunno exactly. Kwazka was learning a group of klooms about the old writing, but then the humans started bringing us stuff and learning us new stuff, and the klooms just stopped hanging with Kwazka."

"Have you seen Kwazka lately? Do you know where I can find Kwazka?"

"Sure," K'pai said. "This time of day, you just need to look around the community structure."

"Thank you, K'pai," I said. "You have been very helpful. Thank you for listening to my story. I can't begin to tell you, especially in Terran, how much it means to me."

"No prob, Duder! I liked your story—it was way koofi! Hey, you should come to the school and tell your story again to all of us!"

"Thanks, Duder," I replied. "I might just take you up on that."

As I walked to the community structure, I felt pleased overall with my conversation with K'pai. Although K'pai obviously didn't understand how right Sam had been, at least he had appreciated my story and experiences.

It was late in the day when I arrived at the site of the old community structure. Like everything else in the village, the building had been replaced with a larger structure made from human-manufactured materials. It was clear that the building was designed to resemble a traditional kloormari dwelling with its walls finished to resemble ksada and its roof of metal strips, reminiscent of k'k'mos leaves. The building was, of course, far larger than any traditional structure. While I appreciated the effort, its appearance reeked of artifice.

I was about to enter when I saw an old kloormar squatting on the ground, leaning against a wall. I had to take a closer look to see that the old kloormar was indeed Kwazka. Kwazka did not look well; in fact, Kwazka looked absolutely awful.

I knelt beside the old kloormar. "Greetings, Kwazka. It's me, Kelvoo."

"Who?" Kwazka asked.

I was deeply troubled and confused to encounter a kloormar with a memory problem. I had never heard of such a thing.

"Kwazka, it's me, Kelvoo. Remember? About seven years ago, I left Kuw'baal with eight other kloormari. You wanted to stay behind to preserve our traditions. We're back, Kwazka! We survived! All of us!"

Kwazka gasped. "Kelvoo! It's you! You're back!" Kwazka said in a quavering voice that was almost a whisper. Kwazka extended a trembling hand, and I held it. "Kelvoo, my friend. I have something very important to ask you."

I leaned close to Kwazka's vocal outlets. "Yes, Kwazka, my old friend. What would you like to ask me?"

"Do you know where an old kloormar could find some vina?"

# FORTY-SIX: HELLO, SAM

Kwazka's apparent vina addiction rattled me. Badly. I ran from Kwazka and found my way to K'tatmal's home. I opened the door and called out for K'tatmal. Nobody was home, so I let myself in. K'tatmal's home was even larger than Kahini's, though not as ornate. It also had a commanding view of part of the village and the plain beyond.

I stood by the window wall and pointed my Infotab's camera toward the location where K'pai said that Sam lived. When I zoomed to maximum magnification, I saw a curved white object that may have been the roof of a fabric building, similar to the old classroom.

I decided to meditate and try to sort out my thoughts and come up with a plan for writing my story. Meditation came more easily to me this time, probably because I had a firm goal and task to accomplish. I was roused by the sound of K'tatmal coming home, and I was surprised to find that night had already fallen.

K'tatmal had an algel dispenser and asked me whether I had eaten. "How was the rest of your day, Kelvoo?" K'tatmal asked while we helped ourselves to dinner.

"Very interesting," I said. "I have an important new task to perform, and I learned a great deal. For example, I learned that Sam Buchanan is living a short distance from here! K'tatmal, I have to ask, why didn't you tell me?"

K'tatmal's logic was inescapable. "Because you didn't ask me! Besides, Sam hasn't been here in the village for the last three years."

I replied that I had to go and see Sam first thing in the morning. K'tatmal's response was similar to K'pai's, warning me that Sam was unstable.

"But don't you admire Sam for trying to protect us from the humans?" I asked.

"Yes, Kelvoo, I really do. The problem is that Sam's approach was 'over the top.' Sam is a very angry human. When I gave him the details of our kidnapping and our treatment on *Jezebel's Fury*, he became even more enraged. He would go around shouting at us to 'wake up,' and then he'd go over to Newton and berate the human residents. I don't like to say it, but Sam was embarrassing. Sam's behavior is what made me decide to become part of the system and try to change it without stirring up too much trouble. Unfortunately, I can't say I have had much success so far."

I took a moment to ponder K'tatmal's statement. "I saw Kwazka today. It made me sad. How did Kwazka end up addicted to Vinamibefentyn?"

"It's a very tragic situation, Kelvoo. Nobody knows who gave Kwazka some vina, and Kwazka won't reveal where it came from, but we know that all of Kwazka's SimCash was spent when some troublemaker humans stopped on Kuw'baal for a few months. When they left, they must have taken their vina with them. Kwazka has been in withdrawal ever since.

K'tatmal changed the subject. "So, Kelvoo, you mentioned that you had an important new task. Would that be writing your story for the Planetary Alliance grand inquiry?"

"Yes! How did you know?"

"I saw Trexelan on my way home this evening, and she told me all about it. I think it's wonderful."

"It's going to require me to bring some very painful memories to the surface," I said. "I will need the assistance of a human that I trust to help me write in a style that non-kloormari will understand and appreciate. That's one reason why I want to visit Sam first thing tomorrow."

"I understand, Kelvoo. I just want you to be careful. Last I heard, Sam wants to be left alone, and he can be very unpredictable. I hope you won't be disappointed."

"Thank you, K'tatmal. I will be careful, and I won't set my expectations very high."

"If you like, I can give you a ride over there in the morning."

"No thank you, K'tatmal. I can't explain why, but I think it's important that I make the effort to walk there."

That night after K'tatmal started meditating, I stared out the windows. A streetlight illuminated the path in front of the dwelling, and hundreds of other lights shone from the village below, from the landing pad and the paths leading there and from Newton in the distant hills. I watched as a small shuttle landed on the pad and offloaded a group of humans who were picked up by a small bus and taken to Newton. Everything looked so calm and peaceful. Even though my village had changed dramatically and would never return to the way it was, I managed in that moment to see a certain beauty laid out in front of me. I stood and watched for several hours before I started my meditation.

When I woke from my meditation, I saw that a heavy rain had fallen, and the plain was covered with shallow briny water. K'tatmal suggested I eat as much algel as possible and then gave me a container full of algel for later. "Use your Infotab to call me if you get in trouble or need a ride back," K'tatmal said.

I walked downstream to the end of the path and beyond. When I thought I was about level with Sam's place I came upon an area where the stream fanned out and became shallower, which was fortunate since the stream was swollen from the heavy overnight rain. I walked across the stream and over the opposite bank, stepped down onto the plain, and then started wading through the shallow water. I could tell that I would have to walk much farther than the "two clicks" that K'pai had estimated.

When I reached a place near the center point between the stream and the bottom of the distant hills, I saw wisps of vapor rising off the water as the day grew warmer, and the floodwater started evaporating and sinking down into the sandy soil. I listened and heard only the splashing of each footstep. I took deep breaths and noticed that the air smelled as fresh and clean as it used to. It felt good to be alone and far from the confusion of the village and Newton.

I paused briefly to appreciate the good things that were left on Kuw'baal, then gathered strength for my reunion with Sam. In the back of my mind, it struck me as odd that this pristine expanse of land could somehow be subject to human governance.

I pressed on. All of the floodwater had evaporated when I finally came to a rough collection of structures at the base of the hills near a small stream. The structures rested on a flat, rocky shelf about two meters above the plain.

The only building that appeared to be habitable was a metal-walled shack that seemed to be cobbled together from scavenged materials. One fabric building with a metal frame contained rows of plants in boxes, perhaps as a food source. Metal troughs diverted some of the water from the stream into a large cylindrical container beside the entrance to the "greenhouse." Another fabric structure was tattered and seemed to have been intended for storing equipment and building materials. Decaying equipment and old materials were piled up or just strewn about on the ground.

I observed the area for any signs of movement. After several minutes, I called out. "Hello? Is anybody here? I would like to speak with you."

There was no response. I stepped closer and called out more forcefully. "Hello? Is anybody there?"

The door to the metal shack started to open, and a decrepit human slowly emerged. When the door was half open, it fell off its hinges and clattered to the ground. The man kicked the prostrate door, injuring his toes in the process, as indicated by a scream of pain and his one-footed hopping. The man's face was creased and adorned with an ungroomed beard. Streaks of grey permeated the hair on the man's head and face. He wore a belt over a pair of filthy coveralls with a blaster pistol in a holster.

"Forgive the intrusion," I said. "I'm hoping you can help me. I'm looking for Samuel Buchanan."

"Samuel Buchanan is over!" the man shouted. "This goddamn place broke him! Now bugger off and leave me in peace."

The moment the man spoke, I knew he was my dear friend, Sam Buchanan.

As Sam turned back toward the shack, I called after him. "Sam! It's me! Kelvoo! I've come back!"

Sam swung around to face me. "Don't you *ever* say that name! Kelvoo the kloormar was killed. Both Kelvoos were taken from me!" Sam grasped his blaster and pulled it halfway out of its holster. "Get out of here, or I'll use this! Go away!"

I could tell that Sam was delusional. *Both Kelvoos? What's that supposed to mean?*

Sam picked the door up off the ground, backed into his shack, and leaned the door back against the opening. I had to think of a way to convince Sam that I was alive and with him again. I thought about our previous shared experiences, which took me back to the day when Sam had tried to use Shakespeare to inspire imagination in us.

A piece of culvert pipe, about 150 centimeters long, was lying on the ground beside me. I knelt beside it, lifted one end, and cradled it in the crook of one of my arms. I tilted my eye toward it, and with all of the emotion I could muster, I began speaking. "Asleep, my love? What, dead, my dove? Oh Pyramus, arise!"

Sam's door crashed back to the ground. He stood in the doorway, gaping at me as I continued.

"Speak, speak. Quite dumb? Dead, dead? A tomb must cover thy sweet eyes."

Sam staggered over to me and fell to his knees. "Kelvoo?" he said in a voice that was barely louder than a whisper. "Is it really you, or is it just the drink?"

"It really is me, Sam," I said, touching his shoulder. "I escaped, and I have come back home."

"Oh God! Oh my God!" Sam gasped, clutching my forearm. "And the others? What about your friends who were taken with you?"

"We're all back, Sam. We outwitted our captors, and we all made it back alive."

Sam broke down. He cried and he cried. "Oh God, Kelvoo! I'm so, so sorry!"

"Sorry for what?"

"For everything! I'm . . . I'm sorry the secret of Kuw'baal got out. I'm sorry I didn't teach you to fear humans. I'm sorry you were taken by the Outliers. And I'm so, so sorry that this wonderful planet, your home, has become so effing screwed up. Oh, Kelvoo, I have failed you and your species at every turn. How could you ever forgive me?"

"Sam . . . My dear friend Sam. There is nothing to forgive."

Sam stared at me, his expression alternating between grief and joy. We stayed on our knees for several minutes, letting our emotions wash over us.

Sam suddenly got to his feet. "You must come in, my friend. You must come into my home." He was speaking frenetically. "This way, this way."

Sam's shack was full of clutter, from the floor to the rafters. A single light hung from the center of the ceiling. Enough space had been cleared that there was room for a small bed and a tiny round table. A half-empty bottle of a brown liquid stood on the table along with a mug, which still held a small quantity of drink.

"We must celebrate!" Sam announced, refilling his mug. "Oh! I wish I could offer some of this cheap swill to you."

"That's alright," I said, pulling the container of K'tatmal's algel from my belt.

"I must make a toast," Sam declared, raising his mug. "Yes, yes, a toast to . . . um . . . oh, I dunno . . ."

"How about to new beginnings?" I asked.

"Yeah, why not, old friend," Sam said. I ate a handful of algel, and Sam took a huge swig of his swill and then shook his head vigorously while sticking his tongue out and expelling a raspy "Ahhhhh!" followed by "That's some nasty rum!" Sam grinned. "So, what brings you to my little corner of 'paradise' today?" he slurred. "Just a social visit, or is there something more I can do for you?"

"Perhaps both," I said. "It was only late yesterday that I learned you were here. That's why I left the village first thing this morning to come and see you."

"You walked all the way from the village?"

"I would have walked for years to see you again, Sam." I could see that he was touched by my sentiment. "It just happens that there is something else that I'd like to discuss with you. When we escaped captivity, a Sarayan vessel came to our rescue. Yesterday, the Sarayan delegation to the Planetary Alliance asked me to write my story from first contact up to the present."

Sam was starting to look wobbly, his eyes closing halfway. "Why?"

"Because the Alliance is re-evaluating Terra's role and place in the organization. They have been watching how the humans have handled Kuw'baal, among other things, and they are not pleased. The Alliance is considering holding a grand inquiry to reconsider Terran membership. The Sarayan delegation wants me to write my story to submit as testimony."

Sam's eyes snapped open. "My God, Kelvoo! Do you know what this means? God, I hate those bastards!"

"Are you saying you hate the Sarayans or the Planetary Alliance?" I asked, confused.

"No, I'm talking about the effing *humans*! Scum, one and all! This means that the Alliance might just do what I tried to do all that time: hold the bloody humans responsible for what they've done!" Sam was frantic. "Please, Kelvoo, you've got to let me help! What can I do for you?"

"Well, I have to write my story in Terran, which is very different from writing for kloormari readers. I want my story to be informative but not boring or pedantic. At the same time, I don't want to leave out anything important. I especially want my story to hold readers' attention. I think it's important that as many beings as possible actually read it. My work will need input and review by a human with a Terran background. You are the only human around here whom I trust completely. I would greatly appreciate your help."

Sam sprang up and started rummaging through stacks of storage containers in the dimly lit shack. He hyperactively pulled lids off bins and rummaged through them, spilling some of the contents on the floor. "I . . . I have recording equipment and . . . and transcription software," he said breathlessly. "I know it's here somewhere. Oh, this is going to be so good. If I can just find it . . ."

"Sam, please stop!" I said. "I don't think you're in any condition to help right at this moment. Why don't you just lie down and get some sleep? I can return in the morning, and we can get started then."

"In the morning . . . yes, yes, that sounds good," Sam said as he started to calm himself. He sat on the corner of his bed and looked at me. "There's just one thing we need to do right now."

Sam downed the small amount of rum left in the mug. Then he took the bottle and its remaining contents, along with two unopened bottles of swill from under his bed, and staggered outside. I followed.

Sam lurched to the edge of a large boulder and threw the bottles at the rock. I had expected to hear a shattering sound and witness breaking glass flying, as I had seen on old human vids. Instead, the bottles bounced off the rock and rolled to a standstill on the ground.

Sam drew his blaster and shot in the general direction of the bottles, missing by a wide margin. He turned toward me. "Guess I'm a little rusty," he slurred. As he spoke, Sam teetered and inadvertently pointed the weapon at me a couple of times.

"May I try?" I asked. Sam handed me the blaster. "Give it your best shot, Kelvoo!"

I fired three times in rapid succession, hitting each bottle. Each one vaporized, and a fine spray of liquid shot out, igniting into a fireball. Blue flame danced on the remaining liquid as some of it bubbled away, and the rest left a sticky brown residue in the dirt. When I had disposed of the final bottle, Sam whooped, jumped into the air, twirled around, and fell flat on his back in a cloud of dust.

I picked up Sam, who was heavier than I had expected, and carried him into the shack, careful not to bump his head on the narrow doorway. Then I placed him on his bed.

"I'll be back tomorrow morning," I said. "I'm going to see whether K'tatmal will give me a ride."

"Don't let K'tatmal see me."

"Why not?"

"I don't want any of the others to see me. Not like this! Please, Kelvoo, wait a few days until I can clean myself up. Then I'll be so happy to see all of you again." He sat up. "No more drinking for Sam! I've got a mission now. You've come back to me, and you've saved me!" He lay back and closed his eyes. "You saved me, buddy," he whispered. "You saved me."

I left the shack, picked the door up off the ground, and leaned it back over the opening as best as I could. I had a quick look around Sam's homestead and then walked a few steps to the small stream. I was overjoyed to see a large amount of living algel growing along its banks. I sampled a small quantity. It had been such a long time since I had consumed wild algel. Kloormari don't really have a sense of taste, as humans do, but eating fresh algel was delightful! Typically, it would have been too early in the day for a meal, but I consumed the "delicious" substance until I could eat no more.

Tired but refreshed, I set off on the arduous walk back to the village.

# FORTY-SEVEN: DETOX

By the time I left Sam's shack, I knew I wouldn't be able to get back to the village before nightfall. Instead of heading directly to the stream and then following it up to the village, I made a beeline across the plain directly toward the village. As the sky grew dark, I hoped I would be guided back by the village lights.

I knew I could contact K'tatmal using my Infotab, but I had never used the communication software before. It prompted me to enter a contact code or select a contact from my list. My list contained just a single entry for Sub-commander Trexelan, and I didn't want to bother her.

Once daylight faded, I walked toward the village lights, but I tripped over rocks a couple of times and had to move slowly and cautiously. About an hour later, my Infotab started making a sound that I had never heard before. The screen showed, "Incoming call from K'tatmal" along with a green "Answer" button. When I tapped the button, I saw K'tatmal's face.

"Hello? Kelvoo?" K'tatmal said.

I held the screen up to my face. "Can you see me, K'tatmal?"

"Not clearly, Kelvoo, but I can hear you. I'm guessing that you're somewhere out in the dark. You should see an icon marked 'Send Location' in the corner of your screen. If you give that a tap, I'll come and pick you up." I tapped the icon. "Got it," K'tatmal said. "Stay exactly where you are. I'll be there in a few minutes."

I was starting to see the benefits of personal electronic communications. Eight minutes later, a car landed right in front of me. K'tatmal invited me in, and we returned to K'tatmal's home.

"I want to know all about what happened today, but first things first," K'tatmal said once we made ourselves comfortable. K'tatmal proceeded to transfer contact information for each member of Sam's Team to my Infotab. It turned out that the Sarayan delegation had provided each team member with a communications package. K'tatmal showed me how to send a notification to each of my friends so that they could add me to their contact lists.

Once that task was complete, I related the entire story of my meeting with Sam.

"It sounds as though Sam may have an alcohol addiction," K'tatmal said. We didn't know much about the subject, so we read about it on our Infotabs.

"It definitely looks as though Sam is an alcoholic!" I declared after about two minutes of research.

As I continued reading, I learned about the severe damage that alcohol addiction had caused to countless humans and the people who cared about them. Like many human traits, I found it hard to fathom why a being would choose to use a substance when there was even a small chance that it could control and ruin their lives.

I learned about recovery from alcoholism and understood that there was only a slim chance of Sam staying sober. If he did, he would be in for a great deal of suffering over the coming days as his body detoxified. I read that there were medical treatments that could ease the dangerous aspects of detox, and I planned to take Sam to a physician in Newton. I realized that if Sam was going to be able to help me at all, I would require his sobriety.

The next morning, K'tatmal drove me to a place near Sam's shack in manual mode since "Sam's Place" wasn't a known location in the car's navigational database. I walked to the shack and gently lifted the door away. Sam was still sleeping. I gently shook his shoulder to let him know I was there. He groaned, then rolled over, and began snoring. I decided to give him time to recover.

I couldn't exactly get to work at that moment, so while I waited, I sent a message, updating all of my kloormari friends on the situation. Each of them said they were eager to visit Sam. I told them of Sam's illness and how he would need a few days of recovery before anyone should consider visiting. I also said that I planned to stay with Sam during recovery, so I might not be returning to the village for several days. I assured my friends that I would be fine since a natural supply of algel was growing close by.

It wasn't until after midday when Sam stirred. I knelt by his bed and held his hand. Sam blinked a few times. "Thank you for coming back, Kelvoo. You're looking well."

"And you, my friend, are looking like you were shot out of an airlock!" I replied. Sam laughed and then grasped the sides of his head and groaned with pain.

"Could you please bring me a mug of water from the stream?" he asked.

I did as Sam requested. When I returned, he was sitting up. He drank the water slowly. "So I don't throw up," he explained.

After he finished the water, I asked Sam whether he remembered what we were planning to do. "Something about writing," he said. "Yes! You've been asked to write your story for the Alliance. They're going to have an inquiry and decide whether to give the Terrans the boot! I also remember you saying that you want my help!" Sam stood up. "That's great, Kelvoo! I'm ready to help!"

Sam grabbed his head again, swayed a bit, groaned, and then sat back down on the bed. "Sorry, got up a bit fast there!" He took a moment before continuing. "I have some recording equipment and transcription software. It's really good stuff that I managed to get off the *Pacifica* when she was decommissioned. It can distinguish voices in a crowded room and record each conversation. I was thinking that maybe you can use your vocal outlets to tell different parts of the story at the same time. The equipment can transcribe it, and then you can pull the different parts together into a single document."

I thought that Sam's idea was nothing short of brilliant.

"Sam, you know you're going to go into withdrawal soon, right?"

"Yeah, Kelvoo. I've been through it a couple of times before. It's hell."

"I've read that there are medical treatments that can ease your suffering and reduce the risks to your health and your life. Perhaps we should go to Newton and get some medical help."

"Not a chance! I'm just going to 'white knuckle' it. I've done it before, and I'm going to do it again. Forever this time!"

"But Sam, I don't want to see you needlessly suffer."

"Suffering is part of it, my friend. I deserve to suffer. I did this to myself, and it's important to me to deal with the consequences. I won't seek medical help, and if you bring any to me, I'll refuse."

"Unfortunately, that is your choice to make, Sam, but I'm going to stay with you during withdrawal, and I'm going to do whatever I can to help, and you can't stop me. So, before we get started, I need to know whether you have enough food and supplies to get through this."

"I'm fine, Kelvoo."

"Alright, show me where you keep your food."

Sam refused. It didn't take long until he admitted that he was out of food. Before I had shown up, Sam's plan was to go into town that morning to buy supplies.

"You stay here and get some rest," I said. "Just give me a list of what you need, and I'll go to Newton and buy it."

"You got any SimCash?" Sam asked.

"I've still got the balance from the *Orion Provider* on my Infotab."

"That won't be near enough. Tell you what, if you insist on going into town, I'll transfer a shopping list and enough funds to your Infotab."

"How do you have any SimCash?" I asked.

"My pension. I got pensioned off by the Terran First Contact Authority, so every couple of weeks they deposit a bunch of SimCash to my account."

I was surprised but relieved that Sam was letting me go into town for him without more pushback. He gave me directions to the shop where he bought all of his supplies. Sam's shack was just a ten-minute walk from the shop at the edge of Newton. Sam sent me a list and transferred the funds to me, and then I set off.

I followed a winding path between two hills where I saw a vehicle repair shop, a building supply store, and the "Newtown Market." When I entered, I was the only patron.

"Welcome!" the shopkeeper said. "We don't get many kloormari customers. What brings you my way today?"

"I have a list of supplies that I need to pick up," I said.

"Can I help you find anything?"

"I am reluctant to accept assistance. The last time I was in a shop, I didn't buy anything, and the shopkeeper demanded payment for wasting his time."

"Wow!" she said. "That sounds like a shady character. Did that happen here in Newton or in your village?"

"Neither. It happened on the *Orion Provider*."

"The *Orion* . . . Wait a minute, are you one of those kloormari who just came back after being in captivity for seven years?"

"Yes. My name is Kelvoo."

"Oh my gosh! You were the one who was interviewed on the *Orion*! I remember seeing that a few years ago. Then you were taken by those awful Outliers. Oh, you must have had such a terrible time!"

"Yes, and all of the trouble started with that interview. The incident also led to a lot of pain for some humans."

"I know! Poor Sam Buchanan! You knew him, didn't you? After the information about this planet leaked out in the interview, there was such a kerfuffle! When the *Pacifica Spirit* returned to Terra, the captain and crew were put through the wringer with all kinds of inquiries. It pretty much drove Sam insane; poor guy was just racked with guilt! Did you know that Sam moved here? He lives just down the path now!"

"I do know that. In fact, I'm here to pick up supplies for Sam."

"Oh, that's wonderful! How's Sam doing? It's been a couple of weeks since he was last here."

"Sam's not doing very well at the moment, but I hope he will be getting better soon. My return seems to have given him a new purpose, so I'm hopeful that I can help him to heal."

I showed Sam's list to the shopkeeper. She said that Sam usually picked up a few bottles of rum, and she wondered whether he might have forgotten to add it to the list.

"No," I said, "Sam says that he is no longer going to drink alcohol. I hope he succeeds."

"So do I, Kelvoo. So do I."

The shopkeeper told me that her name was Brenda. She and I continued to chat while she directed me to all of the supplies for Sam. "So, I guess you noticed a lot of changes when you returned! Do you like what you see?"

"I'm afraid not, Brenda. I think I am witnessing the destruction of my own species' culture."

"Oh dear! I'm surprised to hear that. Of course, Sam used to warn about that all the time to anyone who'd listen. Mind you, he used to say that to those who wouldn't listen either! The thing is, the other kloormari I've spoken to are quite excited about all the goods and technologies that are coming in."

"Well, Brenda, when it comes to the group of us who were abducted, we have a different outlook, partly because the changes came all at once for us instead of gradually over seven years. Our perspective is also different because we have seen some of the terrible things that humans are capable of. That makes us very worried about what might still be to come."

"I hear you, Kelvoo, and I think I get where you're coming from. Hopefully, everything works out well in the end."

Brenda had me transfer the applicable amount of SimCash from my Infotab. The containers of groceries and other supplies were bulky and heavy, so Brenda invited me to take one of the store's hover carts. "Just press the 'Go Home' button when you're done, and it'll come right back here."

I thanked Brenda and then made my way back to Sam's shack. Her kindness and interest in my concerns were very encouraging. It brought back some of the warmth that I had felt toward humans during the *Pacifica's* original stay. I wondered for a moment whether my time on the *Jezebel's Fury* had jaded my perception. I concluded that most humans could be very pleasant individually but dangerous as a group. My resolve to help my people and write my story remained undiminished.

As I approached Sam's encampment, I was surprised to see dozens of storage boxes piled outside on the ground. When I looked inside Sam's shack, I saw that the interior was mostly empty. Sam had set up a folding table and placed electronic equipment there. He had also added another photoelectric panel to the roof with a cable that led to a charging station inside. The bed also had fresh sheets, which Sam had found in one of the storage boxes.

Sam helped me unload the hover cart. I pressed the "Go Home" button and watched it rise and then speed off toward the store.

Sam was working at a frenetic pace to get everything set up. I asked him to slow down, but he said there was a limited time before he would start feeling awful, and everything had to be ready for me to get started. I expressed my concern about so many of Sam's belongings being outside and exposed to the elements.

"Kelvoo," Sam said, "all of this is just 'stuff.' It doesn't matter. In fact, it's been cluttering my life and weighing me down. Would you like any of it? Help yourself! I'm either going to give it away or throw it out!"

Sam opened one of the electrolyte drinks and a nutrition bar that I had just purchased. It seemed that he had come to rely on pre-packaged, processed food. I wondered how long it had been since he had enjoyed a cooked meal, like the ones that Bertie used to prepare on the *Pacifica Spirit*. I reminisced about Bertie's blunt but kind demeanor, and I realized she was one of the most interesting humans that I had ever met.

Sam took me inside and showed me how to use the recording and transcription system with my Infotab. I tried reciting eight sets of sample dialog simultaneously, using all eight of my vocal outlets. The software tried to transcribe my words to eight different documents, but there was too much crosstalk. Sam suggested that I try to speak using a distinct pitch for each voice. After some practice, I had considerable success using four simultaneous voices. I also learned how to merge each transcribed document into a single text. This would let me, for example, narrate the first four chapters at the same time, merge them into my story, and then repeat the process for the next four chapters.

While I practiced, Sam stood beside me and stared intently. I noticed that his hands were shaking slightly, and beads of sweat were forming on his forehead. "Are you alright?" I asked.

"It's starting, Kelvoo, and all I want right now is a drink. Don't let me have one, okay? No matter what, stop me from going into town and buying booze."

"I'll do what I can," I replied.

Sam looked directly at me. "Let me apologize to you right now for my behavior over the next few days. There'll be times when I'm angry, sad, irritable, paranoid, delusional, or all of those things at the same time! Please make sure I stay hydrated and make me eat at least a little bit every day."

"I will, Sam. I promise."

"One more thing, Kelvoo . . . Thank you. You're the best friend I've ever had."

"It's the least I could do for you, my friend."

Sam stepped outside to relieve himself in his ramshackle outhouse. He came back in and changed into some pyjamas that he had found in a storage bin. Sam sat on the bed and consumed the electrolyte beverage. Then he laid down and began his long bout of suffering.

I started narrating my story. I wanted to ensure that I didn't leave out a single detail, so my recounting of events was very thorough.

My efforts happened in fits and starts. When Sam slept, it was usually for just a few minutes. Sometimes Sam was anxious and would respond to the slightest sound with surprise and paranoia. Sometimes Sam would hear sounds that didn't exist. Sometimes I would narrate my story, and Sam would accuse me of lying or saying something hurtful. At times he would think that someone else was in the room.

Sam's physical symptoms were frightening at times. He would have headaches and fevers and shake uncontrollably. At one point, his entire body went into seizure, and I thought he was about to die.

In addition to interrupting his sleep, Sam's insomnia was very disruptive to my meditation. This made *me* irritable. Sometimes I harbored anger toward Sam for putting me through this, but mostly for his foolish selfishness in deciding to consume such a dangerously addictive drug.

During Sam's brief moments of relative calm, I fed him. My knowledge of human nutritional needs was limited, but I knew that Sam's prepackaged protein bars and other processed foods were less than ideal. At one point, while Sam slept after an especially nasty bout of fever and shaking, I ran to the Newtown Market to get Brenda's advice. When I entered, I received suspicious stares from a number of patrons in the store, but Brenda welcomed me.

She was placing items on a shelf. When I started explaining the situation to her, she asked a member of her staff to take over. Then Brenda told me to go back to Sam, and she would come and visit in a few minutes. By the time I reached Sam's encampment, Brenda had caught up to me in a small car. We went inside the shack where Sam was semi-conscious.

"Oh my," Brenda said. "Sam's living conditions are much worse than I had thought."

"You should have seen the place before he cleaned it up!" I replied.

Brenda pulled out a cylindrical flask. "Soup," she said. She asked me to bring a bowl and spoon. The best I could do was to bring Sam's mug and a spoon, which I had seen in a storage box outside. She poured the hot liquid into the mug. Brenda gently roused Sam.

"Who are you?" he barked.

"It's me, Brenda," she said, "from the store. I heard you were having a rough time."

"Dammit, Kelvoo, why'd you have to go telling anyone about me?" he said. "Now the whole damned town probably knows!"

Brenda grabbed Sam by the chin. "I know you're suffering like hell right now, but don't you dare take it out on Kelvoo! This kloormar has been by your side the whole time. You should be thanking Kelvoo for giving a damn about you and for coming to me for help. Now shut up and eat your soup!"

"Sorry," Sam muttered, and Brenda slowly spooned the soup into his mouth. The hot food had a very soothing effect on Sam. When he was finished, he gave her a sheepish look. "Thank you," he said, then laid back down, and for the first time in the last two days, Sam slept for a few hours.

I noticed tears coming from Brenda's eyes, and I apologized for making her feel obligated to help. "No, Kelvoo, that's not it," she said. "What you're going through is all too familiar to me. My dad had the same problem after my mom died. He put me through this more times that I can count. He'd get drunk, I'd get mad, he'd stop and be all apologetic, then I'd come over and take care of him during withdrawal. Then a couple of weeks later, we'd repeat the process all over again. It took a long time for my dad's alcoholism to kill him. When it finally happened, do you know what I felt?"

I gently touched Brenda's arm. "Sad?"

"No, Kelvoo, not even a little bit. I felt relieved. Not long after that, I felt guilty for feeling relieved. Addiction is a terrible thing, Kelvoo. It destroys the addict, but it also causes immense harm to everyone who cares about them. Long before Dad died, he had alienated himself from all of his friends. There was no funeral or memorial. Alcohol had taken everything."

"Brenda, I'm very sorry that you had to experience so much pain."

"Thanks, Kelvoo. I'm sorry if I was rambling, but it feels good to talk about it to someone. I think what I'm trying to say is . . . don't get too emotionally invested in Sam's recovery. Prepare yourself for the likelihood that his sobriety won't last."

With that, Brenda informed me that she had better return to the store. She said she would return the next day with more soup and something a bit more substantial. I asked her how I should go about paying for her food and services. "I won't hear of it!" Brenda said. "It's on the house."

As she left, I thanked her. "You're a good human being."

"You really think so?" she asked.

"Oh yes . . . especially for a shopkeeper!"

Brenda burst out laughing. "See you tomorrow!" As she drove away, I could hear her laughter coming from inside the car.

My thoughts returned to the Samuel Buchanan that I had known during the *Pacifica's* first visit: Sam the scientist, Sam the teacher, and Sam the friend. Sam the addict just made me feel sad.

On the fourth day, Sam was doing better. He was able to sleep longer, and I was able to write more than I had in the previous days combined. Brenda stopped by with more soup along with buttered toast and some scrambled eggs in a "hot pack." I didn't know whether Sam remembered his previous outburst toward me, but he certainly seemed subdued and deferential toward both of us.

On the fifth day, Sam was starting to resemble his former self. He drank lots of water and other non-alcoholic beverages. Brenda came by with a substantial hot meal, and Sam consumed it with gusto. He was very grateful to both of us, and he assured Brenda that she didn't need to come by anymore. Brenda agreed, but she told both of us to call on her if she could help again.

"Alright, Kelvoo," Sam said late that afternoon, "let's see what you've got so far."

I explained that I had written my account up to the part where the automated lander had departed back to the "sky world."

"Excellent!" Sam said. "How many screens of text did that take?"

"Two thousand one hundred and sixty-seven."

"Uh-oh!" Sam said. He read the first two screens and then skimmed over fifteen more. "I'm sorry I wasn't able to help you over the last few days. Unfortunately, I think we're going to have to adjust your writing style for non-kloormari readers."

I was disappointed that my writing wouldn't appeal to other species. Sam tried to explain that humans and other Alliance species didn't have the attention span to read a minute-by-minute account of the finest details of a story.

"I know you've read many human novels, both fiction and non-fiction," he said. "I also know you've read third-person accounts and autobiographies. Think about how these stories, especially human autobiographies, are worded. Think about the style and the level of detail that these writers used. If you can use these stories as a template while telling *your* story in your own words and expressing your true feelings, you will write a good document that many beings will want to read."

"But Sam," I replied, "I don't know enough about what's important to non-kloormari readers. I'm sure I can imitate a human style, but what if I leave out important details?"

"It's about finding the right balance," Sam said. "You need to relate the important events while still including various anecdotes and observations that will hold the reader's interest and make your characters relatable. That's where I can help, Kelvoo, if it's alright with you."

"That would be wonderful," I replied. "When I said I was worried about leaving out details, I was mostly thinking about technical information. Other species don't know much about the kloormari, and I wonder whether the story will make sense if I assume knowledge that the readers don't have."

Sam thought about my concerns for a moment before replying. "How about this: What if you write your story, and then I write a preface? When your story is written, I'll read through it and make a list of questions that readers might have. Then I'll write a brief introduction to fill in any missing pieces in advance. That would appeal to me as a scientist, and hopefully, it will make your story easier to read and more interesting."

"That's a wonderful idea, Sam!"

So, I started writing my story again. The experience was so much more gratifying this time because I wrote with the counsel and support of my good friend, Sam.

# FORTY-EIGHT: SAM'S STORY

During Sam's withdrawal, I had kept in touch with the other members of Sam's Team and provided them with progress reports. Now that Sam was feeling better, all of my friends were very interested in seeing Sam, and he was keen to reunite with all of them. We arranged for the team to visit in the evening. Sam went into town earlier that day with a bin full of clothes and towels. When he returned, Sam had a haircut and was clean shaven. The laundry in the bin had been washed, dried, and folded. Sam bathed in the stream where it emptied onto the plain, using soap that he had purchased in town.

Sam wanted the group to gather around a campfire as he used to do with friends on Terra. Since wood didn't exist on Kuw'baal, he had purchased a substitute called "SimLogs." SimLogs were sticks that would burn for hours with a bright yellow flame. They produced popping and cracking sounds and lots of heat, but they emitted no smoke or pollutants. "Close enough," Sam said. Sam had also purchased four lanterns.

Late in the afternoon, heavy rains started to fall, threatening to put a damper on Sam's plan. Fortunately, the rains passed quickly, leaving the air pleasantly fresh and clean.

As dusk approached, so did all of the members of Sam's Team, including Kwazka! The group arrived on a large hoverlift. Sam waved as the group approached, and they all waved back. Each member of the team stepped off the hoverlift and exchanged greetings with Sam, saying how much they had missed him and what fond memories they had of their time with him. Sam was surprised by the emotions expressed by the team. K'aablart explained that the emotions developed over time and through the hardships we had experienced on the *Jezebel's Fury*, so they had come with a heavy toll on our mental health.

We all gathered around the SimLogs, which Sam had placed in a conical pile. We started engaging in small talk, or more precisely, Sam asked each kloormar questions, and they responded. I was very pleased with how lucid Sam was now and how he could still identify each of us individually and recall specific events from our earliest interactions with him.

When night fell, Sam switched the lanterns on. He took one of the SimLogs a few paces away, laid it on a rock, and used his blaster pistol in

344

slice mode to ignite the end of it. Three of my colleagues closed their eye or put a hand up between their eye and Sam to block the view. It was clear that, for them at least, the sight of blaster fire brought back disturbing memories. Seeing their reactions sparked the same response in me, and I had to fight to push my memories back down deep inside of me.

Sam brought back the burning stick and pushed it into the pile. Unlike blaster plasma, the flames glowed with warm, soft yellows, oranges, and reds. Staring into the fire made me feel calmer and content.

In addition to the events surrounding the *Pacifica's* initial visit, our small talk included our time preceding the visit by "Captain Smith." We learned a lot about K'tatmal's experiences on Kuw'baal after returning from Benzolar 3, and we talked about our experiences in the recent days since our homecoming.

Kwazka opened up about being addicted to vina. "Back when I was one of the last kloormari eating wild algel, I would often see a group of human youth congregating at the part of the stream bank where I would take my algel. Seven weeks after I first saw them, I started feeling terrible; I was in immense pain. "The young humans saw this and approached me. They told me a story about a disease that was spreading through this sector of the galaxy, and they thought I had caught it. They told me that they had a medicine that could treat me. I doubted their story, but one of them pulled a spray bottle out of a bag and squirted a substance into my breathing inlet. Within minutes, I felt as if I had been cured. The youths said they could get more, but I had to keep it secret because the medicine was illegal, and they couldn't get more if I told anyone. Looking back, I think they must have sprayed vina onto the algel along my feeding spot, so I would get hooked.

"A few weeks later, I needed more vina, and they demanded SimCash. This continued for about two years, I think, but I can't remember exactly how long it was. That's right, I—a kloormar—can't remember! That's how badly vina has messed me up! Anyway, each time I needed more, the price went up. It didn't matter to me—I just needed my vina.

"One day, I saw the human security people having a talk with the group of youths. The next day, I saw them hurrying onto a passenger transport heading off planet. I've been in withdrawal ever since, and that was over three years ago. I'm slowly getting better, but I'm old, and I don't think I'm going to live long enough to be fully recovered.

"There is one thing I do know for sure: Seeing all of you return home was the best treatment for my condition. It has brought me peace and eased a great deal of my pain."

We all expressed our sympathy and our admiration toward Kwazka for sharing the story. We continued talking until the conversation dwindled to a stop.

"I see that we've been talking about many things, but we've avoided talking about certain events," Sam observed. "Would I be right in assuming that we aren't ready to talk about our more traumatic experiences?"

"I know we need to talk about these things," Keeto replied, "but I'm not ready yet, especially since we're having such a pleasant time right now just enjoying each other's company. Besides, I think we should wait until Kelvoo's story comes out. I think we should use it as a basis for future conversations as we try to work through our difficulties."

Kleloma turned to me. "By the way, Kelvoo, thank you for doing this. We know it's going to be incredibly difficult, but the story must be told. We all think you're very brave."

"Thank you, Kleloma, and my thanks to all of you for your support and trust," I said. "I don't know whether my writing will be any good, but making the effort is what's important to me."

"What I want to say is tangentially related to our negative experiences," Kroz said, "but I have hopeful news, and I think it's important to share it now. It relates to the two human girls whom we taught to read: May and Brenna."

The subject got my full attention immediately as Kroz continued. "Since the Sarayans were planning to turn custody of the girls over to the human authorities, I wondered what became of them. K'tatmal investigated and has information for us."

"Yes, when Kroz told me about the human children, I contacted the Child Services Agency in Newton," K'tatmal said. "The girls were placed with foster parents while the agency tried to track down any family members in the Outlier colonies and on Terra. Yesterday, it was determined that the girls have no living relatives. I've learned that, during all of their time in the care of the agency, Brenna and May have been asking to see us. The agency won't tell me why we weren't informed or why they didn't facilitate a meeting, but now that we know, I am confident that we will be able to see the girls again, if each of you want to."

"I would very much like to see the girls," I said. "For all of the trauma that we've been through, I suspect that the emotional toll on them has been even worse. We agreed to help them in the first place, and I think that, if we can continue to help and offer them support, it will also help us heal."

Sam didn't know that we had met human children on the *Jezebel's Fury*. He told us that he wanted to learn more.

"That will come," I said, "when you help me write that part of the story."

Once again, the conversation dwindled, but none of us minded. I simply basked in the beauty of the fire and the comfort of existing in the moment with beings that I trusted and loved. Finally, Sam told us that he was turning in for the night. He took one of the lanterns and returned to the shack. That left the rest of us—the original ten kloormari of Sam's Team—gathered around a campfire where we were relaxed, and for the moment at least, at peace.

One by one, we drifted off into a meditative state, not needing to worry about hypothermia in the warm night air of Kuw'baal. The flickering flames had a hypnotic effect on me. After I closed my eye, I could still see the soft flickering light through my eyelid as I slipped into a blissful state of rest.

My kloormari friends and I remained in place until daylight returned. My friends boarded the hoverlift, and I returned to Sam's shack to work on my story.

As I dictated each set of chapters, and the software transcribed it, Sam reviewed the text with me. Since I could turn out four chapters at a time, the reviews took far longer than the actual "writing." In the beginning, Sam came up with so many suggestions that the second draft didn't even resemble the original, but before long, I learned to write in a way that worked for Sam and for me as well.

When I wrote about first contact, my group's education with Sam, and our trip on the *Pacifica Spirit*, Sam was fascinated by my impression of the events. He felt awkward reading about himself and insisted that I was far too kind to him. The first difficult part of the story for both of us was my recounting of the *Orion Provider* interview. Sam told me, as he had many times before, that he had harbored a great deal of guilt about the incident. As I wrote, I realized that I did too, regardless of any logic or assurances to the contrary.

When I wrote about our abduction, Sam was troubled. He was especially appalled that "Captain Smith" had claimed to know him and used his name and image to take advantage of us. At times, it seemed as though he was having as hard a time reading my story as I had writing it.

"There's something I don't understand," I said as Sam and I discussed the abduction. "Shortly after I returned to Kuw'baal, I looked up information about Outlier gangs, the Brotherhood, *Jezebel's Fury*, and related topics on a local InfoServer. I found a great deal of data with many articles predating our first contact. Despite this, I didn't see any such information when I was your student. I suppose it's possible that I never happened upon that data, but it seems rather unlikely."

"Oh, Kelvoo," Sam replied, shaking his head. "I'm so sorry."

"Sorry for what?"

"The data on the original InfoServers was sanitized."

"Sanitized?"

"'Cleansed' by the Terran First Contact Authority. They had no problem including information about humanity's troubled past, and they were delighted to show how Terran humans had overcome their challenges. What they didn't want new species to see was information that could show modern humans in a negative light."

"Why not?"

"I'm sorry, Kelvoo. It sounds so stupid for me to say this now, but they were worried that you would get the wrong impression of humans."

"Well, Sam," I replied with sadness and a touch of anger, "it's clear now that we would have formed the *right* impression of humans. We might even have had the opportunity to see through Captain Smith's ruse."

"Oh my God, Kelvoo. I messed up so badly! Back then, I was so idealistic. I bought into the TFCA's mission, and I wanted so badly to spread their 'gospel' and save the galaxy. You and your friends paid a terrible price for my naïveté."

"Sam, you've got to stop blaming yourself for all of our problems. *You* didn't set the TFCA's policies. If anything, their withholding of important information helps to exonerate you!"

As I continued my writing, I struggled to record some parts of the story, but as I forced my way through each traumatic event, I knew I was that much closer to finishing. Sam's distress, on the other hand, seemed to increase with each new revelation.

He felt nauseated when he read my account of Brawn's transgression with Sandra, the concubine, and the gruesome punishment that Brawn received.

Sam had a lot of difficulty when he read that I had become pregnant with our group's baby. Up to that point, I hadn't mentioned the baby at all. Sam was overwhelmed when he read that I had named the baby "Sam."

"Whatever made you want to name your baby after me?" he asked incredulously.

"I named my baby after my hero," I replied. "As you read further, you'll learn that Baby Sam turned out to be a hero too. That fact reaffirms for me that the baby's name was appropriate." As I said those words, I was overcome with emotion, as was Sam. We both had to pause before we could continue.

Sam didn't ask me why the baby didn't come back with us to Kuw'baal, and he didn't ask what became of Baby Sam. I think he must have known that things didn't end well for the baby, and he didn't want to think about that tragedy. That was fine with me. I didn't want to think about it either, but the story wound its way inexorably toward the horror of our baby's death and all of the terrible events that followed it.

It only took seventeen days to finish my story. During our writing efforts, we took short but fairly frequent breaks. During those breaks, Sam would tell me parts of the events of his life after he left Kuw'baal on the *Pacifica*. As I wrote and revealed new parts of my story, Sam revealed more of his own tale. By the time we had finished writing, I had a complete picture of the main events in Sam's life after he left Kuw'baal.

\*\*\*

Sam's return to Terra had been tumultuous. The same was true for Captain Staedtler, and to varying extents, the rest of the *Pacifica's* crew. "Captain Smith" had been outright lying when he told me that the TFCA had cancelled its inquiry. He had only told half-truths when he said that my interview had turned Captain Staedtler and the crew into celebrities.

When my interview with Kaley Hart was broadcast on Terra, it did garner sympathy from the humans but not enough to stop a full inquiry. The result was that Captain Staedtler was found responsible for the leaked information. He was stripped of his captaincy and took early retirement. Sam was suspended by the TFCA while they tried to decide what to do with him.

Meanwhile, Sam broke his employment contract by making impassioned pleas to the public. He went on a "media blitz," as he called it, saying he should be blamed instead of the captain. From the moment he set foot back on Terra, Sam insisted that Alliance vessels must be dispatched to Kuw'baal immediately to protect the kloormari from exploitation.

Debate over a new mission raged at the top levels of the TFCA, but the leadership was deadlocked, and plans for any possible mission ground to a halt. The non-Terran leaders of the Planetary Alliance were as divided as the Terrans. Taking action would have required an affirmative vote of 70 percent of Alliance delegates, but at least 50 percent thought that, since a Terran mission had resulted in the leak, the Terrans would have to lead and fund any follow-up missions.

Once it was far too late, the Terrans decided to launch a small-scale single-vessel mission to Kuw'baal that would have no decision-making authority once there. The crew's only purpose was to observe and report back.

Sam was a relentless thorn in TFCA's side. Large swaths of the public supported his return to Kuw'baal, but the leadership was embarrassed by his statements to the media and wanted to distance themselves from him.

The observation mission provided the TFCA with a perfect solution to their "Buchanan issue." Sam was more than eager to return to Kuw'baal, and the TFCA hoped he would end up out of sight and out of mind.

Sam's return to Kuw'baal was on a smaller vessel than the *Pacifica Spirit*. The *Cabezon* was a privately owned work barge that would usually make the rounds between communication relays and automated survey stations to perform routine maintenance work under contract. The *Cabezon* was to deploy a communications relay in geosynchronous orbit around Kuw'baal, and the TFCA booked passage for Sam and a small team to establish an observation outpost.

Sam had never expected to see Lynda Paige again. She had been "encouraged" to accept a lump sum and leave the TFCA. Lynda was able to land a position as second navigator on the *Cabezon*. Although the job was a step down from the *Pacifica*, Lynda was interested because the *Cabezon* frequented the area of space out toward Kuw'baal. Sam was beyond delighted when he stepped onto the *Cabezon* and was greeted with a "Hello, stranger!" from Lynda.

On the voyage, Sam and Lynda were together every waking moment when Lynda wasn't on duty. Lynda had been following Sam's struggles in the media and admired his passion and tenacity. She was also disillusioned by the leadership and bureaucracy of the TFCA, so they both had a great deal to talk about. The discovery of intelligent life on Kuw'baal had been the highlight of their careers. The aftermath of that mission had been the worst part of their lives.

Twelve hours after the *Cabezon* deployed the Kuw'baal communications relay, Sam and the rest of the observation team were going to take a shuttle to the surface to set up their outpost. By then, Sam and Lynda had developed a strong bond. "You should come with me," Sam had said half-jokingly to Lynda.

"Just try to stop me!" Lynda replied. She quit her job on the spot and threw her lot in with Sam.

As soon as the shuttle touched down by the mineral plain, scores of kloormari came from the village. Sam had been expecting to see more kloormari, but he hadn't yet realized that another vessel had come and gone just a few days before, so visits by spacecraft were becoming "old hat."

The villagers gathered around Sam and Lynda, offering greetings in rudimentary Terran. They also greeted the six other members of the observation team. Sam was impressed by how much the kloormari villagers' communication skills had developed. As more villagers arrived, Sam and Lynda scanned the crowd for the individuals that they had spent the most time with. Lynda spotted Kwazka first.

Sam asked Kwazka where he could find the rest of his former students.

"Did you think they would still be here?" Kwazka asked. "They have already left with your friend."

"My friend?" Sam asked.

"Yes, your friend, Captain Roger Smith."

Sam and Lynda were panicked. The shuttle was in the process of bringing shelters and supplies over the course of several trips. When the shuttle landed, Sam asked them to bring the long-range communications gear on the next trip. When it arrived, the team made their first use of the communications relay to notify the Terran First Contact Authority that nine kloormari had been taken from Kuw'baal under suspicious circumstances.

The TFCA's investigative division questioned Kwazka, who was able to give a detailed description of "Captain Smith" and his shuttle. Unauthorized jumps had been logged in the vicinity of Kuw'baal, and agents embedded into Outlier gangs had reported sightings of the *Jezebel's Fury*, so it didn't take long to surmise who had taken Sam's Team. Kwazka had said that the group would be back in six months, but the TFCA, along with Sam and Lynda, didn't think that Sam's Team would survive for that long.

Sam fell into a deep depression, and his guilt reached a new level. His demeanor required great patience and kindness from Lynda. It was only with her love and support that Sam got through the worst of his emotions and impulses.

Six months later, after Sam's Team was supposed to have returned, Sam emerged from his bleak state. He assumed that his kloormari friends had perished, and he decided it was time to move on. He was grateful for Lynda's support and amazed that she had managed to stay by his side. Lynda became pregnant, and Sam was looking forward to a new chapter and a chance to have a positive impact on his child's life.

Up to that point, a few human settlers had arrived on Kuw'baal. Sam consulted with the kloormari villagers to warn them of human expansionism, but the influx was just a trickle, and the kloormari found the presence of humans to be interesting, and they enjoyed interacting with them.

One day, a flotilla of nine large vessels arrived and immediately began offloading huge containers of goods, supplies, and heavy equipment along with over 300 humans. Sam and Lynda ran to the scene to try to block the onslaught. Of course, they had no chance. Some of the new arrivals were executives from a mining consortium. Sam told them that they had no rights to the resources of the planet. The executive team included corporate lawyers who pointed out that Terran and Alliance laws did not apply to Kuw'baal since the normal procedures that followed first contact had been suspended, and there had been no formal declaration of Kuw'baal as a legal protectorate.

The kloormari villagers did nothing to intervene. On the contrary, they gathered around what is now the site of Newton and watched in awe as massive equipment was unloaded, brought to life, and used to build homes, bunkhouses, and offices from prefabricated parts. Some of the human arrivals waved at the crowd of kloormari, and they were pleased to wave back.

A contingent of the new arrivals, called the "Outreach Group," went out into the crowd, and later, into the village to deliver their message of "friendship, trust, and cooperation" with their new neighbors. Their job was made simple by the kloormari's existing knowledge of the Terran language and their ability to learn. The Outreach Group was well trained in their mission. Their technique was to inundate the kloormari with technology and commerce, along with large doses of Terran culture and entertainment.

The kloormari were confused by Sam's insistence that the growth of the human population would have negative consequences. Despite the village's loss of nine kloormari to Captain Smith, the villagers were confident in their ability to detect any possible deception from the human arrivals. After all, these weren't the Outlier humans that Kwazka had warned them about. These were Terrans: the "good" humans. The villagers also felt that any risks from

351

the new arrivals were outweighed by all of the benefits that they brought with them.

Once the commercial interests had arrived on Kuw'baal, the observation team was recalled to Terra. Sam refused to return, and Lynda chose to remain with him and deliver the first human born on Kuw'baal. Sam and Lynda used parts of the structures left behind by the team to create a homestead outside of "New Town" at the base of the adjoining hills.

Lynda had wanted to give birth at the homestead, which at that time, was more like a small house and less like a shack. The birth was not an easy one, so Sam and Lynda's son ended up being delivered in the health clinic operated by the mining consortium.

Sam took a few weeks to care for Lynda and their son until new waves of spacecraft started to arrive. Sam was livid. Infrastructure started being developed in the town, and businesses sprang up, lending the town a new sense of permanence. New Town was now being called Newton. It served as a hub for exploration of the planet. Small craft were parked all around Newton. Every day, craft would depart with survey crews to various parts of the planet, and other vessels would return.

Sam would run into town or over to the kloormari village, trying to set up meetings, convince others to join him, or carrying a sign and shouting. Meanwhile, Lynda was left to maintain the homestead while also attending to the baby's needs. Sam's obsession started to wear him down mentally. He would return home in the evening, upset and hardly able to sleep. Since alcoholic beverages were available from several sources in Newton, Sam found it helpful to have a drink at the end of the day. This led to two drinks in the evening, then one or more drinks at midday, then drinks with higher levels of alcohol, and so on.

The day after the baby's third birthday, Lynda sat Sam down and told him that enough was enough. She said it was time for Sam to come to grips with the fact that he had tried, but no more could be done to save Kuw'baal. She explained that there were no schools, or for that matter, other human children on the planet, and they had to think about their son's social and educational needs. Sam was angry and would hear none of it. He told Lynda that the problems with Kuw'baal were his fault, and only he could fix them. "End of discussion!" Sam had declared.

The following day when Sam was having another diatribe in Newton, Lynda took the baby and boarded a shuttle for an orbiting passenger vessel bound for Terra.

Sam started to reduce his engagement with the humans and the kloormari but only because of the severe increase in his drinking and intoxication. Lynda tried to keep in touch via vid transmission. She would call Sam when it was morning at his location on Kuw'baal. She would usually have their son on her lap or close by. The boy had started attending pre-school. He had a good vocabulary, and he was very active, running around constantly.

A year after Lynda's departure, Lynda called Sam after he'd had a sleepless night. Although it was only midmorning, Sam had already been drinking. The moment he received the call, Sam started berating Lynda. He went on a diatribe, calling her the most vicious and vulgar names and spitting out obscenities at the top of his lungs. "Why the hell did you call me anyway?" Sam concluded.

Lynda had burst into tears. "So you could wish your son a happy fourth birthday!" That's when Sam noticed his crying son in the corner of the vid screen. Lynda terminated the call immediately, and Sam had no further contact with Lynda or his son.

That was when Sam completely fell apart. He was no longer a thorn in the side of the humans or the kloormari. Samuel Buchanan had become Sam the Hermit—a hostile, drunken shell of who he once was and could have become. From that moment on, Sam had contemplated suicide many times, but in the blurry depths of his mind, he had always held out hope that someday he might be able to heal and do something that could make a difference. I was pleased that his assistance with my story might just grant him his wish.

***

Sam told me his story, one piece at a time, spread out over many discussions. For me, the most poignant moment came when Sam brought up an image on his Infotab. It showed him with Lynda, holding their newborn son. Both of them were smiling at the camera in front of their tidy little homestead.

"What did you name your son?" I asked.

"We usually called him Kelly, but his full legal name is Kelvoo Buchanan-Paige. We named him in memory of my hero."

# FORTY-NINE: PREFACE

*Note to reader: The preceding chapter marked the end of the story that I turned over to Samuel Buchanan, so he could write the preface for me. My story from this point forward has not been reviewed by Sam. I am confident that I have developed a style that you will find readable. If not, please know that I tried my best.*

After I dictated the chapter about Sam's personal struggles and transcribed it, I provided it to Sam, acknowledging that the chapter contained information that was deeply personal to him and focused on his human frailties. I told Sam that, out of respect for him, I was willing to omit anything about him that could be construed as negative.

"It doesn't matter, Kelvoo," he replied. "Your story is far more important than any individual. I am a flawed person. Humans are deeply flawed and cannot help inflicting pain on themselves, other humans, and all living things around them. I don't hold myself above any other human. Your story tells the truth about your observations of humans and your interactions with them. Please don't sanitize your story the way that the TFCA sanitized the InfoServer data.

"I insist that you include whatever you've already written. Helping you with your story has given me a sense of purpose and is helping me to heal. I'm on my way to being at peace with myself."

Late in the afternoon, I transferred a copy of my story to Sam's Infotab.

"Kelvoo," he said, "I can't begin to tell you how amazing it's been to reunite with all of my kloormari friends, and especially, how rewarding it has been to work with you. If there's anything that can change the tide against the encroachment of humans, your story might just do it. I've messed up a lot of things in my life, but I'm proud to be helping you, and I feel as though I have finally played a role in making a positive difference."

"Sam," I replied, "you have been making a positive difference to me since the moment we met."

After a moment, Sam got down to business. "I'm going to need three days to review your story, look for any gaps, and then fill in those gaps with my preface. It's very important that I work alone without interruption from anybody. Three days from now, I will send the preface to you, and you can incorporate it into your story."

I sent a message to K'tatmal, asking for a lift back to the village.

"I appreciate you, Kelvoo," Sam said as I left his shack, "more than you will ever know." I let Sam know that I felt the same way. Then I walked to the place where Sam's Team had gathered around the campfire and waited there for my ride.

Over the next three days, I stayed in K'tatmal's home. K'tatmal was busy at work, so I spent most of the time walking through the village and talking with other kloormari, especially my friends from Sam's Team.

Each day, I would walk and explore uninhabited areas behind the village. This was not an activity that would ever have occurred to me in the past unless I'd had a specific purpose. I enjoyed the solitude, and I was learning to see beauty in my surroundings. I also sought out valleys and gullies, looking for streams and sometimes finding small areas where pockets of algel were still growing wild. My traumatic experiences had changed me, and I let myself believe that some of the changes might actually help me grow in new and positive ways.

The third day after Sam started on the preface was a Friday. K'tatmal had been very busy that week and was looking forward to two days of rest. Shortly after K'tatmal came home, my Infotab notified me of an incoming document. Sam had completed his preface and sent it to me along with a message: "Thank you for letting me write the attached preface for you. Please don't hesitate to make any changes as you see fit."

"Document received," I replied. "Thank you so much, Sam. I'll see you soon."

I read Sam's preface immediately. I could see how useful it would be for readers who were unfamiliar with Kuw'baal and the kloormari. I realized that some parts of my story might have assumed knowledge that some readers could be lacking, so Sam's preface added a great deal of value.

I made only one revision to Sam's work. The last sentence in Sam's preface was: "I was deeply honored that my best friend, Kelvoo, asked me to write this preface as a final way to show my support for the kloormari and their future." I removed the word "final." I was confident that Sam was going to overcome his addiction and guilt and that he would play a pivotal and beneficial role in my life for a long time to come.

I added Sam's preface to the beginning of my story, and then I transmitted the completed document to Trexelan, so she could provide it to the Sarayan delegation for submission to the Planetary Alliance.

That night, I stood in silence, looking through K'tatmal's wall of windows, taking in the view of the village, the plain, and the lights of Newton in the distant hills.

I had a sensation of lightness that I had never felt before. My mission had been completed. Even if it turned out to have no meaningful impact, a record of my story had been created, and for the first time in years, I had written a historical document. More importantly, writing the story had forced me to recall and confront the horrors that I had lived through. The place deep within my abdomen where I had stuffed down my grief, rage, terror, sorrow, guilt, and regret felt empty—wonderfully empty.

As I stared into the night, I came to terms with the fact that my world would never return to what it was. I was more determined than ever to reclaim Kuw'baal from the humans but not through anger, hate, or violence. Our planet had changed, but I felt confident that we kloormari were going to take back our world, embrace its changes, and determine our own future.

In the days before we knew that anything existed beyond our sky, our world had been a beautiful place, but I came to realize it was still beautiful. Beauty could be found wherever it was sought. I saw beauty in the lights of my village. I saw beauty in the colorful metal houses. I saw beauty in the landing pad, starkly lit against the pure black of the plain. There was beauty in the shimmering lights of Newton, beauty in the flash of blue light on the other side of the plain, and beauty in the departure of a shuttle bound for who knew where.

As K'tatmal settled down to read my story, I effortlessly drifted into a state of meditation. Deep inside my mind, the lights in the vista before me were transformed into a brilliant field of stars and distant galaxies.

# FIFTY: PACHELBEL'S CANON

*N*ote to reader: When I first sent my story to Trexelan, I did not realize that further events would warrant inclusion. After the following events occurred, I transcribed them and sent them to Trexelan to be added as the final chapter in my story.

In my deep meditative state in K'tatmal's home, I had much information to process. For the most part, I basked in the healing knowledge that I had accomplished my mission and could calculate and plan for future actions.

I recalled and cross-referenced snippets of information until, at some point in the early morning hours, I related three things:

1. When I had written the chapter called "Sam's Story," Sam had told me not to hesitate to write whatever I wanted about him, followed by, "I am on my way to being at peace with myself."
2. I thought about the word that I had edited out of the last sentence in Sam's preface: "Final."
3. I recalled the blue flash of light that I had seen in the darkness across the plain.

I flung myself out of my meditation and leapt over to K'tatmal, shaking K'tatmal. "You have to take me to Sam! Now!"

"What's wrong?" K'tatmal asked, trying to regain full alertness.

"I think Sam's in danger! We have to check on him immediately!"

We left K'tatmal's home and ran along the village paths to the garage. We leapt into the car, and K'tatmal pointed the vehicle in the general direction of Sam's shack. While driving, K'tatmal brought up a log of previous trips on the car's console, selecting the outbound trip when K'tatmal had last picked me up from Sam's home. The vehicle adjusted course. K'tatmal selected "emergency mode" on the console, and the car accelerated to high speed.

"What specifically are you worried about, Kelvoo?" K'tatmal asked.

"I don't want to say, K'tatmal . . . I don't even want to think about it."

We approached Sam's location less than three minutes after the car had left the village. From a distance, we saw the light from a lantern placed where our group had once gathered around a campfire. As we neared the lantern, we saw the circle of light that it cast on the ground. At the edge of the circle, we saw Sam's orange jumpsuit—his uniform from the *Pacifica Spirit*. A blaster pistol and a half-empty bottle of alcohol were on the ground close by.

K'tatmal stopped the car, and we got out. "Sam! Sam, are you alright?" I shouted.

I stepped up to the lantern and looked down. A human hand was showing beyond the end of a sleeve of the jumpsuit. I lifted the lantern and saw Sam's eyes staring blankly from his lifeless face. Below that a massive hole with burned edges was torn through Sam's chest.

K'tatmal and I just stood and stared at the shell that once had been Samuel Buchanan. We stood and did nothing for over an hour until the morning horizon of the Kuw'baal sky began its timeless transformation from black to grey.

Finally, K'tatmal broke the silence. "Why did he do this?"

"He couldn't have," I lied to myself. "Someone else must have murdered him!"

I saw a clear, weatherproof envelope on the ground with a rock carefully placed on it, so it wouldn't blow away. A single sheet of paper was folded inside the envelope. A message had been handwritten on the outside of the paper: "If you find this, please take it to the kloormar named 'Kelvoo' in the kloormari village."

I took the paper out of the envelope and unfolded it. A letter had been handwritten in the manner that ancient humans once used.

Dear Kelvoo,

Please share this message with every member of "Sam's Team."

I am sorry to be leaving you in this way, my friends. I hope you will be able to forgive my weakness.

I have been planning my exit for a long time now. My life has been a series of failures ever since we took our brief voyage of discovery together on the *Pacifica Spirit*. I failed to keep secret the knowledge of your planet and species. I failed to teach you everything you needed to know to protect yourselves from human evil and deception. I failed to be a good partner to my beloved Lynda. I failed to be a father to my son. Above all, I failed as a friend and protector of each of you and every kloormar on Kuw'baal.

Despite my failures, I did succeed in my final act. I am proud to have made my small contribution to assist Kelvoo in writing a story that I hope will improve your planet and your wonderful people. I have decided to quit while I'm ahead.

I am very tired. I'm going to take a final drink in tribute to the good times that we all shared, and then I will be gone.

Please know that I am departing by my own choice and not because of anything that any of you have done.

To my friend Kelvoo, I leave you all of my meager possessions. Please distribute or discard them as you wish. The same goes for my body. Please feel free to dispose of it as you see fit.

Goodbye, my wonderful friends. I have loved each and every one of you to the full extent of my mind, my heart, and my soul.

Sam

As I read the letter to K'tatmal, I wondered why my words came out haltingly and why my voice was distorted. Some of the words came out as a whisper or in a higher pitch than I intended.

When I finished reading, I was overcome with fatigue. I laid down on my side on the dusty ground beside Sam's body and stared at it. I was confused by my feelings. More accurately, I was confused by my lack of feelings. I was emotionally numb, and I wondered why. Similarly, K'tatmal was quiet and motionless.

"What do you want to do?" K'tatmal asked finally. "Humans usually dispose of a body with some kind of ceremony, but I've never witnessed a funeral directly."

"Neither have I," I said, "but Sam said that I could do with him as I saw fit. I know what I want to do, K'tatmal. Will you help me?"

"Of course, my friend," K'tatmal said.

Sam's body was rigid when we picked it up. A few charred pieces fell off from the area around the blaster wound. We placed his body in the back of the car, and then I asked K'tatmal to drive back past the landing pad to the rockfall at the end of the plain. As we approached the rockfall, I asked K'tatmal to drive up the steep hill.

"I'm sorry, Kelvoo, but the car won't go there," K'tatmal said.

"Why not? Can't the vehicle make such a steep climb?"

"No, the car can rise vertically if we need it to. It's not that it *can't* go there; it's that it *won't!* The navigation system says the area has been closed to traffic."

"Why is that?"

"I don't know. The nav system just calls it a 'safety exclusion zone.'"

"K'tatmal, I'm not going to expect you to do this if you aren't up to it, but there is a place beyond the top of the rockfall that was very special to Sam. For reasons that I can't explain, I think it would be appropriate to leave Sam's remains in that location. Do you think that you could help me carry Sam's body to that place?"

"If there is a place that was meaningful to Sam, I would be honored to help take his body there."

K'tatmal parked the car next to where the boulders met the plain and the stream emerged from under the rocks. Our immediate task was to carry Sam up the hill, and my attitude was strictly business.

I muscled Sam's corpse out of the back of the car and placed him face-down over my shoulder. The body's rigor mortis was fading, and I could bend Sam at his waist. I held his legs behind his knees while his upper body, head, and arms dangled behind me. I could only climb over a couple of the larger boulders before I had to lay the corpse down and rest. K'tatmal and I took turns carrying Sam. We also tried draping each of Sam's arms over our shoulders and carrying him together. We tried carrying Sam with me holding his arms and K'tatmal taking his legs and vice versa. No matter what we tried, our progress was slow and exhausting.

A violent burst of rain opened up, drenching us, making the rocks slippery, and slowing our progress. K'tatmal and I slipped several times, scraping a knee, bruising an elbow, or twisting a limb. With each injury, the pain that was building in my body was matched by the intensifying pain in my mind.

I started to become aware of the grief, rage, terror, sorrow, and guilt that I thought had been banished when I finished writing my story. My mind had deceived me. All of those feelings were still there in that place deep inside me where I had locked them away.

K'tatmal had just transferred Sam to me when I lost my grip on Sam along with the grip on my self-control. I dropped Sam's body, and it tumbled down to a jumble of rocks below and became lodged between two boulders. Sam's soaking wet face stared blankly up at me.

"Damn you!" I screamed. "Damn you, Sam Buchanan! How could you? How could you do this to me and my friends?"

I crawled down to Sam's body and continued shouting. "You weren't supposed to die! You were supposed to help us! You did something good for us. You accomplished something you were proud of. You were getting better, and you were supposed to work with us and save our planet and save us all! Damn you!" I raised my hand to slap Sam's lifeless face when K'tatmal grabbed my arm.

The absurdity of yelling at a corpse and slapping it suddenly dawned on me, and my rage was instantly replaced with remorse. "Oh Sam!" I said softly. "Oh Sam, I'm so sorry."

I turned to K'tatmal. "What's wrong with me, K'tatmal? This poor, broken man was my friend! How could I treat him like that? Why am I talking to a dead human? Have I lost my mind?"

"There is nothing *wrong* with you, Kelvoo, but this doesn't mean you aren't damaged. Every member of Sam's Team has been damaged by varying degrees of trauma. Like you, I feel anger and deep disappointment toward Sam. He stole himself from us. His suicide was an act of supreme selfishness, stupidity, and cowardice. Like us, Sam was damaged, but that was no justification for murdering himself and inflicting such pain on us. Sam's death was a senseless waste. It has taken away all of the contributions that he could have made to our planet, our species, and our collective healing."

"I should have stopped him," I replied as guilt tore through me. "I should have seen the signs. I should have stayed with him these last three days. I shouldn't have assumed that he had overcome his pain . . ." I halted for a moment. "I also shouldn't have assumed that my pain had magically disappeared."

"Such thoughts have also crossed my mind," K'tatmal said. "After all, I have worked with a wide variety of humans for years now. Perhaps I should have seen signs that Sam wanted to harm himself. The problem with that argument is that we still lack insight into the human mind. We also have no experience with humans taking their own lives. Kelvoo, how many humans have you known who have committed suicide?"

"None," I admitted. "I wish I had insight into the human mind. They are capable of such ingenuity and creativity, but I have never even felt close to understanding humans."

"I'll let you in on a little secret," K'tatmal said. "Nobody understands the human mind—not even the humans themselves! Before the humans arrived, we kloormari understood one another because we all thought alike. We didn't need to struggle to survive. Until the *Pacifica's* lander arrived, nothing much ever happened. When decisions had to be made, we were always able to reach a logical consensus because a manageable number of variables were involved.

"Today, everything has changed. Even if every human disappeared from Kuw'baal at this very moment, we would never go back to the way things used to be. Life is more interesting now, but it has also become infinitely complex. As a result, our species is changing too. We are learning to adapt to our new environment. Some of us have been struggling over the last several years while others, especially our youth, are managing. Some are even thriving. As a whole, our species is becoming more creative, but at the same time, there have been more disagreements and arguments among us. As the only kloormari lawyer, I assure you that I have seen that happen time and time again. We are what we are, and what we are is changing every day."

As I pondered K'tatmal's wisdom, the rain stopped pounding down, and the sky brightened. I could hear the rush of water in the stream below the boulders, and I saw rushing white water emerging between some of the rocks. Far below, the plain had flooded, its waters reflecting the white sky, separating the kloormari village from Newton.

My conversation with K'tatmal had given us an opportunity to rest and provided some temporary relief from the burdens of Sam and our emotions. We managed to extricate Sam's corpse from between the rocks and then continued our climb more slowly and methodically than before.

It was midafternoon when we reached the top of the rockfall, and the slope became gentler. We carefully placed Sam's body on a patch of flat bedrock and then took a moment to catch our breath.

"How do humans cope?" I asked. "How can they coexist with one another when they are so inconsistent and unpredictable?" I turned toward Sam's body. "How could a human be so generous and yet so selfish at the same time? How can they be so wise and so foolish? How does their species not go completely mad?"

"I think that most of them are mad to some extent," K'tatmal replied. "I really don't know how they cope. I feel as though *I* can hardly cope with the loss of our deceased friend here."

"Perhaps that's why humans have historically turned to the concept of religion," I surmised. "Maybe they use superstition to fill the logical gaps in their lives."

"That makes sense," K'tatmal said. "Remember that religions tell their followers that death is not the end of existence. In my current emotional state, I could find comfort in the concept that Sam's existence continues in a much better place."

"Are you considering following a religion?"

"Oh no!" K'tatmal exclaimed. "There is no evidence for any kind of immortality, so embracing such a belief would be to embrace irrational thought. Human history has proven time and again that absolute belief in anything never ends well. I was just saying that I can see why religion could be very appealing to susceptible humans, especially when they are searching for an explanation of the inexplicable."

At that moment a chime sounded on my Infotab. I had a message from Trexelan. I read it aloud to K'tatmal.

Hello Kelvoo,

I received your story a few hours ago. I haven't had time to read it in its entirety, but it was nothing like what I had expected it to be! I thought your story would consist of a factual list of events, outlining what had happened and when.

Please don't take offense, but I honestly didn't realize that a kloormar could express such depths of emotion or that you could convey both the wonder and horror of everything that you had experienced!

I am confident that your story will have a deep and meaningful impact on the Planetary Alliance and anyone else who reads it. I want to congratulate you on doing such superb work.

I will be sure to send my congratulations to Samuel Buchanan. His preface brilliantly sets the stage and provides the background information for your story. Please thank Sam and congratulate him on my behalf.

See you soon,

Sub-commander Trexelan
Sarayan Security Forces

I walked over to Sam's corpse and looked into his dead eyes. "Trexelan sends her regards and heartfelt congratulations," I said, my voice dripping with irony. "Way to go, Sam!"

I sent a reply to Trexelan's message.

Hello Trexelan,

I cannot tell you how grateful I am for your message of support. I don't think I am deserving of your accolades, but I hope my efforts will produce positive results for my planet and my species.

I want you to know that the story I sent to you is not quite complete. A great many relevant events have occurred in only the last few hours. I would like to record these events by adding a final chapter to my story. I hope to send it to you tomorrow.

All the best,

Kelvoo of Kuw'baal

K'tatmal and I lifted Sam's body again. On the gentler slope of the ridge, it was more practical for one of us to take Sam's arms and the other his legs. We followed the edge of a gully, as Sam and I had done before, until we heard the rush of the rapids below. On our way up the hill, two more waves of intense rain fell upon us, with dry intervals in between.

We became more fatigued with each step. Finally, we resorted to pulling Sam by his arms, letting his heels drag behind us. One of his boots fell off, but we were too tired and too focused on our goal to retrieve it.

As we walked, we noticed that some short metal posts had been pushed into the ground, forming a long line. Each post had a strip of bright orange tape tied to the top. "It looks as though someone other than you and Sam have been here before," K'tatmal remarked. "It looks like someone is marking a boundary."

"That's good," I said. "Sam told me that, on Terra, a place like the one you are about to see would be preserved and protected as a natural treasure. Perhaps these posts are marking the border of some kind of park that humans and kloormari will be able to enjoy in the future."

"I haven't heard of such a plan," K'tatmal said, "but I appreciate the concept."

I felt a surge of energy as we approached the viewpoint. "When we round the corner of the hill up ahead, I think you might see why this place was so special to Sam."

As we walked, the view unfolded before us. First, we could see the tops of the jagged hills that formed the geological bowl. As the lower portions were revealed, we saw the bright yellow, turquoise, ochre, and brilliant white of the layers of minerals. Below the moraine we saw pink, purple, and red plants. When the far shore of the milky blue lake came into view, K'tatmal stopped and gasped, releasing Sam's arm.

"This is so beautiful!" K'tatmal said. "I wonder why none of us had ever visited this place before."

"Probably because we wouldn't have appreciated it," I replied. "When I came up here with Sam, he was in awe, but I didn't understand his reaction. To experience beauty, I think that we first need to see and experience ugliness. We've certainly seen enough of that to last for the rest of our lives!"

We left Sam's body on the ground for a moment as we took a few more steps forward to take in the rest of the view.

"Oh no!" I exclaimed.

A huge yellow vehicle with large black wheels was parked on the near side of the lake. Beside it was a partly assembled bunkhouse as well as storage sheds full of equipment, surrounded by a slatted metal fence. Nearby was a landing pad and a tracked vehicle with a tower on top. The stream below us looked the same as before, but it no longer flowed directly from the lake. A large berm of broken rock with gravel on top ran across the end of the lake closest to us. Tracks in the gravel indicated recent vehicle traffic. A large culvert had been placed under the raised road. Due to the recent heavy rain, water gushed from the lake, through the culvert, and into the stream.

"What is this?" I asked, not wanting to know the answer.

"It's a mining exploration site," K'tatmal said. "The yellow vehicle should look familiar—you told me about the mining colony on XR-318. You would have seen similar machines there."

K'tatmal was correct. "The machine with the tower on top," K'tatmal continued, "I've seen such equipment offloaded from cargo shuttles. I was told that's a core-sampling directed-energy drill. It can bore deep into rock to find precious minerals and gemstones. What I don't understand is how such large vehicles got up here since there is no flat area large enough for huge transports to land."

"I can tell you," I said. "Do you see that flat area between two hills across the valley? That space used to be occupied by a smaller hill. They must have removed the hill and built a road through there. The road must come up the back side of these hills. I assume that the road curves around to a place beyond the far side of Newton."

"So, we could have driven up here?" K'tatmal asked, incredulous.

"That seems to be the case," I said, "but I haven't seen anyone else here. I would imagine that the road is closed on a non-workday. I also suspect that your car's nav system shows the area as closed to traffic for safety reasons because this is an active work site."

"You know, Kelvoo, I don't know why, but for some reason, I'm glad we walked up here the hard way."

"I agree," I said. "I think it might have something to do with facing our pain. For me at least, coming up here added to my pain. It brought my suffering and my burdens to the forefront, and in doing so, it forced me to stare my pain in the eye and deal with it directly. Don't get me wrong, K'tatmal, I don't think that bringing Sam here is going to be a magical cure for my pain. Yesterday, I thought that I had put all of my negative feelings behind me. Today has taught me that my healing will be a long and arduous process, perhaps even lasting for the rest of my life."

After a few minutes of reflection, K'tatmal changed the subject. "I can see why the humans would want to explore here. With all of the layers of minerals that we can see in the hills around the lake, this place must be a treasure trove of valuable resources."

"Are you saying this place *should* be mined?" I asked incredulously.

"Absolutely not!" K'tatmal exclaimed. "This place is incredible. It's probably unique on Kuw'baal. Any disruption of this place is a travesty, and it must be stopped!"

"How?"

"I don't know, but we could start by bringing other kloormari up here—as many as possible, so that they can witness this place! I hope our species has changed and learned enough that they will appreciate the real value of this location. I hope that enough of us will be willing to physically block the work here."

"Wouldn't that be against the humans' laws?"

"To hell with human law!" K'tatmal shouted. K'tatmal started making a vid recording of the area to show it to anyone willing to watch.

"Well, I suppose we have some business to take care of," K'tatmal said a few minutes later.

"Let's get it done," I replied.

We picked Sam up with as much dignity as we could manage and made our way down the loose gravel slope to the sandy spot a few meters downstream from the culvert. It was the place where Sam had scattered his mother's ashes. K'tatmal and I laid Sam's body down on the soft sand.

Wild algel was growing along the banks of the stream—not as much as the last time I was there but certainly enough for our needs at that moment. "Did you realize we haven't eaten at all today?" K'tatmal asked.

"I hadn't even thought about it," I replied, suddenly realizing how much I needed some nourishment. K'tatmal and I ate a large algel meal and then rested for a while.

"So, what are we supposed to do now?" K'tatmal asked. "As I said after you read Sam's note, I have never witnessed a human funeral."

"All I know is that we're supposed to say a few words about the dead person," I replied, "but that's only if we were to have a human funeral for Sam. Sam's note said I was to dispose of him as I saw fit, so we're going to lay his body down in the stream and let the nutrients flow into the environment of Kuw'baal, just as we do for our own species. The only special thing that I'm doing for Sam is bringing him here to this place that he loved and where he chose to scatter his mother's remains."

"Kelvoo, you have seen humans die. How do they handle that moment?"

"It depends upon the human and the circumstances. I've seen absolute fear in the eyes of a human just before his head got blown apart by a blaster. On the other hand, when the captain and crew of *Jezebel's Fury* were about to be executed by the Sarayans, they sang a song. Now that I think about it, they shouldn't have known the punishment they were about to receive. Maybe somebody had tipped them off, or perhaps humans just have an innate sense that the end of their lives is at hand."

"Could you please sing the song for me, Kelvoo?"

"Alright," I said. I sang for K'tatmal, and I also sang for poor dead Sam.

At the end of the day, I'll be flying away,
traveling through the great, vast abyss.
I'll be missing you so, with a heart full of woe,
when we're parted and I reminisce.

If my ship's good and true, I shall fly back to you,
to your love and your touch and your kiss.

By your side I shall stay, until my dying day,
with our lives full of heavenly bliss.

But if I should die, I beg you to try,
to forgive me and know that I care.
In the night sky afar, just spy a bright star,
and trust that my spirit is there.

I'll be twinkling, you'll see, with a love that's set free,
as my spirit shines down upon thee.

As I sang, I was surprised that some of my words came out haltingly. I also had trouble maintaining the correct pitch, my voice cracking and breaking into a higher register at times.

"I'm sorry I didn't do that very well," I said to K'tatmal.

"Nonetheless, it's a beautiful song," K'tatmal said. "It makes me miss the sight of the stars against the blackness of space. I think that the next time a shuttle is making some back-and-forth trips, I would like to see whether I can catch a quick ride into orbit, just to gaze at the stars on one side and Kuw'baal on the other, and perhaps sing that lovely song."

"I had trouble singing because the song brought up some traumatic memories for me, and it was hard for me to get through it," I said. "It's strange. I alternate between hopefulness and despair. Is there any hope for us, K'tatmal?"

"There *is* hope, Kelvoo," K'tatmal replied, "especially when you consider all of the positive things that have come from our interactions with the human species."

"Positive things?" I said. "Are you referring to SimCash, material possessions, and new technology? Do you really think the benefits of those things are going to outweigh the loss of our culture, identity, land, and self-determination?"

"Once again, Kelvoo, you misinterpret what I'm saying. I'm not talking about money and possessions as the positive things. I'm talking about other changes.

"As kloormari, studying and learning have always been our purpose in life, but we were limited to studying our historical texts. Of course, our history is still of great importance to our culture, but just think of all the new things we can learn about! It used to be that the sky was the limit because we thought the universe ended at the sky. We have broken out beyond the sky, and now we have discovered an infinite universe that our species can explore and learn about!

"Think about all of the beings that we have met. Not just humans but Sarayans as well. When it comes to humans, we have seen the best and the worst that they can be. It scares me that our people are starting to become more emotional and more like the humans, but human history and our experiences can serve as a cautionary tale for us. I am hopeful that we can embrace creativity and individuality while avoiding the more irrational human traits.

"Think about the moment that we are living in. Every few thousand years, Ryla 6 passes by, and our planet experiences massive geological upheavals that impact our species. For the last seven years, we have experienced a far more massive upheaval than has ever occurred before or ever will again. You and I, and Sam's Team, and all living kloormari are fortunate enough to exist in this historic and pivotal time. As our species makes a challenging transition, just think about the difference that Sam's Team can make. Before your return, the only beings advocating for the kloormari were Sam with his angry ranting, and me, trying to work within the system to little effect.

"In the end, Kelvoo, I am optimistic about our species. Thanks to the terrible experiences that you and our friends endured, and thanks to your courage in writing your story, there is hope. The Sarayans are with us, and I believe that your story will resonate with all of the other non-human delegations to the Alliance. I even think that a great many Terran humans will read your story and demand change. Make no mistake, Kelvoo, rapid change has been imposed on our species and culture, and we can never go back to the way things were. What we can do, however, is incorporate the changes into a new kloormari culture that we can truly call our own. This, Kelvoo, is what I was referring to when I suggested that we consider the positive aspects of human contact."

I could find no fault with K'tatmal's optimism. "Thank you so much, my friend."

"Well, Kelvoo," K'tatmal said, turning toward Sam's remains, "is it time for us to say goodbye to our friend?"

"I think so, K'tatmal. He is, after all, looking rather 'worse for wear.'"

When we stood, our bodies protested with a litany of stiffness, soreness, and pain. The stream was swollen, and the current was swift as we carefully lifted Sam's remains and gently lowered them into the water.

We immediately realized we had made a serious miscalculation concerning human anatomy. When placed in water, a kloormar will sink like a stone and quickly be buried under any loose gravel, sand, or silt. Sam's body, on the other hand, had a lower density than the water it displaced. We nearly lost our grip on Sam's corpse. If we had done so, his body would have been washed downstream into the gully and would likely have been unrecoverable.

We placed Sam back on the sandy bank and painfully set about gathering large rocks. K'tatmal waded into the rushing water, holding Sam's body under the arms and letting the churning water pull Sam's legs downstream. I carried a large, flat rock and put it on top of Sam's ankles so that his feet were pinned to the streambed. I brought more rocks and placed them farther up Sam's legs until the corpse was covered from the waist down.

As I piled more rock onto the lower half of the body, K'tatmal went ashore to fetch a rock to start on Sam's upper half. When K'tatmal released the body, Sam's waist bent as the rushing water forced the body to sit up. I thought that humans would perceive the entire tableau as macabre and undignified. The death of a human was nothing like its usual depiction in human vids. Death was a mess.

K'tatmal and I didn't stop once Sam was covered. We became obsessed with piling more and more rocks on top of Sam's remains until the pile of rocks rose above the surface of the stream, resembling a memorial cairn.

The remains of Samuel Buchanan had been laid to rest.

I didn't know what to do next. What K'tatmal and I had done so far didn't seem like enough. I waded back into the stream and stood in the calmer water on the downstream side of the cairn where the water covered my feet and my legs, up to my lower knees.

As I stood there, I closed my eyelid and began a powerful recitation of the most meaningful music in Sam's life. As my vocal outlets sounded out "Pachelbel's Canon," the music reverberated through the valley. I released my imagination—something that I felt Sam would have appreciated—and cast aside all logic and limitations, opening my imagination to complete freedom and fantasy.

In my mind, I envisioned a shimmering sphere hovering over the cairn. Then I saw the scene from the vantage point of Sam's shining spirit, looking down at two of his dearest friends, desperately trying to honor him and make sense of their loss.

The view changed as Sam's spirit looked up to the sky. In my imagination, I soared skyward with Sam's spirit. We flew up, up, up into the sky world of my planet, immersed in pure white, soothed and comforted by the peaceful strains of the echoing music.

In a joyous and exhilarating burst, we broke through the clouds and into the vastness of the universe. Sam's spirit soared into orbit around Kuw'baal and then joyously flung itself toward Ryla 6. We flew effortlessly through the deep valleys, over the blue ice, and between the majestic deep-black mountains.

We turned heavenward and raced straight toward the brilliant star, Ryla, unimpeded by physics and the immutable laws of the universe. We skimmed over the star's roiling surface, swooping between flares, and basking in the light of the life-sustaining orb.

From there, Sam's spirit was free to roam the universe unencumbered by the limitations of a body—a body whose remnants were buried under an obscure stream somewhere on an obscure little planet in an obscure star system in a tiny corner of a galaxy that was a single, tiny point of light in an amazing, infinite universe.

I imagined Sam finding a place of eternal joy and reuniting with his beloved mother, ready to rejoin with the spirits of those with whom Sam had found moments of joy and contentment.

As "Pachelbel's Canon" reached its conclusion, and the echoes of its final notes faded from the valley, I opened my eye. I saw a huge wave of rain make its way over the lake, accompanied by a rapidly darkening sky and distant thunder.

I closed my eye again. As the rain started pelting down on me, I wished desperately that it could wash away all the anguish that still lurked deep within me. *Why were both Sams in my life taken so violently and needlessly? Why should life have so cruelly conspired to remove both Kelvoos from Sam?*

Once again, I imagined. My inner eye saw my inner demons leaving my body in the form of black, opaque smoke, billowing from every opening. The smoke swirled around me like a whirlwind, blocking out all light and encasing me in blackness.

The vantage point changed. I was looking down from a short distance above myself. Not as Sam's spirit this time but just as Kelvoo the kloormar. The scene appeared in perfect detail with the sound of the rushing water, the frothing of the rain on the surface of the stream, the rivulets it formed in the sand, and the swirling of the current around the cairn and my trembling legs.

I watched with detached fascination as my body transformed into a human shape. The hair on my head was plastered to my scalp by the pummeling rain, water dripped down my face and melded with the tears rushing from my eyes, and my mouth was twisted, forming a mask of wretched grief.

My human form started to resolve and clarify into an image of Sam Buchanan. His fists were clenched. He bowed his head and raised his fists, resting his forehead on them. Sam fell to his knees at the foot of the cairn, the current swirling around his waist.

Sam's body was spasmodically shaking with uncontrollable sobs of despair. He looked up at the sky world. "Why?" he screamed, continuing to sob. "Why? Why? Why?" He laid the palms of his hands on top of the cairn and bowed his head.

My mind then saw Sam dissolving and his body melting away, tiny particles washing off him, forming swirls in the water as the stream carried my image of Sam far away into the natural environment of my tiny planet.

Next, I heard my name being called and my body being shaken. I opened my eye. I was kneeling waist-deep in the stream. The palms of my hands were placed on top of the cairn, and my eye was bowed down.

K'tatmal was standing in the water next to me. The intense rainstorm had passed. The sky was brighter than it had been, but the light was beginning to dim as the end of the long day was nearing.

"Are you alright, Kelvoo?"

I rose and stood next to K'tatmal, touching K'tatmal's shoulder. "No, K'tatmal, I am not alright. But I will be. We all will be. I know that somehow everything is going to be alright."

K'tatmal and I wearily made our way back down the ridge and the rockfall in the fading light.

"You know, K'tatmal, I find humans to be so fascinating, but overall, I can't say that I particularly like them."

"I understand completely," K'tatmal replied.

"Nevertheless," I continued, "humans do have one trait that I would dearly love to possess."

"What's that?"

"Sometimes I wish that I knew how to forget."

"I wouldn't advise it, Kelvoo. Not when we have an entire planet that needs to be healed."

"How, K'tatmal? How are we going to heal an entire planet? Where can we possibly begin?"

"With ourselves, my friend. Let's just start with ourselves."

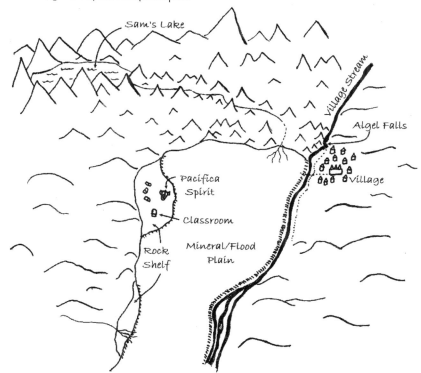

Location of First Contact
During Visit of the Pacifica Spirit

Sam's Lake

Village Stream

Algel Falls

Pacifica
Spirit

Village

Classroom

Rock
Shelf

Mineral/Flood
Plain

Also by Phil Bailey:

# KELVOO'S TERRA

**The exciting sequel to Kelvoo's Testimonial is available now!**

Kelvoo is a survivor. Human first contact had a devastating effect on the kloormari species of Kelvoo's home planet. No kloormar was impacted more profoundly than Kelvoo.

Now, Kelvoo is on a mission to protect two young humans, Brenna and May—orphaned, abandoned, and left in Kelvoo's care. After a generous job offer, pressure from the girls, and the chance to immigrate to Terra, Kelvoo must choose between a life of security and the risks of the human homeworld.

Once on Terra, Kelvoo, Brenna, and May are welcomed with open arms. Terran life is full of wonders until a radical anti-immigrant movement unleashes a violent coup, plunging Terra into chaos and civil war. Will Kelvoo be able to protect Brenna and May, or will they all succumb to the hate and violence surrounding them?

Kelvoo's Terra combines suspense, political intrigue, and personal redemption as it dramatically explores the impact of ignorance and hate, versus the power of family and love.

# Did you enjoy this book?

I can't begin to tell you how valuable a positive online review or social media post is to an independently published book like Kelvoo's Testimonial. Good reviews and positive mentions are the fuel required to compete with millions of other titles – especially when those titles are produced by massive publishing houses with huge marketing budgets and distribution networks.

If you leave a review or make a post, please let me know where to find it and I promise to read it. Your feedback helps me to understand my readers and to improve as a writer for any future books that I may write and you may enjoy.

By aiding in my future success, your reviews or posts will help to enable me to continue my writing and create more books.

You can visit my website and find my social media links at:

**www.kelvoo.com**.

THANK YOU so much,

*-- Phil Bailey*